UNBOUND

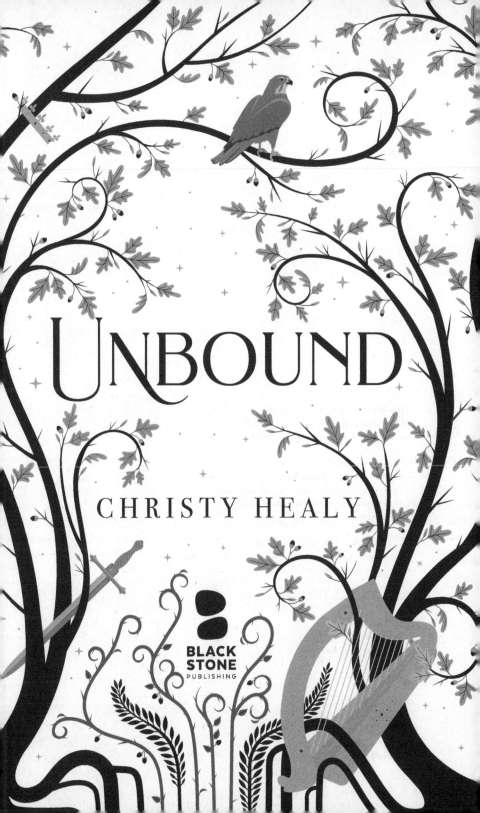

Unbound

CHRISTY HEALY

BLACK STONE PUBLISHING

Printed in the United States of America

First edition: 2024
ISBN 979-8-212-61383-5
Fiction / Fantasy / General

Version 1

Blackstone Publishing
31 Mistletoe Rd.
Ashland, OR 97520

www.BlackstonePublishing.com

For my grandfather, from whom I learned my first lessons of love and of laughter and, ultimately, of loss. We always planned that one day we would visit County Cork, and walk alongside the Blackwater and the Bride together—I hope that when my time comes, you'll be there, waiting for me. I love you.

Inis Trá Tholl

Dúnalderagh

Grianán Ailigh

NORTHERN
UÍNÉILL

Ard an Rátha
Maghera

Latharna

Dubhais

Lough Neagh

ULAID

Cnoc na Loinge
Sliabh Gamh

Bréifne

AIRGIALLA

Lough Conn

CONNACHT

SOUTHERN
UÍNÉILL

Brug na Boinne

Mhám Toirc
Beanna Beola

Tír Sogháin

Vale of Inagh

Tír Sogháin

LAIGIN

Osraige

MUNSTER

Guagán Barra

ÉIRE

SEA OF ÉIREANN

PART ONE

CHAPTER ONE

On the night before her wedding, Rozlyn donned her bridal gown, an elaborate red-and-gold concoction, a delicate thing of embroidered finery, and stood before the silver-coated mirror in her room.

She hated it.

She had asked for black. A night-black gown, with loose, flowing sleeves, no adornments, no trappings—a gown fit for the funeral of a princess rather than the marriage of one.

Rozlyn had said this as Moira brought the dress to her chambers earlier that morning, and the maid had shuddered. "Apologies, my lady," Moira had whispered, tucking her chin against her chest as she spoke, her eyes fixed on the floor and her fingers curled into her palms. "This is the gown that the king, your father, has himself requested for this day."

So she had heard—a dozen gray-haired seamstresses bent over their spindles and their whorls, weaving late into the night by the flickering light of the fire. Rozlyn could all but see them, working feverishly at their looms, their fingers weary and their faces bright with hope.

"He wishes," Moira had continued, "for you to seem resplendent, triumphant." She had flinched when Rozlyn twisted away from her, stalking across the room to stare out her window. "We all do, my lady. After all"—a tremulous half-curtsy, lips trembling—"you are, at last, to end the curse that has plagued our land for so long."

"One-and-twenty years." She could see it reflected in the glass, that hateful gown, lying across her bed, the faint gleam of its golden threads twinkling in the foggy pane before her, taunting her. "A long time, indeed."

Moira had merely bowed her head, but Rozlyn could see her maid's pale fingers quake against the brown fabric of her skirt and relented.

Red it would be, then. Red for guilt, for shame.

For blood.

Rozlyn thought of this again now as she waited for the dawn, standing before her mirror, wreathed in moonlight, her wedding gown weighing heavy on her shoulders—a crimson-gold monstrosity of a dress. She glanced over to the table, at the unopened wooden box that sat there, beckoning to her, and she reached over, lifting the lid to see what gift her soon-to-be husband had given to her on the night before their marriage.

Nestled deep within the downy feathers that cushioned the sides of the little box, Rozlyn could see the faintest glint of gold. Her fingers were steady and ice-cold as she lifted the tiara from its container. What a finely welded thing of beauty it was, with its slim strands woven so closely together, studded with deep-red gems, and at the top, a single rose, crafted from the shavings of burnt-gold leaves.

Rozlyn shuddered at the sight of it, this gift from her beloved, then placed it atop her black hair, which fell loose and unbraided about her shoulders.

She imagined what they would say tomorrow as she descended the stairs, the gold glinting from the threads of her robe and the rose of her crown with equal beauty in the bright light of the day. *She has come to break the curse*, they would whisper, the throngs of people who had not seen her face in all these years, not since the day that her father had locked her away in her tower until her hand would be claimed by another. *Look. There she is*, they would murmur, their eyes growing wet with relief, with joy, to see the end of their suffering after so many long years of pain.

She could imagine, too, the other things that they would whisper.

Why isn't she smiling?

She would look much prettier if she smiled.

She tried it now, watching in the shadowy reflection of the mirror as the corners of her mouth curled. She could see her teeth glinting in the firelight, white-washed fangs bared in a snarl beneath rose-red lips.

Och, they would agree, the people watching wide-eyed as she walked down her father's hall to greet her beloved, whispering behind cupped hands. *But still. She really is a beauty, isn't she now.*

Rozlyn looked at her blurred reflection in the mirror—a gathering storm of red and gold and raven-wing black—and saw only a beast.

She turned away, the gown dragging on the wood floors behind her, and lay on her bed. Her tiara dug into the back of her skull, scraping at her skin, but she did not remove it. She lay in the gloom of her tower, watching the moonlight play across the thick oak beams of the ceiling. With an ease born from years of practice, she lifted her finger and watched as the moonshine swirled across the sleek wooden timbers above her, following the motion of her hand with fluid ease, shifting itself into a myriad of shapes—dragonflies flitting through the reeds of the riverbanks, and silvery horses with tangled, free-flowing manes, and falcons soaring through the winds of a tempest, circling and swooping across the cloud-dark sky with ethereal grace. They flickered through her mind like vague half-formed shadows of memories long forgotten, exploding into life above her, drawn from the cool strands of the moonbeams gliding across her walls.

She laid on her back, her hands twisting in the crimson-stained fabric of her gown, and watched them glide above her, these starlit dancers into whom she had breathed life and beauty, for the final time.

In the deep quiet of the night before her wedding to the man she loved, with only the shadows to see, she said good-bye to them, her constant companions of grace and light, as silent tears spilled down her face.

CHAPTER TWO

She was close, lingering somewhere in the hidden corners of her hall. Jamie could feel the bite of her magic on the air, the sharp nip of its teeth grazing against his skin. He stood still, unlike the others who paced fretfully in front of the stark wooden dais that stood in the center of the great hall. It was a deliberate show of confidence, a false front of bravado and unconcern for the nervous-eyed men who prowled around him, their hands gripping the hilts of their swords. They had, after all, little reason to fear for their lives, despite the rumors, the whispered stories of past horrors once committed by the queen of this very hall.

Unlike him.

Even now, his heartbeat thrummed in perfect time with unseen fangs that curved their way along the side of his throat. They scraped against the lifeblood that hummed in his neck, a teasing threat, and even as his pulse quickened, he could not quite stifle a yearning, a curiosity to know what she would look like now—his serious, green-eyed beauty from over a decade ago.

It flowed through him again, the unbidden memory of her youthful hands, pale against the smooth darkness of the cherrywood, her brows furrowed in concentration as she mimicked his motion of bending the bow and notching the arrow. He steeled himself to remember, as he had so rarely allowed himself to remember for many years now, that narrow face, forever unsmiling, as it studied him with such unerring watchfulness.

He wondered if she would try to kill him as she had once promised.

Most assuredly, she would.

Deservedly.

He ignored the anxiety coiling in his stomach as his men continued to skulk in tight circles around one another, darting suspicious glances at the flickering shadows in the corners of the room, as though she would materialize in their midst from the mere smoke of torches, unleashing havoc and death upon them with nothing more than a flick of her wrist and a wordless command. Not out of the realm of possibility, knowing her as he once had, if the rumors of her sorcery were true.

He wondered, not for the first time, how she had at last learned to master it, that mysterious power within her, and by what means she had come to know how to wield it.

Jamie spun on the heel of his boot, fists clenched in his pockets, the only indication of his unease. He studied the intricacy of the stained-glass window that overshadowed the dais. The podium, bare of any adornments or throne-chair, hummed with the promise of her unseen power, the kaleidoscope of colors glimmering across the polish of its wood from the window above. No trappings or grandiose shows of strength from such a queen as this, he mused. True sovereignty needed no such frills—unnecessary accoutrements to that invisible thrum of power that stalked on invisible paws through the dark corridors of her keep.

As though he had summoned her, the back of his neck prickled. He whirled, his hands moving to the longbow and quiver strapped to his shoulders. His men spun with him, a coordinated movement, and Jamie could all but smell the fear that sprung from the fresh beads of sweat erupting on their brows, could hear the fearful rattling of swords at their sides and the swoosh of arrows being drawn from their quivers.

"Hello, Jamie," she said.

Her face was hidden in the shadows where she stood in the doorway in the far corner of the room, leaning against its frame, her arms crossed across the deep gray and blue of her doublet.

"Rozi." He took one cautious step in her direction as he watched her shoulders stiffen at the casual abbreviation of her name. "I was beginning to wonder if your maid had forgotten to announce us. Hard to imagine that you would keep me waiting, considering how long it has been since we've seen one another."

She straightened, her braid slipping over her shoulder. Jamie eyed her hands as she flexed her fingers against the dark fabric of her breeches. "Not long enough for you to remember to call me by my rightful name, I see."

Jamie laughed even as his men tensed around him, lowering his own hands and sliding them into his pockets with an ease that belied the apprehension rolling through him. "I admit to having been very curious about how you might have changed after all this time, about how you have fared on your own. Although I suppose I hardly need ask. Look at you. The queen of the vale." He wandered a few steps forward, his head tipped back as he studied the wooden beams crisscrossing over them. "Or do you prefer 'witch' of the vale? The reports are somewhat contradictory."

"Why can't it be both?"

"Why, indeed? I, as you know, have always advocated for you to claim your power for your own."

"So you did, right before you attempted to steal it away from me."

Jamie remained still, even as the men behind him staggered backward at the venom threading through her words. "You have your interpretation of certain incidents in our shared history, and I have mine. If you hadn't thrown such a nasty little tantrum and run off, if you had only bothered to ask me why I did what I did . . ." He shrugged. "It's a pity that you didn't linger long enough to hear what I had to say about the role that I played in those unfortunate happenings."

She stepped forward, the light of the torches spilling over her, and despite his fear, despite the anxiety twisting in his chest, Jamie's knees buckled.

At one-and-twenty, she had been a pretty girl, her loveliness underscored by narrow lines and austere features.

Now, nearly ten years later, she was breathtaking.

But it was irrelevant. It didn't matter that the mere sight of her stole the air from his lungs and dizzied his senses. He had never been deceived by the stark perfection of her face, had always recognized it for the mask that it was—beauty, meant only to mask the monster that lurked within.

"I have no interest," she said, "in listening to you wheedle your way through whatever weak-kneed excuses you, no doubt, assume will justify the wealth of lies and deceptions that you practiced upon a naive and lonely child."

"That was quite a speech, Rozi." He clapped, slow and mocking. "Been planning that one for some time, have you?"

"For ten long years."

Don't quail, he told himself firmly. *Don't look away.* The key to surviving potentially lethal encounters with wild animals and former paramours was unnervingly similar, particularly when said paramour was as lethal as she. "Lonely? Yes. I will grant you that—you were a very lonely girl, but there was nothing childlike about you. I remember how cunning you were—how cruel you could be. Perhaps you're merely angry that you finally met a man who was able to match you in those twisted games that you loved to play with your unsuspecting suitors."

Her eyes narrowed. "Tell me," she said, and he braced himself for whatever move she had planned next for him on this invisible board of pieces and pawns she had so carefully arranged. "Who are these men who have come with you to my hall? Did you bother to enlighten them as to the horrors that you knew must be waiting for them here once you dared to show your face?"

Jamie raised his brow, even as the men shuddered as one behind him. "And here I thought we would be given a reprieve from your torments, seeing as we were greeted only by a sweet-faced maid and not your most stalwart soldiers, ready to string us up and dismember us at your command."

"I don't seem to need guards though, do I, when your men shudder at the mere sight of me?"

"Your father's men," he corrected. "He sends his regards, by the way."

She watched him, so still that Jamie could barely detect

the storm of emotion surging beneath the surface. "Is that so." It was not, he knew, a question. "And what is it the two of you have decided that you want of me now? Am I not to be given even this small peace, this parcel of land that is mine and mine alone, as I was promised?"

"By all means." Jamie waved his hand airily. "Once you have done as I ask, you are free to brew your potions and weave your enchantments to your heart's content, to live out your days in this quaint little castle of yours, a bhrèagha—"

"Do not," she said, and the stouthearted men of Éire trembled to hear the whisper of a thunderstrike echo through the room, "ever call me that again."

"—but first, I am afraid your services are required elsewhere."

She drew her shoulders back, and Jamie tensed as her hands clenched at her sides. "No."

"You don't even know yet what it is that I've come to ask of you." Jamie could hear the men behind him shuffling their feet, their fear coating the air with a bitter tang. "Rozi." He lowered his voice. "You need to hear what I have to say."

"I wonder," she said, her teeth flashing as she spoke. "Does the spider wait long enough to listen to the fly explain why it has wandered into her web before she kills it?"

"A fair point. Nevertheless, Rozi," he said again, "do not do something you will later regret." He gestured to the men behind him—these soldiers of unparalleled strength and valor, who had ridden into battle against impossible odds and bloodshed without flinching, and who now shook in terror at the power pulsing in the air around them.

Her attention flickered to the men, and he saw it then, that shadowy scar of grief and guilt shutter over her features. In the swiftest of motions, she raised her hand and flicked her fingers toward them. Even as the soldiers shrieked, the thick branches of a dozen oak trees tore their way through the smooth wooden floors of the great hall, their limbs reaching to the beams of the ceiling above as their broad trunks thundered after them. The men's cries grew muffled as a forest of trees took root within the walls of the castle, settling into the earthen floor that lay beneath the once smooth wood boards, an ominous wall of twisted wood between Jamie and where his men had once stood.

"There now," she said, her eyes glowing with unholy light, her face pale and strained in the early morning sun. "Now it will be impossible for me to have regrets about what I am about to do." She stared at him hungrily.

Jamie retreated three hasty steps, pressing his back against the stone wall behind him, but she merely turned and strolled away, toward her waiting dais, her fists clenched by her sides. From the corner of his eye, he searched the remaining half of the room for shelter from the storm of her wrath that was soon to come crashing down around him.

She had always had a fierce temper, even in her mildest moods, but the gods help the man who rubbed her the wrong way when she felt even the slightest bit under the weather, and Jamie could tell by the way that she flexed her fingers over and over again at her sides that one hell of a headache was throbbing in her temples right now.

And he knew he had irked her in the most injurious of ways ten years ago.

He could very well die today, here in her hall, at the hands of the woman he had loved.

She climbed the steps to her dais, tugging on the end of her braid with her left hand even as she rubbed at her temple with her right. "Do you know," she asked, like a dreamy-eyed girl caught in the throes of the remembrances of her youth, "what I have been remembering since I heard of your intended visit?"

Jamie said nothing. Two doors to the left, one to the right, a set of steps in the far corner leading to a narrow walkway that ran along the length of the upper wall—

"I have been thinking about that terrible Beast. Do you remember it?" She drummed her fingers against the tip of her chin. "Surely you must. How could anyone forget such a monster?"

"Believe me, I've tried."

Her eyes flashed again. "Have you now." Again, not a question. "Regardless, I was remembering how it would terrorize the countryside while I was a girl. Seeking to devour me, my father told me, always searching to find and destroy the irresistible allure of *my* magic, of the dark powers that lived within *me*. It was my fault, I was told, that the people of our realm suffered so greatly, because of the sorcery that pulsed through my veins—this was why the Beast had descended on our lands and wreaked havoc on the lives of so many innocents." She tilted her head back to examine the mosaic of colors that sparkled through the stained-glass window above her. "You remember it, of course—that terrible Beast. But do you recall the full scope of devastation it wrought, the pain it inflicted?"

Jamie eyed the nearby doorway. It was not nearly close enough. Well. Hopefully, it would be quick and relatively painless, whatever she had in mind. "Unfortunately, yes."

She sighed, the sound of a steel trap snapping into place, and another shiver of dread crawled along the length of his spine. "I have always felt so guilty, so racked with shame over the role that I played—inadvertently, it is true—in the destruction of so many lives." She turned to face him. "Do you, I wonder? Do you feel remorse, feel guilt for all the suffering that you and my father have caused?"

"All right, Rozi. You've had your fun, now—"

"I was locked away for fourteen years—fourteen years, imagine that, if you will—in order to protect my people, to lessen the threat of the monster who preyed upon us, was forced to smother, to suppress any signs of my magic that might surface." She lazily traced a finger through the air, and the trees looming around them shuddered in response. "To think that, if the two of you had not been so determined to keep me weak, to stop me from learning how to wield the magic that I was born to possess, so many would not have died." She met his wary gaze, and in spite of himself, he shivered to see the flecks of green in her eyes drowning in a raging sea of unforgiving steel-gray flint.

"I suppose that it is only fitting," she continued, "that you should suffer as they suffered, that you should endure what they endured, don't you agree? I think"—her voice deepened into a guttural growl—"that you should, at last, taste the terror that the Beast of Connacht so loves to inspire."

"By all means, if that's what you desire. But if you could first hear what I have to say, I'd be forever in your debt."

Her lips curled back in a snarl, and she raised her hands as, from the shadowed doorways around her, a dozen lean, lupine figures stalked toward him, teeth bared and hair raised, their winter-blue eyes glowing with preternatural fire.

Gods, no.

A strangled sound escaped him, and Rozi arched her brows, malevolently gleeful at having, at last, provoked a response. "I, too, remember a great deal from our time together—how fond you are of wolves, for example. When I learned of your visit, I decided to call upon some of my acquaintances to ensure that you felt properly welcomed to my hall." She smiled with her lips and not at all with her eyes.

He wasn't particularly inclined to call it a smile.

She ran her hand down the long braid of her hair, examining the loose strands as her wolves prowled into the room. "I hoped that you would appreciate my thinking of you. It's the little things that mean the most, wouldn't you agree?"

Jamie edged away from where he was pinned against the wall, sidling toward the open doorway—his only hope of survival—and eyeing the wolves as they crept ever closer to him, their snouts rippling with snarls. "You know, I do find solace knowing that you clearly have been unable to stop dreaming about me all these years, Rozi. I wonder now, were there any particular parts of me, exactly, that you have been missing? Because if that's what all this hostility is about, a reunion could easily be arranged."

She snarled again, and this time the air around her shivered as her lips turned lupine around newly appeared fangs, her body heaving, growing bulkier, denser, as rough swathes of dark fur sprouted from her arching spine. She fell to all fours, her hands and feet widening to massive paws, claws protracting from underneath black-blue shanks of hair, even as her eyes, bright and gleaming in her half-human face, glimmered at him with unmistakable intent.

"Why, Jamie, you look so very grim," she growled, the sinuous tail that slid across the ground behind her twitching as a pair of black-feathered wings rose above her, shrouding her in shadows, the sharp talons at the crest of each wing gleaming in the sunlight. The wolves advanced on him, their snarls echoing in unison with their mistress's as he shuddered to see the mastery with which she now commanded the Beast who lurked underneath her skin. "Hasn't anyone ever told you that you'd be so much prettier if you smiled?"

Jamie sprinted for the door, away from the wolves that lunged toward him, jaws snapping, away from the raven-haired beast who commanded them.

His wife.

CHAPTER THREE

Rozlyn could remember with perfect clarity the night that the Beast arrived in Connacht.

She was five and had spent the day running wild through the edge of the vale that lay beneath the wide expanse of the snow-tipped peaks of Beanna Beola. It had been a rare day of freedom, her black hair falling loose from its tight braid and her white smock stained with the mud of the river-banks. Her cheeks were glowing and flushed rose-red by the time her nursemaid half-carried her up to bed, her eyelids drooping with exhaustion.

She had fallen asleep, freshly scrubbed and tucked into her bed, laden with pillows and soft knitted blankets. There were no dreams to disturb her that she could re-member, only vague, half-formed thoughts of rushing winds and gurgles reminiscent of a bubbling brook that flowed through the grass as sinister as a snake. Then she was awake, heart pounding in her chest, the sky still dark in the late midnight hours, and she was not in her bed at all but curled on the bench beneath the open windows that overlooked the valley beneath her tower, her hair tousled and tangled, her throat hoarse, as though rubbed raw from screaming.

Her head throbbing, she sat up, rubbing at her eyes, a strange fog misting over her brain. She swallowed against the sandpaper roughness that coated her throat. "Eileen?" she croaked, calling for her nursemaid. Rozlyn swallowed again, the pain in her throat like shards of summer-hot glass, then stood and toddled toward the door that led to the stairwell outside her room. "Eileen?"

She pushed the door open to chaos.

Rozlyn could hear shrieking down below, the sobs of servants and soldiers alike intermingling with one another in the din unfolding beneath her. She stumbled forward to peer over the rail to the great hall that loomed so far below her—tables overturned, benches thrown to their sides, meat and mead spilled across the floor, as though all the warriors of her father's sept had arisen as one and rushed outside to battle an unseen threat that had appeared in the dead of night.

Fear, icy and foreign, shot through her heart. "Father!" she screamed. "Help!"

She could not hear if her father answered over the panicked screams that rose beneath her, a sudden onslaught of renewed terror, as though her childish voice had sparked some new horror in the depths of the castle. She began to cry, deep sobs of fear, sinking down onto the cold stone floor, shivering in her thin nightgown, her arms wrapped around her small body in a vain attempt to soothe herself from the grip of unknowable fear encircling her.

Footsteps thundered up the stairs, and she peeked up to

see her father approaching, his hands trembling as he sank to his knees, and even in her terrified state, she recognized that look on his face, the look that she had seen countless times on her nursemaids and her guards, but here it was now, magnified a thousandfold on his beloved features.

As if, somehow, despite his strength and her smallness, he was afraid of her.

"Rozlyn," he whispered, an awful look on his face, even as a half dozen fully armed men crept up the stairs behind him, their hands resting on their half-sheathed swords. "Child."

"Father." She sobbed, huddled against the merciless stone wall. "What has happened, where is Eileen, a dhaidí—" She barely registered it, the instinctual slipping into that childish endearment that she had told herself she had grown too big, too brave to use any longer. "I'm scared, a dhaidí."

Her pleas dissolved into incoherent weeping as her father studied her, blank and unmoving. Then he turned to the men behind him. "Cormac," he said, his expression dark, the uncontested command of a king. "Fetch the nurse."

"She won't come." The soldier shook his head, his fingers twitching on the hilt of his sword. "She's locked herself away below, crying and screaming. She says that she won't come. After what she has seen, she—"

"I don't care." Her father's voice was the iciest that Rozlyn had ever heard it, and she sobbed even harder, scared of what had caused her father to use such a tone, filled with such terror, such rage. "You tell her she will come to tend to my daughter, or I swear by the might of all the gone gods, her head will adorn my gates before dawn."

Cormac nodded once, refusing to look at where Rozlyn cowered, weeping on the cold stone floor, and vanished down the stairs without another word. Her father's strong arms circled her to lift her into the air, his gentleness returned. "Come now, child. Everything will be all right now. No one shall harm you."

The next few hours passed in a blur. Rozlyn remembered dozing by the fire, wrapped in a soft blanket, blinking sleepily as soldiers came in and out of her room to report to her father, who sat by her side, stone-faced, stroking her hair as he snapped orders to his men in that odd new tone, vibrating with defiance and fear. She remembered too that Eileen had appeared after a while, her face white and withdrawn, as she reached out with tremulous hands to where Rozlyn dozed with her head on her father's thigh to carry her to bed. "Thank you, Eileen," she whispered as those shivering hands tucked the blankets around her. "I love you."

Eileen grew even paler, then turned and fled without answering as Rozlyn dropped away in a dreamless slumber, exhausted and achy, unconcerned that Eileen had not answered.

She never did.

Rozlyn woke the next morning, the sun almost midway through its journey in the sky, and sat up, her head clear, refreshed after hours of rejuvenating sleep. It could not have been so bad as she remembered, she thought as she dressed herself, because look how bright was the sun, how sweetly the birds sang in the trees outside her window. She skipped downstairs with her nightgown tucked under her arm for Eileen to mend, as it was tattered around the hem with jagged holes in the back near her shoulder blades. Perhaps a mouse had been nibbling at it as it lay in her drawer, and she had been too tired to notice it the night before when Eileen slipped it over her head. She jumped down the last step and stopped short as she entered the great hall, the tables and benches still tossed about in disarray, the food grown cold and stale on the floor, the congealed puddles of drink staining the smooth oak boards.

It was empty, the great hall of her father. Eerily empty, when it was always bustling with life.

Rozlyn froze, a shadow of that terror she had felt in the dark hours of the night resurfacing. "Father? Eileen?"

The only answer was the faint echo of their names, so she padded forward, picking her way through the remnants of last night's feast and the overturned furniture, to the doors that led out of the castle. She eased open the door, small hands trembling, then froze in horror.

There was so much blood.

The dirt and the grass of her father's courtyard, so pristine hours ago when she had climbed the stairs after her long day of running through the fields, was rutted with splotches of gore, the crimson stains of dried blood coating the dusty, rock-ridden road that wound its way up the mountain from the valley below. The bloodstains were riddled with strange markings—the gouging claw marks of a terrible monster, odd rippling patterns of something that looked like huge, feathered wings, as though an enormous falcon had descended on the yard and torn into its inhabitants, talons flashing as it fed on dozens of hapless souls.

Rozlyn lost track of how long she stood there in the silent breeze that drifted through her hair, gently lifting its dark strands to brush across her ash-white face, staring at the carnage that scarred her father's courtyard.

Something whispered within her that this was why her father had looked at her with such awful fear, but she shook her head.

A monster had done this, obviously, some horrible beast, and she was only a girl, a pretty, black-haired princess.

She was no monster.

The sound of running boot steps behind her jarred her from her trance, and she turned, her tongue thick with horror, to see her father, his face drawn and tired, rushing toward her. "Rozlyn," he murmured, his hand on her shoulder. "What a terrible night this has been."

Rozlyn sank down on the top step, her nightgown lying forgotten in the blood-smeared dirt at her feet, her fingers clutching at the rough-sawed wood of the cedar boards beneath. "What has happened here?"

Her father sat down next to her, burying his face in his hands. "What I have long feared, child." He sighed and raised his dark head, studying the stains of blood smeared across his home. "The curse you bear has begun to awaken."

Rozlyn's heart stuttered, that unearthly knowing within her whispering again with twisted glee, *I told you so, little monster.* "How?"

"The dark magic within you," her father said heavily, "has lain dormant for the past five years, and I watched in fear for the day that it would manifest itself." His jaw clenched. "That day has come, child."

Rozlyn gripped his forearm. "But I cannot do any magic. I have tried, ever since Eileen told me the story of when I was born, of when the Cailleach cursed me. I have tried and tried, but nothing happens."

Her father stared at her for a long time in silence, something dark and unreadable swirling in his expression, then he ran his large hands down his face. "It is awakening within you, child, whether you feel it or not. Last night's events are proof of that. There are monsters, hideous creatures born of dark magic, that are irresistibly drawn to the summons of that power that lurks within your skin. They sense it and answer its call." He gestured in front of them. "Last night a Beast of terrible size and strength descended on our unsuspecting people. A black-fleeced creature with fangs and claws and huge feathered wings with talons perched atop them, that tore into them with all the fury of a thousand ravenous wolves." He sighed. "That beast was looking for you, child, as you slept in your tower room, safe and sound, while our people died."

It felt like a blow to her face, the punch of a steel-crusted fist across her tiny cheekbone.

She might not be a monster, but she had summoned one—accidentally, to be sure, but brought it here, to her home nonetheless—and it had killed her people because of her.

A surge of nausea churned in her stomach, and the metallic tang on her tongue had the faint flavor of guilt, of shame, if such things could be tasted. "A dhaidí," she said through cold lips. "I'm so sorry. I did not know. I—"

"Hush, child." It was almost growled at her, despite the tender moniker, and Rozlyn's shoulders hunched. "It is out of your control, what has happened." A tight, all-but-imperceptible pause. "For what will continue to happen."

Alarm spiraled through her, her fingers fisting in her skirt. "But it's dead though, isn't it, Father? Surely you killed it—your soldiers killed it when it attacked. It won't come back."

"No," the king said in that same heavy voice, like nothing she had ever heard her father use before. "They did not." He stared at the scars of dried blood that slashed across the grass. "And they will not."

She opened her mouth to cry out in protest, but he

raised a hand. "They will not," he growled. He clenched his fists, then loosed a long breath before turning toward her again. "It is too powerful, child." He stared down into her upturned face. "It cannot be killed by mortal hands. We must wait," he said, laying his hand on top of hers, a wordless promise. "We must endure it until you are of age, when the curse can be broken and your magic destroyed once and for all, as was prophesied on the night of your birth."

Rozlyn nodded, her heart thudding.

She had heard the story so many, many times.

Five years ago, Eileen had often whispered to her, Rozlyn's mother, the queen, was long past her time, and the castle of the king was shrouded in a hush of anticipation as they awaited the arrival of the king's firstborn. It would be a son, her father, Ailain, the great king of Connacht and the chieftain of the Beanna Beola, would boast with utter confidence. A son, who would conquer the known world with his boldness, his bravery, the sheer strength of his arm. Saoirse, his queen, would murmur in agreement, and then would lay her thin, pale hand on her swollen belly in a silent show of acceptance and love, always three successive pats of reassurance.

Yet no child arrived, and the midwives fretted. Her mother quietly roamed the castle, her hand gliding along the stone walls with unruffled ease as the midwives followed in her waddling footsteps, tending to their queen.

"The child will come when it comes." Saoirse soothed all those who fussed over her. "Nature cannot be compelled so easily."

Until one morning, she awoke before the dawn, a strange sensation tugging at her midriff, and with a sob, she pressed her thin, wasted hands to the rumbling body within her, punching and pulling just beneath her skin, and Eileen, Rozlyn noted, would grow melancholic whenever she repeated the queen's words, this benediction that Saoirse had spoken aloud with that intuition that only mothers can know, born of the purest of loves.

"Sweet girl," the queen had whispered, "so you begin, and even so shall I end."

For hours she labored, Eileen would tell Rozlyn by the fire on cold winter nights, when the missing of the mother she had never known threatened to drown her in a deep well of nameless grief. Rozlyn would listen intently, aching to hear it even as she flinched to envision the picture Eileen painted for her—of Saoirse's narrow, fine-boned face distorted in agony as the contractions that racked her thin form heightened to an apex of unbearable anguish, until the midwife, bleary-eyed and bone-tired, looked to the pacing king in the corner of the room, and spoke the truth that they all already knew—"The baby is breech," she whispered. "They will not both survive this night."

Ailain raged, and the midwives shook, but Saoirse closed her red-rimmed eyes and placed her thin hand on her distorted abdomen. "Save her," she said, her voice raw with screaming. "Save my girl."

Rozlyn hated this part of the story and would stare into the fire whenever Eileen repeated those fateful words.

The midwives worked long into the night, twisting and coaxing the stubborn babe buried within her mother's womb, until with a final wrench, they broke the baby free, and even as her mother's lifeblood flooded the sheets beneath her, and her vision grew dim, she sighed at the sight of the red-cheeked, round-faced infant with a swatch of downy black hair. "Little rosebud," she said. "What a beauty."

Then she sighed once more, and never spoke another word, her eyelashes fluttering shut, as the shadows of dark wings against her waxen face.

And there it should have ended—a tragic story, one all too common for the children of Connacht. But then Eileen's voice would drop to a whisper as she knitted by the fire—where Rozlyn sat wide-eyed and solemn at her knee, waiting to hear again the story of the source of all her loneliness—and Eileen would continue her tale, how even as the castle wailed for their lost queen, the wind began to howl, ten thousand trumpets blaring a dreadful alarm, like the Neit, god of war himself, had come bellowing through the cold, star-studded night. The stones of the castle quaked, and the parapets shuddered, and as one, they crouched around one another, the midwives and the king and the squalling infant, their grief forgotten in their fear.

And then in a whirl of icy wind that burst through the rough-hewn window that overlooked the valley far below, she arrived—the Cailleach.

Rozlyn always shivered when Eileen would intone her name, and she would clasp her hands on Eileen's knobby knee. "Tell me how she looked," Rozlyn would say, vibrating with the urgent need to know, and Eileen would sigh and shake her head, her fingers trembling as she worked her needles through the soft sheep's-wool yarn.

It was her skin, Eileen would always say, that was the most horrifying feature of her unearthly presence. Tinged blue and shimmering with an incandescent spark, as though the first frost of winter had kissed her cheeks centuries before, and the chill of that caress had never faded from her features, her skin glistened in the flickering firelight of the hearth. Her hair, ragged and wild, was whiter than the deepest mountain snows, shorn short and jagged along the edges, and it fell across her face as a mist-borne veil over a fearful virgin bride. Her tattered cloak, pulled close around her bony shoulders, was stained and dirty, a garment sewn together with the worn yellow hides of three fallow deer, the threads gnarly and unwieldy, fraying around the sloppily stitched seams. In her right hand, she held a staff carved from the trunk of a willow tree, as polished as stones tumbling throughout an eternal stream.

"What about her eyes? The Cailleach's eyes?" Rozlyn would whisper, and Eileen would always cluck her tongue three times, a warding against evil. Silly Eileen, Rozlyn would think with a roll of her eyes, to be so afraid, as though the dread witch of winter would somehow appear in the nursery only by speaking of such things.

"She might," Eileen would sniff if Rozlyn tried to argue. "Then you wouldn't be so smug when she cuts out your cheeky tongue." Rozlyn would assume a look of penitence, and Eileen would huff and clear her throat, then continue.

Her eyes were hidden behind that sweep of bone-white hair, but as the Cailleach entered the room on the rush of ice-kissed wind, she struck her crooked willow staff against the stone floors of the castle. Three times, a swift staccato of discordant cracks, and across the floors of the room spread a thin layer of silver ice. It crawled across the fur rugs and over the gray stones of the hearth and up the tapestry-laden walls and even over the warm, wet bedclothes where Saoirse lay lifeless, leaving only the humans, who watched in horror unfrozen as winter took hold inside the warmth of the castle walls.

"Hear me." The Cailleach opened her ice-blue lips to reveal yellowed stumps of teeth and an oily black tongue that thrashed and coiled around the nubs of her remaining teeth, as a snake slithers through the branches of a tree. "This child who has been born this night, who has stolen the life breath from the queen of the realm." Rozlyn would always flinch at this moment in Eileen's tale, a sharp stab of guilt burrowing its way into her childish heart. "In her has the power of the gods been reborn, and with her birth shall come the awakening of the darkest and deadliest forces of magic that once roamed the earth, devouring all the kings of the realm and its hapless inhabitants."

Eileen would avert her eyes from Rozlyn's and stare away into the fire that crackled in the hearth. "So you were cursed, child," she would murmur. "Cursed even in the moment that your life began and your mother's ended. We begged your father to kill you then, to send you into the otherworldly realm of Magh Meall, safely wrapped in the arms of your poor mother, but he refused."

Rozlyn had studied Eileen the first time that her nursemaid had confessed her role in this part of the story. "Do you wish that he had let you?"

Eileen returned her gaze to Rozlyn's somber face, far too severe for its childish years, and said nothing.

Rozlyn nodded once, and never asked her again.

Once was enough to hear that her affection for her nursemaid would never be returned. Grumpy, nervy Eileen, who would bring her hot teas when she was sick and braid her hair into pretty plaits, who would rap her fingers with a wooden spoon when she stole sweets from her apron pocket.

Eileen, who would sing snatches of old folk tunes to keep her amused on long, cold winter days and recite the names of the flowering weeds that she would pick by the mountain streams—it was all done from duty, not from love, and Rozlyn knew it.

Eileen would continue her story, her hands trembling a little more than before. "Your father would not allow you to be harmed," she repeated with a sigh, "and caught you in his arms and pressed you to his chest even as we wailed and wept, and the Cailleach loomed by the window still, the ice of her winter-magic swirling around her, drenching us all in the bone-numbing cold of death. He fell to his knees, the great king of Connacht, and begged for a cure, a way to break this curse and destroy the evil magic that lurked within your soul."

The Cailleach, Eileen would say, hissed through her dreadful yellow teeth, that awful black tongue twitching against the stumps of her incisors, and she raised her staff again and struck it against the frost-encrusted wall of the castle, and they watched as an unseen hand began to etch ancient runes into the ice-kissed stone.

Eileen would pause here in the story and eye Rozlyn with familiar wariness, and she herself would stare back unblinking because, even as a child, she knew somehow that it would do her no good to weep, to be weak about the hard truths of her life. "Only the one who learns to love my darkness as their own," Rozlyn would say, "and who willingly binds themself to me shall break the curse."

"Yes," Eileen would answer, shrinking away from her, and Rozlyn would feel every bit the strange abomination of a girl that they all believed her to be, so she would tilt her head and study her nursemaid dispassionately.

"No one has ever loved me." It was not a question, not when she herself could see the answer as she would watch her nursemaid tremble whenever she moved her lips—solemn, unsmiling, childish lips as they were. "Daidí loves me, but he fears me too. Sometimes his hand will shake when he pats my cheek. And you do not love me. No one ever could." Eileen would say nothing, so she herself would speak the truth that none of them ever dared to say. "So then you are all doomed to die."

Eileen would stare at her abandoned yarn, the needles twisted in a disordered mess of distraction. "Yes."

It echoed through her now, this oft-repeated tale, as she sat next to her father in the warmth of the midday sun, staring at the blood that bespattered her childhood home. "No one has ever loved me," she repeated to the king, who flinched at her words. "No one ever will. It cannot be broken."

Ailain opened his mouth to argue, then lowered his head. "We will keep you locked away," he said after a moment. "Hidden in your tower, away from the outside world, to try and prevent the Beast from sensing your presence in our realm again, until the time has come to seek a suitor for your hand in marriage, one who will embrace this darkness that lives inside you and cherish you until the end of your days."

Rozlyn nodded once, then stood, the bits and pieces of what little innocence she had once possessed shattered around her like glimmering shards of tear-stained glass. "A dhaidí," she said without looking at him. "Will it work, keeping me hidden? Will it keep the Beast from preying on our people?"

The king stared at the stairs beneath them, at the thin trail of blood that continued to drip down on the ground beneath it. "No."

The word hung in the air with the heaviness of a great gray stone falling into the bottomless depths of a dark water well, and Rozlyn looked out across the sun-dappled slopes of her childhood romps for the final time. Without another word, she turned and went back inside her tower to be alone with the shadows for the next fifteen years.

CHAPTER
FOUR

THE VALE OF INAGH, ÉIRE, 1017

Jamie ran for his life down the twisting corridors of his wife's castle, the wolves beginning to howl behind him as they hunted him. Panic coursed through him, but underneath it, another emotion hummed, a trace of envious admiration.

She was magnificent, fiercer, and more ferocious than he ever could have imagined, this supple creature of rippling muscle and gleaming fangs, the incarnation of death itself.

He had heard the rumors, of course—that she had somehow learned to wrestle the unruly strands of that magic of hers into obedience, that she had, at some point over the years, broken it to her will, a black-maned stallion careening across the lowlands, eyes wheeling and nostrils flaring, now docile and calm under its mistress's soothing hand. He just hadn't believed it, not fully, until now.

Neither had he believed that she would *actually* kill him, as she had promised, yet here he was, cursing the fool that he had been who had naively believed that the bond that had once glowed silver and bright between them would drown out the darkness of her anger, that he could break through whatever tenuous walls she had built between them and make her remember the sweetness, the potency of what was.

Clearly, he had been very wrong.

He rounded another corner, chest heaving as wolves snarled and snapped at his heels, the wood boards creaking underneath him as he darted into a small side room and slammed the door. For a moment, he leaned against it, wincing as the wolves leapt against the far side of the door, scrabbling at the wood with their claws as they snarled.

It wouldn't hold them long. He panted wildly, scanning his surroundings for an escape.

A tapestry on the opposite wall fluttered on an invisible breeze, and there, he saw it—the flicker of a faint beam of daylight. He scrambled forward, jerking the tapestry to the side, and heaved a sigh of relief at the open window, the waiting grass only a short drop below. He hauled himself over the windowsill even as the door splintered behind him, and he had the briefest glimpse of gray-white snouts and snapping teeth before dropping to the ground beneath.

He rolled to his feet and ran, around the corner of the gray-stone castle, racing for the courtyard, toward the heavily armed cluster of soldiers whom he had stationed outside only an hour ago. He saw them huddled together at the base of the stairs with the now-terrified men who had been bold enough to accompany him into his wife's hall of death, now reunited with their companions underneath the midday sun.

"Arrows!" His hoarse command echoed in the hollow of the vale. "Ready arrows!"

No one moved. Each of the men stood unnaturally still,

their trembling arms raised as if in surrender, staring into the lengthening shadows of the dense trees that guarded the secrets of the vale of Inagh. A low growl resonated through the air above him, and he whirled around to see her, the Beast of Connacht, pacing back and forth on her monstrous paws on the terrace overlooking the front steps of the castle. Even now, that too-familiar gleam was in her eyes.

She was enjoying this, he thought as he wheezed, hands on his knees. She had been waiting, biding her time here in her vale, all these years, imagining this very moment, when she would have him pinned, a moth skewered on the tip of a razor-sharp needle, twitching in fear as he drew his last breath.

He whirled around, scanning the foreboding line of trees, because he recognized that particular look even on her beastly face, and it could only mean disaster for him. "What the hell is this, Bowen?"

The black-bearded soldier at the front of the group raised his head in response, his lips pale. "In the woods." Bowen pointed, his finger shaking, and Jamie saw them, great hulking shades of thick brown fur that lumbered through the brush beneath the trees.

Bears. Of course there would be bears—hungry brown bears and snarling gray wolves and a blackhearted Beast.

Even as sweat poured down his back, his lips twitched.

She had always appreciated the symmetry of such things, had loved to indulge, secretly, her flair for all things dramatic, and here it was now on full display, and almost certainly for his benefit.

"They charge if we reach for our weapons," Bowen said, his face pale and tense, and even as the hot streams of panic bubbled within him, Jamie shivered at the unflinching command that she now wielded over her magic.

However had she managed it, he wondered again, then snapped to attention as the bear closest to him let out a hungry roar.

"She is putting on quite the show for us," he said, his heart pounding harder at the sound of the wolves as they howled behind the front doors. "Though I suspect this is largely for my benefit, Bowen. She won't hurt the lot of you." At least, Jamie thought grimly, he hoped she would not—hoped that whatever other changes her anger and her power and time itself had wrought would not have stripped her of her mercy, her compassion for anyone other than himself.

He shouted up to her as he eyed the hairy brutes prowling among the trees. "Really? Wolves and bears for your execution squad, Rozi? Fitting for a Beast, I suppose."

From above him on the balcony, her voice floated down, coarse and full of thorns. "Well, I did once try fire—with unsatisfactory results, it would seem."

"Both are a bit messy for my taste. I'd prefer an arrow to the eye, if that's all right."

"If you remember," she said, rife with a vicious kind of amusement, "I never had much success with that. Wolves will do nicely enough, I think."

Jamie swore under his breath.

"There's at least a dozen, maybe more," Bowen whispered again, brow wrinkled with worry. "They were waiting for us to come out, then charged us, snarling, until we froze here in front of the hall. They retreated into the underbrush, but if we try to move, they charge us again." He looked at Jamie, the faint scars from past battles blazing livid and bright red under the sheen of sweat coating his face.

Because he was afraid, Jamie realized. Stouthearted Bowen, who had ridden away from a dozen bloody fields of battle without a backward glance, who had not even flinched when Jamie had first told him, months ago, what this might entail, riding here into the heart of her vale and entering the forbidden depths of her castle—Bowen was afraid, trembling with fear, that he might die here today at the hands of his erstwhile princess.

They all might.

Jamie winced at that strident whisper of a warning, a reminder of other, far older, guilt-ridden debts that could never be repaid.

"Rozi," he called, backing away slowly from the tree line and the bears that skulked in its shadows. "Past grievances aside, we really do need to talk."

"I would suggest doing so now rather than later."

A splintering sound, and Jamie whirled to see the wolves clawing their way through the fractured wood doors, snarling as they loped down the steps toward him.

Of all the gods-damned ways to die, he thought grimly, wolves were by far the worst.

"I did promise you once that this is what would happen if you ever displeased me," she said as though he had spoken it aloud, his silent curse, and finally, he ripped his gaze away from the beasts of the wood to instead look up at her.

To let her see him squirm would be his final death knell. It was just another strategy, another premeditated move, calculated and shrewd, in this twisted game of lies and of love that they had always played with each other.

He ignored the wolves that stalked close around him, snapping their teeth a hair's breadth from his knees, and kept his attention focused on the Beast that sat perched above him, her scaly tail thrashing as it dangled over the side of the terrace. "Now, Rozi," he said with a small shrug. "You've made your point. It's true that I behaved abominably toward you. Come on down from there, and we can talk about this like civilized people." He grinned in the way he knew had always irritated her. "Communication is the foundation of every happy marriage, you know."

"We both know that civility has never been my specialty, *husband*."

He sighed, an affectation of weariness, and her tail again lashed through the air in agitated swipes. "It's a neat little trick," he said, waving a hand toward the crouching bears, the threatening wolves, because condescension had always been the weakest spot in her armor, the match with which to strike to ignite the inferno of her rage. "I'll give you that."

"It's not a trick," the Beast growled, and Jamie's mouth quirked up at the exchange, at the memories it evoked, standing in the sunlight, wielding their words as weapons for the very first time.

"I must say," he continued, "I'm somewhat impressed. Better than screech owls and honeybees, I suppose."

She roared once in response, and Jamie staggered backward from the sheer force of it. A shadow fell across him as her wings spread wide, night-black and broad, and she tumbled through the air, landing with a resounding crash before him, her tail whipping through the grass. Her wolves gathered around her, baring their teeth in a silent snarl, their bushy tails low and their haunches poised to pounce, and he again had that unpleasant sensation that this was exactly the endgame she had envisioned for him—helpless and pinned between the flashing teeth of her bishops and the claws of her rooks, and herself the queen, inevitable as the thunder rolling across the stormy sea, advancing on him, the king—her prey.

Match in three moves, a bhrèagha.

He banished the memory as she cocked her shaggy black head and spoke, that hoarse caricature of her smooth tones rumbling through the air. "Tell me," she asked, "did my father ever give you my message from our touching reunion, several years back?"

Three of the wolves broke away from the rest of the pack, stalking toward him, one deliberate paw at a time, slow, hungry steps.

The time for diplomacy—and for levity—was past.

Jamie unslung his longbow from his shoulders and notched an arrow. Guttural growls of warning exploded from the forest as the prowling bears thundered out of the trees as one. He didn't flinch as his soldiers screamed, keeping his gaze locked on hers, and they slowed to a halt a stone's throw away from where his men fell cowering to the ground.

He raised his eyebrows at the Beast who snarled in front of him, a silent question, because he had called her bluff, and they both knew it. She huffed at him once, snapping her fangs. Without another sound, the bears settled back on their haunches and watched him, waiting for their mistress's next wordless command. Jamie eyed the wolves as they continued to skulk around him. "To answer your question"—he lowered his bow a hair's breadth, and he could have sworn he saw the black eyebrows buried underneath the shanks of beastly fur rise ever so slightly at the motion—"no, I don't believe I was given a message," he lied. "I vaguely remember him mentioning something about a giant serpent that crawled out of the loch and into his bedchamber one evening, however, so I can guess that whatever you had to say to me was equally pleasant as that."

"Not a serpent. As usual, my father is woefully ignorant about the true nature of monsters."

"I don't know about that. He warned me from the start that you were such a nasty piece of work that I would most likely end up dead at your hands, and here we are."

The black hair along her spine bristled, and her fangs glistened in the sunlight. "Funny. You were always so very funny." He bowed slightly, mockingly, and he could almost feel the fury pouring off her. It was as exhilarating as he had remembered, poking at this particular Beast. "When I found out that both of you survived the aftermath of my little tantrum, as you call it," she continued, her ears pinned back against her shaggy head. "At first I was furious—then I realized that I was glad. Glad because I wanted to be able to grow this power of mine that you both wanted to deny me, so that I could use it to wreak my vengeance on each of you in a way that you deserve."

"Well, I have seen your father's scars, so I know better than to hope that you are speaking metaphorically. I have to admit that I was surprised you let him live at all."

"A life for a life." The wolves moved in unison with her as she paced back and forth, and something honey-warm surged through him at the sight of her eyes, still so familiar, so strangely human even in the hirsute face of the Beast. "He saved my life on the night I was born, you know. Even when the midwives who pulled me from my mother's womb implored him to throw me, squalling and shrieking, from the top of the battlements, he stopped them." Her nose twitched once in disdain. "I owed him that much at least."

"I suppose it is too much to hope that you will grant me the same courtesy."

Her jaws parted, and she whuffed a harsh sound that he could only assume was a laugh, then bared her fangs at him. Jamie raised his bow again, pulling the arrow taut on the string, and the wolves and the bears surrounding him growled in unison. "Call off your fellow beasts, Rozi. Let my men go. They have done nothing to you. No reason to torment them as well."

She snarled again, and the wolf pacing to his right whined, a plea to his mistress, but the stab of carefully concealed fear eased somewhat in his chest.

If she hadn't killed him yet, then she wasn't going to kill him at all.

Probably.

"Let them go," he said. "Let them go so we can talk, you and I. Ten minutes, Rozi. Give me ten minutes to say what I came here to say, and then you can have your pets rip me to shreds, if you like."

"I hardly need your blessing to do so."

"Yet here I am, offering it anyway. Ten minutes," he said again. "Please." A twitch of the serpentine tail was the only response. He pressed on. "Aren't you even the least bit curious to know what it is that is so desperate that it would bring me here to your home, knowing what must await me?" He held his breath.

The air around her rippled, her lupine features blurring. She rose on her hind legs, her paws dwindling into two pale hands, and Jamie sighed in relief at the sight of her unsmiling face emerging from the tufts of fur. "I would imagine," she said in her own voice again, smooth and thrumming with anger, "that your intentions have not changed from what they were over a decade ago. To make a fool of me, to seduce me into allowing you to steal from me what I never agreed to give you."

"Liar. If you truly thought that, I would already be dead, and we both know it."

For a moment, the only sound was the soft panting of the wolves, then her glare flicked once toward the soldiers hunkering in the dirt. "Go," she said, and Jamie nodded curtly. They scrambled up from their knees, backing away from where she stood, surrounded by wolves, with the brown bears stretched out at her feet. Her nostrils flared once, then turned toward him, her arms folded across her chest. "I hope that you don't expect me to endure another one of your elaborate stories."

"You rather liked my stories, once upon a time, a bhrèagha."

"If you call me that again, my wolves will rip out your tongue."

"I doubt it." He tossed his bow aside with a clatter. "Do you know what I think, Rozi?" he asked, sliding his hands into his pockets. "I think that you have missed our games almost as much as I have, these past ten years, and that is the real reason why I am not lying mangled on the floor of your mead hall even now. We have always challenged one another in ways that no one else ever could." He met her glare with a silent appeal of his own, years of yearning etched on his features. "Don't you remember?"

"I remember," she said, as implacable as the sheer cliffs that loomed above the distant shore, "that you lied to me. There is nothing else worth remembering."

His smile dimmed. "What will it take, then, for me to earn your trust again?"

A pause, then her head tilted to the side, mouth tight. "You weren't surprised that I could summon the trees—you barely flinched at the sight of them." She scrutinized him, searching for any telltale flicker of understanding. "Why is that?"

"I had heard rumors that might be another element of the magic you possess, one that I was rather hoping you had not yet explored." Jamie shrugged. "You will find that I know many things about that power of yours."

She tensed, as he knew she would. "How so?"

"You keep your secrets, and I shall keep my mine. One day, perhaps when we trust each other again"—a scoff interrupted him, but he continued unperturbed—"then I shall tell you all that I know. I think you would find it rather interesting."

"Prove it," she said. "You say that you understand it, the power that I have learned to wield, to command as my own over the past ten years, while you have been wandering the realm, doing the gods know what—"

"Pining after you, obviously."

Her fingers curled into talons at her sides. "Then prove it."

"Prove what? My knowledge or my pining? The latter is very easily provided if you would only—"

Her teeth snapped together, an unspoken, lethal reminder of what lay hidden underneath that mask of seemingly innocent beauty. "Do not dare finish that thought."

By the harp, he had missed this back-and-forth between them, even now, unmistakably overshadowed with the promise of doom as it was. "You want to bargain with me, Rozi? Again? It's never gone well for you in the past."

Her hands flew up, and a spark shimmered for a moment in the air before it faded away, a thin tendril of smoke lingering in its place, evoking memories he had tried hard to forget—a midnight castle engulfed in flames, the scald from the fumes scratching at his throat, kneeling in the rain as he watched what had once been his burn away into ash and embers.

"How did you do it?" The question burst out of him,

his palms sweaty with impatience, that old familiar craving surging forth again. "Ten years ago, you could barely conjure a screech owl without passing out from the pain. How did you learn to control it?"

She lowered her arms, slow and quivering, her face pale with the effort. "It took time," she said without meeting his gaze. "Long days and longer nights of struggling, of fighting with the magic within me, and I—" She stopped, a shadow of uncertainty flitting across her face, then seemed to collect herself, cool and unruffled once more. "Quite frankly, it's none of your business, nor something that I ever intend to share with you, of all people."

"Nature," he said, and her eyes narrowed. "That much is clear. It's tied to the elements of nature, isn't it?" He shrugged. "Don't look so surprised. It has always been rather obvious. The honeybees, all those years ago? Now, they were the biggest clue."

He could have sworn that he saw her lips quirk upward, ever so slightly, at the memory. *There.* A thrill sparked through him. There she was.

She reached up to fiddle with the end of her braid. "The animals and the shifting. That is easy for me now. They do my bidding with only a thought." Her mouth flattened. "The rest is not."

Jamie made a thoughtful humming noise, then held out his hand. "Very well. What bargain shall we strike this time?"

Rozlyn stared at him, unblinking, until he lowered his hand and stepped away. "There is a creature," she said, "of unknown origin, which has been plaguing the denizens of the outermost villages of my vale. It feasts solely on men, no younger than seventeen, no older than forty, and consumes their blood while they are still alive."

"How unpleasant for them."

"Indeed." Rozlyn's mouth shimmered into the contours of what for anyone else would have been the smuggest of smiles. "Many times over the past months have the villagers come to me, pleading with me to stop this monster from preying on the youths of our land, but I have been unsuccessful at luring it out of whatever hole it hides itself in, most likely because I am not the prey it seeks."

Jamie rocked back on his heels, considering this. "Has anyone ever seen it?"

"There have been reports of a young woman with snow-blond hair, dressed in the tattered white rags of a doomed bride, wandering through the trees on the nights in question, when the young men have been found dead and drained of their blood in the early morning hours." She raised her eyebrows. "You are in luck, it seems. The creature chooses to hunt at the waning crescent moon, only three nights from now. Your timing is fortuitous."

"Yes, I was born under a blessed star." He eyed her with a hint of apprehension. "And you believe that I would have greater success than you at tracking this unfair maiden? I'm not the one who is half-wolf, you know."

"No," Rozlyn said with unutterable sweetness. "But I do hope that there is a very good chance that she will kill you if you try."

"My loving wife has such confidence in me. You see, I really am the most fortunate of men."

"This is the only deal that I will make with you, Jamie. Rid my people of this scourge, and I will listen to whatever duplicitous tale of woe that you have come to spin me."

"It's a bargain." He flashed a grin. "Yet another monstrous female for me to woo. Do you suppose that I will have to marry this one as well? Because I have to say, once was enough."

Rozlyn snarled again, vicious and guttural, her claws slipping through the skin of her scarred knuckles. Jamie abandoned all semblance of bravado and fled toward where his men hovered by the tree line, the howls of her wolves echoing behind him.

All things considered, he decided as he reached up to wipe the rivers of sweat from his brow with his sleeve, that went about as well as could be expected.

CHAPTER FIVE

Rozlyn descended the stairs of her father's castle, smoothing her gown with calculating hands, preparing for this next match, this recently arrived opponent who awaited her below, sitting at her father's table—this new contender who presumed to steal her smiles and win her hand.

It made it easier, Rozlyn had long ago decided, enduring this lonely, forlorn existence, hidden away in her gray-stone tower, to imagine that her life was a game, another solitary round of fidchell played on the terrace, the bronze sheen of her figurines glinting in the midday sun as she practiced and perfected the moves and feints and features of her gambits, an endless battle of wits, a struggle of survival, pitted only against herself.

It became particularly useful when her sixteenth birthday dawned, and the suitors began to arrive, their arms filled with flowers and their mouths filled with lies.

Rozlyn hated all of them.

She seated herself at her father's oak table, smoothing her napkin in her lap, over her gown, and peeked up through her lowered lashes. This one, with his nervous eyes and sweat-soaked lips as he hovered in the doorway—he was somehow almost worse than the black-bearded flaith from a fortnight ago, who had crowed about his bravery almost as incessantly as he'd boasted about his well-defined pectoral muscles.

Her somber lips did not waver, but inwardly Rozlyn smiled, remembering the young lord's shrieks. He had insisted that she accompany him on a stroll across the terrace of her tower, as though he were bestowing on her some great favor by allowing her the pleasure of his company. He had droned on as they walked the well-worn wood planks of her prison, bragging about his proficient use of a smallsword, and Rozlyn had smirked privately to herself at the unwitting implication. As he lectured her on the true nature of a great swordsman—how it lay in the adeptness of his beats, in the convincing nature of his second intention—Rozlyn had hummed along in agreement without hearing a word of it, straining to focus those flickers and paltry flares of magic that lived deep within her. It was still so difficult to manipulate anything other than shadows, as though this power within her was an unwieldy spindle-legged foal, still tremulous and trembling in its newborn gait. But it was more potent now than when she was a child, this potential for greatness that slept at the tips of her fingers, ready to shed its frailty and burst from the confines of the fold, a powerful stallion with unparalleled speed.

A horse. The image had hung in her mind, just as her father had described it to her many years ago, the way the wild stallion's legs would churn through the green grasses of the southern lowlands, wild and free, as the bees swarmed up from their nests in protest at the disturbance of their thundering hooves—

There.

Rozlyn had held her breath, ignoring the prattle of the young lord at her side, summoning that faint buzzing that reverberated through her imagination to her now, here on this balcony. In answer, a lazy hum filled the air behind her as a fat yellow-brown honeybee glided toward them to land on the ear of the preening young man.

He yelped at the sudden pinch of its sting, then swore as the shell of his ear grew bulging and red. Rozlyn made a false sound of compassion in this new triumph dancing within her. She reached out again with the faint feelers of this blossoming power within her, calling out to his honey-drunk friends with a low, inviting hum. Another had appeared, bustling through the air in answer, and landed on the young lord's shoulder, and even as he cursed, another crawled up the sleeve of his doublet, and yet another alighted upon the sensitive area at the nape of his neck. He had screeched and slapped and swore, and yet the bees kept appearing, inexplicably drawn to him, a veritable honeycomb of a man. Soon most of his skin was red and raw and horribly inflamed, tears streaming down his cheeks as he screamed, unable even to flex his swollen fingers.

"Perhaps you should seek a healer," Rozlyn had suggested with flawless gentleness, her face as serious and unsmiling as ever. The black-bearded flaith had glared at her, trembling with pain and fury, then stormed away—"damn you, you little *wagon*"—and Rozlyn had waited until he disappeared into the stairwell, then lifted her face to the sky and the buzzing bees that still circled above her, seeking her approval, and smiled.

This one was not so insufferable, but far more pitiable, and with a cool detachment she set aside the memory of her triumph over the small-sworded man and instead focused her attention on how best to destroy the suit of the new-minted earl in front of her.

She watched him greet her father by the door, this young earl, and excitement sang in her blood as he edged nervously toward his seat. It was a game to her, a match of wits, like fidchell, the same sparring and the skewering that she had practiced all her life. It was hardly even a sport, sitting across the board from these suitors. They spread their absurdly translucent nets wide and made them so easy to sidestep, to evade, and all the while, unbeknownst to them, she was quietly launching a king hunt of her own, moving her pieces across the board with expert ease.

She always, always won the match.

The flaith, she pondered even as she bowed her head in a docile greeting to the flaxen-haired earl, had been boastful and a braggart, humiliation being the key to the demise of his courtship, but this man—he was barely more than a boy himself, so diffident and timid and tremulous. He was scarcely able to look her in the eye, even as still and serene as she appeared to be while sitting at dinner, the boards between them laden with baked meats and pies and fresh red berries. So not an attack on his pride, she mused as she savored the spice of the sausage and onions in her bowl of coddle stew, but an assault on the nervousness that radiated from his every pore. For once, it was not fear that prevented him from meeting her gaze—she was all too accustomed to the averted glances of those who feared the latent power that thrummed in her veins, the damnation of their people—not fear, then, in the young earl's face, but true bashfulness, the shyness of a young boy overwhelmed by the presence of a pretty girl.

That familiar anticipation at a new challenge rose within her as she sipped at her sweet honeyed mead. Brashness and boldness it would be then.

She leaned forward and, with the sharp meat knife, speared a round, conveniently shaped sausage with a savage thrust, then lifted it over the table and back to her plate, brutally pinned on the tip of her blade.

The young earl's eyes went wide as he watched her set it down, the knife still embedded in its flesh. She raised her fork with her other hand and drove it into the very center of the crisp pork meat, spearing it clean through to the other side with brutal efficiency. She swiveled her fork so that the elongated sausage stood quivering on its end and, with slow, deliberate strokes of her knife, began to peel the singed skin of the pig away from the juicy meat inside.

Rozlyn looked up from the task at hand, a portrait of innocence, and met the horrified gaze of her would-be suitor. *Check.* "I like to skin them before I eat them," she explained, blinking serenely at the pale-faced boy across from her. "I have been practicing since I was a young girl."

Her father choked into his goblet as the earl swallowed, beads of sweat appearing on his youthful brow. "Rozlyn," Ailain growled, "conduct yourself like a lady."

"Of course," she murmured, demure princess that she was, of course, so solemn and so calm. She laid the half-flayed sausage down on her plate, and with great precision, lifted her fork and knife and began to dice its length, swiftly and surely, into neatly carved slices of meat.

Match in two moves.

The young earl laid his fork down beside his plate with

a clatter, his hand going to rest in his lap with an overtly protective air. "My King," he squeaked, "I am afraid that I am . . . quite unwell. I must take my leave of you."

Ailain shot to his feet, pleading with the pale-faced youth, as Rozlyn continued to chew the carved pieces of sausage with great contentment, and then licked her lips—once, twice—at the earl when he glanced nervously in her direction. He abandoned any pretense at politeness and fled, bolting through the door to the stairs that spiraled down the inside of the tower walls, abandoning his half-eaten lunch on the table.

Match, she thought, and her lips did not so much as quiver at the sight of his empty chair.

She watched as her father stood stock-still in the doorway, fists clenched at his side, his shoulders heaving. "I do hope," Rozlyn murmured, "that the young earl has not taken ill from any food served at our table."

The king pivoted to face his cool-eyed daughter as she ladled the remainder of her stew into her solemn mouth and glowered. "You are a devil-child if I ever saw one."

Rozlyn lifted her brows. "I am sure that I do not know why you would think so."

Ailain flung himself into his chair, the wood moaning under the force of his hefty form. "This is the third one in a month, Rozlyn, whom you have sent running within the very hour of their arrival."

"Perhaps you should seek more stalwart men for my hand rather than silly boys who run away, frightened by their own shadows."

"Was it shadows, then, that landed the young flaith of Bréifne in a healer's home for the best part of a fortnight, swollen and half-asphyxiated by the dozen welts from bee bites that covered his body?"

Rozlyn considered informing her irate father that, in a way, yes, it was shadows that did such a thing, considering the nature of her conjuring. Probably not helpful, she decided, and would most likely drastically reduce her chances of enjoying dessert.

She shrugged instead. "It is hardly my fault that he insisted on bringing me those foolish flowers when every child knows that it is the peak season for honeybees."

"And what about the lord of Fer Teir? Or the prince of Leinster?"

A gratified thrill rushed through her at the latter name.

What a superstitious, nosy, fool of a man he had been. He had quizzed her on her "defect," demanding the details of her "infirmity." Rozlyn had smothered her outrage and instead widened her eyes with an all-too-credible expression of dismay. "My father's dogs," she had whispered, "should they be so unfortunate as to meet my eyes, will run whimpering from the room, never to be seen again, until they are found, cold and dead, their bodies contorted, curled under the benches in the great hall in the throes of unimaginable terror, drowned in their own blood." She had shivered delicately as his mouth fell open in horror. "I fear that one day it will be a man who looks into my eyes and sees his own death reflected within their depths."

He had left an hour later and had not sent word to her father about his supposed suit since.

That game had barely even qualified as a match—it was a rout.

"You must give them a chance, child," her father said, and Rozlyn jolted back to the present, raising her eyes to see genuine pain etched across his face. "You must. It is the only way—". He broke off abruptly.

"It is the only way to free our people from the Beast," Rozlyn finished, her shoulders sagging. She risked another glance at her father's grim face. "Could we not try again, send out more warriors, more experienced hunters to kill the Beast?"

"No," thundered Ailain, his fist crashing down on the table so that the silver plates rattled against the smooth oak planks. "I will not allow those whom I am meant to protect to come to harm."

Rozlyn nodded, her fingers twisting around her fork. The guilt she tried so hard to bury throbbed suddenly, a half-healed bruise newly struck. "I could try," she said hopelessly, as she had pleaded so many times over the years. "I know that I am young, barely seventeen, but I could try and learn how to use it, how to harness this power I have to fight the Beast, if only you would let me."

"The gods damn it, Rozlyn." Her father shoved away from the table, and Rozlyn jumped back in her seat to avoid the mead that sloshed over the side of her goblet. "Do you listen to nothing? There is but one way to break this curse that brings this monster to our lands and looses it on our people, and you refuse to do the only thing that you truly can do to save them."

Rozlyn's eyes burned, so she swallowed thickly, fighting back the surge of tears building in her throat. Her father had always hated to see her cry. "I am sorry, Father," she whispered. "I know I am selfish. Only, it does not seem so evil, this bit of magic that I possess, and I do not—" Her throat closed up, and she cleared it. "Truthfully, I do not relish the idea of being bound to another."

Ailain sighed, then sat down in his chair. He reached across the table and placed his meaty hand over hers, an uncharacteristic show of affection. The lump in her throat grew, and somehow she was five years old again, a bright-eyed child longing for nothing more than to be loved by her father, no matter how many monsters lurked in the shadows of her soul. "I know, child. You were born as wild as the black-maned mares who roam the lowlands in the southern realm, as unbreakable in spirit. It pains me to shuffle you off to another in such a way, as though you were mere chattel, little rosebud." Rozlyn's heart swelled to hear the endearment of her long-dead mother on her father's tongue. "But—" Her father's voice echoed with hollow finality. "It is the only way. You must make one of these men love you, and I would have you cherish them in return. I am trying," he pleaded, "to ensure your happiness. Only the man who will at last bring a smile to your pretty face shall earn your hand. Only he will be worthy of your heart, and worthwhile enough to treasure you as you so deserve."

Rozlyn nodded, even while her heart whispered to her that that was a lie, that no one would ever truly see her for what she was, that none could ever love the darkness in her soul.

And yet, she decided that night as she watched the moonbeams feebly shift themselves across her ceiling under the guidance of her finger, for her father she would try. For her father, who had suffered so much for her sake, who had with tremulous hands taught her to play fidchell, who had been there even on her loneliest and darkest days, who had saved her again and again, when so many had begged for him to put the good of his people over the wishes of his heart and end her life—for him, she would try to let these suitors love her.

For him, she would ignore the inner cry of protest, of pain that arose at the idea of losing this incandescent magic that spun within her veins.

The suitors came and went, and Rozlyn walked and talked with them as solemnly as ever, and when the bolder ones leaned in to kiss her somber lips, she let them, closing her eyes, not in passion but in preoccupation, coolly comparing the slick, wet slide of one's kiss with the open-mouthed groping of another's.

Each time, her revulsion grew so strong that she shoved them all away—unyielding and cold—and each time, they stormed off.

An unnatural monster, they called her. A witch, a wagon, a fiend of hell—hateful, foul maledictions, all.

Yet each night, Rozlyn lay in her bed, tracing the shadows of moonlight on the oak beams of the ceiling, silently marveling at the beauty found within her beastliness.

CHAPTER SIX

THE VALE OF INAGH, ÉIRE, 1017

Jamie was many things—perturbed, amused, resigned—but he could not in good conscience say that he was surprised at his wife's declaration.

Because of course she was exactly that vindictive, to banish him from her home and force him to sleep in the woods.

Jamie huddled beneath the relative shelter of an overhanging crag, which jutted from the side of the rocky knoll in the shadow of the castle, shivering against the blast of sharp, icy rain that blew in his face, a deliberate taunt.

Clearly, this storm was of a personal nature.

She had ordered him to disband most of his men, and only a few of those most loyal to him, rather than to Ailain, had remained—Bowen and Tavin and Hedrek and Nyle, good men all—but their regret rolled off them in waves. Their resentment was far more heated, unlike the relentless sleet that rained down upon them, night and day, while they waited for the third night to arrive so that he could venture forth to confront the monster who preyed upon the youths of her realm.

They were forbidden to approach the hall—on pain of death by dismemberment, Rozlyn had commanded before she banished them into the thickets of the vale—not until the bloodthirsty creature that stalked her people had been slain. Jamie's men had nodded their agreement even before she had finished speaking. Even so, on the second day of unforgiving icy rain, Jamie crept near the walls of her citadel and squinted through the sleet and the gloom until he could see her. She perched on the windowsill with seeming casualness, the tantalizing glow of a warm fire burning in a cheery red-and-gold silhouette behind her. Jamie glowered as she crossed her ankles and leaned against the window frame, munching on bites of barmbrack as she turned the pages in her book, the perfect portrait of unconcerned indifference.

Without a doubt, she knew that he knew that *she* knew that he was there, watching from the woods.

Gods, she was exhausting.

Jamie cupped his half-frozen hands around his mouth and called up to her. "Have you considered that the harvest season is not yet half-passed, and that you are destroying your precious people's livelihood? Or has what little compassion you ever felt for them been annihilated by your loathing of me? Or perhaps it is the pangs of unrequited lust that inspire you to lash out at me like this?"

Her answer floated back down to him, muffled by the sound of driving rain. "As usual, you underestimate me, *husband*. Your understanding is, unsurprisingly, severely limited."

Jamie narrowed his eyes, the icy rain biting into the creases along his temples, then turned on his heel to the nearest pine tree, pulling himself up through the slick, sap-soaked branches until he poked his head out of the top of the evergreen.

The dark gray storm cloud that pelted them with such merciless rain was situated directly over the little copse where they had made their camp, and to the left and right of it, stretching as far as his eye could see, the serene blue sky unfolded, unblemished by even the slightest hint of a tempestuous cloud.

"Well, damn."

Jamie scratched at his jaw and climbed back down the branches, his hands numb with cold, the frosty water trickling down the collar of his shirt and coating his spine with a sharp layer of ice. He jumped to the ground beneath Rozlyn's window seat, where she continued reading her book and snacking on her cake with the self-satisfied air of a house cat having raided its master's store of cream. "Not 'easy' for you, indeed. I suppose," he shouted back up to her fire-warmed window, "that if we were to move our temporary lodgings to the east, we would find ourselves once again in the midst of an unseasonably miserable ice storm?"

"No man can control the weather," she said, and even from far below, he caught her well-satisfied smirk.

"But a woman can, apparently." Jamie threw up his hands, torn between frustration and begrudging admiration. "This is a bit melodramatic, even for you—you do know that, yes?"

Rozlyn took another deliberate bite of barmbrack. "Do try and stay warm, *husband*. It's strangely frigid tonight."

Jamie stalked away, back to his ice-crusted blankets and

his shivering, disgruntled men, trying to hide from them the amusement that her wickedness provoked in him.

At last, the morning of the third day waned, and the warmth of the sun peeked through the heavy black clouds, the icy rain disappearing as mysteriously as it had come. Jamie glowered in the direction of the castle, then shouldered his longbow and leather quiver of thick ash arrows and ordered his men to remain in the valley. As soon as the rain cleared and the sun reached its zenith in the sky, he had ridden away, urging his silver-maned mare toward the outskirts of the village north of Rozlyn's home, wedged into the base of the great mountains of Mhám Toirc that encircled the vale of Inagh to the west, facing the looming peaks of Beanna Beola to the southeast.

The trees grew still and watchful around him as night fell, blanketing him in a shroud of darkness. He stopped to dismount, securing the reins of his horse to a nearby tree. He moved through the brambles and the brush, running his hands and his arms through their leaves, the cool breeze carrying his scent down through the shadows of the trees at the base of the mountain. The moon was just beginning to crest midway in the sky when he slipped back toward his horse and crouched underneath the craggy ridge of a boulder-ridden hillside beside the gentle gurgle of a small rushing stream. There, building a small fire beneath its rim, he unslung his bow and waited.

The black hours of midnight slipped in around him, and with them, on soundless feet, a silent presence lingered there among the watching woods, and he knew she had come. He stood, stepping away from the overhanging rock into the small clearing in front of him. "A chailín," he said, low and soothing, "I mean you no harm. Come and sit by the fire with me."

A long, simmering hiss echoed through the trees from the unseen figure, and Jamie tightened his grip on his arrow, drawing it taut as he scanned the impenetrable darkness of the trees around him. "Come now," he called. "Don't be shy, pretty lady."

There was a rush of motion behind him, and he whirled and there she was—a nightmarish vision of matted white-blond hair and bleached-bone skin, stretched tight and taut over her skeletal frame, her eyes whirling in her skull, even as her mouth gaped wide in an endless scream, her chin drenched in dark crimson blood.

Jamie raised his bow and fired, watching as the arrow passed straight through her emaciated, blood-drenched face, and then she was on him, tackling him to the ground as she tore at the air far too close for comfort to his face with long, lethal fangs. Jamie wrapped his hands around her gaunt neck even as the blood of some poor past victim dripped onto his cheek, and he summoned all his strength to flip her under him as he pressed down, choking at the soft, breakable dent in her windpipe. She kicked and thrashed, clawing at his arms and his shoulders with impossible strength, but he knelt on her stomach with grim determination, blinking away the blood and sweat that poured down his brow. She opened her mouth in a gasping gulp of desperation, and he reared back, jerking her head into the air only to slam it down into the rocky earth with as much force as he could muster.

She lay there, stunned and unmoving for a few brief seconds, and he spun off her to stumble to the small flickering fire and seize a burning branch, his fingers screaming at the scorching heat of the embers. Jamie wheeled around, and as quick as that, she was already on her feet, her skeletal fingers curving in rage as she advanced on him, her mouth foaming with blood and saliva.

"Stop." In a slow, hypnotic motion, he waved the flaming branch in front of her face, and her shoulders sagged as her steps slowed, her deadened eyes following the movement, mouth slightly ajar. "There now," he murmured, as soft as a lullaby. "Rest for a while and listen to my voice." He watched her for a moment, but her enchantment with the bright orange-red of the flame held, and he continued. "Will you answer my questions?"

Her crimson-soiled lips parted. "Yes," she croaked.

Jamie studied her blank expression. "What happened to you, a chailín?" he whispered, relaxing his grip on the burning torch. "Who did this to you?"

Her thin shoulders twitched and shook. "Áthair," she croaked again. "Fear céile."

His jaw clenched. "I have known too many others like you," he said softly. "I have heard their stories and helped them grieve many long years ago, as I would for you." He gestured toward the stream, where it gurgled in rhythm with her harsh breathing, reminiscent of something like sobs. "Show me, and I will help you to find the peace that I have given to your sisters before you."

The milky white orbs in her skeletal face stilled, the cloudy haze coating them cleared, and for the briefest moment, he saw her there, the girl she used to be, trapped within the monster she had become, and she screamed once, a cry of mourning rather than wildness, and he knew that she understood.

She lurched forward, her eyes whirling in her skull, and dropped to her sticklike knees by the banks of the stream and plunged her face into the water. It churned around her, and from the smoky tendrils that arose from the stream, the tragedy of her life unfolded in the smoke before him.

A pretty girl, as he had suspected, with straight blond hair and eyes as clear as the sky in springtime.

She walked hand in hand with a redheaded, freckle-faced boy, his face and hands rough and calloused, his clothes stained with the rich, dark dirt of the land. They strolled together through the grass-green hills of rich farmland, chatting about chores and children—*what would you call our daughter if we have one*, she asked, laughing, and he grinned slyly—*so long as you give me ample chances to try for them, then you can name our pretty girls whatever you like*—and she pinched his arm as she smiled, shaking her head at him in fondness even as she blushed.

The smoke swirled and shifted, and now she was weeping, her hair unbound and unkempt, kneeling before a stone-faced man, unfeeling and flinty, and she lifted her hands in supplication—*please, a dhaidí, please, I beg you, I love another, please do not condemn me to this living death*—but he struck at her pale face, and she crumpled to the ground, sobbing in pain and heartbreak.

Another man appeared, younger and more handsome, but with a hard, cruel face and a jaw of iron, and he stood before the ashen-faced maiden, now decked in the finery of her bridal clothes—a white-and-red gown, with a thin headband of gold placed on her snow-blond hair—as she dully recited the ancient words of the marriage-bond to the cold-eyed chieftain in front of her, and then she was slipping away into the quiet dark of the night even as the cheer and uproar from the bridal feast within echoed at her tauntingly, mocking her lost dreams of a vanished life with the red-haired boy.

She grew thinner and paler, the purloined plaything of a warmongering chief, the dark splotches of black-blue bruises mottling the bare skin of her neck and her arms. Thinner and thinner, her cheekbones protruded from her face as she stared unseeingly at the lavish dinners laid out in front of her as her husband roared, deep in his cups next to her, oblivious to the despair consuming her alive. She withered away in starvation, the sweet-spiced meats and succulent fruits returning untouched to the kitchen on her cold, neglected plate.

Then she was gone, a wisp on the wind, and buried with quick, hurried impatience in her fateful bridal gown, almost even as she breathed her last. She was mourned by none but a solitary, broad-backed boy with tousled red hair, his face snow-white with grief beneath his freckles, kneeling in the mud by her hasty grave, hands pressed into the weeping earth for a final embrace.

Night fell, and that same earth began to shift and shake, and two white hands dug away at the soft black dirt, and she rose with a terrible vengeance, stalking through the darkness to her father's house. He was snoring in his bed, with one arm flung across his aging face, and she sprang, her newborn fangs flashing in the dim light of the hearth. He screamed—one long, terrible scream—and then she was on him, drawing out his thick lifeblood with her knifelike teeth—his life for the life she had desired, the life that he had stolen, for all the little lives of bright eyes and shaky first steps and tiny belly laughs that would now never be.

Then she was moving through the night, swifter than a shadow, her bloodlust rising, the sweet-and-sour taste of her vengeance still burning in her mouth, and there was her bridal home, her erstwhile husband ensconced in her marriage bed, the body of some unlucky girl already pinned underneath his grunting stomach. She struck as swift as an adder, his shrieks mingling with the screams of the terrified girl, and she savored the acrid taste of his blackhearted blood, drawing out his agony and his pain with slow, torturous sips until his sobbing stopped and his body went stiff and still.

She rose, her chin dripping bright crimson with gore, and the girl in her bed shuddered and sobbed, but she turned away with indifference to prowl away in the night, returning only at the first glimpse of the dawn to her bed in the dirt. She lingered only for the soft touch of those warm, calloused hands on the earth above her, growing rarer and rarer as the long years passed, and for the nights when her shallow grave opened wide—those ravenous midnight awakenings, her hunger for vengeance burning anew in her throat—and she prowled the night, searching for new victims to slake her undying thirst.

The smoke vanished, and she lifted her head from the water, the droplets streaming down her corpse-pale face as she blinked at him, purged of her rage by her watery confession.

Jamie inhaled through his teeth. "Show me," he said, and her milk-white stare bore into his own. "Show me where you sleep, and I will help you to rest, a chailín."

She lurched to her feet, and he tensed, his fingers

tightening on the still-burning branch, but then she blinked once, twice, and turned away, slipping into the shadows of the trees, and he hurried to where his horse pranced nervously nearby, tossing her head in protest against the leather strap that tied her to the tree. He swung himself into the saddle and urged her forward, following the unearthly specter skating through the night before them.

It would be far easier to simply kill her again, for good this time. He considered it, watching the tattered hem of her gown catch and drag across the gnarled roots that lined the forest floor. It would be simple enough, an iron stake through where her heart had once been, a heap of rocks tied around her bony ankles before he dumped her emaciated frame into the river to feed whatever fish might be brave enough or desperate enough to taste her corpse-white flesh. It was certainly the blood-price owed to her victims, yet he could not bring himself to do it, to unsheathe the iron spike tucked carefully into his belt underneath his doublet. She deserved this much, this small, insufficient peace, to rest free from violent dreams of the misery that she had endured, of the horror that she had become, and to find shelter deep within the slumbering embrace of the earth-mother herself.

She drifted through the night, over rocks and thorns, across newly shorn fields, through the endless darkness of the night-drenched trees, with Jamie following close behind, until she came to the outskirts of the little village at the edge of the vale of Inagh and crawled into a shallow hole in a long-forgotten, overgrown cemetery. The names etched into the stone markers were faded with hundreds of years of snow and rain and sun. She laid down, her hands crossed at her breast, and closed her wild eyes for the final time.

An hour before dawn, Jamie stood back from the grave,

muddy and exhausted, his hands raw and bleeding from the
rough edges of the dozen flint rocks that he had dragged
from the river to place carefully across the expanse of her
grave. The ground beneath them seemed to breathe forth a
sigh and relax, one final exhalation before it settled down
to sleep at last.

He tilted his head back against the cool mist of the new
morning sky and tried not to weep at how such a little bit of
power could make such monsters out of men.

CHAPTER SEVEN

Most of Rozlyn's memories from her youth were a jumbled, incoherent mass of remembrances. All the days and weeks and months locked away in her tower seemed to blur together, an interminable stretch of years, but there were two in particular that stood out, bright and clear, crystalized in her memory—the day that the Beast first arrived in Connacht, and the day that Jamie did.

She was settled on a particularly sunny nook of the stone balustrade of her tower with a book and an apple, relishing the sweet-citrus tang and the pale warmth of the sun after weeks of rain, when a shadow fell over her, blocking the rays of the midday light. She looked up, squinting with annoyance, and saw him standing there, head tilted to the side, watching her with dark blue eyes.

"Who are you?"

"You do know," he observed without preamble, ignoring

her barked demand, "that it is almost a seventy-five-foot drop off the side, and you are precariously close to the edge."

Rozlyn slid closer to the side until her slippered foot dangled defiantly over the edge of the balustrade. "I asked you a question."

He grinned at her, and Rozlyn acknowledged a begrudging tug of attraction at the way that the faint imprint of the laugh lines at the corners of his eyes creased into deeper wrinkles when he smiled. "Someone who is mildly concerned about what a nasty mess you will make when you are splattered on the ground below."

Awareness dawned, and Rozlyn shut her book with a frustrated snap, her half-eaten apple forgotten on the ledge beside her. "You're a new suitor."

"I'm not slagging about the splatter. I have a queasy stomach and don't particularly tolerate any sort of gruesomeness well, so if you could come away from there, I would appreciate it greatly."

"How do you imagine," Rozlyn asked with great politeness, "this queasy stomach of yours would tolerate evisceration?"

"Probably not well." He shoved his hands into his pockets. "Is that something that happens often in these parts? What a very unpleasant place."

Rozlyn bared her teeth. "Only to those foolish enough to seek to marry me."

The stranger snorted. "Such hubris. Why, by the harp, would I ever want to marry you? You seem like quite the shrew."

"How *dare* you? I am the princess of Connacht."

"You don't say. How odd. You're pretty enough, I suppose, but I had heard that she was quite the beauty."

Her book slapped against the stone wall. "I will have you hanged, you insolent muppet."

"I doubt it," he said, and she bristled at the mischievous glint in his eyes. "Rumor has it that your father's sept does not like you at all, that they are rather suspicious of your little magic tricks."

"They're not tricks, you fool; it's real magic."

"Either way," he said. "I rather suspect that they would side with me, stranger though I may be."

Rozlyn scowled, then opened her book and proceeded to ignore him with pointed deliberateness. She had no desire to acknowledge his cheeky grin and his arrogant drawl or the idle way that he rocked back and forth on his heels, with his hands tucked away in his pockets.

"What are you reading?"

"It's called a book," she snapped. "It seems doubtful that you have ever heard of one," and improbably, his eyes lit up, as though he recognized this opening move of hers as well as the strategy behind it and approved of them both, already knowing exactly how he planned to counterattack.

She disliked the sudden throb of anticipation that this realization evoked within her.

"I am, oddly enough, aware of the existence of such marvels. What is it called?"

She was silent, staring unseeingly at the pages filled with inky scrawls of familiar, much-loved words that were somehow undecipherable at the moment. Still, better not to answer him, not to acknowledge his presence in any way. It was unsettling to be so distracted, so caught off guard, and she would not allow him to fluster her any longer.

"Perhaps it is an entire volume of illustrations for

children. That seems appropriate, given how very underwhelming of an impression you have made thus far."

Rozlyn gritted her teeth, ignoring the brief flash of alarm that he had sprung his trap on her while she was unprepared, with no strategy in place, her pieces in disarray across the board. She swallowed and focused on her book, determined not to be goaded into a response, so that he would give up, like they all inevitably did—he would abandon this foolish pursuit of her, grow bored or irritated with her lack of a response, and he would leave her in peace with her solitude.

She had been alone for years, and that was exactly how she liked it.

"You are scowling quite fiercely. Just learning your letters, are you now?"

The frayed edges of her temper snapped. "What do you want?"

"Currently, I would settle for the bare bones of civility. I asked you what you were reading."

"I am not civil, and I told you. A book."

"How enlightening. You should know that I am very persistent, and I will not be deterred until I am satisfied." She heard the faint rustle of his clothes as he leaned against the opposite wall and crossed his ankles, watching her with apparent amusement. "So. What are you reading?"

She scowled and conceded—just this once. "A poem. From across the sea, about a monster who terrorizes the mead hall of the king and the hero who slays it."

"Ah, I am, believe it or not, familiar with it." He leaned forward to get a better look, and she bared her teeth again in a warning. He smiled, wholly unconcerned. "I shall wager a guess that you most closely identify with the monster's mother in this particular text, given her affinity for be-heading and then subsequently devouring the entrails of hapless young men."

She slammed her book shut again—gods, what kind of man was this, to provoke her so, to fracture her carefully crafted mask of serious-eyed calm, not once but twice, in the short span of a few minutes of conversation. "Why are you being such a muttonhead?"

He barked with laughter. "A 'muttonhead'? Did you call me a 'muttonhead'?"

"Is there a reason as to why you cannot go away and leave me in peace?"

"I am trying," he said, his mouth twitching as she glared at him, "to make you laugh. Apparently, that is the key to winning your hand, dubious honor that it is."

"Well, by all means, abandon your suit and slink back into whatever hole you were hatched in and leave me to grow old as a spinster."

"I fear I cannot do that, a bhrèagha." She frowned at the unfamiliar word, and his lips widened into a small secret smile. "Apologies," he said. "I have spent far too much time across the sea in the land of the Picts, and I'm afraid their ways of speaking have carried over into my own."

"What does it mean?"

"A compliment," he said, a roguish glint in his eye, "in admiration of your fabled loveliness. My presence was re-quested, and so I have arrived to seek your hand, charming maiden that you are, in matrimony. At first I was rather excited by the prospect. After all, as I said, the infamous princess of Connacht was rumored to be quite the—"

"Beauty. Yes, I understand now, thank you," she said in a clipped voice, trying—and failing—to hide her irritation at this idle mockery of her loveliness. She *was* beautiful, and even so, men trembled at the sight of her face.

Most men, at least.

"Indeed," the stranger said, still smiling. "I was, as I said, mildly intrigued by the idea." He studied her for a moment, deliberate and teasing. "Less so now, I must admit. Do you always wear your hair just so? It's not particularly flattering."

This man, though, was bizarre, and attractive, and infuriating. This man did not fear her at all, it seemed.

This man had to be gotten rid of, and the sooner, the better.

Rozlyn readied herself for battle, eyeing him as she considered her opening move. "Who allowed you to come here? This is my private terrace."

"Your father," he said, running his fingers idly through his hair. "Of course."

The stranger pushed off the wall and stepped toward her, studying her as intently as she watched him, each taking the measure of the other. "He is not optimistic about my chances, given both your reputation for emotionally eviscerating—your words, not mine—your poor admirers and my own distaste for the kind of theatrics as you seem prone to engage in."

"Then why are you here at all?"

"To be quite blunt, I have heard that whoever wins your hand shall also win a veritable treasure as your dowry, a bhrèagha," he answered, that mockery of a nickname sliding off his tongue with seamless ease. "And I'm a very mercenary man."

"I find it very difficult to believe that my father thought that you, of all people, would be the one to win my heart."

"It's not your *heart* that needs to be won, so I hear." He rocked back on his heels. "Consider yourself put on notice, Rozi."

"My name is Rozlyn. Not Rozi, not—that other word. Merely Rozlyn."

He only smiled in response. "Regardless. I expect henceforth to be wildly and hopelessly, swept-off-my-feet, madly in love with you. Feel free to start your wooing at any time."

"You can go suck a stone."

"There, you see. I'm falling in love already."

Rozlyn's lips twitched—oh gods, oh no—and she clamped down firmly, refusing to acknowledge the rush of humor that slid through her.

He had taken the advantage from her there, and a reluctant admiration twinged through her. "Leave," she said, flat and cold. "It is not a request, and I will not tell you again."

He tilted his head, studying her like she was a puzzle with too many missing pieces, then his attention latched onto the small round table to her left, coming to rest on the black-and-white board strewn with the small white-bronze pieces on one side, the glinted golden ones on the other. "You play fidchell?"

"With my father sometimes, most often by myself. Not with you."

"How disappointing. Very well, we will save that for another bargain on another day." A hint of a smile glinted at the corners of his mouth, as though he knew that they were already engaged in a match of wits far more dangerous than a few little bronze and gold pieces on a simple checkered board. "Let's make a different deal, then, shall we? I shall go and leave you be, for now. Rest assured, I will be back tomorrow—despite the dubious pleasure of your company,

I am still rather eager to get my hands on that intriguing dowry of yours—but I will agree to leave you in peace for the afternoon, if you will but indulge me for a few moments."

"I would rather indulge in watching a flight of kestrels tear out your tongue."

"What a delightfully bloodthirsty mind you have. No wonder you have such an affinity for tales of monsters and myths." He gestured at the slim leather-bound tome that lay discarded on the wide slab of stone behind her. "The bargain that I propose to you is this: I shall tell you a story, a tale of the old gods and their kind, vanished from the face of the earth well over three centuries ago, and once I have finished, I will go. But"—he added, and she did not like that gleam of mischief in his eyes, not at all—"if you enjoy my tale, and you find that I have engaged your interest, however briefly, you must admit that to me, to my face, and I will return tomorrow and tell you another."

"I already know all the old stories of the gods."

"Do you now?"

Rozlyn scoffed. "I have been locked in a tower for nearly fifteen years, and my only companions are the servants who shudder at the sight of me, and the soldiers who guard me, their hands gripping their swords a little tighter than necessary when I pass them in the corridors. I read"—to her horror, her voice cracked ever so slightly—"constantly."

Damn it. She had made a mistake there, revealed the secret of her private pain, something that she would much rather keep hidden, locked away in the shadowy recesses of her soul, not something that this man, of all people, should be allowed to know.

"What a sad little life," he said, his expression bland, and she breathed easier, because he must not have noticed the gravity of what she had revealed. "If you have finished purging the angst from your system, let us return to the matter at hand. Do we have a deal?"

Rozlyn hesitated, her curiosity and her resentment both clawing at her with equal force. He grinned at her, that knowing smile of his extending a challenge impossible to resist. Here, at last, was a worthy opponent.

"Don't be a coward, now." His expression was rife with amusement. "Live a little—be bold for once."

Her mouth set in its usual solemn lines as she sank back down onto her seat on the smooth stone of the balustrade, conceding the exchange. "Very well. One story."

"And you will admit that you enjoyed it when I am done?"

"*If* I enjoy it, which seems improbable, given how very unpleasant our acquaintance has been as a whole, but yes. If I like your story, I will say so, and you may return tomorrow and tell me another."

"It's a bargain, then." He resumed his casual lean against the wall, folding his arms over his chest as he considered her. "I think," he announced after a moment, "that you would particularly relate to a story about Medb, the first queen of Connacht."

Rozlyn's breath caught, but her face remained bland and uninterested. "Why?"

"Och, you see, dear Medb was well-known for her love of masculine attention, and I hear that you very much enjoy kissing your many suitors before you send them along their merry way. It was"—he ran his hands down the front of his dark-gray doublet—"additional motivation for me to dance with your particular brand of devilry, so to speak."

Truly a muttonhead, this man.

She was almost tempted to kiss him just so that she could kick him afterward.

Almost.

She gave a defiant toss of her head. "Get on with it, then."

He laughed, then unfolded his arms, slipping his hands into his pockets once more.

"Queen Medb," he said, "or so legend has it, was a warrior-queen, golden-haired and dark-skinned, the ruler of wolves. She would walk through the lowlands, her robes streaming behind her in endless grace, and the alpha males would bow before her gait, their snouts buried in the dirt, and as she passed, packs upon packs of them would lift their noses to the skies and howl in reverence of their fearless queen. She was beautiful, they say, hauntingly, wildly beautiful, so much so that the mortal men who dared look upon her face would feel their manhood ebb away from their bodies. They would fall to their knees, blubbering like children for the rest of their days, rendered infantile by the sight of her remote and feral loveliness.

"But Queen Medb was content with her freedom and had no pity for the trail of heartbreak that she left in her wake, until the day that the king of all gods, the Dagda, decreed that she be married, that the wild beauty of her face must be bound to a husband, to harness the devastation that she caused with her loveliness."

Something like empathy for the wild warrior-queen flickered within Rozlyn.

"And so," the stranger continued, watching her with those unreadable eyes, "the Dagda declared it, and Medb gnashed her teeth and raged against the mighty will of the ruler-god. At last, she relented, but only, she stipulated, if she could possess a husband who matched her in temperament with perfect equity. The being who would win her hand, she declared, must never, for her sake, feel fear, jealousy, or unkindness, but should be her equal in all things. The king of the gods reluctantly agreed, and Medb was pleased, convinced that no such man could ever exist."

That same spark, tinged with the faintest touch of apprehension, glimmered again, and she glowered at the stranger who still studied her so intently as he told his tale.

This was no story—it was an attack, calculated and cold-blooded.

Still, she could not yet see what endgame he had in mind, so she settled back and let herself become lost in this world of words he was building just for her.

"Hundreds upon thousands of immortal and mortal beings alike came from all the corners of the world, desperate to be the man who would finally tame that wild, free beauty, and Medb dismissed them all as unworthy in comparison to the majesty of her person. Finally, a lesser god by the name of Eochaid arrived, and Medb remembered his feats of courage and strength on the field of battle, and reluctantly acknowledged the inherent justice of his demeanor, and the adoration within his caresses on her skin, and she at last agreed with great sadness that she would take a husband and bind herself to him for all her immortal days.

"The betrothal was announced and the banns were read, but on the eve before the marriage-bond was to take place, Medb wandered down to the riverbanks of the An Bhearú, savoring her last few moments of solitude, where she came upon the captain of her guard, weeping as though his heart would break—Aillil, the serious-eyed swordsman, broad-shouldered and stoic—until now. Now he wept in despair to see his beloved queen, fierce and bold, brought low by the commandment of the king to marry a man against her will.

"Medb saw his tears, pure with his love for her, and for the first time in her eternity of years, felt the stirrings of love in her heart." Something like triumph flashed across the stranger's face, and Rozlyn realized, mortified, that she was staring at him in rapt fascination.

Rozlyn immediately resumed an expression of polite boredom as he continued his story, a shadow of a smile creasing his lips. "She professed her love for Aillil, low-born though he was, and married him that night. Eochaid roared at her for breaking their promised marriage-bond, but she stood steadfast by the husband of her choice, even when Eochaid launched himself at Aillil in a fury. The warrior drew his long steel sword and in one smooth stroke, cleaved Eochaid's head from his body."

The stranger fell silent, and Rozlyn clenched her fists, fuming. "That's it?" The question burst from her. "That's the grand story of the first queen of Connacht? She marries a man who proves his love by murdering another, and that's how it ends?"

"Of course not." He had the gall to wink at her. "I only wanted to see if you were listening."

Rozlyn glowered, and he edged a little closer toward her, in order to lean against the balustrade where she sat, and continued. "So began their life together, but Medb soon realized that the marriage-bond that she had entered into was not an equitable one after all. Despite his low birth, Aillil possessed a treasure of great renown throughout the realm—Finnbennach, a bull of snow-white skin, thrice as large as any of its brothers, who sired the most-prized calves of any creature in the western world. Despite her love for Aillill,

Medb could not tolerate a husband who held any kind of power over her, and thus she set out to match his bull with one of equal worth and beauty, never ceasing until she had found it—Donn Cúailnge—as black and fierce as his complement was white, both beautiful and unbroken.

"Unfortunately," he continued, idly stroking the smooth sun-warmed stones next to her, "the bull was already in the possession of a great warrior-clan, led by the king of Ulaid, Dáire mac Fiachna, and his young but well-famed fighter, Cúchulainn. Medb sent gold and jewels and fine linens to the king of the Ulaid clans, asking to purchase the bull as her own. But Dáire, in his arrogance, sneered at her offering and kept the treasures while refusing her request, sending back this taunt: that only a woman would be so weak as to sue for his favor rather than simply taking what she wanted.

"Medb was furious at the slight to her womanhood and to her wildness and swore to have her vengeance and her cow both at the expense of the prideful young chief. She summoned her armies and marched on the borders of the Ulaid clans, who met her at the crease of the mountains that divided their realms, and at the front of their army was Cúchulainn himself. Even as they prepared for battle, Medb raised her dark arms to the sky and the entirety of the Ulaid army fell to the ground, Cúchulainn included, groaning in agony as they clutched at their abdomens, racked with the agony of a woman's monthly pains.

"The men writhed on the ground, and in the midst of the madness and confusion, Medb's armies slipped through their ranks, and the war commenced. After hours of heated battles and heroic deeds by some of the most famed warriors of Éire, the warrior-queen at last took hold of Donn Cúailnge and spirited him away to the fields where Finnbennach grazed, and while Ailill, her new husband, watched, she set him upon her husband's most-prized possession. The two bulls clashed and raged, goring at each other in the heat of their rivalry, tearing into the soft, rich flesh of the other, until both lay bloodied and beaten, in the gore-ridden grass, breathing their last breaths in unison together."

Rozlyn let out an involuntary cry. "But why go to all that trouble just to destroy them, the poor creatures?"

The stranger shrugged. "Queen Medb turned to the husband of her heart and gestured to the dying symbols of their respective pride, and said, 'Behold what it means to be equal, Ailill. Let there never again be imbalance between us.' She strode away, her long golden hair flowing on the wind, content with her choice, now that neither had power over the other."

He fell silent, and Rozlyn pondered this, turning it over and over in her mind, the ruthlessness, the relent-lessness of the warrior-queen, lost in contemplation. "Well, a bhrèagha," he asked at last, and when she looked back at him, his eyes shone bright with some unnamed emotion. Odd, that. "Shall I see you again tomorrow, then?"

She hesitated.

It would not be a loss if she conceded. A draw—a stale-mate, until she could reassess and evaluate, unleash that gambit of hers that had never once failed her on this strange, enigmatic man who smiled at her so fearlessly. He might have earned the slightest edge today, but the next time, he would not.

The next match, she would win.

And she very much wanted to hear another story.

Rozlyn raised her green-gray gaze to his face begrudg-ingly. "Yes." She hesitated, unwilling to concede even this small victory, but she had to know the identity of this mysterious man who enthralled her with his words and who laughed at her snarls. "Who are you, exactly?"

"I have been known by many names," he said, the mildness in his tone belied by the triumph burning in his blue eyes, "over the years. But you, Rozi, can call me Jamie."

CHAPTER EIGHT

When she was still a girl, locked away and lonely in her quiet tower room, Rozlyn's favorite part of the day had always been the early morning hours, when the last vestiges of night still hung in the air. She would creep from her bed to read by her window, savoring the way that the first pale rays of the sun cascaded across the page, a secret shared just between the two of them while the rest of the world lay sleeping, and she felt safe enough, free enough to smile at the words that danced across the page.

It was a tradition that she continued even now, with her ever-present mug of tea in her hand as she awaited the arrival of the dawn, so, of course, it would be him, the bane of her existence, her traitorous husband, who ruined this precious moment of stolen peace.

Cocooned in the tranquil warmth of her private solar, Rozlyn looked up from her book when the insistent banging on the door of her castle began, just as the first fingers of the sunrise stretched across the still-dark sky. She sniffed, then returned her attention to the pages in front of her, sipping at the steaming honey-lavender tea that swirled in her cup. There was a brief pause, and then a thunderous, resounding crack shuddered the thick oak of the door, and she scowled.

"Open the damn door, Rozi," she heard him yell. "I'm in a pretty foul mood right now."

She frowned and, marking her page, laid her book aside, then strode down the now-treeless great hall to the mended front doors and eased them open. "It is very early," she sniffed as he shoved past her, stalking down the great hall and into her solar and to the fire still burning in the hearth. "What happened?"

"What do you think happened? I tracked down your bloody dearg-dur, that's what happened."

"A what?"

"A dearg-dur. A bloodsucker, a resurrected corpse." Jamie plopped down in her vacated chair by the fire and began scarfing down her still-warm bowl of well-salted stirabout and soda bread.

"Please, by all means, help yourself to my breakfast." Rozlyn leaned against the hearth and crossed her arms, frowning. "A corpse who drinks blood? You knew such things existed?"

"Of course, I did," he mumbled through a mouthful of porridge, a dab of soft butter cream lingering on his top lip before he licked it away. "I knew exactly what I was facing as soon as you described it." He swallowed, then eyed her tea speculatively.

"Don't drink that."

His eyebrows rose at the sound of her snarl, and she grimaced, squeezing her hands into fists at her sides.

"That's mine," she said, snatching the mug up in her hands, her fingers curling around it protectively.

Jamie leaned back in the chair and raised his hands. "Easy now. A man can be thirsty without warranting murder." He eyed the mug clutched in her hands, and she gripped it a little tighter in response. "I don't suppose you have any mead handy. I could use a drink."

Rozlyn gulped down the final dregs of her tea, then jerked her chin. "In the cupboard behind you."

Jamie swiveled around to rummage through the deep cherrywood sideboard. "A dearg-dur," he explained as he sniffed, assessing the various jugs of mead stored inside the cupboard, "is believed to be a restless soul, one unwilling to enter the otherworld of Magh Meall until the terrible injustice committed upon it has been rectified. Usually, a blood-price of some kind that was never paid. Unfortunately—" His expression was grim as he spun back around in the chair and took a long drink from the brown stone jar of his choice. "Even after justice has been restored and its vengeance administered, the bloodlust that fuels it grows too wild and unruly to control, and it is doomed to continue to wander the lands surrounding its grave at each return of the lunar cycle of its original demise, preying on hapless victims to slake its thirst for revenge."

Rozlyn shuddered in spite of herself. "How is it stopped?"

Jamie sighed as he set the jar down on the table with a soft thud and ran his mud-stained hands through his hair. "They are fascinated by fire, consumed by the eternal chill of death as they are. It is easy enough to lure them back to their grave and then cover the earth with heavy rocks. This forces them to lie restful and still, and so enter the otherworld in a state of peace, their wildness tamed forever."

"And this is what you did?"

"After a sort." Jamie stared unseeingly into the flames. "I first asked her to tell me her tale of woe. I was curious, I suppose."

"She spoke to you?"

"In her own way." He leaned forward to cradle his head in his hands, weary and discouraged.

"You are being deliberately cryptic."

"Yes," he snapped, his head jolting up to glare at her. "And if you would like to know how I came to possess this information, as well as the full extent of my knowledge about such matters, then you will listen to what I have come here to say in the first place, as you promised."

They glared at each other, the air between them rolling with anger and the bitter bite of heartache, until the sound of footsteps in the great hall broke the battle of wills before them. They both glanced away to see a tall, broad-shouldered figure, bleary-eyed with the blond-scruffed jaw of a man who had spent the night entangled in the sheets of a beautiful woman and had no use for a razor's edge, shuffle his way sleepily toward the nook where they sat.

"Good morning, my dear," he yawned, then froze at the sight of Jamie sitting by the fire—dirty and disheveled, his face dark as he stared at the newcomer with dawning comprehension.

A savage twist of satisfaction at her husband's pained expression cut through Rozlyn as the interloper continued. "Oh. Hello."

Check.

Rozlyn rose and crossed to the sleepy-eyed man who stood blinking with confusion and kissed him firmly on the cheek. "Good morning, Padraig. As you see, I have a visitor who has come to help rid the village of the creature who has been plaguing our valley for the past few months." She ran her hand down his broad shoulder and biceps, letting her fingers linger on his burly forearm, and the air tightened with a thunderous warning as Jamie watched with increasing ire. "Why don't you go and wait in the kitchen? I am sure that Ciara will fix you some breakfast before you return home to tend to your fields."

Padraig nodded, eyeing Jamie with justified wariness—Jamie's expression continued to burn with anger, simmering at the edges of his self-control—and he shuffled away with a nervous backward glance as he retreated.

Rozlyn turned to face Jamie where he sat by the fire, and folded her arms across her chest, saying nothing, waiting for him to attack first, to blunder through his moves and entrap his own queen.

She watched the hurt flicker in his eyes. It would always be this way between them—always scheming, always plotting, an endless exchange of battery and binds and soul-deep bruises that they gave to one another with such remorseless cruelty. It shouldn't bother her so much. She should have stopped caring ten years ago about his hurts and his sorrows and his pangs of grief.

It shamed her, pained her, that she had not yet learned how to do so.

"Who the hell was that?"

"I'm so sorry. How rude of me. I should have introduced you properly."

"Rozi." The deep, guttural growl, so foreign to him, reminded her suddenly of the Beast that lurked underneath her own skin. "Please kindly explain why that man was just kissing my wife."

Rozlyn sniffed. "Spare me your outrage, Jamie. I am hardly your wife. Exchanging a few meaningless vows right before you betrayed me for the sake of my 'veritable treasure of a dowry'—a very clever evasion, by the way—hardly constitutes a marriage."

"I'm not in the mood for this, Rozi."

"Well, I have to tell you, *husband*, I was not particularly in the mood for being as humiliated as I was ten years ago either." Her fingers drummed against her thighs. "Padraig is, quite clearly, my lover, a farmer from the village whom I am very fond of. He is sweet and kind and a very satisfying lover, and"—her voice rose as Jamie stood up, chair clattering to the floor, his hands clenched at his sides—"he—and the others before him, for that matter—have only ever looked at me with desire for my body and the pleasures that it can offer them, rather than with a lust for my magic."

"I cannot believe that you—"

"I might remind you," she said with a quietude far more ominous than the snarl of her anger, "that you forfeited whatever say or concern you might have once had in who shares my bed on the night that you tried to *kill* me."

For a tense moment, the only sound in the room was the crackling of the fire in the hearth as they stared at one another, chests heaving in identical motions of emotion, until Jamie's shoulders sagged, and his gaze flicked away from her. "That's not what happened, Rozi."

"I honestly do not care what happened or whatever twisted motivation you might have had for behaving as you did." Rozlyn turned to stare into the flames. It was the heat of the embers that burned in her eyes, she told herself, rather than the sting of tears. "The only thing that we have left to say to each other is your explanation as to why you would impose your presence on my life—a life that I have rebuilt on the ruins of the one that you and my father destroyed—when I clearly have no desire to ever see you again."

Jamie was silent. "Very well," he said at last. "We will discuss the demise of our relationship another time."

"There will be no other time." She pivoted to glare at him, serious and thankfully dry-eyed. "You have five minutes to explain yourself, and then I will unleash all the considerable power I have gained over the past ten years on you, and we shall see how clever you really are at escaping the wrath of monsters."

"Monsters," he said, meeting her glare without a trace of fear, "are exactly why I have come to seek your aid, a bhrèagha."

Her nostrils flared, then she returned to her chair by the fire, a temporary truce. Jamie followed and sat down opposite her, leaning forward with his elbows resting on his knees, his hands clasped loosely in front of him. "The dearg-dur is only the beginning, Rozi. She had slept undisturbed for three centuries, ever since the magic of the old gods disappeared from the world, only to reawaken inexplicably a few months ago. Why do you suppose that is?"

Renewed scars of guilt flared briefly within her, but she shoved them down. "Are you going to blame this atrocity on me as well? How many deaths must be laid at my door before you and my father are satisfied with torturing my conscience, Jamie?"

He raised his hands in the air, shaking his head. "It's not an accusation. But you do carry the power of the ancient gods within your blood, Rozi. Your father was not lying when he said that that force within you calls to the monsters of the world, long lain dormant due to the slumbering magic of the gods. Clearly, it no longer sleeps. You are wielding it, using it with magnificent control, somehow . . ." He paused meaningfully, and her lips curled in an unspoken dismissal. A shadow of disappointment flickered across his features, and he continued, "And with such a gift comes consequences." He stared at her, but she refused to flinch, to reveal that his words slammed into her like a battering ram to her already fragile heart. "I am not blaming you for the fact that such creatures have stirred due to you rightfully mastering the power with which you were born, but I will blame you, should you allow innocents to suffer because you refuse to interfere and use that same power to protect them when they are unable to protect themselves."

Rozlyn's stomach tightened. "That's not my responsibility. I didn't ask for this, didn't ask to be given the magic of the gone gods. It's none of my concern."

"Perhaps not, but it was the responsibility of the old gods, you know, the reason why they were gifted the magic that they possessed at the very making of the world. They served as caretakers, as guardians for the earth and its denizens, and you, like it or not, have inherited that task."

She was silent for a moment, considering.

It would endow her with something, this responsibility he placed on her shoulders, to defend and protect. It would grant her some purpose, a chance to achieve something fine and noble and good in this life, to bring beauty to a world into which she had so far only ushered pain.

Unless he was lying, of course, and he had always been a consummate liar, impossibly skilled at crafting his webs of manipulation and deceit. She had allowed herself to be ensnared once, and she had no intention of doing so again.

"How do you know all this?" Her voice was clipped. "You

have always been so well versed in the knowledge of the ancient gods. Those stories you would tell me, for instance. I have searched and searched, but they are not written down in any volume that I can find. Where did you discover those tales, Jamie? How is it that you know them so intimately?"

Jamie leaned back in his chair and folded his arms behind his head. "Tell me about the ice storm with which you so heartlessly tortured my men. How much did it cost you, commanding the elements of the natural world in such a way? Did you stay up all day and all night for three straight days in order to so wield it, ignoring the agony that burned in your bones from the force of such an exertion? Did you have to lie in your bed for hours after it was done, the ache in your head so sharp that it felt like your skull might split in two?"

Her mouth fell open in shock. "How did you know?"

"Och, Rozi. You turned so very pale that day in the hall when you called forth those oak trees to scare away my poor men—it was obvious." His eyes twinkled with something that looked suspiciously like affection. "You might call it firsthand knowledge. I felt the same pains when I first was learning to summon them as well, hundreds of years ago." He smiled again, wry and a bit sad. "I would advise abandoning that pursuit for a while. I don't think you are quite ready."

Rozlyn lurched to her feet. "You are one of them."

"Of a sort." Jamie rose as well, expression grim as he faced her. "I am—was—an immortal, the last remaining member of the Tuatha Dé Danann bloodline, the race of gods who have slept beneath the surface of the world for so many centuries." He shrugged. "At least, you mortals call them gods, because you do not know what else to call such entities.

Many ancient legends call us elves, as we die far too easily at the hands of other deities to be truly divine." He pursed his lips. "We do pride ourselves on being inherently godlike in nature, but it springs more from our hubris, to be honest, than the actual reality of what we are."

"Hubris, indeed."

Jamie smiled at her, a flash of well-remembered tenderness, then shrugged, turning away to stare into the fire. "Call us what you will—elves, gods, monsters—our blood runs silver in our veins, that folaíocht that grants us immortal life, or close enough to it." He signaled toward his own chest. "I was confined to this body centuries ago, never aging, never dying, but forced to live as a mortal man, void of my powers, condemned to watch as my people were doomed to an eternal slumber beneath the surface of the earth."

Rozlyn stayed quiet for a moment, mind whirling. She had always known that there was something different about him. It was the way that he carried himself, the proud line of his shoulders, the easy, careless grace that extended far beyond a man confident in his own strength—until he encountered a being somehow more inevitable than he and his kind.

"You say you were confined to this body—how?"

"In much the same way that you yourself were cursed."

"By the Cailleach?"

Jamie waved his hand in dismissal. "Och, no. She is merely the voice of doom, not the arbitrator of it, a witch of winter who operates outside the laws of the Tuatha Dé Danann. No, this was someone else, someone far more vindictive at her core."

"Who?"

Jamie met her gaze without any trace of guile. "One of her sisters, and no one you would know."

Rozlyn stared back at him, her hands clenching at her sides. "I have had about enough of your evasions, Jamie, or whatever your name truly is."

"I have been Jamie for three hundred years, so for all intents and purposes, that is who I am." That unfairly charming smile. "Or at least until you succumb to my charms and hand over that magic in your veins that is rightfully mine and my people's."

"Go to hell."

"I have actually. Tech Duinn is, as advertised, rather unpleasant. Everyone is so very gloomy there. I would not recommend it."

"I am not interested in your jokes, Jamie."

"And this is not a joke, what I am asking of you." Frustrated, he ran his fingers through his hair. "You think that the Beast of Connacht, untamed and bloodthirsty, was a terrible sight? You have no idea, no concept of what is beginning to stir in the dark corners of the world, sniffing its way out into the light. After three hundred years, the creatures of the sídhe have realized that there is no one left to restrain them, and they are coming for the mortals here, with all the thirsty vengeance of a thousand years of subjugation burning at their heels."

She could hear the desperation echoing in his plea, and she took a step backward, her palms suddenly clammy. "The sídhe. You mean monsters, like the ones I used to hear stories of when I was a child—the slúag and the bean-síde and the Abhartach that once you told me about."

"Yes. Precisely."

"And," she said, watching him closely, "like this dearg-dur."

"Yes—well, in a way. She was, may the rains fall upon her

and bring her rest, a human girl. She lived and she died here, among mortals, but, Rozi—aithníonn ciaróg, ciaróg eile."

She frowned. "What do beetles have to do with any of this?"

"It's a metaphor, Rozi. 'Like calls to like'—an ancient saying. The dearg-dur may have once been a mortal girl, but the power that brought her forth from her untimely grave was not. Not then, when first she passed from this world, nor now. With the reawakening of magic in the land—your magic, the magic of the sídhe—she rose again, and rest assured, others will follow."

"You don't know that."

"I do know that, Rozi. I was there, the day that our world was divided in twain, the seen and the unseen, a terrible sundering." A haunted expression settled over his features, and for the first time, she could see it, the weight of so many years, lurking in his now mortal eyes. "For so long, they have been locked away, confined to the hidden lands of the sídhe, lands forbidden for mere mortals to enter. They exist both below and above the earth, neither of this world nor apart from it, lands of magic and mystery far too terrible for a mortal to survive. The creatures who reside there were bound to those other-lands by the gods. That bond is gone, Rozi, and now they know it. Soon there will be a terrible reckoning brought upon the unsuspecting mortals in Éire if you do not help me." He remained still, watching as she paced back and forth in front of the fire. "We must awaken the gods, Rozi—you must awaken the gods. Come with me into the northern mountains, to the island of Inis Trá Tholl, where the Court of Shádach—the home of the ancient gods—still stands, and use this power that you have been given for something more grand than curing belly-aches and easing labor pains."

"You needn't be so flippant. Those things matter a great deal to the ones suffering from them."

Jamie ran his hand across his jaw in exasperation. "I'm sorry. I only meant that those ailments will soon seem like a dream of pain if these creatures of the sídhe are loosed on the human world. Surely you must see that. Look at what a fairly run-of-the-mill monster such as the dearg-dur was able to accomplish."

"I don't trust you."

"Rozi, for the gods' sake—"

"Let me finish—I will call back my wolves and a hundred more like them and have them tear you limb from limb right here in front of me if you interrupt me again."

Jamie was silent, and she closed her eyes for a moment, gathering herself back into that impenetrable tower of closely guarded secrets and emotions that she had so carefully crafted over the years.

No more concession of advantages. No more missteps. No more weakness.

Rozlyn took a deep breath and decided. "I do not trust you," she repeated. "You have given me no reason to. But I have seen things over the past few months that have concerned me, unsettled me." She was quiet for a moment. "So this is what we will do. You will leave my vale today, and you will return in one month's time." He opened his mouth to object, and Rozlyn raised her pointer finger in the air, and in answer, the faintest crescendo of snarls rose from the depths of the great hall.

She watched as, with great reluctance, Jamie closed his mouth again and folded his arms across his chest. "You will return in one month's time," she said, "and you will bring me some tangible sign, some proof, that what you say is true—that the confinement spell placed on the monsters of the sídhe by the gods of old is becoming unmoored.

Three signs, Jamie, in three months. That is the price that I require for the use of my power."

"This is my purpose, Rozi." She stiffened at the urgency that suddenly saturated his words. "I have done terrible things, yes. To you, to others, things that you cannot imagine, solely for this reason. I am the last remaining guardian of this world, and my own wants, my own desires must forever be subordinate to this sacred duty that I hold." He exhaled, his face dark with some nameless pain. "You want honesty from me, then know that I would do it all over again—every lie, every trick, every miserably callow thing that I have ever done, to you and to the rest of the unsuspecting world—if it meant that I had fulfilled my duty to my people, who have been doomed to a living death beneath the earth."

Rozlyn studied him anew as the light from the rising sun broke through the windows in her room, so bright and cheery in comparison to the dark tension that reverberated between them.

She could do this. She could yield this sacrifice—a few paltry pawns of her self-respect, perhaps a knight or two of her inner peace—for the sake of her people and give him what he had always truly wanted—the promise of the bronze-skinned king gleaming at the far end of the board, the ultimate prize, and her the hapless queen-piece that he had moved so cleverly into position to bind her into obedience. She would do this, let him plot out his strategy until the finishing moves, and then let her endgame prevail, swiping his pieces off the board in a final flourish, and be rid of him once and for all. She would be free of his bargains and his tricks and his clever games, but it would be on her terms, and she alone would set the pace of play of this never-ending game in which they had long ago embroiled themselves.

So she countered, blockading his queen in a single move.

"I believe that much is true, Jamie," she said. "I do not, and I will not forgive what you have done to me because of it, but I believe that you acted out of duty and a desire to do good for the betterment of the many, even if it meant sacrificing the happiness and well-being of one mortal girl." He opened his mouth to protest, but she held up her hand again, a queen with an implacable will who would not suffer the one foolish enough to challenge her. "This is the only bargain that I will ever again make with you, Jamie. Three months and three signs. Show me that you are genuine, that these threats you speak of are real, and I swear that I will go with you to the Court of Shádach to use this power of mine to awaken the gods of yore to save the people of Éire." She pointed. "And then—make no mistake, Jamie—we will go our separate ways, and you will darken my door no more."

"But—"

"You will give me my freedom," she said fiercely, and something rippled in his expression, something that echoed of amazement, of shock, but she ignored it, determined to win at all costs. "Promise me that, when this is done, then you and I are done, and I will, at last, be free."

He watched her emotionless face for a long moment, his eyes flickering with nameless sorrow; then he bowed his head in a gesture of agreement. "So be it."

Rozlyn loathed herself for it, but as he turned to go, to leave her home and her, standing straight-backed and unforgiving by the fire, she could not help but remember the sound of his soft drawl from that long-ago night that would forever echo in her heart.

Match in three moves, a bhrèagha.

CHAPTER NINE

Rozlyn poked at the stalks of vegetables on her pewter plate and scowled. It was one thing to have to endure the taste of cabbage, but quite another that she was forced to suffer through the experience under the watchful eye of her most annoying suitor.

"If you are going to insist on spoiling my supper," she said, "then you must at least tell me the story that I was promised."

Jamie stretched where he lounged in a chair nearby and yawned. "A bit eager, are you?"

"I don't see what purpose your presence serves me otherwise."

He straightened in his chair, eyeing her as she pushed halfheartedly at the green leaves on her plate. "Eat your cabbage," he said. "It's good for you."

Rozlyn glared at him, a wordless threat, and he lifted his hands in the air and laughed. "Easy. I'm only looking out for your well-being. The Dagda himself knows that I am by no means eager to spend the rest of my life as your vow-bonded nursemaid."

She jabbed her fork in his direction. "Then why are you still here?"

"We discussed this, Rozi. Gold, and lots of it. I shall be a very rich man indeed if my wooing of you ends in success— or your wooing of me, I should say." He gestured between them. "And here I am, two days in a row—clearly, I cannot stay away from you, a bhrèagha. I shall be swimming in gold by the end of the fortnight."

"I fail to see what I get out of this arrangement."

Jamie shrugged. "A reprieve from the dullards who have so frequently darkened your doorway for the past four years, perhaps?"

Rozlyn knew that she would never admit it, but he was right. She had been more entertained during these few fiery encounters with him than she could ever remember feeling.

"Or, if you like"—his voice was careless, deliberately so, and the hairs on her arms prickled—"we could play." He gestured to the black-and-white board pushed to the side of the table, the bronze and gold pieces glinting in the fading late afternoon light.

Rozlyn did not like that idea at all—the quiet intimacy of sitting across from him under the hush of the twilight sky, their fingers dancing over the board, pushing and probing and testing the boundaries of that clever mind of his, move for move, piece by piece—an equal match.

She frowned. "No. But you do still owe me a story."

"Another bargain, then." His eyes gleamed as though he knew exactly why she had refused him, and she scowled at the satisfaction in his expression. "Show me how you sicced those bees on your friend, the flaith from Bréifne, and I will tell you my story."

She hesitated. This was a dangerous request. "Why?"

"Idle curiosity. Nothing more."

She pursed her lips.

Why not, she decided, filled with a sudden surge of reckless determination. Why not let him see what wonders she could create, the power she could wield—the marvels that she could unfold with the mere whisper of a wish. Perhaps he would go if he saw. Perhaps he would at last become unnerved and appalled by her unnaturalness and flee as all the others had fled before him. Even as she told herself that that would be for the best—that this unspoken thread of understanding that flowed between them with such ease could only lead her to ruin—she knew that no conjuring of hers could drive him away.

She refused to consider the dangerousness of it all, how it pleased her so much to know that she could trust him with this, her most prized possession, the songs that hummed so harmoniously in her soul.

She closed her eyes and imagined the night sky and its canopy of stars, the way that the creatures of the earth scampered about freely beneath its shadows, all the while unaware of the one lurking in the trees above them, his night-bright eyes gleaming in the darkness. With a harsh screech, he swooped toward the earth, talons outstretched as the mouse below screamed in a sudden awareness of doom—

Above her, a low hoot echoed across the rafters of the tower, and she looked up, the yellow eyes of the screech owl winking at her expectantly from where it perched on the ledge of the roof, his gray-brown wings tucked neatly into his sides. She cooed at him, a wordless thanks, and he ruffled his feathers and shot into the sky, disappearing into the encroaching gloom.

She swiveled to glare at Jamie in triumph and raised her brows. "I win."

Jamie grinned and settled comfortably into his chair, stretching out his legs and folding his arms behind his head. "Very well," he said. "Since it is so obviously important to you that you be victorious, I concede. Have you heard the legend of the harp of the Dagda?"

Rozlyn shook her head, biting back her eagerness, her hunger for the tale, and Jamie smiled. "The Dagda was of course the father and ruler of the ancient gods," he began. "The supernatural, all-powerful race of the Tuatha Dé Danann, the caretakers and guardians of the earth. Elves, too, they are sometimes called in the ancient texts. Among his many treasures of wonder was an enchanted harp, called Uaithne, crafted from the finest oak and adorned with such gems as would be the envy of the richest mortal king, studded with gold and green emeralds and shimmering diamonds of pure light. The harp answered only to the sound of its master's voice, the raw command that shuddered forth from the mouth of the king of all gods. With its magic, the Dagda could entrance any who heard its melodious tones and enslave them hopelessly to his will.

"The harp produced three kinds of spells—the Music of Tears, which caused its audience to weep with wild abandon, even until the salt tears ran in rivers down their faces, for as long as its notes echoed in his hall; the Music of Mirth, which inspired irrepressible bursts of merriment and laughter in whomever heard its beguiling song; and finally, the Music of Sleep, which swept over its listeners and wrapped them in a warm cocoon of heavy slumber, which endured so long as the will of its maker wished it." A shadow passed over his face. Then it cleared as swiftly as it had come, and he continued. "However, the Tuatha Dé Danann were not alone in their status as immortal, all-powerful beings in the realm of Éire. The Court of Shádach—the hall of shadows, as the mortals once called it—lay tucked away on a hidden island beyond the impenetrable ridges of the northern mountains, but it was not to remain a secret for long. Another race of immortal beings, the Fomorians, sadistic, brutal giants who desired to claim the rich land as their own and impose their vicious will upon its simple beauty, challenged the Dagda and his court in a great war, over a thousand years ago, and the victor, it was decided, would forever rule the realm of Éire.

"Battle after battle they fought, with innumerable casualties and losses on both sides, until the green lowlands of the earth lay bloodstained and savaged with the blood of the immortals, giants, and elves alike. The war continued with no end in sight, as each army's might was equally matched by the other, and soon many despaired of there ever being an end to the bloodshed and pain that so racked the souls of gods and men.

"One day, after a particularly savage battle, wherein the bodies of the dead on both sides were piled so high in the air that the crows did not even have to descend from the trees to feast upon their eyes, a grandson of the Fomorian king, Balor of the poisonous eye, wandered across the field of battle, weeping at the sight of so much devastation. He longed to see an end to this war and threw himself on the ground at his grandfather's feet, pleading with him for peace. But Balor, bloodthirsty tyrant that he was, jeered at him and cast him out from the tribe of the Fomorians, doomed to forever be exiled from his home and his people for the weakness that he had shown.

"Lugh was the young Fomorian's name, known for his cunning and craftiness of spirit, as well as for the gentleness of his heart. In his despair at his grandfather's rejection of him, he went to the enemy of his people, the father of the gods, and stood proudly before the Dagda, offering him a resolution to this war that he fought with the Fomorians. Lugh suggested to the Dagda that he leave his hall unguarded and deserted, the famed harp of legend, Uaithne, hanging vulnerable and exposed on his wall; the Fomorians, he argued, would not be able to resist the temptation and would surely try to seize the treasured instrument as their own and thus wield its power.

"Reluctantly, the Dagda agreed and ordered his sept to desert their posts for the first time in the many centuries that they had stood guarding the sacred walls of the Court of Shádach, and it stood cold and unlit on the island of the gods. Until one night, the Fomorians, led by the tyrant Balor himself, came sneaking in across the peaks of the northern mountains across the narrow sea and into their enemies' home, gloating over their seeming victory, and with his own two hands, Balor seized the harp from the wall and tried to command it to play.

"From the corner of his hall emerged the Dagda himself, regal and tall, utterly alone, without the protection of his kin and his guards, and even as the Fomorians seized their weapons and lunged forward to slay the father of all gods, he commanded to his harp that it begin to sing the Music of Sleep.

"The hypnotic song of the harp echoed soothing notes of peaceful dreaming through the great hall, and almost as one, the Fomorians' knees buckled, and their eyelids grew heavy and dull, their arms and hands turning slack and sluggish at their sides. They fell with a resounding crash in matching motions of hypnotic sleep and lay sprawled on the smooth wood floors of the Court of Shádach, forever entranced by the power of the Dagda and his most loyal harp.

"The Dagda called to his faithful sept, where they awaited his orders some distance away, out of earshot of the fateful tune of his harp, and they entered the mead hall of the gods, carrying off their enemies back across the narrow sea to the summit of Slieve Donard in the northern mountains of the realm, chaining them with unbreakable bonds of iron to boulders that they sank immovably into the mountainous earth, the Fomorians still snoring in their enchanted slumbers, never again to be awakened.

"As a reward for his cunning, and for the peace that his sacrifice had achieved, the Dagda named Lugh a chief among the Tuatha Dé Danann, and Lugh asked for one boon in return: that he be allowed to give the death-stroke to his grandfather, the wicked tyrant of the Fomorian race, in justice for the evil that he had wrought upon the world with his greed. The Dagda agreed, and Lugh awakened his grandfather for his final fight. When Balor saw his grandson, strong and tall and brimming with youth, standing before him, he turned to flee, but Lugh pulled out a slingshot of such unrivaled power that when he launched a stone the size of a house at his grandfather's retreating form, it punched through the back of his skull with such force that his eyes, brimming with venom as they were, fell out of the front of his face to the ground below.

"The Tuatha Dé Danann welcomed Lugh as one of their own, and in return for their hospitality, he taught them the art of the plow and the scythe, showing them how to farm the land and grant it fruitfulness, and he was named the god of the harvest, a lord of unparalleled greatness in the hearts of both gods and men."

The story ceased, and the only sound was the rising cry of the crickets from the trees, faint and distant from where the pair sat atop the high stone tower, lodged away from the rest of the world.

Rozlyn sat in silence for a long while as night fell around them, pondering the story. "I wish I had that harp," she whispered, so quietly that Jamie had to lean forward to hear her. "I would sit out on the moorlands at midnight, or at the bottom of Aasleagh Falls and let the mist soak through my hair, and wait for the Beast to find me, and then I would un-leash its power on that monster and condemn it to sleep for all eternity and never harm another innocent soul again." She stared unseeingly across the small bungalows and huts that adorned the tree-lined mountain slopes of her father's kingdom far below.

"You could not wield it," he at last said, gentler than she had ever before heard him. "Only the father of the gods can do so."

She turned to him, lips curled. "You do not know the depths of this power within me." She could hear it herself, the intensity of her secret anger, born from years of being ignored and belittled and condemned, how it brought to life the thrum of an unfulfilled promise that vibrated through her words. "You do not know what I can do."

He met her glare unflinchingly, and they stared at one another for a long moment, the breeze that ruffled their hair the only movement, until a mournful howl broke through the air around them.

"The wolves," Rozlyn breathed. "They must be coming down from the high mountains for the mating season." She rose and hurried to the side of the terrace, leaning over the balustrade, and peered into the rising gloom below. "There. Look, just south of us, beside the hills of Dunach. Do you see?"

He made a small sound of revulsion as he came to stand next to her, his hands in his pockets, and she glanced over at where he stood beside her scowling. "What's wrong?"

"I despise wolves."

Rozlyn made a small sound of dismay. "Oh, but they are so beautiful. See their fur, so sleek and silver. They are magnificent." The tips of her fingers tingled with the desire to stroke their ears, to feel the rough brush of their silver-gray coats under her palms. "One day, I want to be able to walk free of my tower and call to them. I imagine that they would be the most wonderful of companions for me."

Jamie's lips twisted. "Believe me, they would not. Do you know, wolves scavenge after armies, salivating at the thought of battle. They love nothing more than to prowl among the dead and dying on the blood-soaked fields in the aftermath of war, feeding on the injured and the helpless, devouring them even as they lie screaming for mercy." He shuddered again. "It was almost my fate once."

"What happened?"

He rubbed at his jaw, something she had noticed that he did when he was distracted, absent-minded—lost in remembering, it seemed. "It was a long time in the past, a lifetime of battles ago. I had been wounded in the knee and could not walk. I was dragging myself through the mire of my fallen friends when the wolves appeared in the gloom of the early night and attacked me. They went straight for my bad knee, tearing and clawing at it as I tried to fight them off." He pointed to his right leg. "On cold winter evenings, it still aches where their teeth tore the flesh from my bone."

"How did you escape?"

"My uncle saved me," Jamie said, leaning forward to brace his hands on the balustrade. "War was not a terror to him, but a way of life. He embraced it and became it rather than fearing it, as I did."

Rozlyn recognized it, the grief, the faintest touch of guilt in his voice, so similar to her own. "Was?"

"He died." He spoke curtly. "As did all my family."

She glanced away, unsure of what to say, as he remained silent and still, his hands gripping the wooden railing until his knuckles turned marble white. Rozlyn backed away to leave him with his thoughts, when his face cleared abruptly and he turned toward her, an apologetic smile already curving across his lips. "I'm sorry," he said with his usual lightness. "My emotions get the better of me sometimes."

He looked so vulnerable, a young boy lost in the woods, longing for the simple comfort of his mother's familiar arms. She cleared her throat. "I am not a particularly emotional person myself," she said. "When I was eleven, my governess, Kenai, fell ill. She was the only soul throughout my childhood who did not look at me as though I were an abomination. She taught me to read, and it was she who persuaded my father to build his library—I have always thought that she did it for me, to make me happy." Rozlyn swallowed the lump in her throat. "She was the person whom I loved most in the world, and when I went in to say goodbye, all I could bring myself to say was, 'It's very bothersome for you to be doing this the day before the winter solstice and ruining my favorite holiday for me forever, do you know that?' My nursemaid was horrified, and resigned her post immediately, insisting to Father that I was the most wicked and depraved soul she had ever encountered."

Jamie laughed, and an irrepressible thrill raced through her, the satisfaction of knowing that she was the one who soothed away his pain and made him smile. "Och, your nurse-maid was a fool. Death is a tragedy not so much for those who have died, but for those left behind. It is we who are left to grieve, to learn to navigate our way through the storms of life without them. You were right to mourn the loss of two joys simultaneously." She raised her eyebrow at him, and he grinned again. "But perhaps also a little unfeeling, it is true."

Before Rozlyn could respond, her maid appeared on the terrace, her gaze flickering nervously between them. "Yes, Moira?"

"So please you, my lady." She curtsied, her hands fisting in the heavy fabric of her skirts. "Your father the king wishes your presence in the great hall. A young lord from the province of Ulaid has arrived to seek your hand."

Jamie raised his brows. "I believe that your father is hedging his bets, Rozi. Two suitors at one time. What a popular girl you are."

"Thank you, Moira," Rozlyn said, ignoring him. "Please tell him that I will be down presently."

Moira nodded as she backed away inside. Rozlyn pushed from the rail, her hands smoothing at the loose tendrils of hair that had slipped free from the pins that kept her black locks swept up on the top of her head, tucking them behind her ears with studious care. Jamie watched her as she straightened her skirts, and without a word of farewell, glided toward the door. "Have a good evening, a bhrèagha," he called after her. "I suppose that you shall kiss this one as well?"

"Naturally. I have no doubts that I will enjoy myself immensely."

"Liar. Try not to fantasize about me too much while he has his hands on you."

She looked over her shoulder at him where he still stood, smiling, even though his expression had darkened. "Isn't it time for you to give up this ridiculous suit of yours and head back to whatever hole you crawled out of?"

"That's the second time that you made that joke. You're getting slack, Rozi." He shoved away from the railing and strode toward her, his hands in his pockets. "But no, I am not leaving. On the contrary, I believe that I shall be here for quite some time. Your father, you see, wise king that he is, has invited me to stay and serve as one of his advisers for the time being, in the hope, I suspect, that I shall fall desperately in love with you, since we seem to get along so very well." He leaned forward conspiratorially. "Comparatively speaking, of course. It's been two whole days, and I have yet to run screaming in horror from this castle, nor have I been inexplicably attacked by a sadistic swarm of honeybees. So it must seem quite promising, our star-crossed love match."

Rozlyn tossed her head and glided out the door. "You are mistaken, my lord," she called back. "Our chat tonight has given me some very valuable information. I would never plague you with bees." Her hand brushed across the door-frame. "You would most assuredly find yourself beset by ravenous wolves if you were to displease me."

She slipped through the door but lingered in the shadows of the archway, drawn by the irresistible desire to study him unobserved. She watched as alone on the terrace, Jamie tilted his head back to survey the night sky, and with no one to see, he grinned.

She knew that expression. She had felt the urge to let it creep across her face so many times, while playing fidchell against herself in the early morning sun, when she had at last cracked the code of some new gambit she had been practicing, and her pieces had broken free, wreaking havoc across the board, the tantalizing triumph of a successful king hunt trembling at the corners of her lips.

Match in six.

CHAPTER TEN

Jamie had journeyed the world over, had seen sun-scorched deserts and rain-drenched jungles, the endless stretch of ice-crusted plains and the rolling green hills of the lowlands, but there was nothing like the sight of the black craggy mountains of Éire, bejeweled with evergreen trees and brushed with the pristine shroud of the winter's first snow.

"So," Bowen asked, interrupting his perusal of the snow-kissed scene before him. "Are you ever going to tell us what monstrous nightmare we are hunting, exactly?"

They had been journeying east for nearly five days out of the vale of Inagh into the peaks of Beanna Beola, having left Rozlyn's castle almost immediately after Jamie had agreed to her terms. The wind was brutally cold and fierce, but Jamie relished the slice of its icy knives on his face, welcoming any distraction to the visions that haunted him of Rozlyn cocooned in her bed, well warmed by a masculine body sprawled across her sheets.

"The dúlachán," he said, banishing the unwelcome image of her bare arm nestled against a blond-haired chest.

Bowen yanked on the reins of his piebald gelding, and the three other soldiers who accompanied them all choked as one, unified in the throes of their terrified dismay. "But that's impossible," Hedrek gasped, and Tavin and Nyle murmured fearfully between themselves. "We cannot possibly slay the dread horseman of Crom Dubh himself."

"The lady requested a monster." Jamie saw her again, dismissive and unrelenting, and unconsciously, he dug his heels into the flanks of his horse. The mare whuffed, and he ran his gloved hand down her neck in a silent apology. "And she sure as hell is going to get one."

Bowen nudged his horse after him. "But the dúlachán. It speaks death to whomever crosses its path. We will *die*."

"Don't be ridiculous. Only one of us will die." Jamie glanced at Bowen, who paled even further. "The dúlachán causes the death of whomever it calls by name, it is true, but it can only speak once a night while it rides, and there are five of us, so your odds are fairly good, Bowen, my boy."

Bowen gulped, and the men behind them began to protest in anger, but Jamie merely raised his eyebrows. "Perhaps you would prefer to hunt the Abhartach, then?"

"What is that?" Nyle asked, his face pale with nerves.

"A creature with skin as impenetrable as stone who suffocates his victims under a fire-soaked sky before he consumes their blood while they are still alive." It amused him, a little, to see how they blanched even further at this sparse description—the gods help them if they ever encountered the full extent of its horrors. "At least, that's the legend. No one has ever survived it, including a few of the members of the

long-lost clan of the Tuatha Dé Danann, but who knows?
Maybe we will be the first."

His men exchanged looks, and Hedrek cleared his
throat. "We are okay with the dúlachán."

"Good lad." Jamie sighed then relented, taking pity
on their panic-stricken expressions. "I will deal with the
dúlachán," he said. "There is no need to fear. I know its
tricks, and the secret to silencing it for good."

"What if it speaks your name?" Nyle glanced at him,
searching, Jamie knew, for any outward signs of dread at
facing down the nightmare feared by all red-blooded children of Éire.

Which, of course, he was not.

"I would like to see it try."

Despite the bravado of his words, Jamie could not help
but sneak worried glances at his men as their horses trailed
behind his in silence. So many of the souls he had failed to
protect haunted him as he lay tormented and awake in the
dark midnight hours, and the idea of these men joining the
ranks of that seemingly endless march of souls he'd doomed
was more than he could bear.

There was Bowen, and he smiled at the surge of affection for the staunch soldier. Bowen, bulky and strong, but
with the kindest heart. Jamie knew what he had left behind
in Connacht to journey with him here in this quest for the
aid of his former princess—a widowed sister with two nieces
and another little one on the way, his ailing father and aging
mother, all depending upon the gold gifted to him by his
king for his service and his valor. Their faces would no doubt
haunt his sleep as well should Bowen fall, doomed to die,
starving and alone, were they deprived of his salary.

He must not risk Bowen.

But then there were the brothers, twin boys born moments apart, Hedrek and Nyle, inseparable from birth. He remembered the stories their mother had told, dark-eyed and laughing, as he had sat at the table in their little thatched hut, how the two of them would spend hours chasing and teasing and grabbing at each other in an endless cycle of giggles and tantrums of their childhoods, until, at the end of each day, she would find them curled around each other like puppies in a single cot, slumbering with their dark curly heads resting on one another's shoulders.

He imagined their mother's bright-eyed smile forever destroyed at the loss of her boys, and he shook his head, scratching at his stubbled chin. The twins must not be imperiled either.

Jamie glanced at Tavin.

Tavin, blond of hair and sweet souled, with thin shoulders and a still-reedy voice, barely eighteen, a child who dreamed of adventure and grandeur and heroic deeds. An orphan boy, raised by his grandfather, the last of his line—the clan of Ó Corraidhin must not end with this gentle boy, despite how many long-lost beloveds waited so patiently for him in the shadows of Magh Meall.

Jamie cleared his throat and banished the darkness of his thoughts, focusing his attention on the approaching tree line of the forest of Gougane Barra.

The night fell in soft dark waves around them, shrouding the trees in shadows. The men huddled closely around one another, skittish and jumping at the snap of every twig. Jamie pointed wordlessly toward a clump of large boulders nestled by the side of the wide, dusty road, faintly illuminated by the gleaming stars. The absence of moonlight sent a reluctant chill down even Jamie's spine as they dismounted and hid themselves away among the rocks, settling in to wait for whatever dark passenger might come thundering down the lane.

They did not wait long.

The sound of hoofbeats began to echo in a haunting rhythm down the dusty lane. Jamie edged forward, reaching into the knapsack at his side to close his fingers around the stem of the bright golden goblet hidden away in its depths. The hoofbeats thundered closer, and Jamie could hear the shrill whinnying of the beast's steed as it raced down the lane, seeking some poor soul to devour with its deadly hunger.

Bowen made a small choking sound as Jamie stepped forward to the edge of the lane, the unseen horse screaming in the distance. He could hear Hedrek's bright silver sword sliding from its scabbard at his side. "Stay hidden," he hissed as the hoofbeats grew louder and louder, and there, under the faint light of the stars in the cold, moonless night, the figure appeared.

The hoofbeats slowed, and horse and rider came to a stop, the dreaded weight of their attention fixed on Jamie.

The horse was so black that it was almost indiscernible against the deep darkness of the night sky, the brightness of its yellow eyes the only glimmers of light from where it stood. A stone's throw away Jamie waited, vibrating with tension. Its hooves were deadly sharp and smooth, pawing at the dirt in impatience as it waited for its master to allow it to move.

The rider was hooded and still, his large hands gloved, the left clutching a slender white whip, and Jamie realized with a shiver that it was crafted from the spine of one of the monster's victims—the small joints barely visible, so tightly woven was it against the thin strip of rope.

But the right hand contained something far more horrifying.

Jamie steeled himself to look at the abomination he knew dangled in the grip of the rider before him—the decapitated face that hung suspended from the black-gloved hand of the dúlachán.

The rider held his own rotting head aloft, its decaying lips stretched in a horrific parody of a grin from ear to rotting ear. Green-glinted flies lingered all around its moldy orifices, and worms wiggled in the putrid nostrils of its misshapen nose. Its eyes, blank and unblinking, swiveled ceaselessly in its bony sockets, eternally searching for the name of a mortal soul to speak aloud through its decomposing mouth and thus drain the essence from its body, consuming its life force to feed its own unnatural immortality.

That deathly glower landed on Jamie where he stood, and its black, bulbous tongue rolled forth out of its cavernous mouth. The rotted lips moved soundlessly, rapidly, as though struggling to form the words of a foreign language, and Jamie smiled, a grim victory.

Any being, mortal and immortal alike, who might have once known his true name had not walked the earth in over three hundred years.

"You do not know me," he said, "you black-souled bastard. There is nothing here for you to devour."

Its tongue flicked and hissed, an undead snake without venom or fangs, and Jamie's fingers tightened around the golden goblet in the bag at his side.

The metal felt cold and smooth as it brushed against his skin, a talisman against this particular brand of evil. Even monsters fear what they do not know, and an abomination such as the dúlachán could never endure the light, born into the darkness as it had been, deep in the bowels of the foulest parts of the earth.

"I know what you fear," he said. "I know what haunts you, in that voided place where should be your soul, thief of lives that you are. You thrive in the shadows and in the darkness of the world, and only the gold of the light can harm you."

The dúlachán's eyes bulged and its mouth opened even further in an ear-piercing shriek. Even as Jamie went to draw out the goblet to bind the monster with its golden aura, he heard a branch break behind him and saw Hedrek stumble forward in the shadows, his face contorting at the sound of the dúlachán's scream. The monster's black eyes whipped away from Jamie and lighted on Hedrek's ashen face as he landed on his knees in the dirt.

"No!" Jamie ripped the bag away from the golden goblet, but before its gilded sheen could pierce the darkness of the dúlachán's glare from that rotting head dangled in its black-gloved hand, its putrid lips parted, and its black tongue hissed at the fulfillment of its vicious desires.

Hedrek Mac Lochlainn.

Hedrek fell to the ground, choking on the white foam surging up his throat and frothing out of his mouth, and the headless rider screamed again, a protracted shriek of agony, as the glint from the golden goblet shimmered in the faint light of the stars. Nyle and Tavin rushed forward to cradle the convulsing body of their brother and their friend as his limbs thrashed on the ground. Bowen stumbled to where Jamie stood holding the goblet aloft while the monster in front of them clutched its stump of a throat and writhed, beginning to sizzle with black smoke, until there was nothing left but a faint, acrid tang of ash and bone where it had once sat on the back of its horse. The steed whinnied once, a death-call for its master, then turned and galloped away into the night.

The decomposed head lay lifeless in the dust of the road, its mouth still ajar from its final curse, the black tongue bulging from its mouth. The worms and flies began to devour its putrid flesh in earnest where it lay twitching in the dirt, even as Hedrek's body slowed and then stilled, the shadows of the night settling onto his thin, twisted shoulders with the finality of death.

CHAPTER ELEVEN

Rozlyn laid her aching head against the cold stone wall of the stairs outside her tower, praying for a few minutes of peace in this nightmarish day.

The Beast had struck again in the night, and its savagery was unlike anything that they had seen before—a dozen men and women and children, brutally torn apart by its fangs, the half-grown crops left ravaged in the fields. Her father had been gone for much of the morning and had returned a little while ago, disheveled and infuriated.

Infuriated, of course, with her, his unloving and un-lovable daughter.

They had fought so terribly, father and daughter, when he had come back, his hands marred with blood and his face scarred with pain. He had raged at her, as he so often had before, roared at the top of his lungs, railing against her stubbornness, her pride, which had cost so many lives. Rozlyn's eyes had burned with white-hot tears at the truths in his rage, but she threw her shoulders back in defiance. "We aren't even trying to fight it," she said, because they weren't, just an unending concession of souls, year after year, all on her account, and she was suffocating under the weight of all those doomed lives.

How could he be so blind to her, drowning in an ocean of guilt, so careless with so many of the souls he had sworn to protect?

"We simply hide ourselves away and hope for the best, waiting for some man to fall in love with me, which we both know will never happen."

"You won't *let* it happen."

"And even if it did," Rozlyn snapped, "what guarantee do we have that the Beast will disappear? We are blindly putting our trust in something that we have no real understand-ing of." She shook her head. "This isn't working, Father—it never has. We must do something, not sit idly by hoping that some cryptic prophecy given almost two decades ago will eventually be fulfilled and make everything well again."

Ailain slammed his fist onto the table so hard that the green-glass goblet of mead skittered off the edge and shat-tered on the floor beneath. "I have been doing something, but you, with your ill humors and malicious ways—"

"That's not everything. Let me learn to master this power." She flexed her fingers, ready to show him, to prove to him the strength of the magic that hummed within her veins. "There is another way to break this curse, one that does not involve me having to sacrifice what I was given. You say that I do not have the wisdom, the necessary knowledge to do so. Then call upon the druids. There must be some left, somewhere in the northern realm, to come and give me guidance." She raised her hands, and he flinched, his forearm lifting in an instinctive gesture of wariness, and she lowered her arms again, her throat tightening in response. "I can learn to wield it. I can use it against this Beast. I can save our people. Let me do this, please, because we must do something—"

"I have done everything that there is to do!" She staggered backward at his vitriol. "I have dragged every eligible young man living in the entire realm to this tower and set them on you. I have begged them to please you, to bring you joy, to make you smile, and in return, they shall have my daughter's hand in marriage, a dowry the likes of which mortals can only dream of, and the title of savior of the realm of Connacht. But you"—he pointed at her, shaking with fury—"how many men have you driven away, alienating them with your hatefulness, and how many of my people have suffered for it? How many, Rozlyn?"

She stared at him, her fingers relaxing at her sides.

He would never let her be a savior. He would never allow her to be anything more than a meek and pretty face.

"Perhaps," she said, "you should have let them strangle me in my mother's arms as they so wanted and been done with it."

He glared back. "Perhaps I should have, you wicked child." He turned away from her, his shoulders sagging. "Now get out of my sight."

Rozlyn stalked away, refusing to let her tears fall until she was hidden safely away in the recesses of the tower's spiral stairwell, once again alone with only her guilt and the bedimmed sparks of magic that flitted, barely there, at the tips of her fingers.

She rested her throbbing head on her knees—the crushing headache with which she had awoken had not abated nor lessened in the slightest throughout the day—and drew in deep, steadying breaths, trying to soothe the heartbreak in her chest.

She was so tired of being a pawn, and she would never allow herself to be a king—hapless and weak, moving sluggish and slow across the board, relying on the might of others for survival.

She wanted to be a *queen*.

"There she is." She heard him from a few stairs below, interrupting her thoughts, but did not deign to lift her head to acknowledge him. "I have heard," Jamie said as he sat down beside her, hands loosely clasped in front of him, "that you have had a hell of a day, a bhrèagha."

"I don't want to talk about it with you."

"Shall I tell you a story, then, to distract you from your self-pity and your angst?"

"My father hates me, and I am the ruination of my people. I would think that whatever 'angst' I am feeling is well justified."

"Point taken." Jamie stretched out on his back on the cold stone floor next to her, his hands beneath his head, as he watched her sit, while brooding, on the stairs. "But may I tell you a story, Rozi? I believe that you might find it both meaningful and enjoyable."

"I doubt that you are genuinely asking for permission, so by all means. Do as you please."

"I always do." Jamie sighed a little as he made himself comfortable on the floor. "You have heard of the Mórrígan, I presume?"

Rozlyn lifted her head from her knees, intrigued, in spite of herself. "Everyone knows of the Phantom Queen."

"Indeed. One of her many titles, as befits a goddess of

such unfathomable power. The Mórrígan is the goddess of war and death and should be feared and revered on that much alone, but her true strength lies in her unerring omniscience, for she sees the future of all things, even unto the ending of the world. The problem lies in that she is reluctant to share her power with anyone, especially her knowledge, and thus is reticent and taciturn to a fault, causing the suffering of thousands of souls, both gods and humans alike, even if it results in her own doom. She cares not, so long as she keeps her power as hers and hers alone, only sharing snatches of her visions through cryptic codes of songs and rhymes, and always for a terrible, terrible price.

"It was in the great Battle of Moytura, during the war with the Fomorian giants, that she first revealed the true depths of her power. The gods were lined up for battle in a resplendent display of swords and shields and swift, cunning arrows, and she walked into their midst unarmed and unprotected, dressed only in the flowing night-black gown that always adorned her person. The gods roared to see her, all save her wise husband, the Dagda, who stayed silent and still before the pale face of his wife, and one of the chieftains stepped forward to jeer at her.

"'What strength can you bring to us?' he mocked, gesturing at the males in all their thick-armored might of iron and sword. 'What do you bring besides your bounteous bosom?'

"The Mórrígan looked at him, and in the dark abyss of her gaze he saw his own demise, choking on his blood as a spear protruded from his back. Her stare was bereft of all light as she answered in a voice of pure ice, 'I bring subjugation—and death.'

"No one again questioned the Mórrígan after that.

"The battle raged, and it went poorly for the Tuatha Dé Danann, so many divinities falling on the swords of the giants. The Mórrígan's own grandfather, Nuada the Silver-Handed, god of the hunt, fell screaming under the poisonous eye of Balor himself, and then the Dagda, king of the gods, took a spear to the gut and dropped to his knees, his lifeblood pouring onto the earth beneath him as he clutched his belly in despair, and all the while she watched unblinking with her impervious black eyes as the man who had sired her and the man who had loved her both screamed in the death throes of their agonies.

"She took one step toward the field of battle, her black hair lying loose and sleek on her shoulders, as though the wind itself dare not touch her for fear of her vengeance, and then another, and with each step, the warmth of the summer sun and the blood-soaked earth began to crack and ripple with shards of ice. She walked with impenetrable calm to the very center of the battlefield, and all who would dare to accost her turned frost-white, even as they lunged toward her black-clad figure. She lifted her arms to the sky and chanted, a rhythmic, primal sound, some dark art of poetry never before spoken among the denizens of the earth."

An answering darkness pounded in the pulse at Rozlyn's temples and wrists, a siren's song of a desire that she had never before known she harbored.

This—this was the kind of power that she wanted to wield, the awe she wished to inspire.

"What did she say?" Rozlyn breathed. "In the poem?"

Jamie shrugged. "No one knows. The language was one not of this world, and only the Mórrígan could tell, and she never would, so closely she guards the secrets of her power." He fell silent, lost in his thoughts, until she nudged him impatiently, and he continued. "The battle broke in favor of the Tuatha Dé Danann. The Fomorian giants dropped their weapons and ran screaming, plagued by nightmares unseen by any but themselves, and the battle ended, but even as the gods and their armies rejoiced, the Mórrígan looked at the cheering soldiers with her depthless black eyes and spoke once more.

"'Rejoice and be glad while you can,' she declared, as high and cold as the winter wind, 'for I have seen the ending of all things, and the world crushed to ruin in the hands of a vengeful god more powerful than any being yet born, and all inhabitants that roam about the earth dying, shrieking in the palm of his hand as he wipes the essence of life itself from the memory of the cosmos.'

"The cheering died away as they stood frozen in horror, and she turned serenely and glided to where her husband lay choking on his own vomit and blood, dying on the ground, and bent over gracefully to lay a snow-white hand against the wound in his abdomen. The Dagda screamed with unutterable pain, and she rose and walked away without a backward glance, and where there had been a great gaping wound was now a bandage of ice, stanching the blood and seeping its frigid ointment into the injury and healing the hurt. And thus," Jamie's voice was quiet with reverence, "the legend of the Mórrígan was born."

Rozlyn was silent for a long time. "I have heard that she was a shape-shifter, that she could take the form of ravens to herald the deaths of her victims."

"Yes," Jamie said, quiet and brief. "Only one of two of the Tuatha Dé Danann able to do so."

"Who was the other?"

"A minor lord, relatively unknown and unimportant to

the more formidable tales of the more powerful gods. I will tell you his story some other time."

She nodded, twisting her hands together in her lap. "What happened to them?" Rozlyn asked. "The old gods? Where did they go?"

Jamie sat up and leaned forward, again clasping his hands together loosely in front of him as he rested his elbows on his knees. "Opinions vary. Some say they were at last defeated by the Fomorians, who reawakened again many centuries after being defeated by the Dagda, as I told you."

"The harp. Uaithne," she recalled. "It played the song of slumber and enchanted them into an eternal sleep."

His gaze flicked toward her, piercing and bright, then away again as he continued. "Even so. Others say that they are merely slumbering beneath the crust of the earth, waiting to be awakened again. Still others claim that they still roam the mortal world, trapped in human bodies, incapable of accessing their divinity." He shrugged. "No one knows for sure."

Rozlyn stared at the thick gray-stone wall of her tower, toward the vast expanse of lush green hills rolling into the distant horizon that she would never be able to see as she considered her next question. "Would they be able to help me to better control this power inside me, to defeat this Beast, if they still existed?"

Jamie sighed, then rubbed at the rough edges of his jaw. "Most assuredly, they would." He hesitated, a weighty silence stretching between them, and then he cleared his throat. "But they are gone, most likely distracted by far greater concerns than your own, so it is your power to wield, Rozi, regardless of what anyone says."

"You think that I should use it, develop it, learn its secrets?"

"Of course, I do. Were you not listening to the story I just told you? You must make your own victories in this life when they are refused to you by those around you, just as the Mórrígan did. Why would I deny you any modicum of power in a world that has essentially rendered you powerless? Speaking of which"—he rose, beckoning her to follow as he descended the curving stone staircase—"I've obtained for you a small taste of freedom, an excursion into the world outside this damned tower of yours."

Rozlyn scrambled to her feet, chasing after him. "My father says I'm not allowed to leave. You can't—"

"Your father himself gave me permission," he called over his shoulder as she trailed behind him. "The Beast has just attacked. It is unlikely that it will do so again so soon, and if it does, well. Here I am, ready and willing to die in your defense, Rozi, if necessary."

"But where are we going? What are we doing?"

He turned slightly, grinning back at her. "To give you a little bit of power, of course."

She did not have time to question him further, because then they were bursting into the great hall, surrounded by her father's soldiers, who eyed her with greater abhorrence than usual, the aftermath of the Beast's savagery still raw in their memories, this curse she had brought upon her people. Rozlyn kept her face impassive and grave, refusing to acknowledge their stares, as she followed Jamie, ignoring the urge to slip her hand into his for comfort, for reassurance. Almost as though he heard her stifled longing, he turned back, winking at her with such amiability, such openness and affection, that she could feel it starting to form in her chest, that smile she had sworn never to give.

They came to the looming front doors of her father's

castle and Rozlyn hesitated, flooded with memories of the last time that she had exited through these doors on a morning of blood and horror and hell; then, with a renewed rush of determination, she shoved through them to stand, blinking, in the sunlight.

"This way," Jamie said, seemingly oblivious to the riot of emotions churning within her, the shocked and horrified stares of the people bustling about in the courtyard before them as she stood stock-still, savoring the taste of the open air and the scent of green grass and the shouts of the villagers for the first time in almost fifteen years, and she broke free from her reverie and hurried after him down the narrow dirt path that led to the stables.

"What are we doing?'

"I," Jamie announced, "am going to teach you how to use a longbow."

CHAPTER TWELVE

Jamie stalked down the length of Rozlyn's great hall, his hair damp with the misty rain, and tossed the putrid head of the dúlachán at the base of her dais. She surveyed them both with supreme disinterest from where she stood, both hands wrapped around a brown ceramic mug, her nostrils flaring in protest at the stench that floated up from the monstrosity on her floor.

She raised her mug to her lips and blew on it, eyeing him, cool and unruffled, over the rim of her cup. "Could you not have waited with that thing outside?"

Jamie jerked his chin at the decomposing head. "There's your proof. Now let's go."

"I refuse to go anywhere with you until you bathe." Rozlyn wrinkled her nose. "You smell absolutely appalling."

"Now is not the time, Rozi."

"Furthermore," she continued, teeth glinting, "that is not what we agreed. I'm not even sure what *that* is."

"It's the head of the gods-damned dúlachán, that's what it is, Rozi, and I killed it right after Hedrek dropped dead at its feet. He was by no means the first to die at the hands of its sorcery, and he will certainly not be the last poor sap to suffer such an untimely and gruesome end by the curses of one of its even more devilish siblings if you don't stop playacting at being a queen and actually be one."

Rozlyn's mouth flattened. "We made a deal, Jamie. Three months, three monsters. By my count, this is but one."

"What more proof do you want, Rozi?" Jamie pointed to the rot-blackened head on the floor. "Is this not enough? Hedrek is dead. How many more must die before you will put aside your stubbornness and take responsibility for what is happening?"

Even as the angry words flew out of his mouth, Jamie closed his eyes in regret as Rozlyn hissed. She slammed her mug down on the windowsill behind her and stalked forward, her fingers sharp and jagged as a serpent's fangs, coiled to strike. "How dare you come into my home and say that to me."

"Rozi, I'm sorry, that is not what I meant—"

"I don't care what you meant." He watched the anger rolling across her face in waves and knew there was no apology he could make, no justification that he could give that would win him forgiveness now. "We had an agreement, Jamie, one that I insisted upon because I know far too well how little your word can be trusted. It is not my fault that you so chose to endanger the men whom you command. That responsibility lies with you and you alone, and don't you dare ever try and lay it at my feet again." Jamie's shoulders sagged, but she continued, unyielding and cold. "You have given me the first proof, and I will consider what you have shown me. But you will leave now, and you will not return before another month has passed. Then and only then will you provide me your second proof. Do you understand me?"

He returned her glare, the air smoldering between them with unseen fire. "I understand."

Rozlyn whirled, her long black braid snapping through the air as she stalked away. "Good. Now get out."

Jamie turned on his heel and strode for the door, slamming it behind him with such force that the solid oaken frame shuddered. With a frustrated sigh, he sank down on the stone steps, indifferent to the hint of the cool rain that hovered in the air, and buried his head in his hands, chest heaving in hopelessness.

He did not look up when he heard the clunking approach of booted steps, nor did he stir when a hefty, broad-shouldered man sank down next to him on the stairs, leaning back on his elbows with a quiet cheerfulness. "Och," Padraig commented in a companionable way. "Quite a temper she has now, don't you know." He nudged Jamie with his elbow, a show of friendly commiseration. "Try not to take it personally."

Jamie lifted his head to stare at the blond-haired man who grinned at him so guilelessly—his wife's lover. "You don't say."

Padraig shrugged. "She means well, Roz does."

"'Roz'?"

"Aye, that's what I call her. She's a good woman. A witch, to be sure, or some other equally terrifying thing, and scary as seven hells when she wants to be, but she has a good heart. She'll come around, never fear." He smiled, a winsome, happy smile, and Jamie briefly imagined shoving his knife in Padraig's good-natured gullet and twisting until he hit bone. It would not be the most effective way of regaining his estranged wife's trust, but it might be worth a try.

"How about a drink, then? That should help ease the sting of her bite a bit, I've found," Padraig persisted with a companionable wink, and what little tolerance Jamie had managed to muster for his wife's lover snapped.

What he wouldn't give to be able to shift into a beast of his own making and rip this handsome face to shreds right here on her own damn hall-steps, and his fingers flexed suddenly in that old familiar way, burning with the need to wield something powerful and dark, the half-forgotten remnants of some past life, and watch his wife's lover consumed in an inferno of fire and ice.

Padraig's smile faltered at the prolonged silence, and he squirmed on the stoop. "You don't want to have a drink with me, then?"

A rush of remorse, of shame, surged within him. It was no one's fault, he knew, no one's but his own, that his wife had sought solace in the arms of this kindhearted man, and he had lost all right to his anger and his jealousy the first time he'd looked into her eyes and lied.

"Padraig," said Jamie, "you're a good lad, but get the hell away from me right now."

The farmer blinked, then shrugged and rose. "If you change your mind about a spot of mead, I'll be having one, so you come along and find me, aye?"

Jamie ignored him, and Padraig shrugged and strode away with unflappable cheeriness. Jamie closed his eyes, seeking the calm that he had so meticulously composed for so many years now, but only a few moments passed before the sound of approaching footsteps caused him to growl again. "Boyo, I swear by the sacred harp of the Dagda himself, I will peel your good-natured face right off you with my bare hands if you don't leave me the hell alone."

"Well," an amused female voice responded, and Jamie's eyes flew open to see a wizened, white-haired woman standing before him, hands on her hips, a large wicker basket tucked under her arm. "That sounds rather an unpleasant fate for poor Padraig, sweet-souled man that he is."

"Who are you?"

She sat down on the top step, placing her basket filled with herbs and poultices next to her, smoothing down the hair that had begun to prickle with dampness from the misty air. "Galena," she said. "I am the healer in the vale. The queen is quite the sorceress, her intuition for herbs and potions unparalleled. She lacks experience though, and that is where I come in. We work together very well, you know. It has been a mutually beneficial relationship for both of us, and the people of her vale have profited greatly from our combined wisdom."

Jamie studied her, some of that coiled tension slipping away from his shoulders at the sight of her serene face. "I am glad to hear that she has someone like you." He examined the ground, the damp stain spreading beneath his boots as the misty rain began to fall. "She has spent too many years alone."

From the corner of his eye, he saw Galena incline her head, a wordless agreement, and Jamie swallowed the painful lump of regret that rose in his throat. "Have you lived here long?"

"All my life." Galena tipped her head back and let the soft hint of rain dance across her face. "I was born nearly seventy years ago in this vale in the little village that I now serve. My mother was a healer, as was her mother. My sister and I learned the arts of herbs at her knee, and for sixteen years, we cared for the people of the valley together, curing their ailments and mending their hurts." Her eyes blurred as she remembered some long-ago pain. "I could not save her, though, the one I most wanted to save. It was when her labor pains began for her third child, her boy, that the bleeding started, and I could not stanch it, try as I might. She faded away into the realm of Magh Meall in my arms, and her little son with her. I wrapped them both in linens, his sweet face tucked away in the arms of his mother, and buried them under the green grass of the hills overlooking the river, so that they might watch over us, protect us, even from the otherworld beyond the grave."

Jamie ran his hand over his face. "I'm sorry," he said. "It never eases, the pain of loss, no matter how many years may pass."

"Och, no." She clucked her tongue softly. "There are days when I hardly can even remember the sound of her laugh or the curve of her face, but then I will see a blue-eyed child with dark red curls tumbling down the gentle slope of the hill where she lies, and the hurt is so sharp and so severe, it feels like only yesterday I closed her bright eyes and laid her in the earth." She sighed. "Her daughters are married now, with little ones of their own. It does not seem right that I have seen fifty years on this earth come and go without that other half of me, that long-lost piece of my heart."

Jamie nodded, his own heart shuddering, but said nothing, his fingers twisting in the black fleece of his doublet.

"She is a great lady, you know," Galena said, breaking through the silence between them abruptly. "Padraig, bless his simple soul, is not wrong about that. Aloof, and a bit cold, it's true. She keeps a careful distance from us all, even as she numbers us among her precious few friends. Trust does not come easily to the queen, nor the idea of being—vulnerable, I suppose." A brief pause, and the unspoken rebuke hovered in the air between them. "But," Galena continued after a moment, "a great lady nonetheless." She studied the afternoon sky, heavy and dark with the encroaching storm clouds in the east. "I recognized that greatness in her ten years ago, when I found her shivering, drenched with rainwater, and half-starved, crouched in the crumbling ruins of this old castle."

His chest clenched suddenly, as though he could see her there in front of him, frightened green-gray eyes in a too-thin face. "She was starving?"

"Well-nigh." He ignored her overt scrutiny, but then she laid her hand on his sleeve, a feather-soft reassurance. "It was not an accident," she said, "that she appeared in this place on that day as I gathered my herbs in the cool spring rain. Something led her here, guided her weary feet to my doorstep, so that I could help her. Save her, as I suspect that I was born to do."

Jamie froze. "Save her? Save her how?"

Galena smiled, and for a moment, the only sound between them was the soft whistle of the breeze through the trees as Jamie studied her placid face, suspicion churning inside him. "So, you're a witch," he said at last, his expression hard.

"As is your wife."

"No," he said, and his voice was a snarl, barely audible in the fast-approaching gloom of the evening rain. "She is no witch. We both know that what lives within her is far greater, far more powerful than that."

Her eyes twinkled. "I suspected as much, but it is nice

to have it confirmed." Galena sighed a little, then ran her fingers lightly over the herbs in her basket. "Although I, too, am no witch, though I understand why you would think so."

"What are you, then?"

"Druid-born, many generations past." The tension that had rumbled along his spine eased, and she leaned toward him, bumping his shoulder with hers lightly, a silent reassurance. "I told you that my mother was a healer, and so she was, but she had the wealth of a dozen generations of druid-born lore to help her, to guide her, which she, in turn, passed down to me. It is little magic, barely more than a whisper, especially compared to what the queen wields, but it helps. I can see the pain, the hurts that those given into my care are undergoing, and I alleviate their suffering in their time of need." Galena looked back at him, her head cocked, birdlike. "Or to guide a terrified young girl who possesses a power that she can neither understand nor control and give her the key to mastering that magic."

Jamie's eyes fluttered shut, relief flooding through him. "It was you."

"It was me," she confirmed. Then her expression grew blurred as she stared into the green valley around them. "And what a blessing she has been for us, your wife, as I knew that she could be—not the plague she was raised to believe herself to be. For over fifty years, I have served the people of the vale. I have seen so many births and deaths, injuries and illnesses, and innumerable sufferings. But for the past ten years, the people in this valley have known extraordinarily little of those things. Your brèagha, as you call her, has provided herbs to ease the labor pains of a young mother whose time has come, potions to cure fevers that would have erstwhile carried off the souls of so many sweet-faced babes, poultices that have healed hurts in men's legs that would have rendered them hapless cripples for the rest of their days had they been left to my care alone." Galena shook her head in wonder. "They call her a witch, sure, but you are right. It is far, far more than simple witchcraft that she practices. She speaks the language of the earth in a way that I never would have believed possible. The birds and the beasts of the earth answer her call so fluently, and the plants and minerals speak to her in whispers unheard by any mortal soul."

Jamie said nothing, but his stomach clenched.

Surely there was no way for her to know his secret, this wrinkled woman, even with her witchlike shrewdness. There was no one alive who knew who he was—what he was—the last remaining flicker of light in a dark and dying world.

"She commands the natural elements," Galena continued, and he could feel that same shrewdness wandering over his face, "with such breathtaking power, as though the earth itself were the source and solace of her magic."

"Yes," Jamie said. "I know."

Galena watched him carefully. "Och, I believe you do indeed."

Jamie swiveled his head to meet her calculating gaze, each assessing the other until he dropped his head and looked away into the mist-soaked trees. "She does not know."

"I assumed as much."

He hesitated. "I don't know how to tell her."

Galena pursed her lips. "You will find a way, in time."

They sat in silence for several long minutes, each studying the evening sky as the rain fell in earnest, soaking their hair, the brown and the white, and streaming down their skin, until finally Galena rose and lifted her basket, turning to enter the warm wooden hall behind them.

"Have patience, a dhia," she whispered. "She will soon see the truth of things."

He nodded once, and the old woman disappeared through the doors as Jamie sat alone in the mist and the rain, chilled to the bone by the memories of his past, wishing he could turn back time.

CHAPTER THIRTEEN

TÍR SOGHÁIN, ÉIRE, 1006

A longbow. Rozlyn frowned. This felt like a trap. "I don't want to learn how to shoot a bow."

"Would you prefer to remain helpless, then, a pretty little damsel in distress all your life?" Jamie asked, and she recoiled, her lips curling into a snarl, ready to snap, before she recognized the knowing gleam in his eye.

It was uncanny, really, how he could almost read her innermost thoughts, as though her entire being were a book with pristine, untouched pages, and he could read her face as easily as the flowing lines of script scrawled across the paper, the unheard narrative of her most secret longings.

"One day," he said, and her eyes darted back to see him watching her in that steady way of his, "the time will come when more human monsters might try to prey upon you, a bhrèagha, and when that day dawns, I would prefer to see you able to fight for yourself against them as magnificently as you have fought against me." His mouth quirked. "Metaphorically speaking, of course."

She considered this, the memory of those suspicious stares that would linger in the air when she moved through her father's hall, the hiss of whispers that would echo behind her as she slipped from room to room. "I suppose that is fair."

"Let the Cailleach take note of this day in her diary of doom. The princess of Connacht has openly admitted that I am right about something."

"This could also be the day when she writes that you were strung up in the air and skewered like a fish with my very real dinner knife."

"What a shocking amount of bloodthirstiness for such a pretty lady. I am very optimistic that you will be a natural-born warrior."

They skirted around the barn to where he had set up several rolled bales of hay as targets. A collection of arrows and a slimmer bow, the twin to his own, lay waiting beneath the shade of a looming birch tree.

Rozlyn picked it up, turning it over in her hands. "It's so light, so fluid." She plucked tentatively at the string. "Very well, I admit it. I very much wish to learn how to use this."

"Anything to make you smile, Rozi."

She glared at him, and he laughed, then began to instruct her on how to position her feet and her hands, her posture, her stance. She obeyed, shifting and flexing, but the long skirts of her gown tripped her, and the constraints of her bodice hampered her movements. She stumbled several times as she tried to hold her bow in the position he had requested.

Jamie frowned. "It would be easier if you were not wearing approximately sixteen different articles of clothing." His eyes narrowed as he considered her, the heavy linen of her white gown, the innumerable folds of fabric that swathed her from head to toe, secreting away any hint of skin. "Wait here," he ordered and stalked away, irritation lining the set of his shoulders with every stride he took.

Something about it was familiar, a faded memory from years long lost to time, the determination in his gaze, as though she had seen it once before, in the faint shadows of her memory, that same defiant look on some other long-forgotten face.

Rozlyn shrugged, shaking away the nagging whisper of that strange dream. She retrieved a book from the deep pockets of her gown and settled in to enjoy the rarity of a lazy afternoon in the open air, away from the impassable stone walls that had loomed around her for so many years. The loneliness somehow did not seem so oppressive here under the unfettered brilliance of the sun, and Rozlyn ignored that warning that whispered in her ear—that it was not the faint smell of the cedar-scented breeze or the cascade of sunbeams that pierced the shadows that lingered in her soul, but a pair of steady eyes and a laugh like a summer breeze—and instead focused on her book.

She was jolted from her reverie by a thump beside her. Rozlyn lowered her book to find a pair of dark gray breeches and a hunter-green doublet with two supple black leather boots lying in the grass next to her while Jamie looked down at her, arms crossed over his chest.

"You're back."

He gestured toward the clothes. "Go and change."

Rozlyn lifted the shirt in the air, studying the thin fabric as she ran her fingers across the stitching on the loose sleeve. "These are so small, like they were made for a child."

"They were," he said. "You are practically infant-sized yourself. Come along, then, a bhrèagha."

"I've told you that I don't like it when you call me that."

"Don't be so pretty, then."

Rozlyn threw one of the boots at his head, and he ducked, laughing. "You almost smiled at that, Rozi. You'll cave, soon enough."

She sniffed, then raised her book in a gesture of dismissal. "I've changed my mind. I would rather read. It's far too hot for such activities."

Jamie nudged her with the toe of his boot. "Go and change," he said. "Stop being lazy. You can lounge about and read for days, uninterrupted and alone, when you are cocooned away in your tower, as I suspect you have on multiple occasions for the past fifteen years. I'm offering you the chance to live a little, Rozi, and enjoy the sun on your skin and the wind in your hair. Now get off that adorable arse of yours and get changed."

"Might I remind you that I am the princess of Connacht?"

"And yet you have an arse, the same as any peasant girl, and it happens to be a very nice one at that. Be grateful and get off it and go."

Rozlyn huffed. "One day," she snarled as she snatched up the clothes and stalked toward the barn, "I will see you hanged, Jamie."

"In that case, the least you could do is to let me watch."

She slammed the door behind her, and alone in the gloom of the barn with only the horses to see, she allowed herself the briefest of smiles.

It was much easier, she admitted to herself, to move about freely in the breeches and shirt. The supple leather of the boots bent beneath the soles of her feet with far greater ease than the stiff brocade slippers that she had always worn. Rozlyn closed one eye, her tongue easing out of the side of her mouth as she drew back an arrow until the string was taut and firm, then loosed it.

It sailed clumsily ahead and then clattered to the ground, a pathetic failure of an attempt.

Rozlyn scowled.

"That's all right," Jamie said, a kindhearted nursemaid mollifying a recalcitrant child, and Rozlyn opened her mouth to protest before realizing that her sour expression most likely warranted such a reaction. "We have plenty of time to practice. You are too stiff, too tense though. You need to relax."

"I was perfectly relaxed when I was reading my book a few moments ago. Perhaps I should go back to that."

Jamie leaned over to where the discarded book lay in the sun. "Ah," he said. "I know this poem. An interesting story for you, and one that is rather hard to find in this part of the world." He thumbed through the pages. "Rather gory in some places, too, if I remember correctly. Research for your future suitors?"

"There's a dragon in it." Rozlyn raised her bow again and aimed it with renewed determination at the bale of hay in front of her, picturing his face with relish as the arrow trembled in her grip. It was infuriating, how easy he made it seem, to hold it steady and sure against the taut string. "Amazing creatures, dragons. To consume a person in a single bite, a breath of fire." The swollen and bee-stung face of the flaith from Bréifne arose in her memory. "I do wish they were real."

"What makes you think that they are not?"

Rozlyn scoffed. "There are no such things as dragons."

"Not anymore, perhaps." Jamie leaned forward and adjusted the angle of her bow slightly, and for some inexplicable reason, her skin hummed, and her heart fluttered at the brush of his fingers against her own. "But once there were, those great black-scaled beasts with leather wings and diamond-hard bellies and eyes of fire—the oilliphéists, they were called. Legend claims that a thousand years ago, long before the Tuatha Dé Danann made their way to the shores of Éire, after they first were born of the earth-mother Danu, the dragons retreated deep into the lairs with their hoards of gold and slept, never to wake again." He winced as Rozlyn loosed an arrow with a grand flourish, and it again clattered to the ground before her. "Legend says that only one of their kind remains alive to this day—Lig na Paiste, the last dragon. He slumbers still, under a barren isle of rock and ice in the cold waters of the northern sea, and there beneath the surface of the rock, he lies dreaming on his bed of gold, waiting to be called forth."

"By whom?"

Jamie shrugged. "By whomever is foolhardy enough to consider himself the master of such monsters, I suppose."

"I'm tempted to try just so I could watch it eat you."

"A hopeless endeavor. Dragons sleep deep, a bhrèagha."

"No, *this* is a hopeless endeavor." She notched another arrow to her bow and lifted it again with an exaggerated weariness.

He ran his hand across his jaw in that absent-minded way of his, and Rozlyn ignored the flash of heat that shot through her belly at the familiar gesture, a faint silver thread of intimacy intensifying between them. "Keep practicing and listen. I will tell you the tale of the god of shape-shifting."

"The one like the Mórrígan?" Rozlyn squinted with one eye closed and tried again, and this time the arrow hung briefly in the air before collapsing in the dirt.

"Even so. This is the story of Midir—and Étaín."

Something in his voice changed, turned raw and rough around the contours of the latter name, and Rozlyn glanced at him. "Who is that?"

He raised his eyebrows, and she sighed as she drew another arrow to aim at the target.

She liked it more than she would admit, even to herself, this constant tug-and-pull between them, nothing freely given, only earned.

As though they were equal, the complement of the other. Well matched.

She brushed away the whispered thought as Jamie continued. "Once, among the Tuatha Dé Danann, lived two gods of the Dagda's clan, Aengus and Midir. Aengus was the god of love and summer, while Midir was a lesser god, wielding only a drop of the power inherited from the combined might of his father and mother. One day, the gods were walking through the realm of Brug na Boinne, the birthright of Aengus, when two sprites in the shape of young boys—the púca, mischievous creatures with golden eyes, mostly harmless but known for their tricks and their guile—threw holly branches at the heads of the gods. Midir threw himself over Aengus and shielded him from the sharp briars of the greenery, but failed to protect his own eyes, and was blinded in his left eye as a result.

"Aengus was deeply touched by Midir's gesture of sacrifice and horrified at the injury he had endured. He called forth the most skilled of healers to mend Midir's eye, and then as a sign of his gratitude, promised to secure for him the love of the most beautiful woman in the world."

Rozlyn made a sound of disgust. "He promised to gift him a girl? Any girl? Whether she wanted to be given or not?"

"Just listen." Jamie shushed her, handing her another arrow, and she huffed, but swallowed her objections, focusing instead on the target taunting her a dozen or so steps away. "Midir, however, scoffed at the idea of forcing his affections on a hapless girl and rejected Aengus's proposal, promptly forgetting about the offer entirely, until one afternoon, sometime later, as he rode along the coastline of the great sea to the north. There in the white sand of the beach, the surf lapping at the hem of her white gauzy gown, he saw a mortal girl with raven-black hair that fell to her waist in a waterfall of glossy night, swirling all around her in the warm salt breeze that wafted in from the waves of the ocean. Something stirred within him, a powerful surge of longing that he had never before known, as he saw her standing so still and serene, her face tipped back toward the brilliant blue sky as she breathed in the salt-mist of the sea.

"Midir dismounted his horse and crept closer, his heart thundering in his chest, watching as she meandered through the surf, the blue-green water rising even to her knees, and she leaned down carelessly, letting her fingers run through the sand-swept sea. He watched and watched, entranced by the simple beauty of her graceful form, until the shore echoed with the calls of her handmaidens, seeking their absent mistress. With great reluctance, she strode away from the waves and trudged up the beach, casting longing glances backward at the churning water.

"Day after day, Midir haunted the coasts of Ulaid and watched as the girl returned each evening to dip her slim legs in the sun-warmed waters of the sea. He learned that she was Étaín, the daughter of Étar, a great chief of Latharna; that she loved the freedom of the sea and the wind and the salt-soaked air; that she rode a stallion as fearlessly as any warrior-chief of old; that her eyes were like mirrors to the ocean she so loved; and that she was promised to Eochu, the high king of northern Éire, destined to be his queen.

"Midir watched with increasingly desperate pain as, day after day, she returned to the serenity of the sea, as she wept with sadness over her approaching marriage-bond. For the lovely Étaín, the most beautiful girl ever to be born to the land of Éire, did not wish to leave her father's home, the sea and the sand that she so loved, to marry this iron-jawed king of the high-walled castle in the North. Midir watched and watched as his beloved wept and grew pale and wan with grief, until finally he snapped. He summoned Aengus, the god of love and summer, and called in the favor promised so many years before. 'Her,' he said, pointing to the black-haired beauty where she stood by the shore. 'Win for me her love.'

"Aengus bounded away to her father, Étar, and presented Midir's suit, but the chief refused, insisting that his daughter marry the king and become the queen of the northern realm, thus ensuring the might of his lineage and his bloodline for the coming centuries. Aengus wheedled and pled with the chief, until finally he agreed. If Aengus would clear for him the waterlogged plains of the inland moors of his domain and divert the great rivers of his realm into the lake of Lough Neagh, thus promising his people endless fertility of their lands, then he would grant the hand of Étaín to Midir.

"Aengus returned sadly to Midir, for his power did not allow him to so manipulate the forces of the natural world.

But Midir's love was made of iron and stone, and so determined was he to save this wild, free girl from a lifetime of misery that he began to labor at his task that very night. He called upon all the forces of his power, which burned through his blood, and for seven days and seven nights, he dug at the banks of the rivers with his immortal hands—the Bhanna and the Sámair and the Oichén—until his palms were scarred and bloody and raw with pain, and the mouths of the great rivers slowly turned their courses to pour the wealth of their waters into Lough Neagh. Then Midir grimly bound his mangled hands with ointment and fine linens, and for a fortnight, he labored, building a dam of unequaled proportions against the eastern borders of Étar's land. When the dam was complete, he blew with a mighty breath upon the wet marshes of Étar's realm—the Mag Tóchair and the Mag Muirthemhe and the Mag Lemna and a dozen more like them—and with a powerful gust of his immortal breath, the bogs dried out, blooming with lush grasses and flowers and trees, fruitful, fertile fields, instead of the wetlands they had once been.

"Midir surveyed his work, then strode directly into the hall of Étar and pointed a bloody, mud-mired finger at the chief. 'I have diverted your rivers and restored your lands,' he announced, exhausted but fierce and glowing with triumph. 'Now give to me what was promised. Your daughter's hand in marriage.'

"Étar was stunned to see the promise of prosperity and wealth given to his people, and he called for his daughter. Étaín entered the hall and looked at the mud-stained god before her, her lovely face unreadable and cool. He dropped to one knee and reached for her hand.

"She did not give it to him.

"Instead, Étaín merely studied him. 'What can you offer me that he cannot?' she asked, gesturing to where Eochu, her betrothed, glowered in the corner.

"'Freedom,' Midir promised her.

"She watched him, then put her small hand into his calloused one, stained with the dirt by which he had won her love. 'Then you shall be my husband and no other.'

"They were married within three days' time, in secret haste, for still her father disapproved, and her promised husband raged. Midir, too, had long been promised in an arrangement set by the Tuatha Dé Danann to marry a powerful witch named Fúamnach in order to establish a truce between the warring clans of the immortals—"

"Wait," Rozlyn interrupted, dropping the bow to place her hands on her hips in outrage. "He is engaged to someone else, as is she, and yet he pursues and romances this girl anyway? What kind of deplorable, selfish god-child is he?"

"But he doesn't love her. He loves Étaín." Jamie stared at her, brow furrowed. "It's romantic."

Rozlyn snorted, most unladylike and unrepentant of such. "Romantic? He is an immortal god, and she is an eighteen-year-old mortal girl. What business does he have courting her? She is a mere child compared to him."

"But—"

"And," Rozlyn continued, jabbing her finger at him for emphasis, "lest we forget, he already has an immortal wife of his own—"

"Consort. Betrothed. All those things, but not his wife."

"Spoken like a man. He is not free to be dillydallying with other girls—"

"Dillydallying? He's not dillydallying. It's not a game to him; he loves her—"

"Dillydallying," Rozlyn repeated firmly. "He has no business falling in love with other girls, mortal or not, when he is betrothed to another woman. He sounds like an absolute cad."

Jamie blinked, a shadow of uncertainty shading his features. "You haven't even heard how the story ends."

Rozlyn sniffed. "I don't need to. I'm sure she falls madly in love with him, and all the while we will ignore the fact that he is betraying the woman whom he has already promised to marry, regardless of her feelings, and they will live happily ever after. No, thank you. I am perfectly content not having to suffer through such drivel."

Jamie laughed, but Rozlyn noticed that there was no humor in it, a grim bark of something akin to disappointment. "Duly noted. No more love stories for the princess of Connacht."

"I would appreciate that." She bent down and picked up the discarded longbow, her movements irritated, that brief flash of *something* that she had felt in those few moments gone cold and steely inside her. "I have quite enough of that nonsense in my real life. I hardly need to hear about some other girl's luckless love life in addition to my own."

She lowered the bow as she noticed how Jamie stared at her, his face expressionless and hard. "What?"

He shook his head. "Nothing." Jamie gestured toward the bow, the motion curt, before he shoved his hands into his pockets with considerable force. "Again. And this time, don't miss."

She didn't.

CHAPTER FOURTEEN

"All right," Jamie announced, blowing furious puffs of hot breath into his half-frozen hands. "It's time."

Bowen looked up at him quickly, while Nyle and Tavin paused their card game to swivel around to listen. Jamie sighed and gave up trying to rub any semblance of feeling into his hands, slipping them into his pockets as he paced in front of his men. "The dúlachán, it seems, did not sufficiently impress the lady." Nyle made a noise of contempt, the memory of his brother writhing in pain still fresh and raw, no doubt, and Jamie looked away before continuing. "So we hunt bigger game this month, lads. This time," he said, "we will bring back a bean-sí."

Tavin squeaked, and Nyle tossed the cards on the frosty ground in disgust, while Bowen gaped at him. "You want to hunt the devil-woman of the sídhe? Are you mad?"

Jamie shrugged. "We survived the dúlachán."

"Some of us did," Nyle interrupted, his voice a tremor of darkness, of still-boiling anger.

"It is a relatively similar entity as the bean-sí, speaking death to its victims, so unless you feel the urge to hunt down the aforementioned Abhartach—"

"That seems unnecessary," Tavin interrupted, eyes wide.

"Then the bean-sí it is." Jamie blew out a long breath. "As always, I do not require you to do this, lads. I have told you the stakes at play here, the risks we run both by moving forward, and the risks of doing nothing, but your presence is and has always been entirely optional. There is no shame in being reluctant to face such monsters as these."

Bowen folded his arms across his hefty chest. "But you will."

Jamie rolled his shoulders, ignoring that shadowy tug of guilt in his chest. This was all that was left to him, this need to make right all the things that had gone so horribly wrong because of him. "It's my duty, Bowen, not yours."

"But our people, our families, will suffer at the hands of these monsters if they are not stopped," Tavin said. His boyish features darkened in the soft afternoon light. "And our duty lies with them."

Bowen nodded in agreement, his mouth set in a grim line, and Nyle kicked at the stones lying in the dirt. "I am with you," he grunted. "But I do not see why she needs convincing. It is selfish and cruel to make us do this, when she ought to help those she can with that damned magic of hers."

His hurt was a palpable thing, lingering in the air between them, and Jamie silently resolved to send the boy home after this last quest, to let him heal in his mother's house and under her watchful eye. His grief and his anger would only grow deeper, leave far more jagged scars, out here in the wilderness, seeking the monsters that had killed his brother under the direction of the man who had failed to protect him.

Another name, another face added to his ledger, never to be set right.

Nyle folded his arms across his chest. "She should be here," he repeated. "She is the one with magic, not us."

Oh, the irony, Jamie thought grimly. It had once been his, that magic, and everything would be so much easier if it was again. "It is my fault," he insisted again, "that the queen of the vale is so reluctant to trust my word on this matter. Not hers." He shook his head when Nyle started to object, and the boy fell silent. "The bean-sí hunts at all moons, so we begin tonight. It might take us a few tries to track her down, but by the time we have captured and gagged the creature and dragged her back to the vale, then we should be right at the one-month mark."

He turned and swung himself into the saddle, his silver-gray mare dancing under his weight, and gathered his reins as his men stamped out their fires and mounted their horses, and together they galloped away from their little camp on the outskirts of the vale of Inagh and into the cool, fog-drenched mountains of Mhám Toirc.

The air was colder here, not from the shadows of the looming boulders or the tall fir trees but from the presence of the nameless monsters that lurked among its crevices and crannies. He could taste the foulness of their magic on his tongue, the acrid tang of rot and despair that trailed in their wake, these creatures of evil, and he glanced surreptitiously at his men to see if they could sense what secret danger lurked about them even now.

Bowen was grinning from ear to ear while Nyle teased a blushing Tavin about the attentions of a red-haired tavern girl from a few weeks back, and they jostled one another and joked in hushed voices, oblivious to the stench of evil that rose around them, the faint tinge of poison that lingered in the air.

Jamie hissed out a foul-flavored breath through clenched teeth and rode on, wary of every shadow that flickered in the branches and rocks of the mountain, even as the sun-dappled rays that crept in through the trees winked at him with a deceptively bright innocence. *Nothing to see here,* they seemed to whisper with mischievous malevolence. *All is well, for such beauty could never hide anything as vile as you suspect we do,* and his fingers tensed reflexively around the leather reins. His horse whinnied, shaking her soft silver mane, sensing his agitation. Jamie gritted his teeth and nudged her forward, ignoring the stench of wrongness that grew ever more potent with each plodding step into the trees.

His nerve barely lasted an hour before Jamie yanked on the reins, his mare sliding to a stop, hooves dancing. "We need to leave," he said, his voice urgent and low with warning.

The men's murmurs stopped immediately as they straightened in their saddles behind him. "What's the matter?" Bowen asked as Tavin and Nyle reached for their swords where they rested in their scabbards by their sides.

"I don't know." Jamie's nostrils flared as he surveyed the thick green undergrowth, the faintly waving branches of the sweet-scented firs, the lingering shadows under the gray boulders that loomed along the narrow path through the mountain. "The air is wrong. Something is here that should not be, that we are not ready to face." He moved to swing his horse's head back the way they had come, down the path to the base of the mountains, when, from the cluster of lichen-licked rocks ahead of them, an eerie howl broke loose, and every hair on Jamie's forearms stood on its end at the sound.

"Run," he snapped, whipping the horse back to face the unseen monster ahead. "All of you, run, out of the mountains. Stay away from the rocks. Make for the open space of the meadows."

Tavin turned to flee, but Nyle and Bowen hesitated, watching him in panicked concern. "But—"

"Go!" Jamie ordered. "Before the third howl, or you are all doomed—go!"

Bowen paled. "The cú-sídhe."

"Go," Jamie repeated, his face bleak, even as a second unearthly howl reverberated across the rocks of the mountain. "Wait for me at the base of the mountain." No one moved, and he gestured impatiently, ignoring the grief in Bowen's terrified dark eyes. "I will not see another of you dead because of me. Go!"

Nyle moaned, a sorrowful sound, and Bowen's face hardened as they both wheeled their horses around and thundered after Tavin, their hoofbeats echoing down the mountainside. Jamie drew his longbow away from his shoulders, notched his keenest arrow to the shaft of his bow, and waited with sweaty palms and a thundering heart for that third fateful howl.

It broke across the crags of the mountain with a guttural bark of hunger. The small flint rocks strewn about the dirt path underneath him shuddered as the enormous wolflike creature sprang from its den beneath the boulders and crashed to the ground in front of him, its dark green fur rippling with fury, its pale yellow teeth—tinged with the faint black of its poisonous bite—bared in a promise of slow, agonizing death.

Jamie stared into its black eyes and pulled his bow tight. He snarled back at the wolf, his lips curling, and loosed his arrow right as the enormous green wolf leapt at his horse with a bone-shuddering howl.

The arrow caught the monster in its right shoulder, and it hurtled to the ground, its black-tipped claws scratching at the dirt with pain as it staggered back to its feet, roaring with a black inferno of wrath. Its hair bristled anew as it limped in tight, threatening circles around them. Jamie reached for another arrow as his horse flattened her ears tight against her head and screamed, her hooves dancing unsteadily on the path as she swerved to continue facing her attacker.

The wolf lunged again in silence, no warning snarl this time, with supernatural swiftness, and the mare screamed again, rearing back on her hind legs in terror just as Jamie loosed another arrow. It shot high into the trees, missing its mark. Even as he gritted his teeth in sickened disgust at the sacrifice of his mare, Jamie rolled from the back of the saddle, kicking his feet loose from the stirrups and flinging the reins into the trees, hoping the bait of the trapped horse, screaming with terror, would draw the wolf's attention away from him where he lay, helpless.

He hit the ground hard on his stomach and rolled to his back and sat up, reaching behind his shoulders for another arrow, when the creature's hot breath suddenly cascaded across his face, and it was there, clawing at his chest, and he was thrown back on the rock-studded dirt of the mountain

floor so hard that the air whooshed from his lungs in a painful gust, and he screamed at the fiery scratches of the claws
that penetrated through his doublet to shred the skin beneath. Through the dizzying haze of pain he saw the wolf's
black eyes gleaming as it opened its jaws, fangs dripping with
the green-black ooze of its venomous bite, ready to sink its
teeth deep into the flesh of his right shoulder.

The world went black and woozy around him as his
vision swam, the pain exploding in a blinding inferno of
agony through his shoulder blade, and he screamed again,
piercing and shrill, as the wolf's fangs savaged the soft skin
of his arm. He groped blindly at his waist with his left hand,
shaking with pain, even as the wolf reared back to bite again,
its black glower fixated on the lifeblood that pulsed through
the weak tissue of his throat, and in one swift, desperate
motion, Jamie drew the sharp, curved knife belted to his
waist and drove it into the cú-sídhe's flank.

The wolf shrieked and whirled away, tearing and ripping
with its teeth at the joint where the knife was embedded deep
in the bone, howling with agony, then loped away, whimpering as it fled to hide in some dark corner of the mountain
and lick its wounds.

Jamie watched its dark green form disappear into the
trees, his vision swimming from the poison even now beginning to burn its way through his veins, then rolled onto his
side and vomited on the forest floor before he staggered to
his feet and toward his mare, trembling and ensnared in the
low-hanging branches of the trees. He dragged himself with
ragged, shallow breaths into the saddle, collapsing across her
sweat-soaked neck. "Go," he whispered, and the horse began
to move, her ears pricking forward at the raw command that
thrummed through his strained voice, a recognition of the

lingering shadows of power still sputtering inside him, of the divinity he had long since lost. "Take me home."

He was slumped over her silver-gray mane when the mare emerged at the base of the mountain, floating on a dark cloud of unthinkable pain, when his men saw him, sprinting toward him with shouts of alarm. Bowen seized his arm, his face paling at the sight of the dark crimson blood that stained the front of his doublet, the blackened gash of the poisonous bite on his shoulder, and Jamie raised his head, his vision swirling in a toxic fog. "Take me home," he whispered again as his eyes rolled back in his head. "Take me to my brèagha."

CHAPTER
FIFTEEN

Rozlyn leaned against the balustrade of her terrace, her knuckles white as she gripped the railing, studying the evening sky. She did not turn when she heard his footsteps behind her, even when he leaned against the rail next to her.

"No sign of it," she murmured. "Two months, and no sign of it at all."

Jamie crossed his ankles as he watched her. "That's a good thing, a bhrèagha. Let it stay away, forever if it likes."

"Yes." She hesitated. "It has never stayed away for this long, Jamie. It will, it *must* strike soon." She swallowed. "It seems more terrible each time, as though with each visit it grows more and more violent." Rozlyn squeezed her eyes shut. "It is no wonder that they all hate me so much."

Jamie was silent, then reached for her hand where her nails dug into the wooden paling, prying them free gently before wrapping his fingers around her own. "It is not your fault, Rozi," he said. "You did not conjure this monster, nor did you wish this evil upon them."

"I know." Rozlyn took one last searching look at the sky, the stars just beginning to emerge from behind the velvet blanket of night as it unrolled itself across the firmament, then turned away, her fingers slipping from his. She ignored the soft whine of protest that echoed in her heart, which she had for so long kept hidden away. "You are here late."

"My apologies," he said, but he did not sound particularly regretful to be here, standing so close to her underneath the canopy of midnight stars. "I realized that I forgot to give you this." He reached into his doublet and pulled out a thick, leather-bound volume. "More stories for the princess."

She took it from him, studying it with interest. "A book of war poetry." She raised her eyebrows at him. "Interesting choice."

Jamie pointed a finger at her emphatically. "Not a love poem, you will notice."

"Love is more of a battle than any war that I have ever read about." She tossed the book down, her expression tinged with bitterness. She was quiet for a long moment. "You have told me so many stories over the past year. I have never thanked you for that."

"You still haven't, but nevertheless, you're very welcome."

She continued to stare across the dark shadows of the valley nestled far below the rolling mountains. "You never did tell me," she said, "the rest of that one story, from a few months ago, about Midir and his bride. You said that you would tell me of his shape-shifting powers, but I never heard the ending."

He shrugged, his fingers tapping against the railing. "I did not imagine you would be interested in hearing it."

Jamie examined her for a quiet moment. "You're in a mood this evening."

Rozlyn sighed and wrapped her arms around her shoulders, hugging herself. "I feel tense, on edge, full of an energy that I cannot control." She shrugged. "I need to do something, something wild, to try and siphon it off somehow before I explode."

He made a noncommittal noise under his breath, then after a moment, glanced at her as he rubbed at his jaw in that idle way of his. "I know something wild that you could do."

"What is that?"

His smile flashed in the starlight. "Kiss me."

Something bright and hot flared inside her, something alarming and exhilarating all at once, a yearning and a warning, colliding into one another in a confusing medley of emotions.

This was dangerous territory, unexplored, treacherous ground, where one misstep could cost her everything—her magic, her freedom, all the aspects of her life that had any value to them at all—and yet she found that she ached to explore this strange new world.

Rozlyn swallowed. Be careful, she warned herself. Be wary. "You've never asked me that before."

"I'm not asking now—merely suggesting. It is entirely up to you whether you will or not."

"Why on earth would I kiss you?"

"You wound me, Rozi. Why ever not?"

"Because I don't want to marry you. That's why."

Jamie snorted. "By the harp, who said anything about marriage? Just a quick kiss to distract you from this energy, that's all." He smiled at her, and she recognized it for the challenge that it was. "I know, for a fact, that you have no objections to kissing other young men whom you have no intention of marrying."

Rozlyn scowled, inexplicably hurt. "That does not mean that I have any desire to ever kiss *you*, Jamie." She turned to retreat inside her room when he called out to her again.

"A bargain, then, like on the first day that we met. Do you remember, Rozi?"

She turned around. "I remember." She eyed him. "What kind of bargain?"

He gestured toward the table on the terrace, lit only by the moon's pale glow, and the small wooden box that lay discarded on top of it. "You still play fidchell, yes?" She nodded, and he continued with a shrug. "Then play with me, Rozi—one match. If you win, then I will return half of the gold that your father has so generously given me in return for playing the part of your doting suitor. But if I win now"—he smiled, a dark-haired angel, and she mistrusted every part of him—"then I get my kiss." He paused, studying her intently. "Are we agreed?"

No, she thought. Absolutely not. She should say good night and go inside, back to her room, to her cold and empty bed, to her shadows and her griefs, back to missing a life she had never been given the chance to live.

Rozlyn's breath shuddered out. "I told you. I have no intention of kissing you. It's demeaning to bet on such a thing."

"So I have been told before by a maiden very like you." His lips twitched when she scowled. "Yet I have seen you kissing a half dozen boys since I arrived here." His eyes glinted, and she saw it then, the slow burn of long-restrained jealousy. Jealous—he was jealous that she had let them kiss her, and her heart thundered at the thought of it. "What is one more, after all?"

Rozlyn hesitated. It was true that she could do this, close her eyes and imagine he was just one more in that never-ending line of suitors, smug and self-righteous, seeking her hand but not her heart.

And yet—

There were boys, beardless and self-assured and as much of a threat to her heart as the slime-covered bullfrogs in the black-watered loch far below her tower walls—and then there was Jamie, as she'd come to know him over their idle months together. Tall and lean, with his clever blue eyes and that ever-present scruff that darkened the clean lines of his jaw . . . She felt things when he produced that warm smile—and always, always, her pulse quickened at the way that he seemed to see into the very depths of her soul. She felt as though she were a leather-bound book that was to everyone else filled with foreign ciphers and illegible scrawls, but in his hands, the tome of her secret thoughts and longings fell open, translated into convivial lines on oft-perused pages, well-worn and welcoming.

She would play with him.

It wasn't the allure of kissing him that convinced her, not the image of his lips on hers, but the idea of sitting across from him at this small table under the faint light of the stars, moving their pieces in perfect equanimity, attacking and countering, jesting and teasing, the back-and-forth rhythm of sacrifices and forks, of castling and exchanges, matching her wit to his in the most elemental of ways.

She would win. Her life was too full of disappointments and failures. She deserved a small taste of victory, of triumph.

"Very well." She flipped her braid back over her shoulder. "Then let's play."

Jamie grinned at her, an unspeakably wicked thing, and Rozlyn straightened her shoulders and glided to the table as he sank into the chair opposite her. They set up their pieces in mutual silence. Rozlyn peeked at him, his expression unreadable and calm, as he straightened his bronze rooks on the ends of the black-squared board. He looked up and caught her gaze, then gestured grandly. "Ladies first."

They began to play, moving their pieces with confident speed. The rhythm of the game came effortlessly to Rozlyn, the long years of solitude with nothing better to do than to practice and to plan the strategies guiding her moves, but it unnerved her a little, to see an answering ease guiding his own movements across from her. She pinned his queen with her bishop and her knight with relative ease, but he slipped away from her hold and skewered her own queen only a few moves later. She frowned.

"Try harder," he murmured as he studied the board with mild amusement. "Or I will start to suspect that you want to lose."

Her lips curled, a silent challenge, and their pieces flew across the board in earnest, dancing and dabbing at one another, attack and retreat, and the little piles on either side of the board grew higher and higher with their fallen men until suddenly Jamie leaned back in his chair, folding his arms behind his head, and announced, "Match in three moves, a bhrèagha."

Rozlyn's eyes flew to the board with renewed examination—not possible—and after a moment, she frowned. "How did you do that?"

He shrugged, eyeing her carefully. "I have secrets of my own, Rozi."

She stood, a sudden panic mixed with some other unknowable emotion clawing at her throat, and paced away from him. "You cheated."

"I most certainly did not. Stop stalling, you little coward."

He rose from his seat and slid his hands into his pockets as he watched her.

She said nothing but continued to stand apart from him, staring down at her hands as they twisted together in an involuntary expression of distress.

"It is only a kiss," he said from where he stood across the terrace, careful to keep his distance from her.

"I have kissed dozens of men."

"And I women."

"So it's nothing."

"Nothing at all."

Rozlyn did not move.

Jamie edged forward a cautious step. "Just close your eyes and imagine I'm that scrawny lad from Munster who was here last week. You kissed him easily enough."

"He looked like a frog."

Jamie smiled as he eased a little closer to where she stood. "And what do I look like, a bhrèagha?"

"You look—" Her voice faded away as he moved infinitesimally closer, until the tips of his boots brushed against the fabric of her skirt as it lay on the wooden floor of the terrace.

She could smell him now, that faint whiff of cedar and salt, and something else too, something wild and free and irrepressible, as though the roll of the hills and the whisper of the wind and the thundering of the rivers were captured in the pores of his skin.

"Yes?"

She frowned, bereft of tactics and techniques on this foreign field of play. "I don't remember what I was saying."

He smiled again, not with wickedness this time but with something that made Rozlyn suddenly grow warm all over and woozy on her feet, as though the world were spinning far faster than it had been only moments ago. "That's all right," he murmured as his hands meandered toward her waist. "We'll revisit the topic some other time."

Rozlyn's chest constricted once as he slid his arms around her, his hands latching onto the bones of her hips, and she stared at the black fleece of his doublet, refusing to look into his face. "Let's get this over with," she said steadily, even as her heart thrummed in her chest, and her palms grew slick and heavy with that surge of nameless desire that she had only felt the merest flickers of before now.

She was very much at a loss at how to counter this move.

Jamie remained still, holding her with a feather-like touch, a whisper of a caress, but she could sense his eyes roaming over her face as she kept her gaze averted from his own. "It would help," he whispered, and his breath skated over the wayward strands of her hair as it fell from its pins around the edges of her face, sending the most delicious shivers of that same sparkling desire shimmering down her spine, "if I could see a little more of that pretty face of yours."

She raised her head slowly to meet his eyes, and he bent his head and brushed his lips against hers, the barest touch of a kiss, so soft that she could almost convince herself that it had never happened, if not for the explosion of desire that welled within her.

It was like he could see her, the true color of her, a girl full of smiles, whom she might have been in another world, another life free of cailleachs and curses and mothers gone cold beside the crying bodies of their newborn babes.

A storm broke loose inside her at his touch, and she forgot what it had been like to kiss any other man. Her head jerked back from the force of that rush of emotion, and from deep within her throat erupted a soundless plea for more, and Jamie growled in response, lowering his head further to nuzzle at the curve of her ear with his nose.

"Only one kiss," she gasped as the scrape of his teeth against the soft skin of her neck set fire to whatever strange tempest was raging within her blood.

"Of course," he murmured, nipping at her throat. "That's all I took, wasn't it now, a bhrèagha? I wouldn't dream otherwise."

Her breaths grew ragged and rough. "Although," she said as his lips explored down the curve of her neck to the small strip of skin exposed at the base of her throat, and she fought the urge to moan as he continued to barely brush the edge of his mouth against her sensitive skin, and gods, it was unbearable, this tease of a kiss, this whispered promise of forbidden delights, "we are not married."

"The gods forbid," Jamie murmured, and she frantically swallowed the urge to laugh.

"And you do not love me."

"Of course not." His fingers slid up her back in seductive strokes, and she arched against him. "Not in the slightest."

"So," she whispered, "it might not be so bad."

Jamie made a strangled sound deep in his throat, and his hands tightened a little rougher around her waist, pressing her closer. "It most definitely," he whispered against her neck, "would not be at all bad."

Rozlyn shuddered and then yielded, looking up into a face that burned with the most voracious hunger that she had ever seen, and she raised herself up on her toes, her mouth deepening and molding against his. "Perhaps," she murmured as his touch grew hungrier, demanding, infinitely darker, "we can risk it. Just this once."

And then she closed her eyes and conceded the match.

Chapter Sixteen

THE VALE OF INAGH, ÉIRE, 1017

Rozlyn could sense the change in the air, the way that the rain thrummed more urgently onto the leaves of the forest surrounding her vale and knew that he was here, a full fortnight earlier than she expected him.

She also knew, somehow, that he was hurt.

Turning away from the long table in her solar, its surface jumbled with her collections of dried-out herbs and pestles and potions, she ran through the great hall, her boots tapping against the smooth wood floors in rhythm to the wild beating of her heart, and that primal urge singing in her veins to find him, help him, save him.

She rushed out the main doors and stood silent on the top step, peering into the mist-green fog, swirling in the sheets of rain that showered down from the sky.

There—emerging from the trees, she spotted the gleam of his silver-gray horse just visible through the gloom, his smattering of men on horseback surrounding him. She could see him slumped against the neck of the horse, his left arm clinging to the silver strands of its mane, his right arm dangling by his side. That thread of a pulse between them quickened, and the realization flashed unbidden through her—she had sacrificed him, a knight thrown to the literal wolves, discarded as easily, as carelessly as though he were a pawn.

In the span of a heartbeat, he raised his head and met her gaze through the cascading rain that pelted his face, and something tight and ironclad clenched inside her at the sight of those dark eyes so blurred with pain.

He rode forward into the clearing in front of the steps of her home and slid from his mount in a single motion, stumbling to his knees on the soggy ground. "Here you are, waiting right where I left you," he said with a smile, the clever edges of his voice hollowed out and dull. "Did you miss me so terribly?"

"Almost as much as I'd miss the devils in hell," Rozlyn answered, her heart in her throat, as he pitched forward onto his face in the mud, his right arm flopping uselessly at his side, the reins falling to the ground. His men leapt as one from their horses and lurched forward, clamoring and shouting as they half-carried, half-dragged him forward. Her trancelike state broke, and Rozlyn choked once, then hurried down the steps, out into the sheets of icy rain to meet them, scanning his limp frame.

His right arm was smeared with blood, the front of his tunic ripped and dyed an even deeper black with splotches of wet red gore, and his face was far too pale.

"What happened?"

Nyle growled and spat at the ground even as Rozlyn's eyebrows rose at his boldness. "Do you care?" The boy's eyes burned as he clutched at Jamie's sagging frame, and his face contorted as he screamed at Rozlyn. "You send him off to fight these demons, knowing what waited for him, for all of us, all for the sake of your injured pride—"

Jamie made an incoherent sound of warning, even as Rozlyn snarled, but Nyle soldiered on, his hands vibrating with fury. "You say the word, and off we go to our doom, just so you can watch him squirm. Hedrek is dead." He faltered, the final word shaky on his tongue. "And Jamie will no doubt be as well, so you've gotten what you wanted, haven't you?"

"You have no idea," Rozlyn said, dangerous and low, the faint shadows of great feathered wings rising behind her through the blinding sheets of rain, "what I want."

Nyle stood his ground even as his face paled. "I know that I don't see you out here fighting these monsters."

From the corner of her eye, she saw Jamie lift his head with agonizing sluggishness. "Nyle," he said, and it broke something in her that she had long since buried away, to hear the hollowness, the hurt in his voice. "Enough, lad."

Rozlyn looked to Bowen, willing the feral thundering of her heart to slow, to calm. Too dangerous, to allow herself to become so wrathful, so wild and unrestrained. "I will ask you one more time: What happened?"

Bowen glanced at her, the vague imprint of her terrible wings still lingering in the air, and flinched at the ominous expression etched across her face. "The cú-sídhe happened."

"When?"

"Three days ago."

Rozlyn hissed. Every child born in Éire knew the nightmare of the cú-sídhe, the monstrous wolf spawned within the fairy mounds scattered throughout the realm. Even in a world free from magic for over three hundred years, everyone knew well enough to shudder at the sound of its name. Three days of its poisons running through a person's veins was a dark matter, indeed. "Get him inside. Take him into my solar." Even as she spoke, she pulled her cloak over her hair and ran into the trees.

She did not stop until she came to the small, thatched hut on the outskirts of the village, soaked to the skin with the frigid rain, her boots drenched from the puddles of rainwater pooling in the rocky lane. She banged on the door, and after an interminable moment, it swung open to reveal Galena standing in the doorway, her white hair illuminated by the orange-red light of the hearth burning behind her.

"What's wrong?"

"Jamie," Rozlyn said without preamble. "The cú-sídhe has bit him."

Galena swore, then turned and hurried farther into her house, snatching up her cloak and a handful of herbs and poultices, which she tucked away in her basket. "Is it the neck?"

"No," Rozlyn answered, her fingers sizzling with the roar of that power thrumming beneath the surface of her skin, and for the first time in nearly a decade, that nameless threat swelled, that dark thundercloud of her magic rumbling inside her, dangerously close to bursting beyond the boundaries of her control. "His arm, near the shoulder. Claw marks on his chest."

She needed a cup of tea, desperately.

"That's still too close to his lifeblood," said Galena, swinging her cloak around her shoulders. "He will not last more than a few days if we do not intervene."

"It has already been three."

Galena glanced up at Rozlyn's flat tone, softening as she studied her rigid face. "Then let's hurry." She paused at the sight of the faint tremors rolling through Rozlyn's shoulders, quaking her tightly clenched fingers. "Can you control it?"

Rozlyn pinched at the bridge of her nose, understanding the veiled question behind her words. "I suppose that I must."

Galena hesitated, then turned and hurried back to her table, ruffling through a fresh-picked pile of herbage. She plucked a few thin brown twigs with spiny green leaves and thrust them into Rozlyn's quivering fingers. "Try and eat," she said. "Although the bitterness—"

Rozlyn bit into the branch, gagging at the acrid burn of the juices in her mouth, and forced herself to swallow. "Let's go."

Cramming the rest of the branch into her mouth and chewing grimly, her head woozy from the effect of the sour juices, she backed away a few steps from the door, willing that throbbing surge of power to bend to her will. The familiar stretch and pull rippled along the skin at the back of her shoulders as the great feathered wings protruded through her scapula, and her body grew heavy with the rigid lines of bone and muscle and thick, dark fur, and she drank in the sensation of that wildness rushing through her veins, like fire devouring the dry grass on a sweltering summer's day. She turned and saw Galena standing in the door, her fingers tight on the handle of her basket, watching her. She huffed once, a wordless command, and Galena strode forward into the cold bite of the rain. Rozlyn gently seized the frail frame of the old woman in her massive paws, and with three mighty flaps of her wings, they were soaring through the rain that pelted the earth around them, high above the trees as she arrowed toward her castle with unerring speed.

She dropped to the ground, releasing Galena from the tight grip of her paws. The healer rushed forward, then hesitated. "Will you come?"

Rozlyn shook her shaggy head, and Galena pursed her lips. "Take a moment," she said, a quiet command. "Then come. I will need you."

She turned and hurried inside, disappearing down the hall, a trail of rainwater dripping onto the wood floors after her, and Rozlyn let out a deep huff from her bushy jaws. She stood in the rain for a long time, the chill of the half-frozen water soaking into her thick fur, as she stared into the dark night, searching for a peace that she had only just started to believe possible for her to know.

She should have known better, that for monsters such as her, there could only be chaos, and bloodshed, and pain—could only be the ever-present threat of death.

She shook herself fiercely and wrapped her wings around her beastly form as she shifted, her black hair glossy and smooth once more, and with a deep breath, she strode on her own two legs into the castle. Rozlyn could hear the murmur of voices from inside her solar and she paused in the doorway, soaked to her skin, her cloak and gown clinging to her like ivy on stone.

Jamie was stretched out on her long wooden table, the herbs and potions with which she had been working before his arrival shoved onto the floor in a disheveled heap, and for a terrifying moment, her heart seized in her chest. Then the air burst from her lungs in an uncontrolled rush of relief at the sight of him twisting toward where she stood in the door, eyes hazy with pain, but open and alert.

She cleared her throat, and the other three pairs of eyes in the room swung toward her. "How serious is it?"

"Just a scratch."

"Be quiet." Rozlyn waved a hand at Jamie even before he finished speaking, her attention focused on Galena. "How bad?"

The older woman shrugged, her white hair falling across her shoulders in a sheen of light. "It is hard to say. The infection has settled deep in his blood, but I was able to draw out much of the poison by the burdock root and dandelion poultice. It is fortunate that between the two of us, we had both in our collections."

Rozlyn's lips tightened. "How is it best treated?"

"Nettle tea for fever and infection," Galena said, wiping the remnants of dried blood from the festering wound, blackened and burnt around the edges. "The chest wounds are relatively shallow and should heal easily. The wound in his shoulder, though, is deep, troublingly so. It might be necessary to wrap it in comfrey leaves overnight to try and seal the gash to prevent secondary infection." She looked at Rozlyn, whose shoulders tensed.

Jamie watched them from where he lay on the table, chest rising and falling with laborious effort, his face drawn and pale. "Comfrey leaves can be quite toxic, if I remember correctly."

"Yes." Galena's answer was short and crisp. "I would only advise their use in the direst of circumstances."

"Interesting," said Jamie, faint and faraway with pain, as though the distant shores of Magh Meall were shimmering there before him, and an ice-cold kiss of fear pressed itself against the nape of Rozlyn's neck. "Tell me, Rozi, does the news of my impending demise help or hurt my chances at getting a roll tonight?"

"I suppose," she said, refusing to acknowledge the terror

that still stroked along her skin, "that would depend on exactly how devoted Bowen here is to you."

Jamie winced as he pulled himself up to sit on the edge of the table, his arm ensconced in a linen sling and his legs dangling over the side—his fingers shook, a sick sheen of sweat beading across his ash-white brow. "You mock, but a man could do far worse on the last night of his life than Bowen. Look at those shoulders. The man is built like an ox."

It hurt her all over again to hear it, that wry humor of his, unflappable and steady as the sheer white cliffs that overlooked the sea.

Bowen grinned and flexed quite proudly as even Nyle smirked a little, while Galena eased toward the door. "I shall come back in a few hours, shall I?"

Rozlyn's eyes narrowed to slits as she stared at Jamie, who smiled back, his lips pale and trembling with fever. "Thank you, Galena. That will be fine." She laced her fingers through the age-weathered ones of the older woman, squeezing them briefly, then stepped away. "I asked Ciara to fix you a hot meal, and to make up a room for you in the guest quarters. Go and rest, a chara mná."

Galena nodded and let her fingers, warm with unspoken words of comfort, trail across the back of Rozlyn's hand, and then slipped from the room, followed by Bowen. Nyle lingered, glowering at Rozlyn, who stared back, her face impassive and cold. Jamie reached out with his left hand and squeezed the boy's shoulder in a gesture of reassurance. "It's all right," he said. "Leave us be. Go help Tavin with the horses. The poor lad is all by himself in the rain and the cold tending to them."

Nyle nodded, ducking his head away from Rozlyn's icy gaze, and slunk from the room.

For a moment, they were silent, studying one another, until Rozlyn looked away and walked toward the hearth, removing a tin kettle from the small table beside it and filling it with fresh water from the waiting jug. She leaned forward and placed it on the iron bail inside the fire to heat.

"I want you to know," Rozlyn said at last with great coolness, without turning around, "that I shall be sure and apply the comfrey leaves most generously if necessary."

Jamie barked out a laugh, then winced as his shoulder jerked with the motion. "Och, I would expect nothing less." He loosed a long, shuddering sigh. "I hate wolves, Rozi."

Rozlyn crossed back to where he sat upon the table. "I know." She clenched her teeth and fought back the instinctive urge to run her fingers through his dark-brown hair in a gesture of comfort, turning instead to rummage through her discarded herbs. "You should rest."

He slid gingerly off the table and limped toward the low divan that was tucked into the corner of the room, and her heart beat a little faster to hear the labored breaths that he drew with such obvious pain. "If you are going to make me sleep in the woods again, a bhrèagha, it will have to wait until tomorrow, because tonight I go no further than that couch."

"A bargain," she countered, and watched from beneath her lowered eyelids as he smiled at that, yet another echo of their past life together, despite the agony etched across his face as he eased himself down onto the cushions. "Drink the tea that I'm making you, and you may stay tonight on my couch. Otherwise, into the woods you go. I don't think you will be able to put up much of a fight."

He eyed the kettle warily. "What's in it? Hemlock?"

"That's for next time." The kettle whistled, and she

withdrew it from the hearth, pouring a steaming cup of boiling water over the little strainer containing a dozen sweet-smelling green leaves and crisp, dried red petals into the waiting ceramic brown mug. "This is poppy tea for the pain and to help you sleep."

"I don't want it."

"Then leave. Perhaps you'll catch consumption as well, and I shall at last be rid of you once and for all."

He scowled. "It makes my head feel"—he gestured with his left hand—"swirly." She stared at him, expressionless, and he sighed. "Give it here, then."

Rozlyn watched as he blew on the concoction, then drained the contents of the mug with several long swallows, and she focused very hard on not admiring the strong line of muscle in his throat as he leaned back his head to drink the last drops of the tea.

She refused to consider what that might mean, that something as simple as his throat, for the gods' sake, could do this to her—ignored the fact that she had sent Padraig away again two nights ago when he had come knocking, knowing that it would be impossible to feel his touch and not pretend it belonged to another.

She hated herself for it.

He flipped the empty mug over and waggled it, smiling faintly, even as his face remained that awful ashy-pale hue of death. "Satisfied?"

She did not deign to respond but walked away to the hearth and withdrew a book from the shelves nearby, sank down in her chair by the fire, and proceeded to ignore him.

It was for the best. For both their sakes.

It was a good while later, and she assumed that he had long since fallen asleep, exhausted from the strain of the last few days as much as from the poppy leaves, when he spoke across the darkened room.

"I have another story to tell you, Rozi." The words sounded thick with the effect of the drugs she had given him, and she turned to peer at him in the gloom from where she sat by the fire.

"You should be sleeping."

"Don't you want to hear my story? It's a very good one. I'm sure you'll like it."

"I think," Rozlyn said, "that it is well past the midnight hour, and that I am tired from tending to your wounds, so it is probably for the best if we both sit quietly for a while and rest."

Jamie was silent for a moment. "But I want to tell you my story."

Rozlyn sighed, then set aside her book. "Go on, then, but I won't promise to stay awake long enough to hear it."

"You will." Jamie inhaled, a sharp shudder of pain, then continued, his voice heavy from the potion flowing through his veins. "Once upon a time, there was a princess who never smiled."

It was like he had stabbed her, a sharp knife to the heart. "Go to hell, Jamie."

"Just listen." He closed his eyes, inhaling languorously as he tried to speak. "In her whole life, for years and years, no one had ever seen her smile. It was clear why she never did, this solemn-eyed girl, born motherless and cursed into a world filled with enemies. The denizens of her father's realm, peasants and nobles, servants and soldiers alike, all spoke of their princess only in hushed whispers, in furtive tones of fear and trembling, appalled at the terrible scourge that her birth had brought upon their realm—the Beast of Connacht.

"The king forced his people to pay the price, to suffer at the mercy of the terrible Beast's fangs and claws, to feed its insatiable hunger, while his daughter remained locked away and hidden from the world in her ivy-covered tower in the mountains. The inhabitants of the land wept and prayed for the day when the princess's hand would be given in marriage to a stalwart young lord who loved her, and the curse that had for so long ravaged their land would finally be lifted.

"Despite her curse"—Jamie's voice gentled to impossible depths—"the king cared for his daughter, even when it seemed like he hated her—this somber-souled girl with night-black hair and green-gray eyes the exact same hue as the gray-stone walls of her tower overgrown by the rich ivy leaves—and he wept to see her so solemn and so sad. He called upon all the jesters and clowns and musicians and actors of his realm to come to her tower, to tell her silly stories and sing silly songs, and they tumbled wildly and danced and made cheery faces at the grave-eyed princess, but she never once smiled."

"They weren't very funny," she whispered through stiff lips, and she heard him chuff once, a gentle, wheezing laugh.

"So on the morning of her sixteenth birthday, the king announced that he would only seek for his sad-eyed daughter a husband who could make her smile, who could make her happy, and in doing so, cleanse her of the magic that swirled in her veins. Young nobles came from far and wide, lords and marquises and earls and barons and thanes, carrying cakes and roses and star-studded necklaces to sweeten their words of courtship, but she never smiled at any of them.

She only stared back at them, straight-lipped and sad-eyed, until they grew frustrated or bored, these handsome young men, and one by one they stormed away, flinging on their ermine-lined cloaks and leaving her there in her cold gray tower. She would watch them go, serious-eyed and sad, always alone."

Rozlyn stood abruptly, furiously, overturning her chair with such force that it shattered on the floor beside her. "I see," she said, fingers flexing with a dangerous intent. "But then a handsome young man arrived—is that it?—and he was so different from the others, so very clever, and she fell desperately in love, and if she only had not been so stubborn, or so selfish as to not want to *die* at the hands of this oh-so-charming savior, then everyone would have lived happily ever after. Except her, of course, because she would have been dead, but that's hardly important." She could feel herself shaking, trembling with ten long years of pent-up anger and hurt. "Is that the moral of your story, Jamie?"

"No." His chest rose and fell, in tortured heaves, as he pushed himself up on his elbows. "One day, a man, the last remnant of the bloodline of the old gods, did arrive, and she did fall in love, but he ruined everything, a bhrèagha."

Rozlyn said nothing, her own breaths now coming hard and fast, each a painful blow to her already bruised heart. She would not forgive him. She would not, no matter what story he spun for her.

He was so good at that, she reminded herself, at spinning stories as a spider weaves its web. It was his best, his most powerful gambit on this black-and-white board of their never-ending game, and she would do well to remember it.

"He did come to deceive her," Jamie said, and she flinched at the admission. "He came to steal away her power, it's true, because he was so in love with the idea of claiming that magic of hers as his own, but he forgot his purpose, Rozi. His goal was simple—to win her affection, win her hand, and so win her power—but he found himself idling the time away, delaying the inevitable, inexplicably reluctant to make that fateful move." His fingers dug into the blanket shoved down around his waist. "He had not considered, you see, what would happen if he found something, someone, who was far more precious to him than the power he had craved for so long."

"You were going to *kill* me, Jamie."

"No, I swear—"

"Do not," she said, too low to be safe, "lie to me. I heard you that night, with my father."

"I never would have let you die. As soon as I had the ability to do so, I would have saved you." He swallowed. "I was going to explain everything to you as soon as I joined you upstairs, but you went ahead and burned the entire damn castle to the ground around me, Rozi."

More lies, all of it, an endless stream of deceptions. "I heard you tell my father that I would die, Jamie."

"What did you expect me to say to him? Did you think that I would admit that I was once a god, the last remaining member of the Tuatha Dé Danann, and that I had come to unleash the very magic that he longed to keep hidden away? That would have gone over well."

"Don't condescend to me, Jamie. I have every reason to doubt you. Everything that you have ever said to me has been a lie."

"Not everything."

"Don't. Don't you dare try and make light of this to me, to justify all the terrible things that you have done." Her fists clenched at her sides, because she had given him the key to all the hidden rooms of her secret self, those shadowy corners that she had never shown to anyone else, and he had betrayed her, betrayed her trust and conspired to condemn her to the fate he knew she most feared. She slashed her hand through the air, and the flames in the hearth leapt up in response to her rage. "You mocked me, laughed at me. You told him that you intended to strip my power from me that very night, and to hell with me. Quite literally, as I would have died when it was ripped from my soul."

Jamie shook his head in frustration. "I told him what he wanted to hear, Rozi. That was never my plan. I was going to tell you everything, then spirit you away in the night and take you north, as we had once discussed. Do you remember? I would have brought you to the last remaining druids in the realm so that they could help you control this power of yours, even as you have done."

"I don't believe you."

He sat up straighter, his face pale and drawn, the words stumbling out of him. "It's the truth, Rozi. You would have learned to control it, the Beast would have been gone, and then when you were ready, you could give to me this power without harm befalling you so that I could have released the ancient gods from where they sleep beneath the earth, and we would have been together at last." He looked at her pleadingly. "I loved you, a bhrèagha. I had a plan, the whole time. I would have saved you if you had only let me."

Rozlyn stood still, her hands clenched at her sides. "I saved myself, Jamie." She turned and stalked away from him toward the door, to the open sky that called to her just outside, filled with the clean scent of the rain-soaked midnight air and the soft sheen of moonlight and the utter lack of any painful swirl of emotions that the dark-eyed, ashen-faced man before her evoked. "And I did not need your love to do so."

She stormed away, her fingers flexing over and over again in a desperate attempt to keep the wildness of the Beast that was clawing just beneath the surface at bay, until she surrendered to its call, walking out into the cold night air, her wings exploding from beneath her shoulders as she soared away into the tear-sodden sky.

Chapter Seventeen

TÍR SOGHÁIN, ÉIRE, 1007

Jamie rolled away onto his stomach just as the dawn broke across the eastern horizon, yawning as he stretched. She watched him, the muscles in his back tensing, and clutched her pillow to her chest. "You should go."

He laughed into the soft downy mattress, then turned his head to grin at her. "Good morning to you too, a bhrèagha."

Rozlyn rolled her eyes. "Good morning." A brief pause. "But you should go."

He propped himself up on his elbow, reaching out to stroke the curve of her cheek, flushed and warm from a breathless night of being pressed to his chest. "I see the bloom of romance has already worn off for you. What a shame. You barely lasted two weeks before those stars I put in your eyes disappeared entirely."

She shoved his hand away playfully. "You have been lounging in here later and later each morning. Moira almost caught you yesterday, you lazy fool."

"But she didn't."

"But she could have." Rozlyn stroked her finger across the back of his hand. "She is accustomed to me waking early, and she always has my tea ready for me by the time I awaken."

Jamie grinned at her with all the cheekiness of a man well sated. "She has not thought to question why you have been so very exhausted each morning? Poor little princess, so deliciously sleep-deprived these days."

Rozlyn scoffed, then leaned forward to kiss him again, reveling in the rough graze of his scruff against the silken softness of her face. "You never fully shave this," she murmured. "But it never grows into a beard either. Why?"

"I hate the weight of a full beard," he whispered back, even as his lips became busy seeking something deeper, more urgent than the gentle kiss she had given him. "But I am hardly a boy. This seems like a good compromise."

"Such vanity," she said, and for a few gasping moments she indulged him, his hands sliding into her hair and along the curve of her spine, his fingers trailing down that sensitive path of her skin that he had learned so very fast and so very well. She caught herself right before she moaned at the feel of his nose nuzzling into her neck. "Now go," she ordered, pulling away from him to snuggle back down among her pillows. "Or my father will have you locked away in a marriage-bond before you have time to put your pants on."

"At least I'll be well prepared for my wedding night." Jamie rolled over and stood, reaching for his discarded clothes on the floor, and Rozlyn eyed him appreciatively. He grinned at her as he pulled his undershirt over his head, shaking his dark hair like a dog in the river. "You keep looking at me like that, a marriage-bond will be the least of your worries."

She almost smiled.

She watched him dress, combing his fingers through his mattress-tussled hair. It was so close, that unseen smile lingering on her lips, perpetually it seemed these days. Sometimes she ached with the need to let go, to allow herself to love him without dreading what it would mean for her and her magic, to simply let herself be carefree and happy, as she might have been in some other life. Her chest tightened at the thought—the idea of the life she could have had, born free of curses and stolen magic, a bright-eyed girl free to laugh with the dark-haired love of her life.

The word thudded in the bottom of Rozlyn's stomach, a dull weight of leaden fear.

Love. She did love him, so very much, and it would be her ruin, the loss of her magic, the only true beauty that she possessed.

He plopped back down on the side of the bed to pull on his boots. "Shall I see you at breakfast," he asked, unaware of the turmoil rolling through her chest, "or will you be lazing about in your boudoir for most of the day, pampered princess that you are?"

"I'll be down soon."

He glanced at her, his eyebrows raising at her terse tone, then leaned over to kiss her on her temple. "I was only joking. Get some rest, Rozi. You have certainly earned it." With a wink, he slipped out of her room, peering into the corridor to ensure that no one was watching.

The door snapped shut, and Rozlyn was alone.

Surely, surely, Rozlyn pleaded with herself as she rested her head against the wall behind her bed, he did not love her. He was too careless, too flippant to feel any such thing for her. Surely he did not, and yet—it had been months since the Beast had attacked, as though the pull of her magic was fading, as though the song inside her that called to the evil monsters of the realm was growing weak and thin.

Rozlyn told herself that this was a good thing, a blessing, that her father's people had been safe and unharmed these past few weeks, that perhaps the Beast had given up and skulked off to other far-off corners of the world to stalk other, less human prey, but she knew better. The Beast's absence terrified her because she knew what it meant.

It was growing weak, this beautiful magic of hers.

A viselike pain clenched around her heart, and she pressed her face into the pillow, drinking in the faint cedar scent where his head had rested. It would not be so bad, she told herself, her palms growing sweaty and hot, to be married to Jamie, to love him and be loved in return. She would sacrifice her magic, it was true—she had been told so little of the curse with which she had been born, but a marriage-bond would undoubtedly mean that she would lose that wondrous spark of beauty that shimmered at the tips of her fingers late at night as she brought life to the moonbeams dancing across her ceiling.

Her people would be safe, and she would have Jamie, and it did not matter—she threw the pillow on the ground with shaky hands—it did not matter that she would then be only a girl, powerless and weak—uncursed, but bereft of the one thing about her that was truly beautiful.

Rozlyn threw back the covers in a sudden, panicked moment and dressed herself with frantic fingers, anxious to be gone from the room, away from the mussed bedding and the flattened pillows and the sheets that smelled of salt and cedar and him.

She hurried down the stairs toward the kitchen,

focusing instead on the scent of fresh-baked soda bread and crisp-fried back bacon, when the murmur of voices inside stopped her just outside the door, listening to the whispered conversation between the two maids.

"Months," she heard Moira say, quivering with excitement. "Three months, and she has not changed, not transformed into that Beast."

"It's because of the man," Úna whispered back, raising her voice over the hiss of the griddle as she stirred the potatoes. "The one from the North."

"Och, most surely." Rozlyn remained frozen, her breath caught in her chest, as she heard the clatter of plates as Moira washed the morning dishes. "Every night for a fortnight he has been in her bed. She will marry him soon enough, and we will all be free of her terrors, you'll see."

Rozlyn heard Úna groan. "At last. I had long ago resigned myself that we were all to die one day at her infernal claws. A miracle, that's what it is, that any man could ever love that beastly girl."

"Especially one as handsome as he is," Moira said, and the two women laughed, and Rozlyn's limbs were unnaturally sluggish and heavy as she staggered away, her chest tight, her mind whirling.

That long-buried memory of her father's courtyard, blood-splattered and scarred with horrors, the echoing wails, the look of fear, of foreboding on her father's face as he saw her, crouched in her tattered and torn nightgown by the stairs—

Rozlyn placed one hand against the cold stone wall, her vision spinning, and an unfamiliar harsh sound echoed through the corridor, a strangled, choking sound, as though a fish were flopping about on the riverbank, gasping in pain, twitching in the death throes of drowning in the fresh air, and why, exactly, could she not breathe, force her lungs to inhale and exhale, as the blackness at the edges of her vision crept in—

She shoved away from the wall, reeling down the corridors, blindly seeking a port in this soul-rending storm.

She needed him.

She crashed into the great hall, her face death-white. "Jamie."

And then he was there, even as the murmurs of fear rose from the few servants who dared to enter her father's castle—of course they were afraid, because she was a Beast and could kill them all at any moment, what an unspeakable nightmare of a person she was, to be capable of such brutality against such a wealth of innocents—and then his strong arms were encircling her, cradling her, as he stared down at her face, frantic. "Rozi, what's wrong?"

In the back of her roaring mind, something screamed at her to get away from him, to push him aside and run as far she could from his dear presence, lest she burst into a monstrous cacophony of claws and wings and fangs and tear at his beloved face, but even as she moved to shove him aside, his arms tightened around her, and he dragged her out of the hall, away from the frightened eyes of the spectators lurking around them. "No, you don't," he said. "Stay with me, a bhrèagha. Breathe, my love. In and out, easy now."

Her lungs obeyed, as though the sound of his voice alone poured life into her with its low, steady tones, and she gasped, choking on her rising sobs.

"You have found out, then."

Startled, she glanced at him to find him watching her with an uncharacteristic gravity etched on his face.

"You knew."

"Of course, I did." She made a small keening sound, burying her face in her hands. He pulled her closer, his fingers caressing her in soothing strokes against the small of her back. "We all did, but your father forbade anyone to tell you the truth, and I, for once, agreed with him. Why cause you such grief to know what terrible manifestation your magic took when it thundered beyond your control inside you?"

"I would have done something," she managed to gasp through her sobs. "Something, anything, I would have—"

His arms tightened. "I do not like to imagine what you would have done, which is exactly why I did not tell you." He pressed a kiss to the top of her head. "It was not your fault, Rozi, so why should you bear that burden of pain?"

"Jamie," she choked as the tears streamed down her cheeks, the rainstorm of heartbreak she had kept locked away inside for so many years. "What have I done—vicious, unspeakable things, a Beast, a monster, a *murderer*—"

His hands cupped her face as his fingers stroked at the damp tendrils of hair come loose from her braid. "No," he whispered. "You are a beauty, every part of you, all the way down to those secret corners of your soul, the likes of which this world will never again see." His grip tightened. "It's how I see you."

Rozlyn's breath shuddered out, and she pressed her face into his chest.

"Rozi," he said. "You know what we must do."

She closed her eyes, steeling herself for what she knew his next words must be.

"We must be married, Rozi."

Match in three moves.

Rozlyn remembered it, that triumphant boast under

the stars, now riddled with the tentative notes of a whispered warning, and she swallowed around the sudden lump in her throat. She stepped away from him, staring at the ground, her hands trembling, the heaviness in her chest unbearably painful. "If I do this, if I marry you, then I will sacrifice my power, my magic." She stumbled slightly over the word. "And that's my queen, Jamie." She shook her head, dazed. "I mean—"

"I know what you mean." She knew he was watching her, the air tense between them. "And yes, you would. But it is to protect the king, to save your people. A necessary move, a justified trade."

"But it is all that I have ever had."

His arms slipped around her again, pulling her close, and she clung to the cedar scent of his skin, her nose buried in the warm skin of his neck. "You have me now," he whispered, his breath fluttering against the curve of her ear, and she shivered at the thrill that raced down her spine even now at the warmth of his touch. "Isn't that enough?"

Rozlyn squeezed tighter, fighting against the rising lump in her throat. "Yes," she lied through the screams of protest that echoed inside her skull.

His hands slid up and down her back, across her shoulders, as he continued to murmur in her ear. "You can protect all these helpless souls, Rozi. The Beast inside you will disappear, will be gone from this land, once that magic inside you is destroyed. You will be the savior of your people."

A savior. A protector, as she had never before been allowed to be.

She swallowed. "I don't believe that I can save someone from a tragedy that I myself caused."

His hands continued to stroke her back, and she won-dered, so impossibly tired, if perhaps she should just concede, simply give up and allow herself to be soothed into acquiescence, if only for a reprieve from having to scratch and claw and fight for even the smallest taste of freedom.

"Perhaps," he said, and she blinked for a moment, unsure if she had spoken that weariness aloud, but then he continued. "But I believe that you owe it to them to try."

A moment of silence passed between them, and the foundations of her world shifted and cracked underneath her as she sighed, then nodded once.

Jamie's arms tightened again, and she could all but feel the relief coursing through him. "Good girl," he whispered. "Trust me, only for a little while longer, and then all will be well."

Rozlyn held on to that thread of trust as they stood before her father, hand in hand, as he wept with joy and kissed her cheek with more genuine affection than she had received from him since she had been a child, and no beastly entity yet lurked underneath her skin. She clung to it as the people gathered beneath her terrace screaming with joy and celebration as her father's voice boomed out across them, announcing the marriage that would take place in three days' time. She clutched at it as she saw the eyes of her maid and the soldiers and the servants who skipped through her fa-ther's hall were, for once, bright and unburdened with fear. She hugged it to her chest as she stood before the mirror on the eve of her wedding to the man she loved—because she did love him, this steady, smiling-eyed man—adorned in that hateful bridal gown, studying for the last time the girl she once was, wondering about the woman she soon would be.

She held on to it most desperately as she stood before

him in the bright light of the morning sun, half-blinded by tears she refused to shed, as she stumbled through her vows, her vision swimming as he held her hands in his own, unwavering and calm as he promised her a lifetime of protection and fidelity and love.

She braced herself to feel it happening, the sundering of her magic, as Jamie's vows faded away and her father tightened the embroidered strip of linen around their joined hands, binding them forever with his invocation of the long-lost gods, but the moment passed, and she remained unaffected by the bond set in place by the ancient ritual. She was still blinking in surprise even as Jamie pulled her close and kissed her under the warmth of the morning sun as a thunderous roar arose around them from the throng watching with bated breath, for now the curse had been broken, and they would live, free from fear at last.

Rozlyn trembled in Jamie's arms, because it was still there, that thrum of power deep within her; it lived on inside her, the Beast lurking in the shadows, waiting to strike.

Jamie took her by the hand and led her back into her father's home for the hours-long banquet that had been prepared, and as they entered the banquet room and the room shook with the thunder of a hundred voices roaring with approval, she wondered when it would happen, if it would hurt when it was ripped away from her soul, this secret song that she alone could sing, calling out to the birds of the air and the shadows of the sky. It was strange, so strange that the two could live together in such harmony, this ugly Beast and the beauty that was her magic, the horror and the light, side by side within her soul, for so many years.

They would die together soon enough, she thought even

as Jamie pulled out her chair at the head of her father's table, smiling at her with such honest affection as her father's subjects cheered and drank and laughed and toasted her, their fear already forgotten.

The wedding feast was like ash in her mouth, tasteless and bland, as she waited for the banquet to subside. The dancing and the toasts and the roar of the songs passed by in a blur of sound and hazy colors, a loud, garish dream of carousing and indecipherable roaring, and only the solid warmth of Jamie's hand clasped in hers convinced her that it was real.

As the moon rose high in the sky, he bent over and kissed her cheek, and she closed her eyes, savoring the reassuring caress of his lips on her skin, an unspoken affirmation of his love. He pulled back, ever unruffled and calm, and that dizziness that threatened to consume her steadied for a moment, a near-capsized ship set upright and unscathed on the storm-tossed waves.

"Go on up," he said, and her heart swelled with love, that he could so easily read her and see it, that desperate, clawing desire to be alone, to be silent for a little while and let the panic surging within her subside. "I'll join you in a little while." She nodded, unable to speak through the tears gathering in the back of her throat.

She lay in her bed for a long, long time as she continued to wait, tracing a forlorn farewell to the shadows of the moonlight on her ceiling, conjuring incandescent shapes and stories of horses and hares and dragonflies dancing on the glass surface of the astral water, until unable to bear it any longer, she shoved away from her pillows and ripped off that vile red-and-gold gown, throwing it in a sad heap on the floor, the gorgeous gold tiara with its beautiful, delicate rose falling next to it with a soulless clatter. Pulling on a soft gray gown and fur-lined cloak, she snuck down the stairwell to the terrace below, telling herself she only needed some air, the cool wind of the night sky on her cheeks, and all her anxieties and misgivings and fears would fade away.

She crept out into the darkness of the terrace, watching the people file out of her father's mead hall, dizzy with drink and with joy as they stumbled their way home. It eased the ache in her heart to see them, carefree and lighthearted, free of fear because of her, and she started to turn away and go back to her room to wait for her new husband to come to her when she froze, hearing the faint hum of voices beneath her, from the balcony that stretched out from her father's room below.

Rozlyn crept closer, her cloak pulled tight across her shoulders and hair. She could see them, where they stood on the balcony below, those two familiar forms, one broad-shouldered and bearded, and the other lean and tall and endearingly languid, with his hands thrust in his pockets and his dark head tipped, scanning the star-studded sky. It was such a familiar gesture, so fundamentally Jamie in nature that, safely alone and unseen here in the darkness, she smiled as a surge of love scrubbed at that lingering stain of doubt, and she slid against the wall, eager to hear that well-loved voice that could so effortlessly soothe her fears.

"You are sure?" She heard her father ask. "That it will become yours?"

Rozlyn saw Jamie shrug his shoulders, the movement faint in the darkness of the torchless balcony. "We shall soon find out."

Her father was silent for a moment. "I would have thought the sundering would have happened at the moment of the vows, when the marriage-bond first fell into place between you."

"Don't be a fool," Jamie scoffed, and Rozlyn jolted a little to hear him address her father, the great king of Connacht, with such contempt. "The ceremony is merely that—a symbol, an empty sign, an excuse to dance and make merry. The *real* marriage comes later—truly I am sorry to discuss the awkwardness of this next part with you—when two become one, a vow of words made flesh."

A tense pause. "I don't—"

"I must bed your daughter before she truly becomes my wife, Ailain. Surely you understand the nature of a marriage-bond—there is paper and ink and empty words, and then there is something far more ancient and real, and which I should attend to sooner rather than later, if you would excuse me. She is no doubt anxiously awaiting me in her chambers, and it's rude, you know, to keep any lady waiting, but especially one of your daughter's rather terrifying caliber."

Rozlyn's heart shuddered to a stop.

He was smirking with such arrogance, such smugness, and the dull ache in her heart grew hot and wild, the sadness churning in her gut boiled to a fever pitch as the flames of white-hot, humiliated rage began to build into an inferno of fury inside her.

He had lied to her.

"I have done all that your king has asked of me," she heard her father hiss at Jamie, who continued to lean against the wall with such contempt, such indolence, as though he had never cared at all, as though all his jokes and his stories, all the bargains between them and the bed, all the games they had played together had been just that to him—a well-plotted,

strategic game of rooks and knights and queens, of adjournments and advantages and adjustments, and now he had her
king cornered and pinned.

Match in three moves, a bhrèagha.

"Over fifteen years ago," she heard her father hiss
through the roaring in her ears, "when he sent his envoys,
I have kept my vow, and she has been safe and unharmed.
My people have called for her death for years, even as they
have died in droves, all because of *her*, but I have resisted
for your sake and your king's, so that she would be waiting
here, yours for the taking."

"Don't sound so sanctimonious, Ailain. You were well
compensated for that with gold and lands beyond which you
ever might have possessed otherwise."

"This cannot fail," Ailain said urgently, not with concern for his daughter, she realized as fire began to scream
within her, but with the desire to see her gone, as dead as
they had always wished her to be, these people who had
birthed her and feared her and hated her for the beauty
in her blood with which she had been born, and Rozlyn
shook with a terrible, unnamed emotion. "I will grieve for
my daughter. I have grieved for her, ever since that damned
witch laid this curse upon her, and it comforts me to know
that she has had some small glimpse of happiness with you
before she must join her mother in the realm of Magh Meall.
But"—his voice became strident and tense—"I will not see it
be all for naught. You must truly love her. You must, or we
are all doomed to fail."

Jamie shrugged again, and Rozlyn's heart shattered, a
jagged, ugly fracture filled with splinters and glass shards,
because it was so careless, so callous, that dismissive gesture from this man she had loved. "In truth," he said,

"it matters little. The prophecy states that I must love her magic in order to possess it, and make no mistake, Ailain, I surely do." He drew in a satisfied breath. "I have waited so long, so patiently for the chance to command it as my own."

Ailain seized his sleeve as he turned away. "We had an agreement," he said. "You will possess her magic—there is no avoiding that aspect of this miserable curse—but you will take your magic, this dowry I give you in exchange for my daughter's life, and you will go back from whence you came."

Jamie brushed off his hand and turned to stroll away. "As you wish."

Ailain called out to him before he disappeared into the door beneath, and Rozlyn braced herself against the tidal waves of rage that were rushing through her, even as her fingers crackled and sparked with that primal power flowing within her veins. "You truly were never afraid of her?" her father asked, and it was his curiosity that broke her, that severed that last remaining thread of love between them, this confirmation that he had always feared her far more than he had loved her. "Knowing the Beast that resides within her, that explodes from her so furiously, without warning?"

Rozlyn could no longer see Jamie, but she could hear him: a scornful dismissal, drifting backward to the king. "I have feared many things in my life," she heard him say, even as the haze of her revulsion blurred her vision as she stared out into the vastness of the night sky. "But a pretty little girl of one-and-twenty is not one of them, Ailain."

She heard her father give a huff of surprised laughter and watched as he braced his elbows against the balustrade and rested his head in his hands, weariness written across the lines of his posture. Even as she acknowledged it, the raging inferno within her reached a crescendo of flames, and she turned, eyes blazing and fingers sparking, and strode back through the castle, trailing her fingertips against the finely woven cloths of the tapestries that lined the walls, leaving behind her a churning trail of hot orange sparks rising in their wake. She glided into her father's throne room, tendrils of smoke and fire swirling around her hands, even as the air about her smoldered.

They had lied to her, betrayed her—these two men whom she had loved, and the nursemaids and the servants, who fed her sweet treats and told her stories and plaited her hair, and the soldiers who had prowled her halls with their hands on their hearts, swearing to protect her—they had all soothed her and sang to her and smiled at her, knowing all the while that they were enticing her to her doom, coaxing her to cause her own ruination for their own ends.

Let them all burn as she had been burning inside all these years, consumed by that loneliness she had endured all her life.

They believed that she was a Beast before, but now she would show them what power a true monster could wield.

Becoming a Beast had always been her endgame after all, it seemed.

She raised her arms in the center of the great hall and, even as her head screamed with a strange new agony, crimson flames leapt from the torches that lined the cedarwood walls and bounded into the palms of her hands, dogs writhing with delight at the long-awaited return of their beloved mistress. She flicked her fingers toward the timbers of wood beams crisscrossing the ceiling. The flames raced outward, leaping from her side to crawl across the floors, devouring the long wooden tables and benches that lined the room. With a final, vengeful flutter of her fingers, she pointed her hand at the towering throne, looming above the rest on its wooden dais, its oaken surface polished and gleaming in the growing firelight surrounding it. Her flames writhed around it, and she could hear it now—the secret language of the power that had slept latent for so long within her, and even as the idea flickered through her, she watched as the flames twisted around themselves, becoming lupine in shape, and they grew fangs of fire as they snarled. They flung themselves on her father's throne, ripping and tearing into the solid wood, and it crumpled into ruin around them as they gorged themselves on the cinders and ash of his throne, the heart of his pride and his home.

The fire-wolves raised their heads and watched her, hackles raised and fangs bared, and a savage thrill roared to life within her, that this was the shape that her magic had taken, the form of the creature he most feared, and she pointed toward the door, a wordless command. They bounded away, and she savored it for a moment, the smell of the smoke and the roar of the fire and the idea that they would be the last thing that he ever saw before her creations closed his hateful blue eyes forever.

Flames of orange and red and gold unfurled around her in a triumphant crescendo of song, and Rozlyn's lips parted in a snarl of a smile. He thought that he had won this game of theirs, with his pinnings and his bindings of her all-powerful queen, this power in her veins, but he had misjudged her, as everyone had always done, and now she would burn the board before he ever would have the chance to make his final move.

Match in three moves, indeed.

Rozlyn turned and walked down the length of the great hall, her face an unmoving mask of fury as she heard screams erupt from all corners of the castle, the flames screeching in delight as they consumed the bones of the building. She did not hesitate as she strode out into the night, her head splintering with the pain of her newfound powers. Down the steps of her father's castle she glided, her vision blurred, not with tears, but with the sharp pain of her vengeance, away into the woods that waited for her patiently in the shadows of the night, and she did not look back as the building crumbled behind her, its stones crashing to the earth with a final thunderous boom.

Match.

CHAPTER EIGHTEEN

Rozlyn soared through the night sky on a crosswind breeze, her black-feathered wings shuddering as they cleaved through the air with smooth strokes.

He was a *liar*, had always been a liar, from the very beginning.

Her jaws parted, jowls lifting in a snarl, but even as her claws curved over the great bearlike paws of her feet, she remembered the fear she had felt, the panic when he had stumbled forward in the mud, stained with blood and nearly robbed of life. She could almost see him there before her, so pale and pallid and pained, his arm sagging uselessly where the monster's fangs had savaged him.

Something thick and cold thudded in the pit of her stomach as she remembered in the dim recesses of her memory—*it was almost my fate once*—the raw, quiet honesty in his voice as he whispered of battlefield horrors and his greatest fears. She could see him there too, leaning on the balustrade against the fading darkness of the twilight sky, as he told her tales and brought her books and shared his smiles with her sadness and, day after day, made her feel so much less alone in her narrow world of ivy and stone and shadows.

She snarled again, the rage inside her seeking a far darker and more deadly target.

He must have been so afraid, alone in the woods, those merciless teeth tearing at him as he stared into the face of his worst nightmare come to life.

Another memory flickered through her, of him lying on the couch in her solar, reaching out a shaking hand toward her, his eyes clouded with so many hurts, right before she snarled at him again, just like the Beast that she was, that she had always been.

He had loved her. He had, she knew that now, at least a little bit, even in the midst of his plots and his schemes and the arranging of his pieces in this game they had always played together, and oh, gods, he was the only one who ever had loved her in her whole life, even when she was so fundamentally unlovable—a Beast, a monstrous Beast, for gods' sakes, who could blame them for fearing her, hating her—and then something inside her twisted until it snapped, like a cracked tree branch laden with too much ice, its broken ends jagged with razor-pointed shards.

She swerved and fixed her gaze on the fast-approaching mountain ridges of Mhám Toirc.

She landed with a crash on the boulder-strewn side of the mountain, searching the gloom for this monster, this creature that had savaged the man she had once loved so very much.

It had tried to take her knight, and for that, it would forfeit its king.

Rozlyn threw back her head and roared, the trees shuddering in their roots in response to her challenge, and whatever dark beings of the night prowled among the roots and rocks of the craggy mountain went silent in fear of a creature far more terrible than any other monster that roamed these woods.

She roared again, an insistent challenging, and from faraway, a long, unearthly howl answered. She stalked toward the sound, claws protracted and fangs gleaming, her wings crashing through the brush with no care to be stealthy as she hunted her prey.

She could smell it on the air, that foul odor of its wrongness as it plunged through the forest, seeking her as intently as she sought it, and her snout wrinkled in revulsion even as it howled again, closer this time. She braced her muscles, crouching close to the ground, shuffling her hind legs as she prepared to lunge.

Rozlyn focused on the underbrush ahead of her, and she could hear its loping strides as it sped toward her, the air growing heavy with the unbearable stench of decay that wafted from its poisonous jaws, and a third howl reverberated through the air as it burst through the trees, galloping straight for her.

She saw the powerful stride of its lean legs, the sheer strength of the musculature hiding beneath its dark green pelt, the drip of the poison from its putrid fangs, and that wild rush of rage burned anew within her, imagining him pinned underneath it, fighting for his life in the face of certain death.

Rozlyn leapt.

They crashed together with a tree-shattering force in midair, snapping and snarling, and its teeth grazed against the thick fur of her pelt, its claws scratching at her face. She snapped her own razor-sharp fangs in return, snagging the thick fur of its throat in her teeth as she ripped at its jugular. The cú-sídhe yelped as her fangs sliced through the soft meat of its windpipe; then it wheeled away, choking and gagging as it whined.

Rozlyn lunged again, a relentless force of unnatural swiftness and brutality, her wings propelling her toward the wolf in an explosion of speed, and she pounced on his broad back, digging into his ribs with her claws as deep as they would go. The wolf screamed, snapping at her as it twisted his head desperately, trying to free itself from her merciless grip, but even as she drove her claws further into its contorted body, her great feathered wings scissored forward, the gleaming talons at the tip of each wing glinting ominously as she slashed at its snout and soulless eyes.

A violent spray of black blood, reeking with the unbearable stench of corruption, exploded from its left eye as her talon drove deep into the center of its bottomless pupil. The wolf gagged, its legs crumpling underneath it as it collapsed on the ground. Rozlyn sank her claws further into its bloody ribs and withdrew her talons from its face as she tucked them behind her, settling herself more firmly atop the cú-sídhe, preparing herself for the final, fatal blow. Her jaws parted, gagging on the overpowering stench of putridity that poured from its wounds, as the wolf growled underneath her, twitching helplessly. With the swiftness of an adder, she struck, her fangs sinking into its exposed throat as it lay pinioned in the dirt. She ripped once, twice, with her powerful teeth, the fangs that had once torn apart so many innocent lives, and oceans of thick black gore poured from the gaping wound in its craw.

A guttural rattling sound echoed in its throat, and then its black eyes slowly dimmed, the unnatural light fading from their depths.

Rozlyn slowly retracted her claws and slunk away from the reeking, black-bloodied corpse of the green-pelted monster and prowled about it, her nose twitching in protest at the foulness of the odor that saturated the air. All around her, the trees and rocks and bushes seemed to loose a collective sigh as she stalked in circles around her kill, the muscles jumping and bunching beneath her glossy blue-black fur, and suddenly, she roared again, a bellow of triumphant defiance, a reverberating challenge to any who might still dare to test the might of the Beast of Connacht.

Utter silence prevailed, and the shapeless shadows that had clustered unseen around them during the battle retreated into the depths of the forest out of which they had slunk to acknowledge the new-crowned monarch of monsters.

Rozlyn stood alone, her eyes glowing with supernatural green fire, the undisputed queen of the beasts, and she roared once more, a final warning to all who lingered in the shadows of her vale, then threw herself into the sky with an exultant flap of her black-feathered wings.

CHAPTER NINETEEN

The small castle before her was in ruins, its silver-blue stones crumbling and half-hidden under the soft green moss and looping vines meandering their way over the rotting wood beams that once supported its weight. It was haunting and beautiful and heartbreaking, the sad remnants of some long-lost king's might and power, reduced to a crumbling heap of foggy rocks and decomposing wood.

It was perfect, an apt metaphor for what she had become.

Rozlyn wrapped her arms around her torso and trudged forward, her eyes burning with exhaustion, soaked to the bone with mud and rain. She had lost track of the days since she had left her father's hall in flames behind her, the ash and embers floating through the trees to kiss her skin in a silent farewell as she had fled through the woods toward the valley that lay just beyond the distant mountain ridge.

She had been too afraid to sleep, terrified that the Beast prowling within her on its padded black paws would come roaring to life as soon as she drifted off, shrieking with hunger as it took to the skies to hunt. She shivered at the thought, stumbling over the wet hem of her gown, her fur-lined cloak heavy with rain on her shoulders, and she knew that she would have to sleep soon, that the pull of exhaustion tugging at the back of her skull would overwhelm her soon.

And she would be a monster again.

Rozlyn let out a little cry and sank to her knees in the middle of the ruined, once-great hall, burying her face in her trembling hands. Her stomach rumbled, and her sob became a bitter laugh. The red berries and dandelions and tender green leaves from hawthorn trees that she had devoured as she foraged in the forest had barely kept the sharp pangs of starvation at bay, but soon enough, she would sleep, and when she awoke, no doubt her belly would be full from unremembered, unnatural feasting.

She risked it for a moment, closing her eyes as her breaths grew hoarse and ragged, listening to the rain drumming against the ground around her, its cold drops sliding down her face and mingling with the warmth of her tears.

She could hear the distant roar of the river, its banks swollen with rain, churning with whitewater rapids, crashing against the unmovable boulders buried in its depths. It would be a fitting way to go, pulled under the dark waves of the angry water, smashed against the unforgiving stones—the blood-price paid for so many lives she could not remember taking. At least she could take no more after her own was lost.

The idea had hardly finished echoing in her mind when she heard shuffling behind her, and she whirled around on her knees, heart thrumming, because he had found her, he had come to claim her power, here in this rain-swept wilderness, and leave her lying lifeless in the dark as he strode away, careless and cruel in his triumph.

She didn't mind dying, but she very much minded letting him win this new deadly game she had started with fire and smoke and bloodthirsty fury.

The blurry figure at the other end of the ruined hall sharpened and came into focus, and she almost gasped in relief at the sight of the slight, white-haired woman who studied her in silence, head cocked to the side. "Who are you?"

The woman drifted closer, her silver brows arching in something like amusement. "I might ask the same of you, child." She paused, and Rozlyn realized suddenly how suspicious she must look—bedraggled and covered in mud, dressed in fine linen and a regal fur cloak. She stood, staggering a little as she steadied herself on her weary feet.

"I'm Moira," she lied, the memory of her pale-eyed maid flashing before her. "I live in a nearby village and simply got lost in the rain." She raised her chin defiantly and stared down at the older woman. "I am sure that my brothers will be along soon to find me and take me home."

The woman merely shook her head. "And do your brothers keep you starved to nothing but skin and bones as well, child? Come now, you'll have to do better than that if you want to fool a wise old woman." She winked, and Rozlyn's heart lurched painfully at the easy friendliness of the gesture. "Whatever lies you tell, I no doubt told the same ones myself once as a young girl, and whatever mischief you have made, I can promise you that I made the very same myself many years ago."

The hazy memory of her father's bloodied courtyard, the black smoke rising from his battlements, flickered through her. "Somehow I doubt that."

"Perhaps not," she said. "Sure it is that I'm no princess, a rebellious girl who set fire to her father's castle and fled into the night."

Rozlyn staggered backward, panic surging anew. "I don't know what you mean."

"The rumors have already spread far and wide, child." The old woman shifted the weight of her basket to her other arm. "All of Éire has long known the legend of the beautiful princess who transforms into a Beast at night, but that same princess thumbing her nose at her father and new husband and disappearing into thin air? That's the far more interesting tale, don't you know."

She should run, Rozlyn thought wildly. Run before she was caught, dragged back in chains to that ruined mead hall, the horror of the realm.

How he would laugh at her, laugh with his beautiful blue eyes.

She took another step backward, preparing to flee, when the woman held up a hand. "Easy, child," she said, and it was like a balm soothing those new-bruised parts of her heart, the gentle warmth of her voice. "I've no griefs with you." Her eyebrows lifted slightly. "Your father, on the other hand—well, that's another matter."

Rozlyn hesitated. "What do you mean?"

The woman laughed, then turned away, tugging her cloak closer around her. "Come along, child. There's a bit of roof still intact in the far corner. Come, sit and dry yourself, and let Galena tell you her secrets, and then perhaps you can tell me some of yours."

Maybe she was a witch, Rozlyn wondered fuzzily to herself as she followed the older woman's shuffling steps without question. As soon as they settled in under the sagging canopy of decomposing wood beams and waterlogged straw—Galena dug into her basket for a loaf of brown soda bread and a bit of dried lamb, handing both to Rozlyn without a word— Rozlyn found the tale spilling out of her, her whole history, a waterfall of words oozing of betrayal and anger and guilt, thundering their way through the soft silence of the tumbledown hall.

Galena sat quietly as Rozlyn stumbled her way through her story, shaking with shame and hurt, the food lying forgotten on her lap. "I don't know what to do," she concluded, and her voice crumbled as she dropped her head into her hands. "I can't control it. I don't know how, and I will hurt so many more people, ruin so many more lives if I can't master it." The sobs built up in her chest with a viselike grip, threatening to choke the air from her lungs. "I don't know what to do. I think it would be better if I . . ." She trailed away, leaving the air heavy with the unspoken conclusion hanging between them.

There was a long silence as the rain continued to fall in soothing, rhythmic waves on the unsteady roof above them, and then Galena cleared her throat and leaned forward slightly, her hands clasped over her knees. "Child," she said, and Rozlyn raised her head at the iron threading its way through the simple word. "I do not believe that you have come this far only to fall so low."

Rozlyn stared at her, and Galena reached out and laid her blue-veined hand over the top of the princess's clammy one. "Listen to me. The gods may be long gone from our world, but there is still an ordering to it, a symmetry to the seemingly arbitrary wreckage of life. How else could it be that you have stumbled your way here, child, to the vale of Inagh, to this ruined heap of stones and wood, the sole spot in all the valley where the meadowsweet herbs grow, the very ones I need to ease the aches and pains of my old bones?"

"But—"

"You found your way here," Galena repeated, ignoring Rozlyn's weak protest. "It is no coincidence, child, that you have come to this place, to me, perhaps the last remaining descendant of the druids of the western realm."

Rozlyn leapt up, her heart pounding. "A druid. You're a druid."

"No." Galena rose as well, her hand braced against the small of her back. "The druids have long since vanished from the land, soon after the gods themselves, and so much of the world's magic with them. My ancestor was Cathbad, who long ago served the high king of Ulaid in the North, before he was forced to flee here after his ill-fated prophecy of Deirdre of the Sorrows provoked the king's wrath."

The name was vaguely familiar to Rozlyn. "I have heard her story," she said slowly. "Before she was born, it was foretold that she would be the most beautiful woman of Éire, that her beauty would bring suffering and strife to her people." Rozlyn frowned, remembering. "They went to war over her, the high kings of the realm, and she died, throwing herself from a chariot to die upon the rocks rather than be handed over as a prize to the man who had killed her lover." Rozlyn stepped back sharply at Galena's nod. "I thought that was only a story, a legend."

"No, child," Galena said, settling down on her knees on the ground and rummaging through her basket of herbs. "Poor Deirdre and her lovely face were all too real, as were the greed and the lust of the men who brought about her undoing. There are far too many similarities between the beautiful Deirdre and yourself, child." Rozlyn tensed, but

Galena continued her perusal of her basket, unconcerned. "But do you know what the greatest difference is?" Rozlyn shook her head, and Galena's lips curved into a smile as she lifted a few slender rods of deep-brown branches. "You can, with a little learning, at least fight back."

Rozlyn stared at the slim twigs that Galena held out to her. "What is that?"

"Slips of the rowan tree." Rozlyn ran the tip of her finger down the smooth bark of the branch and shivered a little at the touch. "We healers simply call it witchwood." Rozlyn's fingers closed around the branch and she held it up in the dim light, scrutinizing it, as Galena continued. "In the lore passed down to me from my mother and her mother before her, all the way from Cathbad himself, it is said that the gods first formed the human woman from the bark of its tree, and in its juices lie the untapped power of the first goddess of creation. There is no greater protection, no more potent guardian against evil than in the sap that flows beneath its bark. Its juices will grant you clarity, consciousness, if you will, whenever the magic within you threatens to take hold." Galena shrugged. "In time, you might find it will do more—expand on your other powers, help you to wield the elements more efficiently—although you seem to have burnt your father's castle easily enough." She hesitated for a moment. "It is possible that one day you could even be able to summon this Beast of yours at will, to take its shape as you please, for whatsoever purpose you require."

Rozlyn's knees grew weak, and she sank down onto the ground next to Galena, her fingers trembling as she stroked the slender branches. "Can it be so simple?" she whispered, as her throat burned with a wild, fierce hope. "All this time, all this pain, and this little thing is the answer?"

Galena held up a finger. "No, child, of course not." She wrapped her fingers around Rozlyn's wrist. "You will have to work hard, toil through lonely days and dark, terror-filled nights, pour your sweat and blood and tears out on the earth as you wrestle with the magic inside you, to learn to wield it as part of your own self—and not allow it to overwhelm you, to again become a feral monster seeking to ravage and destroy." Rozlyn shuddered, and Galena's fingers tightened around her wrist, squeezing in a wordless reassurance. "You are the answer, child, your determination and your will. This"—her fingers gently unlatched from Rozlyn's wrist to stroke the branches clutched in her fist—"this will just make it a little easier to arrive at."

Rozlyn swallowed, sweat beading on her forehead. "Should I eat it now?"

"I would not recommend it." Galena winced as she stood, beckoning for Rozlyn to follow. "It's horribly bitter when raw. Best to sweeten it with honey, perhaps some lavender to help calm your nerves." She gathered her basket and straightened, smiling down where Rozlyn still crouched in the dirt, grasping at the slender branches, her face stained with tears and rain. "How would you like a hot cup of tea, child?"

"Dear gods," Galena said as Rozlyn collapsed against the trunk of the smooth birch tree, panting with exertion and clutching at her sides. "What a monster you are."

Rozlyn could barely hear her over the ringing in her ears. "I did it," she panted. "I did it."

Her knees shook and her back was soaked with perspiration, her head throbbing from the overwhelming force of her shifting, but Rozlyn wanted to scream with exhilaration, with triumph.

After months of long days and endless nights, scratching and clawing in the dirt as she wrestled with the magic inside her, the Beast had at long last answered her call.

She sank to the ground, her back sliding against the smooth trunk of the tree, her legs sprawled out in the dirt in front of her as she gasped.

Galena rested her hand lightly on the top of Rozlyn's sweat-soaked head, tucking a damp curl behind her ear gently. "Well done, child," she whispered. "You have been far braver than you will ever know."

"Not alone." Rozlyn's eyes remained closed as she spoke, her fingers curled in the damp black dirt next to her. "Without you, I would have been lost." She opened her eyes and looked up at Galena. "I owe you a debt I can never repay."

"Nonsense," said Galena briskly. "There is no debt between us." She tilted her head, considering. "Although it is a pity that you are not on better terms with your father. We need an advocate who will speak to him for us, as we are all but forgotten here in the valley, neglected and unprotected. We do not have the wealth or the provisions of those living under the banner of the king, but he does not regard our cries for help."

Rozlyn's chest twisted painfully. She could almost see them hovering before her, the faces of her newfound friends—boisterous Teagan, with her love of raunchy jokes; and the wood-carvers, Aidan and Ruari, and their sweet-scented hut filled with cedar shavings and fresh-baked potato cake; and golden-haired Fiadh with her five children—all the gentle, unassuming souls who had welcomed her into their homes, who had shared their bread and their meat without a hint of revulsion or fear. They had embraced her as one of their own, the dread Beast of Connacht, and she would repay them thousandfold.

This magic of hers would no longer be a scourge in this world, a blight upon her people, but a weapon to be wielded, by her, in defense of those she loved, and woe to the fool who crossed her.

The words burst from her, fierce and full of savage devotion. "I can protect you now, Galena. All of you."

The older woman stroked Rozlyn's raven-black hair with a gentle hand. "I know, child." Her eyes filled briefly with shadows. "I hope that now you shall at last find some peace, little rosebud."

Rozlyn reached up and squeezed the older woman's hand. "I do not suppose," she said quietly, "that I will ever truly know peace, not after what I have done." Galena made a wordless noise of protest, but Rozlyn shook her head, her lips pressed together, and she fell silent, waiting. "I can win for you—for all of you, I suspect—independence from my father and give you the security that you need, but first . . ." She tilted her head back and stared up at the dark clouds rolling toward them from the east, a gathering storm, as Galena's hand continued to caress the thick strands of her hair in gentle, soothing strokes. "But first there is something that I do want, that I have wanted for a long time, and I think that gaining that will be the key to securing your freedom, your safety."

Galena's hand stilled on the top of Rozlyn's head. "What's that?"

Her teeth flashed in the late afternoon gloom as she snarled. "Revenge."

There was no moon on the night that Rozlyn returned to the charred remnants of her childhood home to see her father, almost a year to the day after she had left it billowing with smoke and engulfed in flames.

She flew through the pitch-black sky, the darkness unending, as though the stars themselves sensed the all-consuming blackness of her rage and hid themselves away behind the clouds that drifted across the firmament. Her wings beat in a rhythmic motion, steady and sure, as she arrowed her way past the familiar lakes and cliffs of Connacht and landed at the edge of the loch that bordered the remains of her father's castle.

She studied it for a long moment, the half-built walls barely visible in the blackness of the night, the smooth timbers leaning against the fresh-cut beams of oak that lined the charcoal-smeared stone walls of her tower, ready to be restored to their former pride, as though nothing had happened, as though she had not been lied to and deceived for so many years.

Her tail snapped in renewed anger, and she prowled about to face the dark waters of the loch and the monster that she knew lurked beneath.

For years, it had called to her, the murky waters of the lagoon that slept there at the base of the mountain. For years, she had sat by her tower window, watching it with bated breath, inexplicably entranced by the faint ripples that would slink their way across the water, yearning to dip her fingers into its waves and feel the caress of the cold black water slip across her skin.

She had never known why, never was sure what had always drawn her so inexorably to its black-glassed depths, but now as she tasted the wet, malodorous odor of the loch, she knew what it was that had called to her with such insistence—a siren's song of black magic, from one monster to another.

She knew he was there, waiting and watching. She could sense him with the feelers of this newfound power of hers. She stalked forward, her front paws sinking into the black mud of the loch, and let its dark waters creep in around her. She quivered at the whisper of power in its depths as the loch water soaked into her fur. She let out a low growl, a call of sororal likeness to the creature that slithered within the depths of the lake. A rumbling pulse of answering power shook the muddy ground beneath her paws as it emerged.

Even in her bestial form, Rozlyn shuddered a little at the sight of it.

Its deep-brown fur glistened in the dark night as it crawled through the mud of the foreshore of the loch, its heavy body squelching as it approached. Rozlyn eyed it as it dragged its lumbering frame toward her, its bright, sharp teeth bared in a snarl, and Rozlyn's hair bristled in a silent warning to the dobhar-chú to come no closer.

It was the first time that she had tested this part of her power, the summoning of her own kind, her fellow monsters who prowled about in the dark corners of the world. It was risky, calling them forth, but she could not resist, and she watched the dobhar-chú's snarl fade away, its beady eyes sharpening with recognition.

She loved Galena, and she loved her newfound village, the good-hearted people who embraced her as one of their own, but she would never be like them, never truly be one of them. Monsters, she thought as the dobhar-chú dragged the rest of its heavy body out of the loch. She belonged to the clan of monsters, the vile, twisted offspring of the earth, her one true kin—the only way for her to feel a little less alone in this world. At least they could understand her, to know what it was like to be reviled and condemned.

The dobhar-chú halted, flipping its wide, flat tail back and forth in impatience, and a wordless agreement passed between them. The dobhar-chú bowed its head, and Rozlyn turned and prowled away, her wings flapping in a soundless command to follow her.

Together they slipped through the dark toward her father's half-built hall, the great winged bearlike beast and the gargantuan otter-fish, making their way through the shadows. It followed her up the grassy knoll to the charred balcony that stretched out from her father's chambers.

Rozlyn looked back at her monstrous companion in a silent question, and in answer, the dobhar-chú padded over to the rough stone wall. Digging its sharp claws into the crevices of the stone, it began to lurch and pull its way up the smoke-stained walls toward the room where her father slept. Rozlyn chuffed once, then rose into the air after him, her wings beating soundlessly against the stillness of the night air.

She landed on the fire-warped wooden boards of the smoke-blackened balcony, the weakened timbers creaking in protest against her weight. She shifted, gasping aloud as her pale fingers emerged from underneath the dark fur of the Beast, her newfound prowess over her power still agonizingly painful to wield. Rozlyn exhaled through the pain, and then she straightened her slim shoulders and tied back the shower of raven-black hair that cascaded around her face, even as the dobhar-chú slithered its hulking frame over the balustrade to stand next to her, twitching at the scent of the pulse of hot, human blood within.

Rozlyn eased forward into the room with a subtle motion

to the dobhar-chú to wait, to stay for a moment, and there
he was, illuminated by the low-burning embers of the hearth
fire—her father, dreaming and peaceful and unmarred by
flames or guilt.

She stepped forward, and with a vicious shove, pushed
over the tall mahogany chair that sat by his desk. It fell to
the floor with a harsh clatter.

Ailain bolted awake, sitting up in his bed, wild and hands
whirling in panic. "Who—Cormac, Eomain—someone—"

"I would suggest," Rozlyn said, stalking forward into the
dim light of the fire, "that you keep this interlude between
us, unless you truly do relish the sight of your men's innards
splayed across the floors of your chambers." Her fingers
quivered, aching to lash out with this newfound strength,
to take the revenge she had craved for so long. "Do you,
Father? Is that the reason behind this abomination that you
have inflicted on your only child? Did you enjoy seeing the
bloodshed that I wrought upon your people?"

Ailain sat frozen, the bedsheets twisted around him as
he stared at her. "Rozlyn," he gasped, "my little rosebud."

She snarled, and the shadows of her feathered black
wings loomed across the flickering firelight reflected on
his walls. "Don't you dare," she growled, "condescend to
me, *Father*."

"Rozlyn, please," her father pleaded, and that beacon of
anger burned brighter inside her, that he would be tender,
be gentle with her now, after everything that he had done,
all the years of screams and threats and breaking her, piece
by piece, into that shattered mess of shame and despair that
she had been so close to becoming. "Please listen to me. It
is not what you have been led to believe—"

"Quiet." At her unspoken command, from the shadows

of the balcony, the dobhar-chú came slithering in, an ominous hissing escaping through its sharp teeth, and Rozlyn relished watching her father's ruddy face turn bloodless and pale at the sight of the loch monster. "I have come for my vengeance, and nothing more. No excuses or pleas or protestations of love." Her voice thickened over the word. "If it helps," she continued with renewed smoothness, belied by the viciousness swirling in her belly, "you are not my primary concern this night." Her chest tightened, and the flames of her wrath licked their lips greedily, ravenous and aching to feed on the true source of their vengeance. "Where is he?"

Ailain swallowed. "Where is who?"

Rozlyn's lips lifted in a sneer. "My *husband*, that's who." The dobhar-chú swung its head toward her at the promise of violence in her tone, and she could see an answering hunger reflected in its eyes.

The same. A whispered purr of an unknown dark voice bled through her. They were the same, these monsters and her, savage and half-mad for the taste of blood.

"Rozlyn."

Her attention snapped back to her father. "Why else would I bother myself with the likes of you? I will see him dead," she snarled as her claws shoved their way through the delicate skin of her knuckles unbidden, so wild was the rage that stormed within her, "and I will secure my freedom if it is the last thing that I do."

She could feel the truth of it, that veiled knowing that he was the only threat left that could do her harm, that could take this power away from her. She was strong now, as she had never before been allowed to be—an invincible force— and once he was gone for good, all traces of him erased from existence, the magic would be hers and hers alone, forever.

Ailian held out his hands, pleading with her. "He is not here," he whispered, shaking as the dobhar-chú lurched its way closer to the bed where he still lay, eyes gleaming. "He is gone—I swear it. He has not been here for at least a year."

Rozlyn growled, a guttural sound of rage, and the dobhar-chú lumbered closer, a thin trail of thick white drool slipping from between its jaws, down the contours of its sleek coat.

She turned away to stalk toward the balcony when her father called out to her, his voice breaking.

"Rozlyn, child. I'm so sorry. It was never my intention to see you so hurt, and if I had thought there was any other way—"

"There was always another way," she said, her back to him as she stared unseeingly into the night sky. "You just did not care enough to search for it."

"Rozlyn, child—"

"Such a simple fix," she mused. "So many innocent lives, so much suffering, all because you never cared enough to look."

"Please. Rozlyn, please, I am your father. Spare my life, sweet girl, my only child, my rosebud—"

She held up her hand, a seemingly lazy gesture, and a vicious streak of white-hot lightning split the deep night sky, illuminating the terrified face of her father in an explosion of blinding light, even as her head throbbed with that now-familiar shredding of pain whenever she called upon those newly discovered corners of her magic. He fell silent, shaking in his sheets as the dobhar-chú continued to drool and chuff its teeth in anticipation as it studied him.

"How long did you know?" she asked, as though it were nothing, an inquiry about the kind of meat that he had been served at supper, or the spices in his mead. "For how long were you aware that you would doom me to die on the day that you gave away my hand in marriage to the man of your choice, and that he would strip from me this power embedded within me, that its loss would leave me broken and bleeding in my own home?"

Her father made a soft choking sound. "Rozlyn, daughter, please."

"A father's duty is to protect his child. Do not call me daughter again. How long?"

Ailain shook at the ice-coated bite of her words. "Since the beginning," he whispered. "It was part of the prophecy given by the Cailleach. I forbade them to speak of it, forbade them to tell you—"

"That will do." She shrugged. "It hardly matters now anyway."

It didn't, she assured herself—it did not matter that this man who had procured her chocolates from across the ice-cold sea and brought her flowers and taught her the rules of the game by which she navigated the stormy waters of her life had all along been counting down the days until she would die.

She would not allow herself to care, to grieve for him. For either of them.

"Keep to your realm, and I shall keep to mine." She turned to face him, her face a cold mask of hatred. "I have claimed the vale of Inagh as my own. The people who live there are under my protection, my rule, and you will collect no tax from them, nor will you or your armies so much as raise a finger against them, or you will pay for it far more dearly than with a few burnt towers and a smoke-filled hall." He nodded once, his fingers trembling as they clutched at the sheets, and she threw her head back, her black hair swinging proudly behind her, a flag of victory waving from the bows of a homecoming ship. "The Beanna Beola are yours, as are the Mhám Toirc to the west of my vale, but the narrow strip between them is mine. Skirt around them as much as you like, but if you step foot across their borders into my realm, I will claim your life as forfeit with all the fire and fury of this magic that you so long fought to deny me." Ailain made an involuntary whimper of fear, and she turned away, ignoring his distress. "Do we have an agreement, King of Connacht?"

"Rozlyn." Her father eyed the dobhar-chú looming patient and still next to his bed, then bowed his head. "We are agreed."

Rozlyn huffed once in disdain as she shifted, her body growing heavy with blue-black fur, her feathered wings unfurling behind her as the dobhar-chú reared up on its hind legs, its front paws landing on her father's mattress with a thump. "Stop sniveling," she said as her father sobbed, scrabbling backward away from the monster's gleaming teeth. "He will not kill you. I owe you that much, at least, for having the most basic shreds of decency and choosing to not hurl me from the tower in the first hour that I was born." She paused. "He will, however, leave you a simple reminder of what power the daughters of men can possess when they at last break free."

The dobhar-chú began to salivate in earnest, and her father's sobs turned to heaving cries of terror as Rozlyn padded out into the night. "Tell him when he returns," she called back over her shaggy shoulder, even as her face elongated into a lupine shape, "as we both know that he will, that whenever I see him again, he will die wishing those wolves had ended his life on that battlefield so long ago."

Behind her, the dobhar-chú hissed and lunged for her father's face with its sharp teeth, and Rozlyn did not wait to hear his screams, but threw herself into the night sky, that endless thirst for vengeance still burning within her, never to be quenched.

CHAPTER TWENTY

Rozlyn tucked her wings onto her back and sprawled on the sun-warmed boulder outside her home, her paws twitching in her enjoyment of the midday warmth, napping after her battle with the cú-sídhe.

She had flown back in the soft light of the newly wakened dawn, landing among the copse of trees that shaded her courtyard. With only a twitch of her head, her transformation seamless, she straightened her cloak around her shoulders and slipped into the stillness of her hall, down the quiet corridor to her solar, the fire burning low in the hearth.

She had lingered in the doorway, studying his pale face, peaceful and boyish in sleep, with a detached coolness.

Galena had risen creakily from the corner where she sat, and Rozlyn had jolted a little at the movement. "The fever is broken," Galena had whispered. "The wound still looks bad, black and oozing of that foul venom, but the herbs have done their job so far." She tilted her head, examining

Rozlyn's drawn, exhausted face. "I thought I might find you here when I returned a few hours ago, but he was alone."

She stopped, the silent question hanging in the air between them, but Rozlyn had turned without answering and stalked away. "Call me if there is any change."

She had headed straight for the kitchen, and almost sobbed with gratitude at the sight of a hot kettle of freshly boiled water waiting for her tea, and as she squeezed in the juices of that life-giving herb, mixing in a liberal amount of honey and lavender to distill the bitterness of its taste, she loaded a plate high with crisp sausage and black pudding and soft, oat-laden soda bread. She carried her breakfast outside in the cool damp air, the mild mist welcoming and warm compared to the icy sheets of last evening's rain, and settled on a nearby boulder to devour her feast, ravenous after the strain of the previous night.

She had finished with a sigh, then stretched out on the flat surface of the rock, hands behind her head, to watch the sun begin to break free of the handful of dark-gray clouds that hung in the sky.

She had awoken hours later in the full light of the sun, that surge of wildness still thrumming through her veins with revitalized intensity. She yielded to the urge and shifted, flexing her limbs across the sun-dappled boulder, stretching her wings with unconcerned ease to savor the rarity of such warm golden rays in the late autumn months.

She would no longer pretend that she hated this Beast who lived underneath her skin. She loved it, as much as she loved the beauty of her spells and her charms.

It was only at the sound of those familiar footsteps—a little slower, a little shakier than usual—that her ears pricked, and she raised her head to survey him as he approached.

Jamie halted beside her, his dark hair disheveled, his face still so pale with his arm slung tight against his chest, but his eyes were clear. Some of the lingering tension in her chest eased at the sight of them, twinkling at her in that affectionate way of his. "You look," he announced, "like an overgrown house cat who has just made a meal of some hapless mouse caught in a trap."

Rozlyn's jowls twitched, remembering the savaged body of the cú-sídhe as it lay sprawled in the blood-soaked dirt beneath her, then sat up, yawning as she flashed her sharp fangs at him.

He grinned. "What big teeth you have, a bhrèagha." He winced as he sat down on a low crag of rock that jutted from the grass across from her, his face creasing with the exertion, then sighed. "I was hoping that we could talk."

She growled, reluctant, then with a heavy sigh, she twitched, and her body bent and molded itself into slighter, paler contours, and in a blink, she tossed her raven-black hair over her shoulder and scowled at him. "What?"

He studied her, and she tried to ignore the admiration apparent on his face. "I shall never grow tired of watching you do that." She merely raised her brows, and he grimaced again as he adjusted his arm against his chest. "Right. I'll get on with it then. Very well. First, I suppose I should say thank you."

She started a little, her memory flashing back to the bloody body of the cú-sídhe, when he clarified. "For saving my life, with the herbs, the poultices, and the tea, I suppose. I slept like the dead." He grimaced. "Although it might be too soon for me to comfortably utilize that analogy."

"Oh. You're welcome."

Jamie sighed again as he shifted on his perch. "Second,

we need to discuss this—situation between us, Rozi. I am willing to venture out a third time, to see what monsters I can carry home to you, if that is what you need for your own satisfaction, but I must ask you to reconsider. I have already failed poor Hedrek, and I came perilously close to losing the others to that demon-wolf."

"You came perilously close to losing yourself," she said, and he smiled. She scowled at him. "Not that I care."

"Of course not." His face grew serious as he watched her. "Is it not enough, Rozi, the terrors that I have shown you? What more must I do to prove to you how desperately I need your help?"

"No more." She stood up, her hands clenching at her sides. "I believe you."

Jamie lurched to his feet as well, then yelped at the sudden slice of agony that ripped through his shoulder with the abrupt movement. "Then let's go, Rozi. There is no time to lose."

"You are hardly"—she gestured to his bandaged arm—"in a position to go anywhere, Jamie."

"A week, then, and I shall be fine." He blew out an impatient breath. "Damn that wolf. I told you. They really are the most depraved of creatures."

"Sit down, Jamie." Rozlyn's voice was firm. "Why the urgency? Why are you so insistent on this? I understand that it is the duty of your people, but you almost died, Jamie. Surely you realize, must see the need to wait, to take some time and think this through."

"We do not have time, Rozi." Jamie paced in front of her, and she watched him with raised brows. "We need to leave now if you are finally agreeing to help me."

His movements were jerky and uneven, but not from pain.

There was something frantic about the way that he prowled across the grass, back and forth, his uninjured hand clenching and unclenching itself in an unconscious movement of desperation.

He was hiding something from her.

Again.

She was quiet for a moment. "Jamie," she said at last, soft and pleading. "No more lies. Tell me the truth. What is really happening here?"

He stared into the distance at the far-off peaks of the snowcapped mountains, his face remote, and she stepped closer, reaching out to lay a hand on his left arm where it hung by his side. "Talk to me, Jamie."

He looked at her, his stare boring into hers, and it still thrummed between them, that tug of attraction, that shimmering silvery thread of—something—that ran far deeper beneath the surfaces of their skins, that called to each other in insistent voices of longing and need.

Jamie's eyes dimmed and he bowed his head with a sigh. "It is my fault, you know, that all of this has happened to you." He ran his good hand across his chin. "It is in her pursuit of vengeance of me that you were cursed at all."

"What do you mean?"

"Remember the stories I told you, Rozi. They were not chosen idly."

"What do you mean?"

He made a motion as if to roll his shoulders, then winced with remembered pain. "You were not wrong," he said heavily, "when you accused me of manipulating you. I was, I admit it—and all those stories were told to you with a very specific purpose in mind." The words fell heavy on her ears, an ominous toll of doom. "Particularly the tale of the god who betrayed his betrothed for the sake of a mortal girl and doomed us all."

A faint bell of recognition rang in the back of her mind at the name, a rush of blurred remembrances—memories of stories of shape-shifting and dragonflies and rerouted rivers and inexplicably, a tiger with bright orange eyes and teeth bared in a grin.

That couldn't be right. She shook her head, trying to clear her brain of that strange fog. "Midir," she said slowly. "I remember this. He was a son of the Dagda. What does he have to do with me?"

Jamie grimaced. "Quite a lot, in fact." He made a feeble attempt at a smile. "That would be me."

"*You* are Midir?" Rozlyn frowned, first in disbelief, then in consternation. "You absolute *bastard*. How dare you trifle with me, marry me, whilst you are promised to another woman!"

"You defend her still, I see, as you did when I first told you the tale well over ten years ago."

"You told me many stories of the old gods."

"So I did," he said, flexing the fingers of his uninjured arm idly in the sun, testing their strength. "But only one that concerned myself. I have been locked away in this mortal body for nearly three hundred years, forced to endure a mortal life that never ends, all the while knowing that my father and mother, my sisters and brothers, my friends, my entire race of people are cursed to eternal slumber beneath the bowels of the earth because of me, while you hapless mortals have had free rein over the natural world and been left to fend for yourselves against the remnants of the most evil sorcery that this land has to offer."

Rozlyn stared at her husband, assessing and thoughtful.

He was a prince, one of the immortal gods, the most powerful beings in all Éire. She should have known that, she
realized. She should have known from that first day on the
sunlit terrace of her father's home, when he smiled at her
with absolutely no trace of fear in his eyes.

No man had ever before met her gaze without trepida-
tion, without fear.

She sank down onto the lush green grass, folding her legs
underneath her gown. "I didn't really believe you when you
first told me. You truly are one of the great gods of yore."

"Once. No longer though." Jamie huffed, disgruntled,
and slid his uninjured hand into his pocket, the gesture
so familiar that her heart cracked down the center all over
again. "I told you as much. This human body is my prison,
denied my divinity but doomed to an interminably long
life." He let out a bitter laugh. "Why do you imagine that I
tried—quite unsuccessfully—to tell you that particular story
so many years ago? It is my magic you wield, Rozi, and very
ineffectually at that." He slid down against the boulder to sit
next to her. "You cannot imagine the depths of the power
that you have left untapped and unexplored all these years.
Even now, you can barely even summon the elementals."

Maybe some of the poison from the cú-sídhe had leaked
into her skin, because his words hung in the air before her,
a jumbled, disoriented heap of memories of truth and lies,
facts and fictions, embellished stories and distorted realities.

She blinked, latching onto the last strange word. "The
elementals?"

He jerked his chin at the trees, the sky, the forest around
them. "Your magic—*my* magic—is fundamentally tied to the elements of nature, Rozi. You were right about that much. The
shape-shifting—always in the form of some animal or beast,

just as you can summon them to do your bidding. The most powerful piece of that puzzle, however, is how to command the elemental features of nature itself and reroute its course, to bend its power to your wants instead of the will of the seasons and the earth-mother herself." He shrugged. "You may be able to make it rain, or call to the wolves, or command the bears and the trees of the woods to terrify the hearts of the unsuspecting men who dare to venture into your vale, but believe me when I tell you that is the barest fraction of what you could be capable of with this magic of mine in your soul."

"That's hardly my fault. I'm a mortal woman. You had centuries to master it—an immortal prince of the Court of Shádach, Jamie."

Jamie snorted. "'Court of Shádach.' What a ridiculous name given by ridiculous humans to the realm of the most powerful entities in the universe."

"Says the *god* afraid of a few wolves."

"Believe me, I have my reasons. Regardless," he continued, "we did not have a court that was separate from the mortals where we remained aloof from the concerns of the rest of the world. That is only a legend. The Court of Shádach was merely where we would gather together as one for our meals and our rest—but for all the days we ruled over the realm of Éire, we walked among you and around you, guiding and teaching and caring for humans, as we cared for all the elements of the natural world. We are guardians, caretakers of the earth and its inhabitants, not monsters."

"I have heard stories that say differently."

"Well, it is true that we can be a bit nasty when irritated, but when sufficiently flattered, we really are a remarkably pleasant people."

"Again," she said. "That was not the impression I was given."

"The Mórrígan, if that is to whom you are referring—and I will allow that she is rather horrifying—does not abide by the same laws as the rest of the Tuatha Dé Danann. She is powerful and terrible enough that none of the others object to her ways, even the Dagda, ruler of the gods."

Rozlyn frowned. "Was it she, then, who locked away your magic along with the rest of the ancient gods? The Mórrígan?"

"By the harp, no. She is confined, as the rest of them. Och, what a terrible day for the cosmos that will be, indeed, when her rage is loosed upon the world."

"Who, then? Who did this?" She sat up straight. "Wait—I do remember this tale. Your betrothed, the cailleach whom you jilted for the princess Étaín—her name was Fúamnach."

"Indeed. What a nasty witch she turned out to be, and I mean that quite literally. She is an incredibly powerful witch, and she has done some very nasty things with that sorcery of hers, you know, so please refrain from glowering at me like that."

"If I am remembering correctly, nothing that you did not deserve."

Jamie huffed again. "A discussion that is perhaps best left for another day."

"Why would you not just tell me this? Why lie to me?"

"I swear by all the gods, the family that I lost, Rozi, don't you understand how hard I tried to do exactly that? Every story that I told you was hinting at, leading to this very moment. Queen Medb, the harp of the Dagda, the Mórrígan, the story of Midir and Étaín, all of it. But you—" His face grew grim. "You were not very receptive toward the latter story, nor were you especially sympathetic to me. I decided it was best not to risk you rejecting me due to your admirable loyalty to your fellow female."

The realization hit Rozlyn like a blow to the face. "The shape-shifting. You never finished your story, but that is how—" She stopped, horrified.

He nodded. "The Beast of Connacht is a perverse, evil manipulation of that power. Not," he said hurriedly, "one of your making, but a callous idea of a cruel joke, courtesy of my former fiancée."

A stab of revulsion. "She gave your power to me? Why?"

Jamie studied the bruised knuckles on his uninjured hand with sudden interest. "That is a very long story, Rozi."

"We have time." She jerked her chin toward his injured arm wrapped in the strips of white linen. "At least a fortnight, judging by the ooze seeping out of your wound through your bandage."

Jamie looked down and swore. "The short version, then, before I bleed to death against this godsforsaken rock." He sighed, stretching out his legs, and she watched him wince at the answering pull in his shoulder. "One night, after I had gone to sleep next to my mortal bride, my jilted fiancée slipped into our chamber through the window and used her dark arts, the witchcraft of her kind, the callieachs, to siphon my power from me—namely, my shape-shifting, and the command I wielded over the natural world and its elements." He raised his eyebrows at Rozlyn, and she remembered the startling accuracy of his description of the aches and pains that had plagued her for so long whenever she tried to call upon the forces of wind and fire and rain. "She then used my gift to transform herself, to mimic the figure and pitch of my father—the Dagda, king of the gods—and entered the great hall of the king to command the harp that hung on his wall."

"You told me this. Uaithne was its name, and it answered only to him, to sing the spells of sadness and mirth and—"

"Slumber," Jamie finished. "She shifted into my father's form and tricked his harp into believing that she was him, and thus cursed the entire court of the Tuatha Dé Danann to an eternal slumber, dragging their corpse-like forms beneath the crust of the earth, wherein she locked them away for all eternity, while I watched, helpless to stop her, to save them, trapped in this feeble mortal form as I was."

"How did she trap you?"

Jamie's face darkened. "My divinity is tied to my power, and without it I am a mere shell of my true self. She drained my soul, powerless and weak as it now was, from my immortal form and confined me to this"—he gestured with mild disdain to his body—"as punishment for so humiliating her by my preference for another wife. Her art keeps me young and healthy, never aging, never dying, doomed to wander the earth for all eternity, a shadow of the deity that I once was, forever grieving the loss of my family, my fortune, and my love." His mouth twisted. "I was wrong to so abandon the promise that I had made to her, Rozi, regardless of how little I cared for her, or of how deeply I loved my mortal wife, but I would argue as well that the punishment I have endured does not fit the crime."

Rozlyn was silent, considering this. "What happened to her, then?" she asked, deliberately, impassively cool. "Your actual wife, as apparently I am the second to hold that title."

Jamie stared at her, utterly devoid of emotion. "She died."

It was cruel, irrational to feel it, that swift twist of petty relief that this long-lost love of her husband's could serve as no rival to her own beauty. "Fúamnach did it?"

"Yes." Jamie's voice was curt, and she knew that there would be no more answered questions about that long-dead first wife. "She savored every aspect, every moment of her revenge, and that is all that I wish to say on the subject, Rozi."

She nodded reluctantly, a selfish desire within her itching to hear more about this wife of her husband's, whose loss still so clearly haunted him, but she ignored it. "How did I end up with your power, then? Did she intend for me to have it?"

"Och, most certainly." Jamie closed his eyes. "Perhaps she had grown bored after three hundred years of watching me squirm. Who knows? She has never bothered to explain her reasoning to me. But I felt it reborn within you that night so many years ago, as did her sister, the Cailleach, as you well know. She felt the need to show herself for the first time in centuries to announce its presence within your blood." Jamie sighed again, his pale face scarred with regret and exhaustion. "I heard rumors of the prophecy that she had made about you, and for the first time in three hundred years, I felt the stirrings of hope—hope that I might recover my power, the very essence of myself, and save my family from the doom that I had brought upon them. I waited and I watched and then I presented myself to your father, a mysterious man from the northern realm, claiming to know the secrets of your magic—not a lie after all, you see—and I swore to him that I would win your hand as no other man could, because I alone could truly love that darkness that swirled within your veins." He watched her, but her face did not flicker at the confession of his indifference toward her, his admittance of his true apathy for their erstwhile love. "And the rest, as they say, is history."

Rozlyn was silent and still, her face a mask of coldness, and Jamie leaned forward, grimacing as his arm seized up in a fresh convulsion of pain. "Do we still have a deal, Rozi? Will you help me to right this terrible injustice that has been done—to your people and to mine?"

Rozlyn stared into the trees as she processed this revelation—not the news of his godhood, nor of his centuries of grief, nor even that soft throb of pain as he told her that his heart had never really belonged to her after all, but to that long-lost bride of yesteryear, a sweet girl who could smile back at him without scowling, who was happy to be helpless and play the part of the blushing bride to his savior-prince.

All these years, she had been caught up in their game, their matches of wits and wiles, when her pieces had never even truly been on the board. He had been playing against some other far more sinister opponent, an unknown face with cruel witchy eyes, surrendering pieces and plotting strategies against someone other than she, and she had never known. A sudden stab of grief sliced through her. There was no match between them, no possibility of equity. She had moved along the path that he had predetermined for her, focused on an entirely different endgame, never seeing her own.

Rozlyn's shoulders sagged.

She might be his queen, but she was an expendable one, for he was hunting a king.

In her mind's eye, she rose from that little wooden table on her father's terrace where they had started their games so many years before, and with a flick of her finger, she conceded her bronze-coated king, and he tumbled against the black-and-white board with a clatter.

There was no match to be played between them any longer.

She looked at him with her ever-serious eyes, her lips firm and unsmiling as ever. "Yes," she said, "I will help you." She rose from the grass and turned to go back inside to the soothing quiet of her solar. "You should rest. We will leave as soon as you can ride."

Jamie loosed a breath of relief and stood to thank her, stretching out his left hand in a heartfelt expression of gratitude, but she strode away without another word, disappearing into her castle without a backward glance, showing no outward sign of the heart that he had just broken all over again.

After all, she had conceded the match.

PART TWO

CHAPTER
TWENTY-ONE

Midir rode along the white-sand beaches of Ulaid, his brown mare snorting as she sprinted over the dampness of the shore, his shoulder-length golden hair streaming in waves behind him.

By the harp, he loved the sea.

He loosened his grip on the reins, and the mare slowed to a gentle lope along the shoreline, and he closed his eyes against the brilliance of the sun reflecting off the shimmering water, drinking in the salt scent of the waves as they rolled in on the ocean breeze.

Here it didn't matter that he was but a minor lord, an oft-overlooked prince in comparison to the might of his far more formidable half brothers. Here, he was a king, the lord of the sea and sand, and his heart quickened with the thrill of the sweet-citrus tang of the ocean air on his tongue.

He rode for a long time, the tide lapping at the shins of his glossy brown mare, and he savored the heat of the midday summer sun on his golden skin, relishing his freedom while it was still his and not at the beckoning of a black-haired, orange-eyed, soon-to-be wife.

Midir banished the image of Fúamnach from his brain, tall and sinuous creature that she was, and focused his attention on the seemingly endless stretch of shore that wound its way down the brilliant-white beach in front of him, unbroken for as far as even his immortal eye could see—

Except, he realized, for her.

He tugged on the leather reins in his hands, and his mare again slowed to a stop. His attention latched onto the slim form wading into the water in front of him, tossing aside her gauzy white gown with careless abandon as she strode into the waves, naked and unashamed as the day her mother must have borne her into this world.

He shifted uncomfortably in his saddle, even as he ached to steal a glance at the lithe form he had glimpsed before he had averted his eyes, but he rebelled at the idea of spying on such an obviously maiden-like figure as she frolicked among the waves.

He should warn her, he decided, announce his presence so that she could protect her modesty from other, less conscientious stares. The Dagda forbid that someone else should see the pale shapeliness of her legs, the supple slant of her shoulders, the way her black hair cascaded down her back toward her—

Midir cleared his throat and nudged his horse forward. "My lady," he called, "pardon me. I cannot help but notice that you have lost your gown."

"I haven't lost it, you fool," she called back as she floated in the waves of the low tide, her feet waving gracefully in the air. "I left it there on the beach, unless you have since stolen it away."

"Of course not," he huffed, affronted. "I would never so shame a maiden."

"How do you know I'm a maiden?" She stretched her arms above her head, and he snapped his attention away from the sight of her exposed skin, her curves, mingling with the waves. "Perhaps I have taken half of Ulaid's army into my bed. What then? Am I less deserving of your respect, of your deference?"

Impossibly, sweat began to pool at the base of his neck—him, an immortal god, and her, a skinny, brash human girl. "Of course not, my lady. As you please."

She stood up in the waist-deep water, her black hair streaming about her, clinging to her curves far too closely for him to dwell on without embarrassing himself. "Who are you? Who is so unmoved by my brashness? Most of the men who have come calling for my hand would have run screaming for the door by now."

"I do not seek your hand," he said, uncomfortable with the myriad of visceral images exploding in his imagination at the full sight of her slender form, her shapely curves. "I simply wished to spare you the shame of being seen in a state of undress by a man other than your husband."

She placed her hands on her hips—by the Dagda's harp, those hips—and strode out of the water. He swallowed again and averted his eyes as she stormed up the beach toward him. "I have no husband," he heard her say, a bite in her voice so incongruous with her youthful innocence, her fresh beauty, "so look as much as you please, but know that if you so much as lay a finger on me, my father will have you torn to pieces and set the dogs on you to devour your flesh even as you lie dying in the dirt."

He glanced at her, careful to keep his gaze focused on

her narrow face and wide eyes—those eyes, as gorgeous as the
sea kelp lolling in the waves behind them—and he allowed
himself a hint of a smirk. "I doubt that, my lady."

She combed her dark hair away from her face with her
fingers, squeezing out the seawater and sand as she tussled
the thick wet strands. "My father," she said, "is the high chief
of Latharna, and my betrothed—" He could not help but
notice the scorn that coated the word even as she narrowed
those sea-swept eyes at him. "He is the king of the North
in Ulaid, with armies upon armies at his command." She
sniffed. "I do not imagine that you would fare well against
their wrath, a chodáin."

Amusement surged through him at the insult. Her chin
jutted forward, an unspoken challenge, and his mouth
quirked up.

What a bold little thing she was.

He looked her up and down, a begrudging hint of
admiration threading through him when she did not so
much as flinch under his slow perusal. "Well," he said,
his eyes returning to meet hers. "I suppose we shall soon
see, won't we?"

She scowled at him, her annoyance flickering across
her finely honed features. She tossed her wet hair in his
face, spraying him with seawater, and sashayed to where her
discarded gown lay in the sand. She bent to snag it in her
hand, and he averted his eyes again, grimacing as he strove
to avoid lingering on those interesting curves so brazenly
on display, even as she pulled the sand-soaked gown over
her head in one fluid motion.

He eyed her, the thin gossamer material that clung in
such enticing ways to her wet skin, then cleared his throat
again. "What is your name?"

She glared at him through the waterfall of black hair. "None of your business."

Midir raised his golden eyebrows in mild surprise. "I can easily find out, you know."

"Suit yourself." She tipped her head to the side, sliding her fingers through her hair as she plaited it into a long smooth braid with practiced ease.

He watched her with growing amusement. "I'm not sure," he said, gesturing to the way that the fabric molded to her damp form, "that your gown is much of a deterrent in defense of your modesty."

She scoffed, then whipped her braid behind her back and turned on her heel to storm away across the sand. "Then I suppose that you will have to do something utterly unheard of for a man and practice a little bit of self-control over your urges, won't you?"

He watched her go, this scornful, green-eyed girl, and for the first time in his immortal life, he fell just a little bit in love.

CHAPTER TWENTY-TWO

Jamie extended his right arm tentatively, flexing his fingers, then heaved a sigh of relief when no lancing pain ripped through the tendons of his biceps. He raised his head and grinned at Bowen. "And to think that you were so deathly afraid of magic when we first began. Look," he gestured to his arm, whole and hale. "Not so bad after all, is it now?"

Bowen grunted as he continued to wrap strips of dried meat and linseed crackers in scraps of linen, packing them into the saddlebags in front of him. "Your arm wouldn't have been festering in unnatural poison for the last fortnight without that same cursed magic either, don't you know."

Jamie merely smiled as he surveyed Bowen's work. "I was thinking," he said after a moment, "that you should remain here, you and Tavin and Nyle, while I accompany the queen north."

Last night as he had lain alone on the cot in the damp

little room in the castle, which Rozlyn had pointed him to two weeks before, determination had grown within him. No more dead men. No more burdens of guilt to carry on his shoulders for the rest of his days. He was already burdened enough with such sins, enough failures to last for an eternity of lifetimes.

Bowen again grunted, sneaking a glance at him out of the corner of his eye. "If you are that desperate to be alone with your lady so you can enjoy that neglected marital bed of yours, you could just say so."

"Not likely, to my everlasting dismay."

Bowen's rueful smile faded. "I don't like the idea of you going alone."

Jamie waved his hand. "I won't be." His attention wandered across the yard to where she stood with Galena, the two of them huddled together in a sort of sisterhood, their gestures intimate and their brief touches full of affection, one so young and vibrant and the other careworn and wrinkled. As if sensing his perusal, Rozlyn glanced away from Galena and met his gaze. "I shall have the dread Beast of Connacht to protect me if any threats arise."

From behind him, Nyle snorted. "To kill you and feed you to whatever monsters she befriends along the way, more like."

"Now, Nyle," Jamie said as Rozlyn stalked toward them. "Just because my loving wife might have tried to murder me once or twice in the past does not mean that she will do so again." She halted before him, her hands on her hips as she scowled at him. "Or at the very least, be comforted by the fact that her track record in terms of successfully killing me is egregiously bad. You are not a particularly adept assassin, it would seem, Rozi."

"The people of Connacht," Nyle said, flint-hard and furious, "who still grieve for those who perished at her monstrous claws would beg to differ."

There was a tense silence, an ominous rippling over Rozlyn's stony features, and Jamie moved between the two of them, reaching out to place an idle hand on Nyle's shoulder as he shoved him away. "Be a good lad," he said. "Run along and fetch my longbow and quiver where Bowen has stored them away while I've been lounging about as a helpless invalid, will you?"

Rozlyn's eyes flared at the tawny-haired boy, who huffed but stepped back before turning and loping away on his errand. Jamie eyed her with mild reproval. "He is only a boy, a bhrèagha, and still grieving his brother."

"We are all grieving our own losses. He can learn to hold his tongue and show some respect."

Jamie smiled. "Someone once told me that respect must be earned, not deserved."

"What wise soul was this?"

"A girl," Jamie said smoothly, "whom I was trying to sweet-talk into my bed."

Rozlyn's lips flattened before she gestured toward Galena. "She says that your arm is somewhat healed but still weak, and too much strain could aggravate the wound."

"And?"

"And," she said, a ripple of irritation roughening the smoothness of her voice, "do you intend to be a fool and insist we leave now, or can it wait another week?"

Jamie folded his arms across his chest. "I have waited three hundred years. You may safely assume that I have long since exhausted what little patience I was born with."

She looked him full in the eyes at that, for the first time

in a fortnight. She had been distant, too remote, since their fateful conversation that day by the boulder, and he had ached with missing her, a far more poignant pain than the agony in his arm.

It seemed impossible that he had survived so long without her.

"One hour," she said, a clear dismissal. "Have it your way." Jamie watched as she turned on her heel and stalked away, aloof and again alone.

The last minutes before her departure flew by with impossible swiftness, and Rozlyn stood for a long moment in the middle of her beloved hall, this once decrepit structure, abandoned years ago by some unknown and long-forgotten clan of yesteryear. It had welcomed her into its cobwebby, mildewed depths, had given her shelter and solace in the darkest hours of her girlhood. She had met Galena here, she thought, as she surveyed the room, sturdy and lovely in its second life, and she almost smiled, remembering the frightened girl that she had been, how she had blossomed and come to life under the warmth of Galena's love.

She had never known her mother, but at least she knew what it felt like to love one, thanks to Galena.

She reached into her pocket and rubbed the collection of rowan branches she had gathered and twined together with a wire, more than enough of a supply to last her for an extended journey. She closed her eyes, remembering her despair and her grief, and the hope that had bloomed so wildly in her chest the first time Galena handed her that steaming mug of tea, rich with honey and lavender and life-giving, albeit unbearably bitter, herbs.

This was the only real home that she had ever known, the only one in which she ever wished to live, and it broke her heart to leave it, however briefly.

She ran her hand down one of the smooth oak beams in the center of her hall, restored by the hours and hours of backbreaking labor and sweat and magic and tears, all of which she showered on it in those early, grief-filled years. "I will come back to you," she whispered, and she could almost hear the reassuring murmur of the wood and the stone as they bade her farewell, for now.

She stalked outside and down the steps, her black braid slipping over her shoulder as she descended to where Galena waited at the bottom.

She said nothing, but the older woman's face was warm, her eyes swimming with unshed tears, and her heart throbbed at the sight of the only mother that she had ever known already grieving for her, as though she, too, knew that there would be no return for Rozlyn, at least not as she now was—free and wild and boundless.

Rozlyn jerked her head at her, an unsteady gesture of farewell, her throat too clogged with emotion to speak. Without a word, she turned away to where Jamie waited, clad in black fleece with his bow slung over his shoulder, his arms crossed as he stood next to their horses.

Rozlyn eyed them, the mare and the gelding, with uncertainty. "Why can't I simply fly us there? It would be much swifter, and we—I—could be back here, could be home again, within the week."

"Because." Jamie grunted as he heaved himself into the saddle, and she could see how even now his weakened right arm trembled from the exertion. "We will also need your magic to call out whatever monsters are lurking in their dark holes along the way, so we can protect whatever poor souls on whom they are now feeding." He raised his eyebrows. "Unless you find my presence so very loathsome that you are willing to leave them to their fates. After all, what are a few hundred more human lives worth anyway?"

She scowled at him. "You are so sure that they will be drawn to confront us, then?"

"To confront you, my lovely wife—without a doubt," he said with that unflappable cheeriness of his. "Your father did not lie to you all those years ago, Rozi, as I warned you after I tracked down your friend the dearg-dur. Your magic calls to theirs, and they will be drawn to you as hideous moths to such a pretty flame."

She huffed once in disdain, then without another word, swung herself into the saddle of the black gelding, gathering the reins in her gloved hands. "I can hardly contain my excitement."

Jamie nudged his gray mare forward, and the two horses trotted side by side down the road ahead. "Who knows," he said. "Perhaps we will even encounter my old friend the cú-sídhe along the way."

Rozlyn glanced at him, her mouth opening to tell him of what she had done on that rainy night a fortnight ago, then she snapped it closed and fixed her attention on the road ahead. "Maybe."

She turned and looked back one final time at the figures still standing at the base of her steps in the pale light of the morning sun, and as she raised her hand in a final, silent farewell, she saw light gray clouds gathered in the far northern corners of the sky, the subtle threat of a slow-brewing storm hovering on the horizon of her home. She swiveled around in the saddle, her heart clenching in his chest, and urged her horse forward after Jamie.

They were quiet for a long time, their horses trudging down the deserted stretch of road, the only sound the birds chirping in the few trees and the rustling of unseen animals in the undergrowth as they rode through the valley, away from the receding shadows of the Mhám Toirc mountains. They paused only when the midday sun reached its zenith in the pale-blue winter sky. Rozlyn perched on a mossy boulder by the edge of the river as she ate her lunch, while Jamie lay sprawled in the grass, his arms folded behind his head, drowsing in the sun.

She rose and nudged him with the toe of her boot. "Are you dead?"

A smile curved across his lips. "Don't sound so hopeful," he said without opening his eyes. "You need me, you know. You may have my power, but only I have the knowledge needed to defeat the monsters that are prowling toward you even as we speak."

"It's my power, and in that case, perhaps this would not be the most ideal time for a nap."

"I'm an invalid recuperating from a terrible wound. I need my rest."

"I believe that I told you exactly that before we left, and my opinion was ignored."

"Worried about me, are you, Rozi?"

She did not answer, just stared into the churning water of the river as it roared past them, winding away into other worlds that she had never even seen.

"You're in one of those moods again." He watched her as he stretched out like a cat in the grass. "Is it that time of the moon for you?"

She whirled, lips curling in outrage. "You bastard, how dare you assume that just because I am in no mood to fawn all over you, it must be because I am otherwise indisposed—"

"Wind your neck in, Rozi. I was simply trying to get a rise out of you."

Her teeth bared. "Oh, were you?"

"I have thirteen sisters, Rozi," he said, as though he were talking to a petulant child. "An unholy number of cousins and aunts and nieces to boot. Do you imagine that I do not know exactly how to most thoroughly distract a woman determined to brood?"

She whirled on her heel without deigning to respond and stalked away, ignoring his lopsided grin.

The afternoon was waning as they climbed out of the slopes of the vale of Inagh and circumvented the vast expanse of the Lough Conn. As the twilight whispered its low-pitched warning of impending night in her ear, they reached the northern regions of Connacht, where the hills of the valley grew steeper, less lush and green, and sharpened into slabs of mountainous rock that rose ominously into the sky until they seemed to touch the very tips of the white-gray clouds that clung to their apexes. Jamie slowed his silver mare to a stop, glancing at Rozlyn, who watched the looming peaks of the Sliabh Gamh with sharpened intensity. "Best wait until dawn to venture into this particular stretch of mountains."

She nodded as she studied the mist that slithered across the cliffs and crags of the colossal expanse of barren rock that waited so patiently, so menacingly before them. "Something is in there."

Jamie made a soft sound of agreement. "Let's wait until morning to find out what exactly."

They built a small fire, banked low to avoid the unwanted attention that its flames might attract, and she sank
down next to it, resting her chin in the cupped palms of
her hands, idly watching the dance of the fire. A tremulous
wisp of a memory snaked its way through her—the flames
leaping from the torches in a darkened mead hall to her
outstretched palms, a glorious crescendo of fury and fire.
"Jamie," she said, "you told me that the ice storm I once
teased you with—"

"Tortured me with, is what I believe you meant to say."

She ignored him. "That was part of your control over
the elementals, was it not? From when you were Midir?"

Jamie straightened from where he crouched next to his
saddlebag, rummaging through their stores of dried meat
and fruit. "Yes. Why?"

She continued to stare into the rhythmic weave of the
orange-and-red flames. "How does it work?"

He rocked back on his heels, his face tilted up to the dark
sky above. "It's hard to explain," he said at last. "It is like
when a brass key snaps into an ancient lock, and you hear
the click as it turns in the palm of your hand, and the door
creaks open and reveals a treasure trove of infinite wonders
you never dreamed existed."

"That's very pretty. Supremely unhelpful, but pretty."

"Fair enough. Think of it this way. I—you—can easily
command elements that are already in existence, in the
natural course of their progression. The ice storm, for instance. It cost you greatly, with the headaches and the level
of concentration needed, but it should not have. It should
have been as natural as breathing, a mere thought come to
life. You were honestly only able to do so even then because
the elements of winter were already whispering in the wind

around you, waiting to be called. Had it been the midsummer months, I imagine you would have been forced to settle for a particularly nasty heat wave."

Rozlyn considered this, a faint prickle of rightness in her fingers at his description. "And the fire in my father's hall? My head ached so terribly, but it worked. The fire obeyed me when I asked it to."

He glanced toward her, and she could tell he was wary now, that they were on dangerous ground, discussing that long-ago night of fury and heartbreak. "I would assume the torches helped—and the fact that those flames were the manifestation of your very real, very profound rage, which had been brewing inside you for well-nigh twenty years by that point."

She ignored the twinge in her chest at the gentleness in his voice. "Will I ever learn, truly, to summon the elementals, to bend the forces of nature to my will, as you could, without pain or repercussion?"

"I suppose that depends," he said, turning away from her again to resume his perusal of the contents of his saddlebag, "on how much more time you have left with which to master it."

A shiver of something very close to dread trickled down her spine. It was a timely reminder not to let down her guard, to be wary and watchful toward him, that they were enemies, each seeking the most prized possession of the other to claim as their own. They ate their meager dinner in silence under the stars and, as she swallowed her last bite of dried mutton, Rozlyn shivered in the winter cold that crept in around them with the deepening night. Jamie shuffled closer to her where she sat quivering by the fire. "Would you like me to keep you warm, a bhrèagha?"

Rozlyn glowered once before yanking her cloak up over her head to block out his bark of laughter, resting her head against the sap-soaked trunk of a pine tree as she tried to sleep.

She awoke with a start sometime later, the fire sizzled out to a mere handful of embers glowing orange and red, the night far too dark, with only a few glimmering stars and the sliver of the waxing crescent moon shining in the far-off distance. She sat up straighter, brushing at her dirty cloak, and saw Jamie standing by a tree across from her, his shoulders tense, staring toward the looming mountain range. "What is it?"

He did not answer for a moment, then jerked his chin toward some unseen presence in the distance. "The slúag," he said shortly. "I can hear them."

Rozlyn rose, frowning at the vaguely familiar name. "What are they?"

"They look like, sound like birds," he answered without turning to face her, his attention fixed on the far-off mountain peaks. "Great gray birds with molting feathers and the faces of human corpses. The ancient lore says that they are condemned souls, spirits of the damned too evil and depraved in this life to be allowed to enter into the otherworld of Magh Meall, so in their rage, they swoop about in the night from the far western peaks of the mountains, seeking the souls of the brokenhearted and the despairing to feed upon."

An icy chill that had nothing to do with the coldness of the winter night slid down her spine. "Why from the west?" she whispered.

"The borders of Magh Meall lie to the west. They cannot look upon its light, or they will shrivel and die, so they fly with their backs to the western sky, only emerging in the night or flying low through the undergrowth of the trees to avoid being burned by its blaze."

Rozlyn considered this, that icy grip of fear tightening around her spine. "You said that you can hear them. What, then, are you listening to? Their screams or screeching or—"

"Their songs," he said. "They call to the heartbroken fools of the world, whispering promises of happiness and contentment and the restoration of all their joys, right before they snatch them away to carry them into the air and drain the essence of their souls."

Rozlyn watched his stony face, devoid of all emotion. "What do they say to you?"

He didn't answer, and she hugged her cloak tighter around her. "Can I hear them?"

"Why would you want to?"

"Perhaps," she said, "I want to know if they would even bother to sing to me."

He looked at her then, his expression blank and unreadable. "Come here."

She edged closer to him, and he placed a steadying hand on the small of her back, his touch feather-light and unsure against her cloak, and before she could stop herself, she relented to it, that brief warmness, the faintest shadow of a memory of far more heated touches.

As soon as her eyes fluttered shut in the surge of that long-dormant ache, she heard it.

It was faint at first, just the whisper of a sweet, sad melody, only one voice to start, and then slowly, surely, one by one, more honey-warm purrs of harmony began to rise, a euphonic soaring of song. *Lovely, lonely girl*, they sang, and a sob rose in her chest at their words. *Why so sad, sweet girl? So alone, such a beautiful beast. No one sees you, lurking underneath*

your fangs and your claws and your scowls, you, the girl who can become the
sky and the stars.

Rozlyn began to shake from something far darker and
more ominous than the deep cold of the new winter night.

Why don't you smile, pretty girl? Someone might love you, as you have
always longed, if you did.

She was wrapped in a cocoon of mist and fog, dreaming
while awake, their beautiful melodies chiming in her ears
like a thousand silver bells of light.

Come home now, Beast of Connacht, and she was too far lost in
their song to hear the menace that bled through into their
voices. *Come home to us, and we will at last give you peace.*

Dimly, she could hear Jamie calling her name, could feel
him shaking her shoulders, could perceive the fading sounds
of his voice roaring at her from a great distance away—*wake*
up, wake up, Rozi, don't listen to them, come back to me—but she was
already gone, floating on the gentle breeze of their song,
humming promises of satisfaction and desire and belonging, and she opened her arms to welcome it, this dispersal
of the numbing sadness of never being seen, for so many
long years, an eternity of lives. She closed her eyes against
the rush of the icy wind, savoring freedom that she had never
truly known, and she flipped lazily to lie on her back as she
glided through the skies like starlight and rain.

A bhrèagha.

It was the faintest whisper of a wail, a strange yet familiar
voice, broken with sobs, with heart-wrenching, unbearable
pain, a remembered cry from some other life, from another
time, some shadow-man of the past, fallen to his knees as he
clutched, inexplicably, at a dark puddle of water pooled on
a white marble floor, and she suddenly wanted to see him,
this wrecked soul that had been so irrevocably shattered.

He was important to her, somehow, in some way, and she needed to see him.

She opened her eyes.

The world around her was howling with wind, the blackest night she had ever seen, the whip-thin branches of the fir and pine trees lashing her face in agonizing stripes of pain. She looked up, her hands flapping helplessly in the cold rush of the wind, and saw them—monstrous, gray-feathered creatures with inhuman faces with faintly human features—the twisted knot of where a nose used to be, blank pits of bone that used to be eyes, a jagged scar that stretched upward from a sharp bony chin. She screamed, but it vanished in a soundless echo on the wind as they whistled her through the trees to the doom lurking just ahead.

She tried again to scream, but even as her lips parted and her mouth stretched wide, no sound emerged, and the slúag that held her gave her a violent shake. She thrashed wildly in its taloned grip that sliced through the thick wool of her cloak and into the soft fleece of her doublet, but the monster held her fast, a squirming mouse caught in the talons of the hungry-eyed falcon.

She was going to die.

She remembered then, as though she could almost hear him murmuring in her ear—*the west, a bhrèagha, look to the west*—and she drew in a breath of icy wind. She threw all her might into her shifting, narrowing and tapering and constricting every drop of her power into the idea of the Beast, its raw power and rage. Like a match striking in the darkness, it stirred within her, an answering roar, and her limbs cracked and twisted in that blessedly familiar way. Then her own wings, darker than the night itself, burst from beneath her shoulders. The trees echoed with screams—not hers, but the shrieks of the slúag—as she roared in fury and snagged them, one, two, three monstrous birds fluttering helplessly against the bite of her claws into their molting flesh.

Rozlyn burst out of the trees in a thunderous crash as the slúag writhed and screamed, flying as swift as the mountain wind, arrowing her way toward the western skyline, the faint purple glow of the horizon glimmering just beyond the ridge. The slúag trapped in her unforgiving grasp twisted into unnatural shapes of terror and pain as the faint purple glow slid across their sluff of bone-gray feathers. She soared higher, her muscles straining with the exertion as they fought against her savage intensity, and then the light washed over them, its pale golden rays seeping into their monstrous pores. As one, they began shaking uncontrollably, writhing in pain under the cleansing light of the sunrise, choking on the vomit and bile pooling in their long-decayed throats.

She reached the pinnacle of the sky, and that luminous purple glow washed over them with renewed force, bathing them in the pure light of the waiting otherworld. The slúag slumped in her claws, their feathers drooping, and she watched as beneath her, their very limbs groaned as they molted, legs and talons and wings and heads falling from their thick, feathered bodies to crash to the ground beneath them.

Rozlyn loosened the grip of her claws, and they fell to the earth, silenced at last, the rotted remnants of evil and heartache that they had inflicted on so many lives, and she watched as they crashed into the craggy rocks of the mountains below, then turned her wings to the east and flew back to Jamie.

CHAPTER TWENTY-THREE

Midir watched from a distance, his heart pounding with ungodlike excitement, as the girl emerged among the jagged black rocks that scarred the otherwise flat white coastline.

She had come back again.

It was the third day in a row that he had watched for her, heedless of all other responsibilities and affairs, and now he at last allowed himself to relax at the sight of her youthful form making its way down to the beach. He reclined on his elbows in the warm sand, the sea breeze ruffling his long golden hair, his deep-purple cloak spread around him as he watched her skip through the hot white sand to the shore, her hands reaching up to her raven-black hair, pinned in an intricate coronet of glossy braids on the top of her head, pulling and tugging at it until it cascaded down about her shoulders.

His chest shuddered. She was even more beautiful than he had remembered.

He just needed to know her name, he promised himself as her gaze locked onto where he lounged on the beach
a little past where the high tide licked at the sand. She
frowned at the sight of him, and his pulse quickened, the
immortal folaíocht that flowed through his veins growing
hot and wild at the sight of her face. It was uncomfortable, unfitting his dignity as one of the immortal gods,
a member of the almighty Tuatha Dé Danann, to feel so
strongly for a mere mortal girl. He could almost hear his
brothers' scorn, their jeers, could almost hear his father's
heavy disapproval, that he should be so enamored by the
brief beauty of a human girl.

He would find out her name, he swore to himself, that
was all—he would learn who she was, this serious, unsmiling
beauty, and then he would be gone, content with the knowledge that she existed in his world, this wild creature of grace
and fire, and go back to the world in which he was supposed
to belong and to the wife who was promised to him.

Soon, he amended as he watched her stalking through
the sand toward him, her hands clenched at her sides as her
half-unpinned hair fell in loose curls about her face. He
had, after all, an eternity to spend in the arms of Fúamnach, under the stern eyes of his father and his kin. A few
days spent in the company of this girl, he promised himself, could hardly matter.

She halted just in front of where he lay, her bare feet
coated with specks of white sand, and he smiled even as
she frowned down at him. "Go away," she ordered without preamble.

He settled back onto the beach, folding his arms behind
his golden head, humming in enjoyment of the midsummer
sky. "You do not command me, my lady. No mortal does."

He heard her shift in the sand. "You are the Tuatha Dé Danann, then."

"One of them." He peered up at her, shading his eyes from the brilliance of the sun with his hand. "Are you now going to treat me with the respect that I so clearly deserve?"

"Respect is earned, not deserved, a dhia." She crossed her arms. "You have an infinite number of beaches on which to lounge in this realm, and the power to carry yourself to any of them forthwith. Go and leave me in peace to enjoy what little time is left to me here on the shore."

Midir sat up, shoulders tense. "Where are you going?"

She huffed. "I am promised to the high king of the northern mountains of Dubhais." He watched as she dug her toes into the sand, and her expression dimmed a little. "I am to be married at the end of this summer's season, and I shall live out the rest of my days in the gloom of his high stone walls and the cold of the sunless mountains, and never again see the sea."

"So do not marry him, then, if you are so disinclined to it."

She sneered. "My feelings," she said, "were not consulted."

"Och, an arranged marriage." He thought of Fúamnach, the hard lines of her bloodred mouth and her nails curving like talons over her long fingers, and his heart clenched again as he studied the girl in front of him. "So you do not love him, then."

She scoffed. "Eochu? That muscle-bound, brainless brute? Hardly. He has spoken but a dozen words to me since our betrothal, and at least half of those were indistinguishable grunts."

Midir made a wordless noise of disdain, then drummed his fingers against the sand as he watched her in silence. "You have not yet told me your name, my lady," he said at last.

"If you have not the wit to figure it out, then that is hardly my concern."

He barked with laughter. "Betrothed to the mighty king of the mountains of Dubhais, the daughter of the chieftain of Latharna—I know who you are, but not what to call you."

"Neither I you, a dhia, and so we are equal."

"A bargain, then," Midir suggested as he rose in a swift, fluid motion to tower over her. She peered up at him, her lips pressed tightly together. He took a slow step backward and smiled again, gentler this time, a silent encouragement. "If you cannot guess my name," he said, folding his arms across his chest, "then you will tell me your own and grant me one kiss before you run home to the arms of your betrothed, but if you do happen to stumble upon the truth of who I am, then I shall leave this beach, never to return, and shall leave you in peace for the rest of your days."

"You want to kiss me?"

"Most assuredly. You are without question the most beautiful maiden whom I have ever seen."

"Mortal maiden, you mean."

"I said what I said."

She glowered at him, her toes digging into the sand as she braced herself to bargain with the divinity in front of her. "My counteroffer. If I cannot guess your name, I will tell you mine, and then I will not kiss you, but I will agree to return to the beach tomorrow at this same time to try and guess again the truth of your name." Another defiant toss of her head. "However, if I do guess correctly, you will grant me one wish, whatever request I so desire, with whatever power you possess in your veins."

Midir's eyebrows raised, surprised. "Very well. We are agreed, although unless you wish to transform into a dog or a horse, or to have me manipulate the course of the seasons as they naturally so fall in the orderings of the universe, your options will be somewhat limited."

She considered this, her lips pursing in contemplation, and he eyed them with increasing interest. What would it be like, he wondered, to feel those stern lips curve against his own in a smile?

"Could you transform me?" she asked abruptly. "If I wished to be something other than myself—temporarily, you understand—could you do that?"

"Yes." He inclined his head. "But let us not be too hasty. First," he said with a shrug, "you must guess my name."

"I want a hint, a clue of some kind to help me guess."

Midir wagged a finger at her. "That was not part of our bargain."

"There are hundreds of you," she protested. "Gods and demigods and minor lords of the Tuatha Dé Danann. It is only fair that you give me a hint."

He considered, then bowed his head in acknowledgment. "You have me there. Very well. My power is lesser in scope than many of my kinsfolk, but it is of the most fundamental kind. My greatest gift," he said, "my most prevailing trait, is this: I can summon the elemental forces of nature to bend themselves to my will."

"You mean the rain and the wind?"

"Among other things, yes, but on a far more fundamental level than those alone."

"But—"

He raised a hand. "That is the only clue that you will get from me today, my lady." She was quiet for a long time as she considered, and he could almost hear her mind racing as it flew through all the known names of the many, many gods of Éire.

At last she frowned, straightening her shoulders as though preparing for her inevitable failure. "You are Lir," she said, even as her eyes glinted with uncertainty. "The great god of the sea."

Midir shouted with laughter. "Och, how he will scream with merriment when I tell him this tale. No, my lady, I am not so worthy as to command the depths of the sea. I am far, far less important than that, I fear." He crossed his arms, pleased at her failure. "Our bargain, then. Your name, if you please."

She scowled, and it thrilled him, the sight of her irritated face. "I want a different clue."

"Tomorrow you shall have it. For now," he said with a satisfied smile, "your name, my lady."

He held his breath as she remained silent, her jaw twitching in annoyance, until at last she sighed and ran her hands down the front of her gown, smoothing the pale green fabric as she spoke. "I am Étaín," she said reluctantly. "And I will return tomorrow to this same spot at this same time to continue to guess your name, as I will eventually do, because I will become something other than what I now seem to be." She lifted her chin and met his gaze unflinchingly, fearlessly. "I will be something greater, something more than what is planned for me to be."

Midir studied her, his amusement fading. He reached out slowly, tentatively, with infinite gentleness, and brushed a long strand of raven-black hair away from the curve of her cheek. "I would not wish to see you be anything other than what you are, bold, beautiful-souled Étaín," he said, and she shivered once as his palm came to rest against the skin of her cheek. "You are quite perfect as you are, a bhrèagha."

CHAPTER TWENTY-FOUR

"The peak of Cnoc na Loinge," Jamie said, pointing to the looming stretch of rock as their horses slowed to a stop. "The highest point of the Sliabh Gamh." His glance slid to her. "From there, you will be able to see the ocean, if you like."

Rozlyn's heart stuttered in her chest and her breath caught as the sudden image of green-blue waves, endlessly churning with white-frothed tips as they rolled in from the horizon, flashed unbidden through her brain.

The sea. She would again see the sea.

The black gelding underneath her whinnied softly, breaking her reverie, and she shook her head, frowning at herself for such a nonsensical thought. "I have never before seen the sea," she said, more to herself than to Jamie, who sat quiet and watchful on his mare beside her.

He rolled his shoulders restlessly. "Let's amend that, shall we? Fancy a climb?"

Five days had passed since Rozlyn had escaped the slúag

and returned, shaken and stained with blood, to Jamie, whom she found screaming her name as he raced through the trees. She had landed in a graceless crash before him, branches snapping and rocks shuddering as she collided with the ground and shifted in one trembling motion, and before she could protest, he was on his knees before her, his arms encircling her as he gasped for air, running his shaking hands down her wind-tossed braid, across her shoulders, down her arms, as though he could not reassure himself enough that she was here before, whole and unharmed.

She was, after all, she had remembered dimly, his most precious, his most vital pawn in this game he was playing against an unseen foe.

She had allowed herself the indulgence of burrowing her aching head in his throat, to breathe in that pine scent of his skin that she had loved so long ago.

They had stayed there for a long time, until the forest around them began to rustle with the stirrings of life, streaks of sunlight breaking their way through the heavy canopy of the overhanging trees, and she had at last pulled away from his arms. "Well," she had whispered. "I suppose that answers that question."

His worried eyes had searched her face. "What question?"

"Apparently, seeing how eager they were to steal it away from me, I do have a soul after all."

Jamie had laughed breathlessly as his hands fell away from her shoulders. "You scared me, Rozi. I'd appreciate it if you'd not dance with the devil again during our time together."

"I wasn't planning on dancing with you at any time."

He had laughed again and stood, extending his hand to her in a tender gesture, and she had refused to let herself consider how easy it had been to reach for it, entwining her fingers with his as he pulled her up.

She shook her head, dispelled the memory of his warm fingers entangling with her own, and studied the dreary gray cliff in front of them. "Climb it, if you like," she answered in response to his challenge. "I prefer to fly."

She leapt from her horse and shifted, transforming in an explosion of wing and fang and fur. She shot into the sky, soaring past the gray boulders of the mountainside and the sporadic splotches of grass and undergrowth that decorated its stony sides, until she broke over the uttermost peak of the cliff and hung in the air, her feathered wings flapping, as she stared at the sea.

She sank to the ground, prowling forward on her black paws, her tail twitching behind her. She reached the edge of the cliff and stood impossibly still, staring across the waves that rolled toward her, away on the distant horizon. Rozlyn shifted, a sudden longing to savor the gust of the sea breeze on her own skin racing through her, and she sank to her knees, tilting her head back as she relished the taste on her tongue of the salt air and brine-soaked mist.

It was, inexplicably, as though she had at long last come home.

It was a long while before she heard him as he scrambled up the cliff to where she knelt, silently watching the waves crashing into the rocks far below, frozen in awe, her black hair floating on the soft salt wind that blew across the cliff overlooking the surf of the sea. "Look," she whispered. "Look how beautiful." She sighed. "I have always longed to see it, dreamed of how it would be, yet somehow it is a thousand times more gorgeous than I ever imagined."

"You like it, then."

She turned to look at him, the lack of a question in his flat tone puzzling. He stared at her with an odd intensity, his dark hair ruffling in the breeze.

"Yes," she said, turning back to stare across the blue-green water, the crest and fall of the white-tipped waves as they crashed toward the rocky shores of the beach. "It is so magnificently unchained, so free, so—unbound."

Jamie stepped forward to stand next to where she still crouched on her knees on the stony cliff, his hands in his pockets as he studied the ocean stretching out beneath them. "So it is indeed."

It seemed as though hours had passed before she could manage to tear herself away, drawn as she was to the crash of the waves, and when she finally shifted to fly reluctantly back down the stony side of the cliff to their waiting horses, Jamie gripped tight in her retracted claws, it was all that she could do not to weep at the loss of its sweet sea breeze and the limitlessness of its beauty.

She was quiet and dull for a long while afterward as they rode down the slopes of the outermost ridges of the Sliabh Gamh, until hours later when Jamie reined in his horse and dismounted. "Dinnertime," he announced, and a faint twinge of affection, of gratitude, shot through her, that he was kind enough to avoid commenting on her obvious distraction. "I can't bear another night of dried strips of mutton. I believe I shall test the strength of my arm and shoot us a hare." He glanced at her, studying her abstracted expression. "Does that sound all right?"

She roused herself enough to look back at him. "Yes," she said, then once more sank away into herself, lost in this baffling fit of brooding that she could not seem to shake.

Rozlyn could feel him watching her as he walked away.

"Try and rest, a bhrèagha," she heard him say, his quiet voice laced with sympathy for this ache inside her heart, this hurt that she did not herself understand. "I'll be back soon."

He disappeared among the trees, and Rozlyn was alone.

All she could think of was the sea—its ceaseless buoyancy, the interminable roll of those cerulean waves, the never-ending stretch of its vastness. She craved the rough-sand texture of the shore on her bare ankles, the crash of the surf against her legs, and it was all that she could do to remain there among the shadowy trees, her head leaning against the rough bark of an oak tree, and not fly straight for where it still called to her, summoning her, so that she could bathe herself in its briny embrace—

Something snapped in the trees in front of her.

Awareness flitted across her skin—she was no longer alone.

There in front of her squatted a dark-furred rabbit with golden eyes, studying her intently, its gray nose twitching.

Barely daring to breathe, Rozlyn reached out her hand for her own bow where it lay next to her, the leather quiver filled with arrows, when the rabbit tilted its head as it watched her. Its furry haunches shook with what Rozlyn could have sworn, in a jolt of shock, was a fit of uncontrollable laughter.

It bounded away, and she thumped the back of her skull against the tree, cursing at herself that she had so foolishly let a potential dinner escape her, when she heard a rustle in the brush behind her. She whirled, and there he was—not a rabbit but a small boy with dark-brown hair and those same golden eyes, grinning at her with unearthly mischievousness.

Rozlyn stared at him wide-eyed, and he spoke in a high, teasing voice. "Hello, witch."

"Watch yourself, boy."

He laughed, the tinkling sound rebounding off the rocks in gleeful echoes. "Now, now," he said as he crept toward her on tiny feet. "Not so fast. I am no child, silly witch."

Rozlyn searched through her memories, the thousands of stories from her books, from the tales Jamie had told her so many times in those long months of their friendship, until it came to her, a half-remembered story of holly branches and an injured god and a naughty boy with golden eyes. "A púca," she cried.

"That is what the gods call my kind, indeed." He twinkled at her. "They hate us, you know, because we are so much cleverer than they, so much shrewder, for all their pomposity and self-importance." He leaned forward ever so slightly, a naughty conspirator. "They also despise to be reminded that we were once as they are, my sisters and brothers and I. All our monstrous selves were once kin to the Tuatha Dé Danann, before they exiled us, confined us to the sídhe, the other-realms, forever condemned to be neither of the earth nor apart from it." His head tilted to the side as he studied her. "You are like them, but not at all like them, witch."

"I am neither a god nor a witch, you little fool."

He laughed again. "Perhaps not, but there is no other word for what you are, so let me ask you this: Are you hungry, witch?"

Rozlyn eyed him, suspicious of the sudden non sequitur. "A little."

He smiled, and it was not to be trusted, a smile that beatific. "A token of my goodwill." He removed his hand from his pocket. "Eat."

He held out to her a cluster of blackberries, their glossy skin glimmering in the late afternoon sun, and her stomach grumbled at the sight of them. She hesitated, trying to recall any snippets of stories about the benevolence of the púcaí, and sensing her indecision, he smiled at her again, with innocence and razor-sharp incisors. "You have no way to know until you try me, witch. I can be friend or foe, and my feeling changes as the wind in the sky."

She looked him over once more, from the tips of his pointed ears to his dirt-brown toes, then reached out and plucked a single berry from the palm of his outstretched hand. "Know this," she said, in what she hoped to be an effectively menacing manner, if such a creature as the púca could even be truly menaced. "If this is poisoned"—she waved the glossy black fruit in front of him threateningly—"my last act on this earth will be to take on a form more monstrous than you ever could imagine, demon that you are, and rip your pretty eyes right out of your head."

He grinned at her, nonplussed. "Sister," he cried, "for so I consider you, shifter of shapes as you are. I give you my word that you will not suffer death at my hands."

She scowled, searching his words for a trap, a hoax or trick of any kind, and finding none, popped the berry in her mouth.

An explosion of flavor washed over her tongue, at first tangy and sweet with the ripeness of the fruit, but just as she hummed in pleasure, the taste shifted, turning to flakes of ash in her mouth. She gagged, spitting onto the ground in disgust as he fell back in the dirt on his back, clutching at his stomach and pounding the dirt with his heels as he shook with peals of laughter. "You brat," she said, fingers curling. "I swear by the harp—"

"Ah," he chanted, sitting up and wagging a gleeful finger at her. "Not so fast, sister. I promised that you should not suffer death, and see? You have not." He grinned again, teeth gleaming. "You have only tasted the flavor of it, and now you shall know how to recognize it when at last it comes for you in the night."

"Leave me alone, demon, before I lose my temper and shred you limb from limb."

"Not yet." He leapt lightly to his feet, tugging at the hem of his doublet as he skipped toward her. "First, I have a proposition for you."

"I'm not interested."

He continued, unperturbed. "I will make a bargain with you, sister." He rocked back and forth on his heels, hands on his hips. "You lack understanding, you see, of this vast world of yours, and I hold its mysteries locked away in my chest as greedily as the dragons lurking underneath the barren isles of the northern seas hoard their gold. My greatest treasure, you see, is secrets, the whispered riddles that the earth-mother hummed to me in my cradle a thousand years ago." A stirring of interest, of excitement built inside her, but she kept her face neutral and bland as he went on. "Such mysteries are my birthright, little witch, and I only part with them very rarely, indeed. But I will make a deal with you, sister shaper. You ride on my back through the hills without falling, and I shall whisper to you the answer to whatever question you ask of me."

Rozlyn studied him, a contemptuous retort hovering on her lips, but something deep within her stopped her. The mysteries of the earth-mother. It was all well and good to have power, to be able to take the shape of a terrible Beast, to command the rains and speak the language of the trees, but this—this was true power, the knowing of such hidden depths.

It was a fool who made a bargain with such a creature as the púca, yet still she hesitated.

"Sister, sister," he said coaxingly as she wavered, "come now. I have proven that I mean you no harm, merely to give you an understanding of things that you do not yet know. You have never died, yet now you have tasted its flavor in your mouth so that you might recognize it when it comes for you on some distant dawn. I have already helped you, sister, and I wish to help you now." His eyes gleamed. "Just a little ride, and then imagine what wonders I will unlock for you."

A thrill rushed down her spine. A game, she thought. He wanted to play a game.

It had been a while since she had felt this, the exhilaration and the rush of a well-matched game, not since she had conceded her king and turned her back on the board that Jamie had so carefully staged. She hadn't felt that yearning since, that burning desire to match her wits against another's, to strategize and plot, to force moves and sacrifice rooks, to trade piece for piece, swap blows with another, to feel the flood of adrenaline coursing through her veins in that inevitable moment when her opponent raised their eyes to hers and knew she had them pinned.

But she was yearning now, aching to play.

She stood, her fingers trembling. "One ride," she said, "and then you will answer whatever question I ask of you. No jokes, no puzzles, no cryptic riddles or incoherent jibes. You will answer me right away, straightforward and honest, and then our bargain will end."

He bowed at the waist. "So we are agreed, then, sister."

The púca whirled and was gone, disappearing into the trees, and Rozlyn turned and was searching for the dark-haired figure when a black-skinned stallion burst from the woods and wheeled about her in tight circles, nostrils flaring and golden eyes blazing. Their own horses, grazing placidly nearby only a moment before, reared up on their hind legs in alarm, whinnying at the sight of this unearthly steed, then fell silent and still, their twitching nostrils the only outward sign of their discontent.

The golden-eyed stallion inclined its head in a silent invitation at Rozlyn, and she hissed between her teeth when she saw no saddle, no bridle—only a sleek black back and glossy mane for her to grasp. "Naughty boy," she murmured, then slid her hands along its powerful shoulders, gripped its mane, and threw herself onto its back.

She shrieked as it shot away, impossibly fast, the wind whipping through her hair, and her teeth chattered from the force of its hooves pounding on the ground beneath them. She slipped to the side on his slick back, and she clutched at his sleek mane, clinging to him, bracing herself against the powerful muscles straining in his neck.

She heard him snuffle to himself in what she could have sworn was a mocking laugh. Then he jolted to a halt, his hooves skidding along the flat shale rocks scattered across the ground. Rozlyn gasped as she almost flew over his head at the suddenness of his stop, and without warning, he bucked and thrust his broad back into the air. Rozlyn's teeth dug into her bottom lip as she bit down, struggling not to scream at the blinding pain racing through her spine as her neck snapped back and forth.

The copper taste of blood filled her mouth, and her panic turned to rage.

She would not lose to him, this malicious, clever, little monster.

Rozlyn raised her hand and shifted.

The púca shrieked, collapsing under the sudden weight of the Beast, and his knees buckled, the full girth and bulk of her transformed body bearing him to the ground as he lay pinioned beneath her, her tail thrashing in triumph.

He squirmed, whimpering softly, a wordless concession, and she rolled away, shifting as she did. She stumbled to her feet with a muffled groan at the ache in her bones from his wild ride, even as he groaned in the dirt, boyish and slim once again. She pressed a hand to her lower back and winced, then looked up to see him watching her. He wheezed a laugh. "I told you, witch," he panted. "Truly you are my sister in all things."

She scowled at him where he lay chuckling on the ground. "We could not be more different, you little demon."

He sat up, wiping the sweat from his brow with the back of his hand. "You are wrong, sister. Just because you do not show the joy that you take from your art does not mean that you do not embrace it." He grinned at her. "You are the mother of all monsters, little witch, and I am their uncle who teaches your children naughty words and sneaks them treats at bedtime."

Rozlyn huffed and folded her arms across his chest. "I have no idea what that is supposed to mean."

"One day you will."

It was no use trying to decipher his riddles, trying to make sense of the foolishness of his ciphers. "You still owe me an answer."

He stood up, still giggling, brushing the dirt and leaves off his pants. "Ask away, sister-witch."

She pondered for a long moment. "If I give up this power to him—" She stopped, her cheeks flushing to hear the vulnerability revealed by her question, laid bare for him to see. "What will then happen to me?"

The golden eyes of the púca dimmed. "If you cede this

power of yours back into the control of Midir, son of the Dagda the just," he said, "then Rozlyn Ó Conchúir will cease to exist, and fade into the ether as though she had never been born."

Rozlyn nodded even as the leaden weight of her despair settled in the pit of her stomach, and the púca backed away into the trees. "It was lovely to meet you, after all these long years," he said, a twinkle of his merriment returning to his face. "It is good to no longer be alone." She looked up sharply to where he lingered at the edge of the woods, the shadows dancing across his dark face. He winked. "Live well and die happy, little sister." Without a sound, he disappeared into the trees, leaving Rozlyn again alone.

CHAPTER TWENTY-FIVE

Étaín truly was a beast.

Engaged to another man—albeit one whom she did not love nor wish to marry, but engaged nonetheless—and she had fallen madly, hopelessly in love with this nameless, light-hearted, golden-haired god beside her.

It was irrelevant, she told herself. He was a god, and she was a mortal maiden, and this would one day be a bittersweet memory with which she would enchant her grandchildren when she was old and gray in her husband's cold, stony castle, while he—the immortal object of her affections—still splashed in the surf under the summer sun, forever golden and eternally young.

"Three weeks," her god said as they waded through the crash of the surf, the foamy water lapping at his knees and soaking the hems of his breeches. "Three weeks, and you have not yet guessed my name, a bhrèagha. I must confess to being rather hurt. Am I so insignificant in the stories of mortals that you cannot even venture to guess at my identity?"

"I would imagine," Étaín replied, the hem of her light pink gown swinging carelessly in her hand as she walked beside him, "that is more of a reflection on how very dull of a god you are rather than on the merit of our stories."

The god tilted his head back to warm his face in the sun. "Fair enough," he conceded. "But I find that I am relatively unconcerned with having my name immortalized in the stories of your kind. I will surely outlive any record of their tellings anyway."

"Such presumption. I hear that the Tuatha Dé Danann are just as susceptible to an arrow in the throat or a sword in the gullet as any mortal, and you do seem to enjoy your wars, as you fight in them with great frequency."

"Not at all. We despise war, ugly, brutal thing that it is." He paused. "All except for one of my uncles, that is. Neit does rather enjoy it." The god grinned down at her, as golden and glorious as the sun itself high above in the summer sky. "I am not him either, in case you were wondering."

"The god of war," she mused, squinting against the sun reflecting off the blue-green waves. "I did not bother guessing him. It did not seem to suit you."

"I shall, of course, take that as a compliment rather than a veiled insult to my virility." He huffed once, a soft sound of amusement. "He is not so bad, Neit. He has a kind heart, despite his rather insatiable battle-lust. He saved my life once."

Étaín looked at him curiously. "How?"

He sighed. "During the great Battle of Moytura, in the war against the Fomorians, centuries ago. I had been wounded in the knee and could not walk. I was quite literally dragging myself through the mud, through the gore of my fallen friends and family, when the wolves that prowl the fields of battle to feast on the injured and the dying found me. They lunged at me and would surely have killed me as I lay there, too weak to defend myself against the onslaught of their teeth. My uncle saw me and broke away from where he was fighting three giants at once and soared into the wolves' midst to carry me to safety." He broke off, distant from the memory. "Of course, he returned to the battle immediately, warmongering, bloodthirsty god that he was, but the giants had gathered their strength while he had exhausted his own in saving me, and they drove three spears through his gut almost as soon as he reentered the fray."

She gasped. "He died?"

"Briefly. He was saved by the Mórrígan. She healed his wounds even as she healed my father's, but because he had already died, his soul floating in the air above the shell of his body, my uncle was never again the same, only a vague, half-formed shadow of his former self. He still fights with as much ferocity as he did before, but when he has no sword in his hand or enemy to slaughter, he is less than he was. Diminished, somehow."

Étaín was quiet for a moment. "I'm sorry," she said at last. "You must feel terribly guilty."

"I do a bit," her god said, "but not enough that I wish he had left me to die. Being devoured alive by wolves is a terribly nasty way to go, so I hear."

Before she could answer, his spine snapped into an impossibly rigid line, and his body flooded with tension as he scanned the horizon. "What's wrong?"

"I must hide you, a bhrèagha," he said, and fear trickled through her at how hard, how ice-cold his voice had become. "I must hide you right now. Do you trust me?"

Étaín stared at him. "I—"

"Do you trust me?" he repeated, his hand encircling her forearm in a tight, demanding grip.

She swallowed then nodded once, and he raised his other hand and snapped his fingers. She felt herself shrinking and folding in upon herself, her limbs and fingers and hair dwindling into spindly legs and gauzy wings and razor-thin antennae, and then she was flitting through the air, hovering before him. "Stay close," he whispered. "Do not leave."

She could see the reflection of her strange new form shining in his eyes.

A dragonfly. He had turned her into a dragonfly with a mere flick of his fingers, so easily, as though it cost him but a mere thought, and then his will was made whole.

She had no time to wonder at the awfulness of such power, because the air around them shuddered, and the sand split into pieces right in front of where he still stood in the surf, and from the earth rose a tall, sinuous form with flaming orange eyes and midnight-black hair.

Étaín studied her in fascination, this tiger prowling within a woman's body.

The tigress stepped forward, and the sand closed back up behind her seamlessly, as though it had never parted. "Midir, my love," she sung out, "I have missed you in our bed these past few weeks. Is this where you have been hiding, then, from the warmth of my embrace?" She smiled, a calculating smirk. "Surely it was not too terrible for you. I seem to recall you made noises of great appreciation for some of my more delicious tricks."

Étaín hovered nearby, watching with shock as he—Midir—folded his arms across his chest, seemingly bored as he surveyed the tiger-woman. "Fúamnach," he drawled, his golden hair shimmering in the light of the sun as it fell in waves over his shoulders. "How lovely to see you. And so unexpectedly too."

She smirked again, a cruel twist of her crimson lips. "My betrothed has forsaken my arms for nearly a month now. I deemed it wise to hunt him down and see what exactly has been keeping his attentions elsewhere." Her gaze roved across the shoreline and the waves, lingering for the briefest moment on Étaín as she drifted through the salt air near Midir's sleek blond head, her wings and heart beating in a furious rhythm. "I must say that I am unimpressed, my love. I would have thought that I would find you cocooned within a harem of beautiful women, surrounded by barrels of the richest mead that Éire has to offer, and here you are, taking a leisurely stroll on the beach." Her nostrils flared. "How very dull of you."

He shrugged. "I had a hankering for some time spent by the sea, I'm afraid." He smiled, and it, this cold curl of his lips, was nothing like the smile that she had come to know, warm and open. "Nothing more."

She studied him, her dark ringlets unfurling in the shimmering heat of the sun, then lifted her lips in a sneer. "Take all the time you need, a fhir chéile," she hissed.

"Soon-to-be husband," he corrected. "Not yet."

She laughed, a humorless sound. "Soon enough, my love. Your father is quite insistent." Her lips were a cruel slash of crimson fire. "Imagine how happy he will be to see peace restored between our peoples."

Midir said nothing, only stared at her in an expression of infinite boredom, and she sniffed and swirled her dark-gray skirt around herself in a fit of irritability. "Return to my bed tonight, my love," she ordered. "Or your father will hear of your neglect, and no doubt have some angry words for his youngest, most unillustrious son."

Before he could answer, the tigress slashed her hand through the air and spoke a long string of garbled words in a strange guttural tongue, and the sand split beneath her feet anew. She vanished from sight, the ground shuddering as it swallowed her whole, even as it mended the jagged breach in the white sand as quickly as it had first appeared.

She watched as Midir bowed his head, then looked at where Étaín still flitted nearby, an incandescent blur of gauzy wings and blue-green skin, then snapped his fingers. She tumbled to the sand, coughing and sputtering as her hands and her legs and her neck lengthened and softened into their former shape, her hair cascading in a waterfall of ink-black hair around her heaving shoulders.

She sprang up even as she choked down the slight tang of nausea that followed her transformation. "You are engaged."

"So," he said, a strange look on his face, "are you, I might remind you."

Étaín threw her head back, stung. "Unhappily so! Begrudgingly engaged to a man whom I do not love and did not choose. It was forced upon me."

"Do you imagine that my situation is so different from your own?"

She shoved at his shoulders in a sudden burst of anger. "You are a prince of the Court of Shádach, the son of the Dagda himself, king of the Tuatha Dé Danann, and here you are, dallying behind your betrothed's back!"

"I am not dallying with you. Do not be so dramatic."

"You, an immortal god, are *dallying* with an unsuspecting mortal girl. Do not compare our circumstances."

Midir threw out his hands in frustration. "Do you think that because I am a god I can do as I please, that I can choose where I so desire? I am bound by the same obligations as you yourself are."

Étaín scoffed. "You have no idea what bonds I endure."

"Believe what you like." His eyes were swirling with angry storm clouds, thundering to break free. "There is little difference between us, Étaín, save that of our mortalities. This magic of mine does not mean that I am any less powerless than you."

"That is an excuse," she spat at him. "An excuse for you to justify your dalliance with a foolish mortal girl who cannot even begin to comprehend the infiniteness of your nature."

"On that," he said, "we can agree. You most assuredly are a fool."

She glared at him, her black hair whipping about her face in the sea breeze. Without another word, she turned and stormed away down the beach, leaving him standing in the surf, staring after her. She stomped up the narrow path that led to her father's castle hidden behind the hills that overlooked the shore and disappeared without a backward glance.

It was for the best, she thought, stomach churning and eyes itching with unshed tears as she stumbled back to her father's house. He was a god, and she was a girl—a fool, just as he had said. Any bond that might have been forming between them, whatever shaky thread of affection and admiration that might have existed in their shared smiles and lingering looks and brushing fingertips as they walked along the beach—a bond like that would inevitably be broken, she assured herself as she fled into her room that night, resting her forehead against the rough wood of her door, tears sliding down her cheeks.

The gods did not marry mortal girls, and if they did, tragedy always ensued.

Everyone knew that.

CHAPTER TWENTY-SIX

"It's so beautiful."

Rozlyn sat astride her mare, staring in awe at the towering waterfall. "The Devil's Chimney," Jamie informed her. "That's how it's known here in Bréifne. And that means," he added, "we are beyond the border region of Connacht. Congratulations, Rozi. You are officially seeing the world."

Rozlyn almost smiled.

Instead, she forced her lips into their usual severe line and raised her eyebrows at Jamie. "Why the dour name?"

Jamie shrugged. "Too many tales of local lads drowning in its depths. The residents of the surrounding region whisper that the devil prowls about its rocky ridges, shoving unsuspecting youths from the ledges, and thus they fall to their doom." A sly grin. "I would imagine it's far more likely that they stagger up here while deep in their cups and drunkenly slip over the edge."

"You needn't sound so gleeful about it."

"At least they die happy, Rozi. There are far worse deaths than to drown in one of the most beauteous wonders of the western world with a mead-addled brain."

"Spoken like a true man of Éire."

Jamie barked with laughter. "What can I say—the last three centuries of mortality have rubbed off on me a bit." He surveyed the beauty of the waterfall before them, dark head tipped back, the golden warmth of the sun playing across his well-formed features. "It is not so bad, this brief, beautiful existence you lead."

"It is not so beautiful for some."

"Nor for me either. I spent many dark years wallowing deep in my rage and grief and self-loathing. But here I am, on my way home with my lovely wife by my side, prepared to free my family and restore the realm to its former state of peace and prosperity." He grinned at her. "A truly inspiring tale of endurance, if I do say so myself."

She huffed, urging her horse onward with a swift nudge of her heels, and Jamie idled after her, the reins loose in his gloved hands. "I am just glad," Jamie said sourly, "that we have no need to journey south to the plains of Osraige." He shuddered. "Once in my long lifetime is more than enough from me."

Rozlyn looked at him as they began the steep climb up the narrow dirt path that wound its way alongside the falls. "What is in Osraige?"

"More miserable wolves, that's what. One day, when I have my power again—" He cleared his throat when he saw the tension that snapped through Rozlyn's spine. The presumption of it, she thought. The arrogance. "The first thing that I shall do is rid my homeland of those nasty beasts. We would be far better without them."

Her fingers trembled with resentment at his words, as though it were a foregone conclusion that she would cede this power to him at the end of their journey.

It was *hers*. She had earned it, fought for it with blood and tears, and she would not give it up so easily.

She forced herself to ignore the anxiety, the anger suddenly surging through her. "What do you mean, the wolves in Osraige?" she asked instead.

"Man-wolves." Her eyes widened in genuine surprise at that. "Although they consider themselves blessed, daft dogs that they are, the leaders of the Ossirians are cursed to take the form of wolves in times of war and famine. Their human bodies grow cold and still, as though they were corpses, while their souls fly from their bodies to infiltrate the minds of wolves. Thus, they hunt their enemies and their prey in that unnatural form, possessing both supernatural strength and cunning. They are fearless warriors, and few escape their wrath."

A sudden stab of envy for these half-human, half-beast creatures coursed through her, that they refused to be victims, but weaponized their monstrosities against those who would subjugate them.

"The only way to defeat them," Jamie continued, "is to find where they have hidden their human bodies, and either stab them through the heart with a blade made of silver, or—the less violent option—remove the human corpse from where they left it and hide it away so that when the soul of the Ossirian leaves its wolven host, it cannot find its human half. If that happens, it will be forced to wander throughout the world in its incorporeal form until its human body shrivels away into dust."

"That's the less violent option?"

"Less violent, yes, but far crueler." Jamie sighed. "They

are not so bad, I suppose. They are simply striving to do as we all are, to defend and protect what is most precious to them. Who am I to blame them for seizing whatever chance they may have of best doing so, regardless of how distasteful it may be?"

Rozlyn stared into the distance, the cool caress of the wind lifting her hair gently from her shoulders and swirling it about her face. "I should like to see them."

"They are likely long gone from this world." Jamie shrugged, a little sadly, despite his earlier distaste. "Whatever magic fueled their transformations was lost when my kin were locked away below the earth. There is little to be found of it now in Éire—magic and wonder. Sad, when once it was nothing but, back when I first knew it."

"There will always be magic to be found in Éire," Rozlyn said, lifting her hand to study the seemingly innocuous tips of her fingers—seemingly so frail and powerless, yet could set castles aflame and conjure storms and summon trees from the nothingness of the earth. "If one knows where to look."

Jamie's melancholic expression lightened at that, his face growing soft and fond as he watched her, and she looked away, a faint flush burning high on her cheeks. "Still," she said. "I would like to go to Osraige, and Bréifne, and beyond. I have seen so little of the world, for all my power. Locked in a tower, hidden away in the vale. I have always been bound to some small corner, away from the rest of the world." Her fingers curled. "I have only ever wished to be free, and I never can be."

"Save the gods," he said, "and restore the balance in the world, then you will be free. I swear to you. Whatever you desire, you will have."

"I don't know what I desire," she said, so quietly that she

wasn't sure he even heard her over the thrum of the water and the low whistle of the wind.

Peace, perhaps—the steady calm of a quiet and easy life, sure, but more than that. Peace of mind, the ease of a clear and unburdened conscience, free from fear of both the ghosts of the past and the secrets of the future. Perhaps he was right, that once it was done, she would at last know what it meant to lie down in the deep quiet of the night and slip into sleep unplagued by the thought of all the souls she could not remember dooming to die a horrible death. Perhaps she could be free of that, and soon. She said nothing else, however, as her horse climbed the steep path by the falls, letting the mist from its thundering waters wash her face clean of her doubts.

They camped that evening on the opposite side of the cliffs of the falls, and as she rolled her meager bedding onto the ground, Jamie pointed to the distant edge of a thick line of trees. "The border of Ulaid," he said. "I am almost home, Rozi."

She ignored the pang in her chest and flopped down on her makeshift bed, grimacing at the soreness in her body from a fortnight of sleeping on the hard earth. "If there is an actual bed anywhere within its vicinity, then the sooner, the better."

He grinned, sly and teasing. "That most certainly can be arranged."

She stuck her tongue out at him, a childish gesture but immensely satisfying, and he smirked and sauntered off into the woods to hunt their dinner, swinging his bow in his hand.

As soon as he disappeared into the trees, she sat up, and reaching into her pocket, withdrew the rowan branches she

kept tucked away inside. Steeling herself for the now-familiar foulness of the bitter herb, she chewed on the end of the
stalk, gagging on the acrid tang. She forced herself to swallow it down, letting the restorative juices roll through her.

She carefully returned her precious stash of herbs to the
safety of her pocket and swallowed the lump in her throat.
She should tell him the truth of her triumph, the secret to
her mastering her power. She wasn't sure why she felt compelled to keep it hidden from him, this secret antidote to
her wildness, but something whispered to her that it was
sacred somehow, this gift of control, of power that Galena
had given to her, not him, and that if he wished to know
the secret to her mastery of his magic, then he would have
to earn it, as she had earned it through the long days and
endless nights of sweat and blood and tears.

Rozlyn flopped back down on her blankets and lay on
her back for a long while, arms crossed behind her head,
watching dark clouds full of rain begin to roll in from the
southwestern sky, and she sighed, resigning herself to another long night huddled beneath a stony ledge in a vain
attempt to keep dry.

"Such a sad sound from such a pretty lady."

Rozlyn shot up, her fingers flexing, ready to shift and to
spring at the unknown threat, when she saw him.

He was tall and fair-skinned, with a wealth of crimson locks that rained down across his brow and his cheeks,
dressed in a gorgeously crafted doublet of the finest silk
and dark linen breeches. He was leaning against the smooth
trunk of a birch tree, and her knees turned strangely wobbly
at the sight of his beauty. He raised a hand and perched a
clay pipe in his sensual lips, still smiling at her as he sucked
on the pipe's broad lip.

"Hello, pretty lady," he repeated, and his words ran like silver through her blood, as a rush of images began to bombard her—a wide mattress with soft silk sheets, wildly mussed and entangled about a pair of muscular legs, a broad chest sprinkled with auburn hair, powerful hands that gripped her bare waist as she threw back her head and moaned—

She jolted as he spoke again, his words blurry in her ears. "What?"

He smiled knowingly at her. "I asked, are you all alone, pretty lady?"

"Yes," she said, her tongue fumbling stupidly over such a simple word, and of course she was alone, she was always alone, she would always be alone—

"That's so sad, sweet girl," he murmured, and she jerked awake again, unaware that she had spoken aloud. "The weather is turning quite nasty, you know. Why don't you come along with me to my home and rest there until the storm has passed?"

She nodded, an idiotic puppet bobbing her head. "Of course."

"Good girl," he crooned, the pipe still hanging between those luscious lips. "Such a sweet, pretty lady. You'll do just as I ask, won't you, my sweet?"

"Yes," she breathed. "Anything."

His dark eyes gleamed. "Anything?"

She nodded, her breaths coming quick and ragged, and another myriad of vivid images battered through her skull. She was sprawled on the mattress, her arms stretched above her head, fingers clutching the cold iron bars of the bed frame, as she sobbed in an ecstasy of delight as his clever, silver-soft tongue curved around the most sensitive areas of her bared flesh, and she shook and trembled at the dark sensation of his fingers brushing against her thighs, nudging them farther and farther apart, and she let them fall open with a blissful moan—

He laughed, a low, evil sound, and her eyes opened dizzily to find him standing in front of her, his hands stroking her face with the pipe still perched in his lips—unlit, she noticed, how odd to smoke a pipe with no flame inside it. "Well, we'd best be hurrying along, then," and his mouth parted on a cruel, lustful sigh. "You seem a bit eager."

He slid his hand down her arm sensually, a silent promise of the delights to come, and Rozlyn moaned again at the pressure from his fingers caressing the downy fleece of her doublet, and he grinned. "Oh, you are going to be a treasure, pretty lady," he crooned. "I shall keep you for at least a month or two."

She nodded again, her tongue too swollen with desire to answer, her brain addled with the fog of unslaked lust, and she began to follow him with unthinking obedience, placid as a broken-eyed doll, as he led her away toward the darkening shadows of the trees beyond the falls. He eyed her for a moment, then shoved her against a nearby tree. "Perhaps a quick taste," he murmured to himself, his hands reaching for the buckle of his breeches. "The rain won't arrive for a little while yet." He jerked his chin at her, the pipe bobbing in his lips as his dark-red curls danced with the motion. "Undo your blouse."

Unbidden, her hands moved toward the fastenings of her doublet, and his tongue licked hungrily as he saw a glimpse of her skin appear at the edge of her shirt, and he lurched forward, fingers greedy. Even as his hands reached for her waist, there was a shout from across the glen, and he lunged away, growling with irritation. Rozlyn stared at him patiently, a docile plaything, waiting for his touch, when through the haze that clouded her vision, she saw his face pale with fear as he turned and ran into the trees.

She looked around and through sluggish blinks saw Jamie in a cloud of smoke, wielding two smoldering branches in both of his hands as he stormed toward her. Once the strange man with the pipe had vanished, Jamie dropped the branches and rushed for her, seizing her face in his shaking hands. "Rozi," he choked. "Rozi, are you all right? Did he hurt you? Did he—" Jamie's voice broke off, his face white with rage at whatever dull desire he saw still lingering in her eyes. "I will kill him; I will kill that fairy—"

Rozlyn shook her head slowly, trying to clear the haze that hovered around her brain. "Fairy? What fairy?"

Jamie did not answer, but wrapped his arms around her, a terrified embrace, and pulled her into his chest. She closed her eyes, moored in a bay of shaky tranquility by the faint scent of cedar, listening to the hammering rhythm of his racing heart. "Never mind that now, a bhrèagha. Just stay with me. It's all right now. I've got you."

She stood still, the fog receding, and her hands began to tremble as her awareness came flooding back. "Jamie," she whispered. "What was that?"

She felt him swallow as he bent his head to place his cheek against hers. "The gean-cánach," he said, and she shuddered to hear that vicious snarl of loathing. "One of the nastiest, most depraved creatures of the sídhe. He and his ilk can't stand smoke. They fear it, for whatever reason. They wander the land seducing young girls with their arts, through their powers of persuasion and manipulation, making them bed slaves for a time, until those foul fairies grow bored and discard their victims without a second thought." He swallowed again, and she could feel the rage still coursing through him. "But they are never the same afterward, those poor enchanted girls, blinded as they are by lust and desire. After they are abandoned, they roam the woods searching for him, until they are finally driven mad by their unrequited lust and die, usually at their own hands."

Her fear subsided, and an answering wrath exploded within her, a dark and terrible fire, thirsting for blood. "I saw myself," she said, "in his bed. He put his hands on me, in my head, made me believe that I wanted it. But I didn't," she whispered, tears spilling down her cheeks. "I didn't."

Jamie's expression was as hard as steel when he pulled away from her, his face tight with fury. "Stay here," he ordered, pulling out an arrow and nocking it to his bow. "I'll be back. Just stay here and don't move."

"Where are you going?"

"I'm going to find that twisted, nasty creature and put an arrow through his brain."

"No." He stopped and turned back toward her, waiting for her to continue. She straightened her shoulders and wiped at her tears with a trembling hand. "I'll do it."

Jamie looked at her intently. "Are you certain?"

"He didn't touch you," she said, her cheeks flush-stained from the hot rush of her tears. "He didn't put his hands on your body, violate *you* with his sick, twisted magic. He did it to me, and only the gods know how many other poor girls, and for their sake and mine, I will make him pay."

His face ignited, a dark, vengeful fire, but his only answer was to lower his bow to his side, the taut string going loose and lax in his hands. "Then go and get him."

Rozlyn stared back for a brief moment, and that thread of understanding, of awareness, went taut between them. Then she raised her hand and shifted. She lowered her lupine head to the tree on which he had leaned, and sniffed, the faint, acrid scent of sweat and sex and corruption rankling in her nose. Even as the tears still shimmered on her shaggy cheeks, with a quick, powerful thrust of her hind legs, she shot into the sky and inhaled the cloud-heavy air, intent on tracking his loathsome scent before the rains fell and washed it away.

There. She caught the faintest whiff of rank sweat and arousal on the breeze below, and she tilted her wings and dove for the earth, a silent plunge toward the monster below.

He was loping through the trees, his useless pipe still hanging from his lips, when she slammed into his back and sent him careening to the ground, the pipe skittering across the blood-splattered rocks.

He whirled with preternatural speed to face her, his gorgeous face distorted with rage and blood, and she saw with grim satisfaction that his two front teeth had been jarred loose from his jawline by the force of her blow. He snarled, and she snarled right back, her jowls parting to reveal the glint of her fangs.

She focused all her power into a single, slight shift, willing her body to bend to her will and hers alone, and the lupine snout and hirsute face of the Beast twisted and shrank until her own countenance, pale and vengeful as a queen, appeared atop the winged Beast. "Not so pretty now, am I?"

The gean-cánach yelped, but before he could turn to flee, she leapt, digging her claws into his handsome features, smooth lips and sharply honed jaw, ripping at the elegance of his skin, scalping the locks of red curls from his head, until nothing remained of that devastatingly beautiful face but a grinning skull, the caricature of the gorgeous predator he once had been, now the ugly remnants of her rightful prey.

She stepped away from the carcass and pursed her human lips, flapping her feathered black wings in contempt, then spat once on his corpse before she rose into the air and flew away, leaving him behind to whatever scavenging beasts so chose to feed upon his rotting flesh.

An hour after she had wept in Jamie's arms, she landed in front of him with a resounding crash, her blue-black fur splattered with blood and tangled locks of crimson hair. He watched as she shifted, then threw back her hair in a gesture of unmitigated pride. "I am no one's prey."

Jamie grinned, a savage sight, then stepped forward and brushed a stray lock of hair behind her ear. "Welcome back, my brave brèagha." He leaned in and pressed the barest hint of a kiss against her brow. "Dinner's ready."

CHAPTER TWENTY-SEVEN

Étaín had not spoken to him in two weeks.

Midir watched her each day as she slipped down to the edge of the sea, eyes downcast. It hurt him more than he liked to admit, this clear refusal to so much as scan the shoreline for a hint of his presence. He accepted it, even while her evasion of him tore at his heart, and he stayed hidden away among the rocks and the tall grass of the sand-banks, once as a crab, then a gull, and even as a clump of tangled kelp that brushed against her ankle.

He stood by as she grew paler and sadder, until one day as he watched from beneath the murky waves of the low-tide surf, shivering inside the scales of a blue-skinned bass, he saw her sink to her knees in the sand and weep as he had never before seen her weep, silent tears streaming down her cheeks to mingle with the ocean brine that surged around her on the shore.

Midir could bear it no longer, and shifted, rising from the sea in one fluid motion, his shadow falling across where she knelt in the sand. "Étaín," he whispered, drops of salt-water slipping down his face. She raised her face to his, red-rimmed eyes and swollen nose and tears still glistening on her cheeks. "Tell me what I can do to make you smile. I cannot bear to see you so sad."

She shook her head, refusing to speak, and he crouched next to her, stroking the loose tendrils of hair that curved behind her ear. "What is that you want, Étaín? Tell me what it is that you desire, and I swear by all the gods of my home that I will obtain it for you, whatever the cost."

She swallowed and stared out at the sea for a long while. "I want," she said, "freedom. I want to be free—to choose, for myself, what my life shall be."

Midir studied her intently, then rose. "You shall have it, a bhrèagha," and her face paled at the ferocity in his tone, the visceral command of undying gods. "I swear by all the gods, you shall have it."

He turned and stalked away before she could answer, down the long stretch of sand to a little cove that nestled in the rocks and crannies of the shoreline. He lifted his gaze to the skies and thundered out across the horizon, "Aengus!"

It echoed back to him faintly, reverberating off the mountains in the far distance, and he shouted again in an unimpeachable command. "Aengus!"

With the faintest rustle of feathers, he appeared, soaring across the sky, his white wings gliding on the breeze, and with a huffed plop in the sand, Aengus landed next to his brother, his pale gold eyes bright and cheery in his keen, angular face.

"Midir, my friend," Aengus said, centuries' worth of warbling love songs and sweet-versed poems drenching his voice. "At long last, you have summoned me. I am thrilled, dear boy, thrilled, I tell you. I have long wished to repay the debt of your injured eye, so tell me. What lovely maiden shall I seduce to your will today? I do hope she is a bit more sweet-tempered than that fiery fiancée of yours."

"No girl." Midir folded his arms across his chest. "I have something else in mind."

Aengus's brow furrowed. "But I promised you the love of whatever maiden you wanted."

"No. You promised," Midir said, "to ensure for me the love of whomsoever I chose, and I choose for you to win the love of Étar, chieftain of Latharna, for his daughter, Étaín, that he might learn to care for her enough to spare her this misery of a marriage that he forces on her."

Aengus stared at him, his mouth ajar. "That is not what I expected when I made you this vow, Midir."

Midir's expression was crafted from unflinching steel as he stared at the god of love and summer. "And yet you so made it. Now fulfill your bargain and pay your debt."

Aengus shook his head in bewildered wonder, then shrugged. "If that is what you want."

"It is."

"Then so be it." Aengus shook out his wings from beneath his shoulder blades and prepared to leap into the sky. "I'll be back in a moment."

He soared away, disappearing into the endless blue of the sky, and Midir sank down into the sand, burying his head in his trembling hands to await his brother's return.

He did not wait long.

Not a full hour had passed before he heard the faint rustle of wings, and Aengus floated in on a swift ocean breeze to land in front of where Midir still sat, his face tilted up toward the pale-eyed god of love.

"I'm sorry, friend," Aengus said without preamble. Midir opened his mouth to protest when Aengus raised his hand. "I have to tell you, this is not my usual line of work, so perhaps my powers of persuasion were not what they normally are, but Étar sends you this message. Well, to be fair, he gave it to me, as he is laboring under the false delusion that I am the one lusting after your little paramour." He paused, considering. "Although she really is quite pretty, so if you do not object—"

"What word?" Midir growled, and Aengus grinned.

"He says that he has no desire to see such an advantageous match slip between his fingers The fiancé is, it seems, the king of a very powerful and warlike clan in the northern mountains."

"Does the fool not realize that I am a god?" Midir slammed his hand on the sand. "How is that not more advantageous for him, to win the gratitude and friendship of one of the Tuatha Dé Danann?"

"Everyone knows that we gods only but dillydally with mortal maidens, Midir. It's not as though you'd marry the girl yourself," Aengus said, his eyebrows waggling, and Midir's jaw tightened. "He has no sons, you see, only daughters, and it is important to him, apparently, to see the continuation of his line through the guarantee of a powerful alliance."

"Surely there is another way," Midir broke in. "One that does not come at the cost of her happiness."

Aengus shrugged. "He believes that it is a small price to pay, these tears of his daughter, and she is but one of many, so he is not particularly attached to the girl." He yawned once, an eternal force long grown bored with the feeble sorrows of the mortal world. "He did mock me and say that if I so lusted after the girl, then I should be prepared to pay a

price worth her weight in gold for the honor of her maidenhead, but that is the only way that he would consider
breaking the promised marriage-bond."

Midir shot to his feet. "I have gold. I have jewels and
silver. I can buy her freedom."

"Will you listen, you overeager boy, until I have quite
finished?" Aengus huffed, then fluttered his wings. "He de-
mands," he continued, "not gold or jewels but something of
far more lasting value. He ordered that I drain the swamps
of his land and divert the rivers into the mouth of the loch,
and thus grant unending fertility and riches of harvest to his
realm and, in so doing, ensure the prosperity of his people
for generations to come." Aengus waved his hand in the air
contemptuously. "I, of course, informed him that I am far
too pretty to dirty myself with such earthbound work, and that
such feats lie outside the scope of my powers, so he sneered
at me and declared that the girl shall be married to Eochu,
king of the northern mountains, within a fortnight's time."

Midir said nothing, staring across the waves, and Aengus
again flittered his wings, impatient to be gone. "I truly am sorry,
Midir," he said as he floated away, his pale-gold eyes already
wandering away from his half brother who stood silently in
front of him. "But you know, there are plenty of other mortal
girls if you desire a bit of fun before your union with that snake
of a witch. Pick someone else, and I will win for you her love."

He soared up, unconcerned, disappearing among the
clouds. Left below, Midir clenched his fists, then turned
from the sea, determination rising in his soul. He sprinted
from the shore toward the marshy, waterlogged lands to the
south, gathering the deepest dregs of his power to the tips
of his fingers as he prepared to fight for his love.

Chapter
Twenty-Eight

"A village," Rozlyn sang. "Thank the gods, I can have a hot bath."

"Three weeks of fighting monsters of unparalleled evil, and you are concerned about a little pampering?"

"I have been bathing in frigid streams for over a fortnight, Jamie."

"I know. You spent more time shrieking at me to look away than you did actually washing yourself—most unnecessarily, I might add. I have already seen all that you have to offer, a bhrèagha. Perhaps you've forgotten."

"I want a bath," Rozlyn said, ignoring the glint in his eye, the underlying dare in his words. "A bath, and then a whole kettle of piping hot tea, perhaps some bread pudding, or biscuits with kerry-gold butter, or, oh! Spice cake!"

A week had passed since Rozlyn had ravaged the face of the gean-cánach in the misty shadows of the falls, and they now approached the outskirts of the small village of Ard an Rátha, nestled among the green-sloped mountains by the sea. Rozlyn felt a surge of excitement at the sight of the villagers bustling through the town, a craving for the companionship of others that she had never realized she needed until this trip.

They swung down from their horses by the hitching post at the center of the village, but even as she went to tie her reins around the post next to Jamie's, she saw the cluster of whispering locals eyeing them with red, suspicious eyes.

Jamie tensed next to her, and she steeled herself for the inevitable, bracing for the wary stares, the trembling lips, the unabashed loathing on the faces of any who beheld the infamous Beast of Connacht, scourge of all Éire.

"Stay here," he murmured, and strode toward them, his handsome face warm and sunny, and she scowled at how, as one, they melted at the sight of his easy wave, his cheery grin. She wheeled around to look toward the crashing of the sea just beyond her sight, the faint sound of its waves soothing the sharp edges in her soul.

What must it be like, she wondered, to greet a stranger with a carefree smile and an outstretched hand, and not have to worry that they would recoil in terror at the sight of what lurked underneath. Galena, she thought, and it steadied her, the memory of her friend, like a soothing balm to new-resurrected scars. Galena was the only one who had not feared her, who had not shaken in her presence and swore in her absence.

"Rozi."

She jumped, her reverie broken, when he called to her after a few long minutes of murmured conversations, punctuated with the muffled sound of a woman weeping, and she hesitated only a moment before approaching them.

They turned toward her as she neared, and smiled—polite, perhaps a little strained, but, she realized, with a fear for some other threat than herself.

"This is my wife," Jamie said, removing one hand from his pocket to wrap it about her wrist as he pulled her to him. "Rozi, my love, apparently some nasty creature has been plaguing the children of the village."

Rozlyn looked up at him sharply, but his face remained unreadable and bland as he continued to regard the gray-bearded man with a look of deep concern. The older man nodded, chin trembling. "They go down to the beaches, to the strands of Maghera, and disappear into the caves, never to come out again."

"It's witches, is what it is," an equally gray-haired woman interjected, her thin, blue-veined hands trembling. "Witches always steal away the children, looking to feed off their innocence. Och, the little lad—" She broke off, weeping into the bedraggled hem of her skirt, which she pressed against her face to muffle her sobs, and a younger, pale-faced man rubbed at her shaking shoulders.

"Maimeó is heartbroken," he whispered. "Her only great-grandson, my sister's child, went missing the day before yesterday, and we can find no trace of the lad anywhere."

Rozlyn sucked in a breath even as Jamie's hand tightened around her wrist in a wordless warning. "It's a tragedy," he said. "I promise, Fearghal, my friend. We'll keep an eye out for the lad as we make our way north." He turned to Rozlyn. "They offered us a room, but I told them that you would be hesitant to linger. Your sister's time will come any day now, and you promised that you'd be at her side for the birth."

"Oh!" Rozlyn cleared her throat. "Yes. For the baby. I

love them—the babies. So soft and squishy, and their squalling. It's so sweet." She hesitated as the villagers looked at
her, expressions of confusion marring their erstwhile concern, and she added hurriedly. "I'm very excited to see it
happening. The birth."

Jamie coughed. "She is tired," he said, his expression
an exaggeration in ruefulness. "Women. Such tender, weak
things. They were not made for arduous travels."

The men murmured in agreement as even the few
women nodded, and Rozlyn fought the urge to glower at
him as he pulled her away in the direction of their horses.
"Slán agat," he called with unshakable cheeriness.

"Slán abhaile," they called back, watching them go with
wide eyes.

"For the love of the Dagda," Jamie whispered. "'Squalling'? 'Excited to see it happening'? Are you mad?"

"'Not made for arduous travels'?" she hissed back.
"'Weak'?"

He pursed his lips. "Very well, we will consider this a
truce for now, but for the harp's sake, Rozi, pull yourself
together. Perhaps try not to draw attention to your presence
and the fact that you are one of the more dangerous embod-
iments of sorcery currently walking the realm. Humans have
been largely unexposed to magic for three centuries now,
and what little they have seen of it has been egregiously evil,
as those poor villagers can attest."

Rozlyn shivered. "What is taking these children, Jamie?
We have to stop whatever it is."

"Where do you think we're going in such a rush?" He
swung himself into the saddle. "Two days since the last boy
was taken. It might not have eaten him yet."

"Something is *eating* those poor children?"

He gestured at her in a silent hurry-it-up motion, and she scrambled to leap onto her gelding's back, following Jamie out of the borders of the village and down the dirt road that led to the beaches of Maghera. "Before you arrived and bedazzled everyone with your undying affection for screaming infants, they told me that there have been rumors of corpse-white horses sighted, roaming through the woods near the village on the nights preceding each child's disappearance." He grimaced. "Such horses always eventually return to the sea, Rozi, and those are the monsters we must face this time."

Rozlyn frowned, remembering a whispered story of sea-ghosts and full moons told to her by a former nursemaid as she sat wide-eyed at her knee. "I thought that kelpies lived in the realm of the Picts across the sea of Éireann."

"Not kelpies," Jamie corrected. "These nasty beasts—present company excluded, of course—are far more vicious and predatory. Kelpies," he explained as they trotted along the road that dwindled down to the shore, "live in the rivers and streams in the kingdom of the Picts, and hunt for love, in a twisted sort of way. They select their victims and carry them into the water to be their soul-bonded mate. Our version, in typical Éire fashion, has much more sinister intent. The each-uisce, as we call them, stalk and seduce their prey solely for the sake of their own greed and carnal appetites. It uses the young women it snatches for its own dark pleasures, then drowns her beneath the surface of the water and eats her."

Rozlyn shuddered. "Then why are they taking the children?"

"I am fairly certain that we are going to find out, Rozi, even though I very much do not want to know."

"How can it be killed?"

"Not easily, but the same as any horse." He patted the silver mane of his mare as he spoke. "Only imagine that your steed were three times as fast, as strong, with a hide of thick leather rather than soft skin. Stab it, strangle it, rip at it with a pair of beastly claws. They would all work eventually if you kept at it long enough."

Rozlyn was silent for a moment. "You have saved my life several times with this kind of knowledge," she said. "With the gean-cánach, obviously, but even after that, when I hunted him—I heard what you said about those poor doomed girls, and I was filled with so much rage that I had to go after him—I had to make him pay for what he had done. And then with the slúag as well. I remembered what you said about the western sky, and I pulled them toward it. And even the cú-sídhe—" She broke off.

Jamie twisted in his saddle to stare at her. "Yes? What about it?"

"Nothing. I only meant that I knew to find Galena and have her help me, knew what herbs to give you, because of what you had told me in the past."

Jamie grunted at this, mollified, and the tightness in her chest eased a little as he continued to ride down the road. "So it goes, Rozi. I am the brains and you are the brawn. We make a good team."

Rozlyn scowled. "I have brains."

"And I'm sure that they are just as pretty as the rest of you."

They reached the edge of the white-sand beaches of Maghera and halted, surveying the strand in silence. Rozlyn savored the rush of the cold sea breeze on her face, reveling again in that inexplicable sensation of rightness, that sense of home that flooded through her even as the briny air filled her lungs. Jamie nudged her impatiently, and she blushed. "What?"

Jamie pointed. "The caves."

Rozlyn followed the direction of his finger and saw them.

There were at least a dozen of the creatures—tall figures with the heads and shoulders of bone-white horses, save for the razor-sharp teeth that protruded from beneath their lips. Below their shoulders, they bore the well-muscled, hard-boned bodies of men, warriors of unparalleled strength. They stalked on bare feet through the wet sand, pacing back and forth as they stared out to sea, whinnying to each other in some secret language.

Rozlyn hissed. "There are so many."

"Quite the conclave of evil that they have gathered here." Jamie's face was grim and set. "And yet—"

She glanced at him when he fell silent. "What?"

"And yet I hate this. I told you before we left that you would attract such creatures—wicked monsters of the worst magic that the earth-mother has ever brought into being—but I never imagined that we would find ourselves so embroiled in their ugly affairs as this."

Rozlyn frowned. "You had no way of knowing that we would find them here when we stopped in the village."

"Perhaps not exactly. But I knew they would come out for you, the monsters hiding in the dark corners of the world." His jaw tightened, and she could see the muscles jumping below his chin. "They hear the call of your power, the song of your magic. They would never be able to resist trying to take it for themselves, the each-uisce included."

"I sense a pattern emerging among the males of my ac-quaintance."

"Save your jokes for when we might not be about to die, Rozi. Focus now."

It unnerved her, the uncharacteristic gravity in his face. "What do I do?"

"Find the boy, Rozi." She could hear the urgency in his voice and sat up a little straighter in her saddler. "Look at them, at how red and ravenous are their eyes. They have not yet fed on him. You find the boy, and I will deal with the each-uisce."

"I can handle them, Jamie."

"Do you think that I doubt you? Finding the boy is more important than battling these beasts. I trust you to find him more quickly and ensure his safety more absolutely than I could do."

Rozlyn nodded and turned to creep away when he grabbed her by the arm. "Do not trust any man who speaks to you," he warned, "nor any horse, or bird. They can assume all these shapes. When in doubt, look at the hair, Rozi. If it is truly an each-uisce, their hair, no matter how lovely, will be matted and marred with sand. Look closely at the hair, Rozi, before you go to save some young boy."

She nodded again, her chest tightening, then slipped away as he withdrew his longbow and arrows and began to stalk toward the creatures who hovered at the mouths of the caves. Rozlyn watched him for one anxious moment, then turned to creep down by the shore in search of the lost boy.

Her boots splashed through the surf of low tide as she snuck along the beach, and even in her anxiety and fear, she could not help but savor the sensation of the cold briny water seeping in through her boots, or the way that the water swirled in a myriad of patterns across the sand before slipping away to rejoin the sea. She drank in the salt air with relish and had just squatted to scoop a handful of sand in her palm—a moment's indulgence that she could not bring herself to resist—when she saw a dark shape break through the waves just off the reef of the shoreline.

Rozlyn rose, her hands reaching for the longbow and quiver strapped behind her shoulders, when the figure disappeared beneath the surface. Rozlyn stood in the surf, her arrow nocked as she waited, scanning the waves for any further sign of the mysterious half-human shape.

"A deirfiúr."

Rozlyn whirled at the sound of the melodious voice, and there, on a salt-soaked rock that jutted onto the shoreline from the waves, lay the most beautiful girl that Rozlyn had ever seen.

Her hair was a deep, rich green, cascading in shimmering waves across her back and shoulders, with expressive sea-blue eyes, her skin a dark, creamy brown. The girl raised a hand, and Rozlyn's breath caught at the delicate webbing that expanded between her fingers as she reached out toward her.

"Deirfiúr," the girl sang again. "Sister."

Rozlyn's heart stuttered a little, the memory of the púca's golden eyes as he called her that same name flashing through her mind, but Jamie's final word of caution made her hesitate. "I am no sister of yours," she said. "Where is the boy you and your kind have stolen away?"

The girl tilted her head, her green hair tumbling across her bare shoulder, then wriggled on the rock. Rozlyn saw a fishlike tail covered in pale blue-and-pink scales curve about the boulder as she spoke again. "The each-uisce do not consort with me, nor I with them," she crooned, as vibrant as the sea itself. "I have come to help you, sister, in return for a price."

Rozlyn studied her, searching for any sign of duplicity in her cerulean eyes. "What price? Who are you?"

The girl let out a low hum. "I was Lí Ban," she sang, "once a mortal girl, born to a simple farmer of Ulaid, content with the lot of my life, until the day of our doom arrived. The rains and the rivers flooded our home and washed my father away. I floated in the waters for two days and two nights, a corpse in all but breath, until I awoke to find myself in a cave deep under the sea, lying on the floor next to a man with brine-soaked hair and bright black eyes, his skin as pale as the first green leaves of spring. He had saved me, this god of the sea, and taken me to his home to be his lover and his bride."

"Lir, the keeper of the sea," Rozlyn said, and the girl bowed her head in acknowledgment.

"But I mourned too much the loss of the sun, the feel of the wind in my hair, and the god of my heart pitied my sorrow and my tears. 'Too much salt resides in the sea,' he whispered as he kissed my tear-soaked cheeks one night. 'I will not add yours to its number.' He could not restore to me my mortality, too long without breath had I gone in those long hours I floated among the waves of the sea where the raging rivers had carried my lifeless form, and so he granted to me this half-life, the being of a mortal girl mixed with the salmon of the sea."

"A merrow," Rozlyn cried. "I remember now."

She inclined her head, watching Rozlyn with a keen intensity as she continued to sing her song. "I bear within my blood a drop of the magic of the gods, deirfiúr, as do you. We are sisters in this life as surely as we were when we were first restored from death."

Rozlyn frowned, confused, but before she could speak,

the girl continued. "I will help you find this boy, sister, but the price that I ask is this: Set free the ancient gods, the caretakers of the earth and sky and sea. Too long have our kind run feral among the hapless mortals of the earth, their vicious appetites unchecked by the restraining hand of the gods, and I pity them, those humans among whom I used to walk and talk and live. They will perish without the magic of the Tuatha Dé Danann." Her sharp teeth flashed in the sun. "Free them, deirfiúr, for all those who will languish and die in this world without their care."

The surf thundered around them as the sisters stared into one another's eyes. "Tell me where the boy is," Rozlyn said at last. "And I promise you that I will free the gods from their slumber."

The merrow nodded, satisfied, then raised her slender brown arm and pointed to the far end of the cove at the mouth of a dark, looming cave. "Tonight the high king of the each-uisce, at the first hour of the setting sun, will claim the heart of the village boy. Long have their kind fed on the hearts of children, to draw from them their life's energy. Once a decade, they steal away a child for their dark desires. But the high king grows feeble in this new age, and his lust for the hearts of mortal children has grown wild and unrestrained—he feeds more and more often, his appetites insatiable. He will not cease to prey upon these mortal children until he has devoured every last one." Her graceful nose wrinkled. "He keeps the boy in the cave there at the center of the cove, bound to a great limestone rock deep within its gloom, until the hour arrives for him to perform his dark rite." Her pale green lips trembled. "Slay the high king, deirfiúr, or the horrors of his reign shall never cease."

Rozlyn swallowed, studying the cavernous mouth of

the cave. "How do I get in? Surely they are guarding him closely."

"You command the waters of the seas and the lochs, deirfiúr. The might of a few warriors of the each-uisce is no match for the mistress of the ocean."

She flipped her dark-green locks over her shoulder and dove back into the waves, vanishing beneath the churning foam, and Rozlyn looked toward the beckoning shadows of the cave in front of her, the final words of her sea sister ringing in her ears.

It was exactly as he had said, on that cold night all those weeks ago.

As though a bronze key had at last snapped into the rusty gears of an ancient and enigmatic lock.

They were but pawns, these monsters who fed on the blood of innocents, and she—she would be queen and knight and rook and bishop as one all-powerful entity, armed with the might of the sea and the sky, storming across this board of sand to take the head of their monstrous king.

She flexed her fingers, a strange new awareness of that power swirling in her veins rising to her wordless call even as the sweet-salt taste of the sea flooded through her mouth, the taste and flavor of its potency shimmering on her tongue, and the waves of the sea growled in response to her summons as she stalked through the sand toward the menacing figures that appeared in the mouth of the cave.

They lifted their savage, equine snouts and saw her, and with whinnying screams, they charged.

Rozlyn lifted her hands and the sea rose with them, and with a roaring crash, it thundered down around the each-uisce, a sea-storm of razor-sharp waves and catapults of sand. Their screams turned to airless coughs as the water

grew merciless hands and wrapped its fingers around their
necks and garroted them where they stood, on the once dry
sand, until they collapsed to the ground in lifeless heaps of
horse and man.

A single figure appeared in the mouth of the cave, a lean
man who turned his corpse-white horse head toward where
she still stalked in his direction with murderous intent.
With a flick of her wrist, the boulders of the strand rose
up against him, clashing against one another even as she
strode toward him, her arms outstretched. The high king of
the each-uisce screeched once as the stones hurtled across
the sand to pinion him against the cliffs, his blood flowing
down the cracks and crevices of the rocks as it spilled onto
the ground.

Rozlyn glided into the cave, past where his body still
writhed in its death throes, without glancing at his glassy-eyed
face, his misshapen mouth shattered and ajar. She ventured
deep into the cave, until at last she sank to her knees before
the blond-haired boy who trembled against the wet slab of
rock at the back of the cavern, his wrists raw and bleeding
from the bite of the seaweed entwined about his arms. She
lifted her hand, and his bonds shivered in response to her
wordless command, sliding away to droop limply on the
floor of the cave. The boy lifted his frightened eyes to her
face, and she raised a finger to her lips. "Don't be afraid,"
she whispered. "No one shall hurt you."

She walked out again, the boy's head resting against her
shoulder as she carried him from the cave of death, past
the ruined body of the high king, into the light of the pale
winter sun and the pure air of a fresh sea breeze, then halted
abruptly.

Jamie stood at the mouth of the cave, surveying the

carnage that she had brought down upon the each-uisce and their king. He was bruised and bloody, a long, shallow scratch curving down from the edge of his cheekbone to the nape of his neck, covered in sand and mud and blood, his quiver empty of arrows.

"You've started to figure it out," he said without removing his gaze from the misshapen bodies of the monsters of the sea. "How to summon the elementals."

He raised his eyes to hers where she stood in front of the cave with the bright-haired boy weeping onto her shoulder, and she could see it then—that greed, that longing for the power in her veins that was once his to wield, and she knew beyond a shadow of a doubt—in the surge of this new thrum of power that rolled through her blood—that a new match had started between them, between her and this man whom she had loved so much, a game that could only end in the most finite of ways, because he would never stop trying to take from her something that she would never willingly give.

Chapter Twenty-Nine

Midir surveyed the dry, seemingly endless stretch of land in front of him, and rubbed the back of his mud-stained hand across his cracked lips.

It had taken an entire week—seven grueling days of backbreaking labor, seven nights of incantations and summonings, each hour spent wrestling and coaxing the might of the natural world to submit to his will—but here he stood, bone-weary with bloody fingertips and burning eyes, and it was finished at last.

Seven mighty rivers flowed into the gaping mouth of the black-watered bay of Lough Neagh, and looming above it, a new-built dam of cedar and ash stood tall and unyielding against its flow. The earth, freshly aerated, sighed with relief as it breathed in the crisp scent of dry air for the first time in a hundred years.

He had done it.

He lingered for a moment longer, savoring his success,

the thrill of pride at this manifestation of his power. Then he turned sharply on his heel and shifted, a golden-feathered falcon screaming through the skies, arrowing its way toward the castle of Étar and his daughter.

Midir circled the timbers surrounding the fortress of the chief before he glided down toward the grassy courtyard below. In a smooth, twisting motion, he shifted into his own tall, purple-robed form, his golden hair matted with dirt and leaves where it fell across his shoulders. He clenched his hands as he marched past the stunned stares of the hall guards and the villagers who stood clustered at the base of the steps. He strode into the great hall of the castle itself, to the broad base of the dais where Étar lounged on his throne, roughly hewn from the trunk of an alder tree. The chieftain drummed his fingers against the armrest of his throne, eyeing Midir as he stood, tall and straight-shouldered, before him. "Who the hell are you?"

Midir flicked his fingers at him, and the chieftain shrieked as a dozen hoot owls descended from the rafters, screeching and clawing at his silver-lined hair with their curving talons. With an idle flip of his wrist, the owls retreated, floating upward to perch on the rafters of the hall, watching and waiting for their master's command.

"Do not," Midir said, "disrespect me again."

The chieftain and his soldiers stared at him, and the guards surrounding him sank to one knee. "A dhia," they chanted, their eyes downcast and their palms spread flat on the hard-packed dirt floor.

Étar watched him, still trembling from the onslaught of a few moments before. "Forgive me," he said, but his face remained sullen. "I did not realize. Your clothes are so torn and muddy, and I—"

"I am here"—the chieftain's sneer was drowned out by the thunderclap of Midir's voice—"to secure your promise to set your daughter free of this marriage-bond that is so hateful to her, as you swore you would. I have completed your tasks." He drew himself up to the full extent of his godlike height, and the guards crouched even lower at the radiance pulsating from him as he spoke. "I have come to claim what is owed to me—your daughter's freedom."

Silence thundered through the room, until a broad-shouldered, bearded man stepped forward from his place of honor beside the throne of Étar, his mouth set in a thin line. "I am Eochu Eichthighearn, son of Eamon Eichthighearn, horse lord and high king of the North. The girl is promised to me."

"And I have come to release her from that promise." Midir folded his arms across his chest, unperturbed. "As was sworn by her father." He turned to stare unblinking at Étar. "The marshes of the lowlands are no more, the rivers that slogged into their fields now pour their water into the depths of Lough Neagh, their fruitfulness forever ensured." A low murmur rose throughout the hall. "Keep your bargain, Chief. Release your daughter."

The soldiers and men whispered in excitement, even as Étar stared at him, his fingers digging into the unpolished wood of his throne. "Indeed," the chief mused. He turned to gesture to one of his hall guards. "Fetch the girl."

The soldier began to hurry away, but before he could approach the doorway that led to the inner chambers of the castle, she appeared in a violet gown of fine linen, her hair pinned against the nape of her neck. She lingered in the shadows, and he could feel her perusing him, his haggard face, his bedraggled clothes. "Father," she said, "here I am. What is your will for me?"

Midir's jaw tightened at the uncharacteristic meekness in her tone, but Étar waved his hand irascibly. "Do you know this god, child?" His tone was clipped, impatient, as though the answer was immaterial to his judgment.

There was the briefest of pauses. "No, Father. I have never seen him before in my life."

A horrified murmur rumbled through the room as Midir stared at her where she still stood in the doorway, her features shrouded from the torchlight of the mead hall.

Étar shrugged. "Do you object, you little fool, to marrying the great king of the North, to being the mother of future kings?"

"No, Father." It was a cool and expressionless answer, and Midir's stomach churned, his palms growing slick with sweat. What was wrong, what had they done to her, his bold, brave girl—

"There you have it, a dhia. Not even a god can break a marriage-bond, no matter how you may rage, and that bond still holds if the girl has no reason to object." He swiveled in his thronelike chair to glare at his daughter still shrouded in shadow. "Come out here where your lord"—he gestured at Eochu, who leered at her with yellowed teeth—"can admire what his dowry has bought him."

Étaín stepped forward, her gaze fixed unwaveringly on Midir's, as the light from the sun streaming in through the open windows draped over her exposed neck.

It was pale and mottled with dark purple bruises, a perfect twin to the hue of her gown.

He stared and stared, a jumble of thoughts tumbling through him—the deliberate coloring of her robe, the carefully pinned hair, the way it framed her slim throat, calling attention to the wounds marring the smoothness of her skin, the exaggerated meekness. It was all for him, somehow, as though she were speaking to him and him alone, in a secret language that only the two of them shared.

"You see." Midir dimly heard Étar gloating in the background even as Eochu leered at his promised bride, who stood with her hands clasped, eyes now downcast in a convincing display of demureness that he never before would have associated with her. "I told you that all the girl needed to come around was a firm hand. Tell this god, girl, what it is you have decided that your destiny shall be."

It smoldered within him, the dangerous spark of his power, hissing and snarling at the sight of her skin, blemished by the vague outline of violent hands. His jaw clenched as she stepped forward again, her meekly bowed head lifting so that her eyes, wide and unflinching, once more met his.

He could almost see it then—that slender, intangible thread of understanding stretching taut between them.

"I choose him." Her voice did not waver as she spoke to Midir but pointed to where Eochu stood on the dais beside her father. Their stares met again, and that faint thread sparked between them. It ignited, unbreakable and white-hot, an iron rod glowing bright in the roaring forge, as a strange new bond roared to life. "I will stand before him and him alone in tomorrow's morning light, and to him will I make my vows and promise my love."

Midir's eyes flashed and he nodded once. Without another word, he turned and slipped from the room as soundlessly as a shadow.

The next morning dawned and Étaín stood, silent and stone-faced, surrounded by her maids as they dressed her in the flowing white-gold bridal gown, when one of her ladies stepped forward timidly. "My lady," she whispered, holding out a small wooden box, "this arrived for you this morning. A gift from your groom."

Étaín raised her eyebrows and waved a hand at her. "Thank you, Aibreann," she said, then reached forward and lifted the lid of the box.

There laid a circlet of gold, a gorgeous piece of unearthly finery, the thin strands of gold entwining around one another, embossed with dozens of crimson-red rubies that sparkled in the sunlight. At its peak lay a single golden rose, ensconced with delicately welded leaves.

Aibreann squealed at the sight of it even as her other maids murmured in admiration. "Such craftsmanship," one whispered. "He must have commissioned the finest goldsmith in all of Éire to weld such a thing of beauty."

They all nodded, cooing with delight, and Étaín lifted it from its box and placed it atop her loose black waves of hair. "Truly," she said, "it is a gift fit for a princess."

They proceeded down the stairs to the great hall, and her father reached for her hand, dragging her into the early light of the morning, down the steps to the grove of fir trees that stood in the front of the castle. Étaín lifted her downcast eyes and saw him standing there, a broad-shouldered, black-bearded man, waiting for her by the druid, who reached with outstretched hands to grasp her own and place it in the meaty palm of her bridegroom.

Étaín raised her eyes, shining with emotion, to the face of her chosen husband and recited her vows of eternal love and loyalty, never wavering, her gaze never swerving from his own. His vows echoed hers, his deep timbre unfamiliar and grating to her ears, and the druid recited the blessing of the gods upon their union as the people cheered, and her father smirked.

Even as the intonation of the priest fell away, she watched as the body of her bridegroom trembled and shifted, and there he was, his hair falling long and golden across his shoulders, his purple robe slung across his back, and the blue eyes of Midir blazed into her own.

A roar erupted from the crowd, and her father shrieked in protest, even as she stepped toward her chosen lord, her immortal husband.

"I knew it was you," she whispered with her face pressed against his neck, breathing in the faint aroma of sap and pine bark that still clung to him, and the ever-present salt of the sea. "Even in your borrowed form, I knew you, and I chose you even then as I choose you now." His hands tightened on her waist as she whispered, soft and full of warmth, and he stared down at her unwaveringly. "I shall always so know you, and I shall always so choose you, until the end of my days."

Midir pulled her close to his chest, his raven-haired bride, adorned in her gown of white and her circlet of fine-crafted gold, and kissed her with unutterable tenderness, as a mother-mare nuzzles a newborn foal as it takes its first hesitant steps across the lush green grass, blinking in awe at the miracle of life. His heart soared as her arms encircled his neck, her slim fingers entwining in his hair, and she pressed her lips to his, a kiss of pure love, of gratitude and adoration.

His wife.

Chapter
Thirty

It was not that dire, Rozlyn tried to reassure herself, as they rode away from the village of Ard an Rátha the next morning. Surely, he would understand. Surely, he would concede that this power that he once had wielded belonged now to her and her alone, that he would come to accept that, and would no longer plot and scheme and conspire ways to steal it away from her.

Although it had seemed calculated, a deliberate challenging of her self-control, a subtle move of entrapment—the way that he had stood so casually this morning in the dim light of the dawn, his shirt tossed aside as he leaned over the basin, scraping at the scruff darkening his jaw with a steel shaver, as though he knew she was watching from the bed in the corner where she had slept all alone, watching the way that his fingers moved, the way that those silver drops of water slid down the contours of his throat, slipping across the planes of his chest until they disappeared down into the waist of his breeches, which hung half-open and loose on his hips. Surely, he had known that her palms had gone sweaty at the sight, imagining and remembering and wanting—

"Well, Rozi," said the now fully dressed Jamie, and she jolted awake from the memory of her early morning fantasies. "I rather imagine that they will be singing songs of your heroism for centuries to come."

Rozlyn rolled her eyes, determined to ignore that lingering clench in her gut. "They believe that it was you who saved the boy, Jamie."

"Technically, we saved him together, although I will allow your work was far more impressive than my single-handedly slaughtering a dozen sea monsters with only my bow to protect me."

"How very manly of you." Her lips flattened. "I'm fairly certain that they would not have been so effusive with their praise if they had seen what I truly am."

The people of Ard an Rátha had wept with joy at the sight of the lost boy nestled in Rozlyn's lap when they had ridden back to the village just as the twilight deepened into night. The boy had been returned to his sobbing mother's arms, and his father had wrapped each of them in a bone-crushing hug, disheveled and dirty as they were, choking on barely audible words of thanks. Jamie merely waved his hand sheepishly, and Rozlyn could not help but admire it, the effortless way that he smiled and deflected and deceived.

"It was nothing. We found him on the outskirts of a cave near the sea," he had explained to the weeping parents, the wide-eyed villagers clustered around them. "He was a bit dazed and disoriented. He might have hit his head on a rock and is clearly in need of some water and his own bed."

"The horse-men were going to kill me and eat my heart,"

the child had announced from his mother's bosom. "But the witch-lady crushed them with rocks." Rozlyn bit back a gasp, but Jamie had only shrugged and mouthed to his father, "Delirious."

Rozlyn had very much wanted to smile at that.

Instead, the boy's uncle Fearghal had ushered them into his thatched hut and called for a healer to tend to Jamie's face. "What happened here?" the healer had asked when he arrived, lingering on the green tinge of the shallow scratch, and Jamie had shrugged again.

"The rocks by the cave were quite slippery with algae."

"Och, I don't recall that," their host had mused as the healer continued to frown at the unusual coloring of the scar. "That particular strand of Maghera usually stays quite dry. How odd."

Rozlyn cleared her throat. "Fearghal," she had murmured, batting her eyelashes where she sat by the fire. "I so hate to bother you, but my throat is quite parched. Do you mind?"

Jamie glared as the young man nearly fell out of his chair in his eagerness. "Whatever you like, my lady. Tea, mead, wine?"

"Some hot tea with honey would be so lovely," she said, brushing her fingertips over the back of his hand, and the young man looked as awestruck as though the gods themselves had appeared in his hut and bestowed on him the wisdom of the world's creation.

"I," Jamie interrupted, his knuckles white as he gripped the edge of his chair, "would also enjoy some mead, if that's all right."

"Hush," demanded the healer as he dabbed at the wound. "You'll tear it open again. No talking, no drinking."

It had been his turn, however, for smugness as midnight drew near and the healer left, declaring Jamie's wound to be relatively minor. The poultice that he had applied had siphoned away that worrisome green tinge, and as soon as he left, Fearghal had turned to where the two of them sat by the fire, sipping their drinks and munching on potato pancakes and barmbrack, and announced that he was leaving to sleep at his sister's and that the soft bed in the corner of his hut was theirs for the night.

Rozlyn had coughed as she tried to swallow the bit of fruit stuck in her throat as Jamie patted her on the back, the portrait of an adoring husband. "How kind of you, Fearghal," he had said, satisfaction rolling off him in waves. "Your hospitality is unparalleled."

Fearghal had bowed, the tips of his ears reddening. "For the life of my nephew, all that I have is yours." He winked at Jamie. "And there's fresh sheets on the bed too."

She had fumed even as Jamie grinned. "They might not be so fresh for long now, my friend, don't you know."

Fearghal had roared with laughter and slipped away with a wave of his hand.

Jamie turned to Rozlyn and opened his mouth to speak, but she reached out and twisted his ear. He yelped. "Sleep on the floor, you donkey," she snapped, moving toward the bed, and she ignored the sound of him laughing to himself as he stretched out before the hearth, his arms folded behind his head.

They had left a little after dawn, their saddlebags loaded with food and water, courtesy of the teary-eyed villagers. They trotted down the road toward the fortress of Grianán in Aileach, a journey of four days, Jamie informed her as they set off. "The king and I are old friends," he said. "He'll grant us passage to the northernmost part of his realm, to Dúnalderagh, where we will sail for Inis Trá Tholl and the Court of Shádach."

Rozlyn frowned. "You know the king of Aileach?"

"Very well. It is in his court that I was serving before I came to woo your hand all those fateful years ago—"

"Ah yes, the one who bribed my father to let you be the one to kill me. I remember."

Wisely, he ignored this. "—and it was to his kingdom that I returned after you jilted me so cruelly on our wedding night."

"Again, I think what you meant to say was, on the night you tried to kill me."

"Just another day of marital bliss, I suppose. Do you know, now that I think about it, I have not had much luck with wedding nights. Ironic, considering it is the night that a man should have the most luck, wouldn't you agree?"

"I can't speak for that other poor girl, but in my experience, your marital troubles are of your own making, Jamie, so forgive me if I don't feel much sympathy for you."

Surprisingly, he was silent for a long moment, his eyes distant. "You might someday." She looked at him curiously, but he only smiled at her, sad and soft, and then continued. "Flaithbertach, despite his unfortunate name, is a good king, and will make the final stage of our journey much simpler. And you shall have another bath to look forward to as well in his fortress. He does enjoy his luxuries."

"Thank the gods for that." Curiosity nibbled at her in spite of herself. "What did you do for him, while you served at his court?"

"Many things. Flaithbertach is an ambitious king, but a good-hearted man—an odd combination in a chieftain of

Éire, sure now. His court is often at war with neighboring clans and regions, yet always with just cause. The overthrow of a petty tyrant, rectifying some abuse of power, an encroachment on his own lands, those kinds of things." He shrugged. "I am a very able warrior, as you know, but I am also in the unique position of possessing centuries' worth of knowledge of battle formations and strategies and such, and the king is more than happy to take advantage of that wisdom for his own purposes."

"He knows who you are?"

"Not by name, of course—not my true name. It was his forefather, Niall Frossach, who first christened me Séamus, which then, in time, became Jamie when I traveled across the sea to the realm of the Picts. I rather liked it, so it has stayed with me, all these years, that naming." He was silent for a moment, lost in memories that, she realized with a start, had occurred long before she had even been born. "So no. He only knows who I am in a very broad sense. I had to explain my presence to his forefathers somehow when I arrived on the doorstep of their ancestral fortress."

"Why did you not stay here, at Grianán? Why did you leave?"

"Various reasons," Jamie said, and she gritted her teeth again at the elusive answer. "I often had other business that took me elsewhere, for varying stretches of time, but it has been, for all intents and purposes, my home since the night that Fúamnach destroyed my family right in front of me."

"Oh." Rozlyn paused, hesitating for a moment on whether to question him further. "Why did you choose Grianán?"

Jamie's face shuttered. "Ancient history."

"Don't be cryptic, Jamie." She leaned forward in her

saddle to peer at him. "It's a long journey. You might as well tell me the story to pass the time."

He smiled a little even as the shadows continued to flicker across his face. "Always begging for your stories. All right then, but when I become moody and my company somehow becomes even more unbearable for you than it now is, you have no one to blame but yourself."

"I'll remember that right before I steal your wine and toss you over the cliffs."

He huffed a reluctant laugh, then settled into his saddle. "I have many half brothers and half sisters, as you know, the legendary sons and daughters of the Dagda. I am a minor one, relatively unimportant and fairly forgotten in the stories of yore, content as I have been to observe the machinations of my countless family members, occasionally being called upon to pass judgment on some petty crime or slight that one has committed against another."

"Why? Why did they ask you to judge them?"

He shrugged. "Perhaps because I was so aloof from their doings, they trusted me to be unbiased. Or perhaps I was simply born impartial, an arbitrator in my soul." The corners of his eyes creased faintly. "It's there in my very name, you know. Midir, the judge—the midithir."

"I hadn't thought of that."

"Thus my mother named me. Only she knows why, and she would never deign to explain—she so rarely does." He ran his hand through his hair, an absent-minded movement, then continued. "Regardless, there I was, overlooked and forgotten, and quite frankly, content to be so, as I was only needed in those rare instances of pettiness, free to go where I pleased and do as I liked. So the years passed, and then the Fomorian giants declared war on the Tuatha Dé Danann, and we were all called to fight, forgotten sons included. At my father's summons, I returned from the corners of the world in which I had spent my days ambling about, growing and shaping and mastering my magic, much in the same way that you have these past few years. I spent centuries wandering the vastness of the world, but no more, for now, I was forced to rejoin my family in the North.

"The war," he said, his face growing pale, "was the most horrific thing that I had ever before witnessed. The blood and the gore and the screams of dying gods and giants, strewn across the blood-smattered fields of the earth, befouling the waters of the rivers. It destroyed it, the natural world that I loved as my own. Again and again, I was sick at the sight of it, never able to purge myself of the nausea that consumed me before such horrors."

Rozlyn sat up straighter in her saddle. "That first day at my father's castle, when I was sitting on the ledge. You said that you were squeamish, that you did not care for the sight of blood."

"I rarely lied to you, Rozi, regardless of what you have always thought," he answered without looking at her, and she frowned as he continued his story without elaborating further. "It came to a climax, though, after ten years of war at the Battle of Moytura. My father still served at the time under the rule of my grandfather, the elder king, Nuada, who had already sustained serious injury over the course of the war, including the loss of his own arm. But on that day, they both rode into battle side by side, and they both fell at the hands of the Fomorian giants—but only my father rose from the dead to rule as king."

"I remember this!" Rozlyn broke in. "The Mórrígan, she saves him."

"Indeed. And in the sorrowful aftermath, Lugh, the son of Balor, tyrant of the Fomorians, comes to my father in the night with his cunning and his cleverness to win the war once and for all for the Tuatha Dé Danann through the enchantments of Uaithne, the famed harp of the Dagda."

"I don't understand. What does this have to do with Grianán?"

"The Dagda built Grianán," Jamie said, and she could hear it now, that loneliness, the grief that came with centuries of solitude. "It is not so much a fortress as it is a tomb—a monument to the many gods who fell that day on its ground, staining its earth with their immortal blood. My half brother Aodh lies even now under its stone floors, killed by the Fomorian chief Corchenn of Cruach, with a single blow to his brain." He looked at her. "I crawled there, sobbing and heartbroken, three hundred years ago, because it was the only home left to me in this world, savaged by the brutal memories of death and destruction as it was. I threw myself on the ground at the mercy of its king, Niall Frossach, and my first friend in this mortal form that you now know me in."

Rozlyn was silent for a long time. "Jamie," she whispered. "I'm so sorry. I never thought to imagine how you must have suffered all these years, how lonely you must have been."

He continued to look straight ahead, his face expressionless. "It doesn't matter, a bhrèagha. We will make it right soon enough, you and I." He exhaled, like the rising wind before the first thunder of a sudden storm. "I did lie to you about one thing."

She tensed. "What?"

Jamie hesitated, and her fingers tightened on the reins. She would not like it, she knew instinctively, what he was about to confess to her, some new crime that he had committed against her, yet another sin for her to resent and mistrust. "When we first left the vale of Inagh, you asked why you could not just fly us to the Court of Shádach, and I told you that we must journey like this—" He gestured to their plodding horses, tails twitching behind them. "I said that we should take the horses so that we could draw out and subdue the monsters on our way."

"Yes?"

"That was a lie." There was a long moment of quiet between them as Rozlyn processed this revelation, her brow furrowing. "I was selfish," Jamie said, but she refused to look at him, focusing instead on the leather reins clutched in her trembling hands. "I thought that I could persuade you to surrender your magic—*my* magic—back to me so that I can be the one who wakes the gods from their slumber. It is my right." The word shuddered in the air between them, the first sluggish slide of an impending avalanche, and she pressed her lips shut as she listened. "The earth-mother gave it to me, Rozi. Hundreds of years ago, she gave to me the care and the command of the natural world. I wielded it well for hundreds of years before it was taken from me, and you cannot even begin to fathom the triumphs, the joys that I have won for myself and for those I love through its art. What you have in your veins is pilfered power, Rozi, and you will not long keep it after we have done our duty and raised the gods from the earth where they slumber."

Her heart thudded as she imagined her hand drawing back from the board in surprise. An ambush, a decoy—that was what his story about his brother had been, and here it was now, the true move—a skewer thrust right at the heart of her queen.

There was no mistaking the underlying meaning of his words.

Rozlyn pulled on the reins sharply, and her horse snorted and tossed its head as she leapt from the saddle and faced him with her hands on her hips. "Don't threaten me, Jamie."

"It's not a threat." He swung off his mare to face her. "It's the truth." He rubbed his face with both hands. "I said that I am sorry, Rozi."

"But we both know that you're not, Jamie. Not really."

"Fine. I am sorry, more than you know, but only that this is what it has come to between us, this hostility, this mistrust that you have for me."

She threw out her hands, and he flinched at the motion. "How can I trust you, Jamie? Over and over again, you have deceived me, tricked me, all for your own ends. What am I supposed to believe, as I clearly cannot trust anything that you say to me?"

He stared at her and said nothing, and she turned away, eyes smoldering. Air, she thought dimly. She needed air, and space, and the solitude of the trees. She stalked toward the wooded slope to her right, pushing aside the branches with shaky hands as she disappeared into the thicket. "I'm going for a walk, Jamie. Don't follow me."

She climbed up the hill, the winter wind whipping at her hair and flushing her cheeks, and she told herself that it was the icy sting making her eyes prickle and burn, the exertion from the climb that stole the breath from her lungs and caused her heart to pound so wildly in her chest. She reached the top of the knoll and leaned her forehead against the smooth trunk of a birch tree, her arms wrapped tight around her waist, searching for any remnants of calm that might linger in her soul.

Rozlyn heard his footsteps behind her, and she growled, the flicker of black feathers and talons flashing in the shadows behind her. "I said not to follow me."

The footsteps stopped. "I'm sorry, Rozi."

"So you keep saying. You lied to me, Jamie. There is no apology for that."

"That's not why I'm apologizing."

She whirled to face him, her teeth bared in a snarl. "For what, then? What, Jamie? There is an unending myriad of sins for which you should apologize, so choose one and get started because if you intend to go through all of them, then we will be here all night."

Jamie stared at her, his expression dark and unreadable. "I am sorry." It was said with such flatness, so utterly devoid of emotion, that Rozlyn shivered in spite of herself to hear it. "I am sorry that I ever knew you in the first place."

Rozlyn flinched. "None of this is my fault, Jamie."

"I know." He dropped his gaze to the ground and slid his hands to his pockets, and her heart ached, a single painful throb. "It's mine. I know that."

She folded her arms and waited, bracing herself for manipulation and lies, for whatever move he intended to make that he thought would bring him one step closer to victory.

"I should never have even tried," Jamie continued, and she couldn't see his face, dipped down to stare at the ground as he spoke. "I should have seen you and loved you, and then walked away, left you alone, let you marry another man and live out your days in peace, to find contentment in someone else's arms."

Rozlyn's frown deepened. "What are you talking about?

If I had married anyone else, I would have died. The curse would have killed me."

"No." She took a step backward at the word, hollow and defeated, not a triumphant king but a pawn, marching across the board to his doom. "Not then. Not that time." He raised his dark blue eyes to her face, swirling with centuries of regret and pain. "I meant that day on the beach."

CHAPTER
THIRTY-ONE

Midir lay next to his sleeping wife in his chambers in the Court of Shádach, listening to the waves rolling in the narrow sea that surrounded the island, admiring the curve of her cheek, flushed from his caresses. In the dim light of the hearth, he smiled to himself with all the satisfaction of a man well satiated. Three times, and gratification hummed in his chest at the memory. Three times she had turned to him, hungry and burning for his touch, even as he had settled back on the pillows, determined to let her rest. He closed his eyes, contentment flowing through his veins.

He had known, from the first moment that he had seen her, that she could match him in every way, as seamlessly as an aerie of falcons soars across the sky, slicing through the air, side by side. It was there even now as she slept, that wordless bond of unbreakable trust still humming between them.

He leaned over her, tracing the veins in her arms with the tip of his finger, and pressed a kiss to her temple. It was indissoluble, a thing of unrelenting permanence, this thread of true love between them, and he would—he knew it, beyond a shadow of a doubt—be true to her forever.

He fell asleep next to her, his hand entwined in hers and drifted into dreams with a smile on his lips.

He awoke to chaos.

Étaín was screaming next to him, the sheets of their marriage bed clutched to her chest, her tussled black hair streaming about her. He jolted up, his hands flexing, and he must still be dreaming, a nightmare of some kind, because his strangely sluggish fingers were robbed of their fire as they groped at the sheets, until he saw the sheen of her ebony hair glimmering in the light from the low-burning hearth.

"I hear congratulations are in order, my love, although I must say that I am rather hurt that you did not bother to invite me to your happy day."

"Fúamnach."

Even before the final syllable died away from her lips, Fúamnach snapped her fingers and spoke in that hateful, guttural-sounding language of hers, and then Étaín was hauled screaming from their bed by an invisible hand, dragged by her beautiful black hair. Midir shouted and tried to lunge after her, but fell to the ground, his body jerking haplessly in response to his efforts.

"Mortal bodies are terribly fragile, my love," he heard the witch say over Étaín's sobs. "I'm afraid that it will take some time for you to grow used to it."

He raised his head, which throbbed with unfamiliar pain, and looked at his wife, white-faced and terrified, as she stared at him in horror. "Midir," she gasped, "what have you done to him?"

"Don't be so horrified, you stupid girl. He is one of you

now. A mortal man, as you should have contented yourself with the first time, rather than stealing away my promised husband with your whorish ways."

Midir raised his trembling hands and looked at the exotic bend and flex of these strange new hands, cursing their feebleness even as he clenched them into an imitation of a fist. "What have you done, Fúamnach?"

"I have taken your power, you fool." It was a crow of triumph, a tiger's snarl of victory as it ripped the throat from its hapless victim. "I drained it away from you as you slept, exhausted, no doubt, from ridding your precious wife of her maidenhead so thoroughly—she is very loud, you know, for a virgin. I have your magic as my own, you see, and locked you away in one of these pathetic mortal forms that you seem so fond of."

Midir looked at her pitiless orange eyes and then at his wife, his beloved Étaín, and a bone-wrenching fear, the likes of which he had never before known, flooded through him. "Let her go, Fúamnach," he said through stiff, cold lips. "This is between us and us alone. Let her go."

"Of course," Fúamnach said, and he quailed at the way her lips curved into that snakelike smirk. "Whatever you like."

She turned, and Midir knew to keep his gaze fixed on hers, to hold fast to Étaín's beseeching stare in her final moments, those sea-deep eyes that he adored. "A bhrèagha."

He did not look away as the witch flicked her fingers at his wife, who shimmered in the air before him for the briefest of moments before she cascaded to the ground, a dark pool of water, puddling onto the cold stone floor.

"I'm doing you a favor, you know," Fúamnach said as he fell to his knees, screaming, while his wife dissolved into nothingness there on the floor. He could feel the loss of her, the loss of his magic, the agony of each one like tender red welts left by the savage strokes of a leather whip, and he keeled over from the pain of it all—the death of his wife and the demise of that power that was so bound to his very personhood. He rested his head on the floor, fighting the nausea that surged within him. "She never could have been your equal. The two of you would have been forever un-matched. Now though?" She gestured toward the watery remains of his beloved Étaín. "Now at least you are some-what more equitable—you, a pitiful excuse for a mortal, and she, a puddle of dirty water that you might shake from your boots." She smirked. "The two things are essentially the same, you know, compared with the splendor of an immortal being like myself, the wife you so thoughtlessly threw away."

"Fúamnach," he choked, raising his head to stare at her gloating face. "Fúamnach, I did not mean— I did not intend— Please, Fúamnach, please. You must stop this."

She laughed, shrill and mirthless. "I must do nothing of the sort," she said, brushing her fingers against the top of his head, and he shuddered as her sharp fingertips dug into his scalp. "Long have I waited for just such an excuse, my love, and here you have so kindly handed it to me upon a silver platter. Behold." Her nails slipped under his chin, and she forced him to look up, to stare into her orange eyes, gleaming with unholy fire. "See for yourself the power that you have given me, the power with which I shall command the entirety of the Tuatha Dé Danann and all their realm."

She stepped back, then raised her hand and flicked her wrist through the air. Before Midir's blurry vision, she shifted, growing broad-shouldered and tall with a braided dark-red beard, and eyes as dark as the northernmost lochs of Éire, a cruel parody of his own father standing before him, shuddering with laughter. "Imagine what power I can now wield," she boomed in his father's voice, fathoms-deep, the commander of the world. "Imagine what shall happen to that sanctimonious, insufferable family of yours—the so-called, self-appointed keepers of the earth—when I stride into your father's hall and command his own precious harp to sing for me the eternal death of his wife and his sons and his daughters, his sisters and brothers and cousins, the doom of all his kin."

"Fúamnach, *please*."

His father's lips parted in a savage parody of a grin. "How shall you feel, I wonder, when I make you watch as everyone you have ever loved is condemned to a fate far worse than death, centuries upon centuries of endless pain, knowing all the while that it was your selfishness that has caused the doom of your kind."

Midir closed his eyes, his grief too overwhelming to endure, and collapsed on the floor, his fingers trembling as he reached out to caress the surface of the pool of water, the remnants of his wife, in a final caress. "Just kill me," he whispered to the witch. "Kill me now, Fúamnach, so that I can join my wife in the realm of Magh Meall, to hold her in my arms for all eternity, whole and unbroken."

She laughed again, a thunderous laugh that seemed to shake the very foundations of the home of the gods to its core. "Your little wife is not dead, you fool," she jeered at him. "Were you not listening? This is your fate, to watch as all you love—all, I said—endure a fate worse than death, for centuries untold. Your precious mortal trash," she hissed, jabbing a thick finger at the puddle on the floor, "will live forever, but not in her own form. I shall force her to be reborn and to die, again and again, in a thousand different forms—a rat, a cow, a snake, or a crow, each one more demeaning than the last—for all eternity, and you will watch as what is left of her soul withers and dies inside whatever beastly form I grant her."

Midir moaned, and Fúamnach continued, her words dripping with ruthless malice. "She will not remember you, sweet lord, not your kisses or your sweet promises of love or your soft touches on her pretty skin. She will remember nothing of herself or of you, not even her own name." Those full lips lifted into a sneer. "At least, not until you free her, my love. If you can, that is." Midir looked up sharply, his heart seizing in his chest, and Fúamnach snapped her teeth together in an imitation of a smile. "This is her curse—she shall remain doomed to live out an eternity of lives, lost to herself and to you, until you can win her hand, just as you once did, whilst you are confined to this mortal body that I have bestowed upon you. Do this, and she is yours, her memory and her heart restored to you—but if you fail?" That deep voice rose several octaves, and he braced himself for her glee, the trapdoor fail-safe that she had surely established, because she would never let him win, never willingly grant to him even a chance at happiness. "Well. Then she will continue to endure whatever shame I choose to lay upon her, and you shall continue to watch every new life of hers flicker and die."

Midir slammed his fists against the floor, his face soaked with tears, but Fúamnach merely laughed. "But I have been so generous, my lord," she crooned, still in his father's voice. "Just look at how handsome I have made you. I have given you every opportunity to win her heart—again—and secure her as your own forever. I have been"—his father's stolen eyes narrowed to snakelike slits—"far fairer to you than you were to me."

"Spare her," Midir begged. "She has done you no wrong. It is only I—it was always I—who hurt you, who humiliated you. Let her be, Fúamnach, I beg of you."

Fúamnach hissed, then abruptly shifted into her sinuous body once more as she towered over him where he crouched on the floor—so weak, so pathetically weak. She grinned, teeth wicked-sharp and gleaming. "Just you wait, my love," she whispered, leaning in to run her finger down the side of his face. He jerked his head away, snarling, but she straightened, smiling as she turned away from him. "One day, after you have suffered enough to slake my thirst for vengeance, I will give you that same chance that you have just begged of me—to spare her, at the cost of your own happiness, your own life—and you will not heed your own plea any more than I."

A fierce surge of rage broke through the cloud of despair that hovered over him. "Never." He stumbled to his feet, his head woozy and his knees trembling. "I will never harm her, no matter what price I must pay."

Fúamnach smiled again, the toothy grin of a tigress on the hunt. She patted him on the cheek then turned to stalk away from where he stood, hands clamped into white-knuckled fists at his sides. "Never say never, my love." She vanished through the doorway, her answer echoing back to him as she strode away into the darkness to curse his family to an eternity of slumber and pain. "Never say never."

Chapter Thirty-Two

Rozlyn stared at him, her mind whirling, and he reached out to take her hand in his.

"It's true that I am Midir," he said. "But you are also Étaín, the wife whom I chose, whose love I won all those centuries ago, my brave brèagha. I have watched you be born and reborn a hundred times—as a dragonfly, a cat, a white-maned horse with eyes bright as the sea, even once as a waterfall that cascaded over the An Bhanna—over and over, until finally, you were born, this green-eyed girl whom you were three hundred years ago."

Her hands trembled, and the breath rushed out of her lungs, because she could almost see it, the peaceful, winding beauty of the wide-mouthed river, the soft churn of the white-water falls on its smooth gray rocks.

"I tried to tell you," he whispered. "Years ago, I tried to tell you the truth of us, but you were so dismissive, so scornful. So I lost my nerve, Rozi, and I could not bear to bring myself to tell you what we once were to each other, what you still are to me, even all these centuries later."

"But why?" She shook her head, fighting the fog swirling through her, threatening to swallow her whole. "Who did this?"

"Fúamnach, of course. She was furious that I chose you, a human girl, over her, and she cursed me, cursed us—she doomed my people to a living *death*—all for the sake of her revenge. Only if I could gain your love and your hand in marriage, as a mortal, not as an all-powerful god, would I break the curse and restore your memory of who you truly were, who we were, together, to each other." His chest heaved. "But she took precautions. After three hundred years, she finally allowed you to be reborn as you truly are, but she cursed you as well, doomed you with a few drops of the very magic that she had stolen from me centuries before, that she had kept hidden away by her arts, and threatened to destroy it, to destroy *you*, if you ever married and ceded your power to your husband." He swallowed again. "To me."

The Cailleach, Rozlyn thought dimly. The Cailleach's prophecy that presented her on a silver platter to her father and her husband, a sacrificial lamb for the bloodlust of the witch.

"Don't you see, Rozi—a bhrèagha? I had to do it. I would never be able to make you love me in the way that she required to bring back your memories, not with the threat of you losing magic constantly looming, which she knew you would learn to treasure so dearly. It was always a dead end, Rozi, a trap with no escape." He blinked, and something akin to tears shimmered in his eyes. "We were never going to be allowed to be together, Rozi. It is not our fate."

Her heart shuddered once, then cracked in two, rupturing along the familiar lines of new-healed scars. How many times, she wondered, had she endured this pain? How many times had she lived through this anguish, this grief? How many more times could she survive a shattered soul before it became too broken, too damaged, to heal?

"Unless." Her eyes cut back to Jamie as he spoke, still watching her, guarded and wary. "Unless you give it back to me, this power, this shred of my divinity, Rozi. It is mine by right, the only way that I will ever free my people from this sleeping death to which they have been condemned." A brush of his fingers against the back of her hand, tentative and soft—persuasive, she thought dully. Coaxing.

His specialty. It had always been.

"It will be better this way," she heard him say through the dull roar of hurt, of confusion throbbing in her temples. "We'll go together to Inis Trá Tholl, to the Court of Shádach, and then we will set this right. We will free them," he continued, that smooth slide of his fingers against her skin so unbearably, achingly persuasive, "and they can save you, restore you to your former self, as you once were, and we—we can have the life we wanted, the life that was stolen from us. Everything will be as it was."

"I won't give it to you." She whirled away, stumbling toward the side of the cliff, her head shaking furiously. "It is all I have, Jamie, all that I have ever had. I have been despised and loathed my whole life, locked away and lied to, abused by everyone who has ever claimed to love me, and this is the only thing that has kept me sane, kept me whole, given me any taste of peace, no matter how brief, and I will never give it up."

"Rozi," he pleaded, his footsteps falling fast behind her. "You have to trust me. You must trust that I will protect you, that I will care for you, no matter what. Once the powers of the Tuatha Dé Danann are awakened, you can be shielded, protected from death when this magic is ripped away from you. I would never allow you to die. I love you. You know that I do."

"Don't talk to me about love." She spun around to face him and shoved at his shoulders, sparks flying from her fingertips. "You are willing to destroy me, Rozlyn, all for the sake of your precious power."

Jamie seized her elbows in his hands. "Do you know what I have sacrificed for you, Rozi? For three hundred years, I have followed you from one end of this realm to the other, devoted to you and you alone, regardless of what form you manifested in. I have loved you as a dapple-coated mare, running wild through the plains of the midlands. I marveled at your speed, your strength as you galloped through the cool wet grass, your mane streaming in the wind." She whimpered, and he loosened his grip on her arms. "I have loved you as a scarlet-winged dragonfly, flitting through the reeds of the river as I lay on my back in the sun, watching the light reflecting off the surface of the water, bedazzling your wings." His hands slid up and down her arms, gentle and slow. "I have loved you as a falcon, screaming on the wind, a glorious force of nature, unparalleled for your grace and your speed." His hands drifted up to cup her cheeks, and she fought back the tears rising in her throat as she stared at him. "Even as a waterfall, inanimate and senseless, I would rest my head against the moss-covered stones underneath your misty rain and dream of you. For three hundred years, I have waited and watched and been loyal to you, to the vows that we swore to one another centuries ago, and finally, you reemerge into this world as I first knew you, and I watched and said nothing as you dallied with and kissed dozens of other men before my very eyes. I have lied to you and deceived you, it is true, and I know that I shall have to atone for that in ways that cause me such great pain that this mortal chest of mine aches as though it would shatter into thousands of bitter shards, but do not—" His voice deepened, thickened with emotion as he dropped his hands and stepped away from her. "Do not lecture me about the depths of my love for you, a bhrèagha."

Rozlyn's breaths came fast and furious as an explosion of vague, half-formed images flashed through her memory. She remembered lying on her bed in her tower room, painting snatches of stories on the beams of the ceiling with the remnants of moonlight that streamed in her window—always, it was always falcons and horses and dragonflies that came to life under her wandering fingers. Even as the memory flickered through her mind, there came a surge of new remembrances—racing through the snow-crusted lowlands as a brown-spotted hare, ears and nose twitching, leaping through the current of the river, pink-gray scales flashing as a cold-skinned trout—and through it all, a tall shadow, watching from a distance. It crouched before her in the grass, offering leaves of cabbage to her tentatively twitching nose, or a hand that stroked the tip of her snow-white snout. Her vision blurred with the onslaught of long-unused tears, and she made a small choking sound as he waited nearby, hands clenched and chest heaving, tortuously still as he watched her relive in flashes and flickers the lost years of their love.

"I remember," she whispered. She lifted her shining gray-green eyes to his face. "I remember you."

Something splintered across his tense face, and in three swift steps he was there, his arms encircling her, and she lifted her lips to his, their heartbeats singing in perfect harmony at long last.

CHAPTER
THIRTY-THREE

The next four days passed in a blur, full of entwining fingers and whispered secrets and stories of transformations and lonely ordeals, of legs lingering against each other's as the horses jostled together, an unending thirst for closeness, this constant longing for the other's touch. The nights were hazy too, arms and legs wrapped around each other, cocooned in a single blanket, full of deep kisses and gasping sighs and soft touches that would slowly begin to quicken into harder, more urgent caresses, pushing the boundaries of where they both so desperately longed to go, only to pull away, hot-cheeked and frustrated.

Jamie had only once suggested in the quiet hours of that first night, with her head on his chest and his fingers in her hair, that they could leave the horses, and she could shift, fly them through the night to the Court of Shádach as she had first suggested, but she interrupted him hurriedly, protesting that it would be cruel to abandon the horses, that they would surely suffer a terrible fate if left to wander the northern realm in the midst of winter on their own, and he had agreed, because even if they gifted them to a farmer along the way, he reasoned, there was no guarantee that the man would not turn out to be a cruel master and torture them, abuse them, and after all, they were such good mounts—surely they deserved far better than to have their happiness risked so needlessly.

They both recognized the lies in their assurances but said nothing.

They never spoke of the decision—or why, exactly, they pulled away from each other so abruptly in the middle of the night—nor of the ever-present shadow of that thrumming magic in her veins, even as it sang to him with a siren's call of desire and yearning.

They rode and they walked and they ate and they teased and they kissed and they held each other close, serenely happy for the little time that was left to them.

No more games. No more matches. Both of their kings had toppled over and lay inert and unprotected on the board, gathering dust.

The day dawned when they halted before the gray-walled fortress of Grianán, their fingers linked, knees brushing, as their horses snuffled one another's noses.

Rozlyn fidgeted in her saddle, and Jamie glanced at her. "Nervous?"

"No. Yes. Are you so sure that he will want to welcome the Beast of Connacht into his home?"

"He would damn well welcome my wife even if she were a two-faced hag who ate her own toenails," Jamie answered as their horses plodded their way toward the drawbridge that stretched across the moat next to the thick stone walls of the barbican. She tried not to flinch at the sight of the silent, ironclad soldiers with their thick metal helmets and long wooden spears that stood along the balustrade, watching them approach.

Before she could venture to whisper a word of warning to Jamie, the drawbridge creaked and rumbled as the mechanism by its side began to turn, whining in protest as it wound its way around the thick metal chain that bound it. Down, down it went, until it landed with a thud on the ground at their feet, inviting them to cross.

They dismounted, and Rozlyn's fingers tightened around Jamie's, her other hand gripping the leather reins of her black gelding a little tighter, aching to escape, to flee, before she could again be caged by a powerful king behind high stone walls, when a booming voice rang out across the bridge. "You stupid son of a bitch, you really have gone and got yourself caught in a marriage-bond, haven't you?"

Jamie waved cheerfully in response even as Rozlyn tensed, and the man behind the voice appeared above the balustrade, leaning over the tall stone wall, his bright red beard fluttering in the breeze. He whistled. "Well, at least you picked a beauty, I'll give you that."

Jamie laughed and slipped his arm around Rozlyn's waist. "Content yourself with your own wives, Flaithbertach, and leave mine be."

The king of Aileach snorted. "I can't keep one long enough to be content, you mucker. They keep leaving me for handsome men."

Rozlyn could not help but feel a throb of sympathy for these wives as she studied him, because he surely was the ugliest man that she had ever seen, with a bulbous nose and flat lips and wide-set eyes, with a mass of unkempt bright-red hair. Jamie shrugged. "You need to find a girl who values power over beauty, Bertie," he called up, and Rozlyn jolted to hear the casual affection behind the nickname. "That one you might keep."

"True, true," the king replied, slinging his arm companionably around the silent, stone-faced soldier next to him. "Och, have you heard though? Mackey here has gone and knocked up the bread-maker's daughter. He'll be joining you soon enough in the living hell that is a marriage-bond."

"Condolences," Jamie said with a grin, and Rozlyn shoved an elbow into his ribs. He cleared his throat in a silent apology. "Are you going to invite us in, Bertie, or are we to sleep in the moat tonight?"

"You can sleep in the moat. Your wife can sleep wherever she so pleases, although you should know, pretty lady, my room is by far the most comfortable." His bushy red eyebrows waggled at her, and a surge of something like begrudging laughter stirred inside her at his ugly, honest face.

Jamie rolled his eyes. "I'm coming in." He stalked forward, one hand on the reins of his mare, while the other slipped down to squeeze Rozlyn's own. "If you tell your men to shoot me, at least have the decency to have them put one through my brain and not my gut."

"I'll tell them to aim a bit lower than that, you mucker." The king disappeared behind the wide expanse of his tall stone wall, and Jamie turned to grin again, this time at her.

"That's the king of Aileach?" Rozlyn whispered as they led their horses across the wooden drawbridge, the black water of the moat stirring beneath them.

There was something down there. She could all but hear it, the purr of its black teeth, see the shine of its waterlogged eyes, and she shivered. Perhaps this was one monster they could forgo fighting.

"Not what you expected, I take it."

"He is very, very different from—from other kings."

"He is not your father, Rozi. He would not lock you away, and even if he tried"—his voice hardened—"you are hardly that girl again, unskilled in magic and unaware of the truth of your world. You could crush him like a bug if you so choose, and believe me, he knows it."

She choked as they entered under the portcullis. "He knows what I am?"

"Of course he knows." Jamie shrugged even as the mechanism beside them groaned once more, the drawbridge beginning to rise back up over the waters of the moat. "I told him years ago."

Rozlyn jerked her hand away, her fingers flexing. "Jamie—"

"Let me look at you!" The king boomed out again as he tripped down the steps, an ungainly, broad-waisted man, his freckles glowing in the pale sunlight. "You don't look much like a monster, I must say."

"You might say differently if she does not get her breakfast on time in the morning," Jamie said, and the king roared with peals of laughter as Rozlyn swiveled around to glare at him.

He winked once, then jerked his chin toward the king.

Rozlyn turned back to face Flaithbertach, straightening her shoulders. "A rí," she murmured, bowing her head, trying to will the stiffness in her shoulders to ease, the panic hovering just below the surface to subside.

The king snorted. "What good manners for a Beast." He gestured toward her, an impatient child demanding a trick. "Come here, girl. Let's see it."

Rozlyn froze, a flare of irritation, of resentment dancing

up her spine. She was no one's puppet, nor an abomination to be ogled.

"I don't—" She trailed away, and Jamie moved closer to her, hovering a hair's breadth away. His finger traced the inside of her wrist, coming to rest over the fluttering beat of her pulse, a silent reassurance.

Flaithbertach huffed, then turned to Jamie. "That's it? That's the Beast that so plagued Connacht? What a region of weaklings they are."

Rozlyn bared her teeth in a hiss. "No king commands me," she growled, and the guards around her tightened their grips on their spears even as Flaithbertach barked a sharp laugh.

"She's as brazen as you said," the king said to Jamie, amused. "But so far, I'm not particularly impressed. She's not so scary. Far too pretty."

Rozlyn glanced at Jamie, who gently pulled his hand from hers and crossed his arms over his chest, waiting. He lifted his brows at her, and that silver thread of understanding between them snapped tight once more as they watched each other.

Without warning, she shifted, exploding into the sunlit sky with the blackness of night. All around her, screams erupted from the denizens of the castle as her black-feathered shadow of talons and claws fell across the courtyard while she soared in predatory circles above them.

She dove, faster than the arrows that flew around her. Even as she heard Jamie's shouted warning, she reached out and gripped the woolen doublet of the king in her claws and tore away into the sky with Flaithbertach tight in her grasp.

He bellowed as she flew higher and higher, faster and faster, the wind screaming through her wings until she leveled out among the clouds, the looming sprawl of his stone-walled fortress a mere dot on the ground beneath him. He gasped wordlessly in her grip as he clung to the black fur of her legs. "What the hell—"

She dropped him.

He fell screaming, whistling toward the earth, and she tilted her massive head to the side and watched him, then bent her wings in a sudden dive, careening toward him, and snatched him up again in her claws right before he crashed to the earth at the feet of his hall guards.

She caught the briefest glimpse of their wide-eyed, horrified faces—the faintest flash of Jamie's grin—then she soared away again, the king limp in her clutches, to the top of the tower that loomed at the center of his castle. She unceremoniously plopped him down onto the slate-tiled roof where she perched next to him, tucking her wings against her shoulder blades, and then lifted a thick black paw to her jaws, licking at it with her tongue as she proceeded to wash her face in supreme indifference to the white-faced man who shivered next to her.

He sat up, his hands quivering, and then he rolled to his side and vomited off the roof onto his terrified hall-troop below. Rozlyn grumbled deep in her throat as he gagged twice, wiping his mouth on the sleeve of his coat, then twisted to stare at her, white-faced but bright-eyed. "Gods be damned," he panted, "now that is what I call a beast."

Her jowls parted and she grinned at him in her blue-black haired form, then stretched out a black-feathered wing and tapped him on the back, and he waved his still-trembling hand. "Apology accepted. You proved your point, girl. Now, if you don't mind—"

Rozlyn snatched him so swiftly that the words still seemed

to hang in the air between them as she tumbled off the roof in a freefall of wings and talons and fur, the king shrieking in her clutches, this time in delight at the raw force of her strength. Her wings parachuted out as they floated to rest on the floor of the courtyard, the soldiers and servants and peasants and nobles standing stock-still, frozen in terror, as their king pushed to his feet and brushed the dirt and vomit off the front of his dark-red robe. She twitched her nose and shifted in a single fluid motion, shaking out her long black hair with a careless hand, then stalked over to where Jamie still stood, hands in his pockets, grinning at her wickedness. She looped her arm through his, and he bent his head to brush a kiss against her cheek. "Will there be anything else, mo rí?"

The king raised his beefy arms above his head. He threw back his head and shouted, "Behold, the Beast of Connacht! Let's have a drink!" The crowd around him exploded, a deafening roar of celebration, for clearly, the infamous Beast of Connacht was no more, and the queen of monsters, regal and tall, had taken its place.

CHAPTER THIRTY-FOUR

"Thanks again, Bertie." Jamie clasped the meaty hand of the king in his own.

"Och, it's nothing, you mucker. I know how long you have waited for this day." Flaithbertach rubbed his beefy hand across his beard. "Be careful though. There's a reason no ship has ever returned from its shores in three hundred years, don't you know."

Jamie nodded. "I know what is waiting there in the court of shadows." His face hardened. "I can handle it." Flaith-bertach nodded, and at the outskirts of Cionn Mhálanna, they stood together staring down at the misty stretch of the peninsula, the last remaining strip of land that stood be-tween him and home.

It was there, waiting for him, his ancestral home—the thrum of magic that danced along its marble walls, the cold bite of the air of this northernmost isle, the sound of the bustle and clamor of a great hall full of gods at the apex of the earth.

Soon enough, all that glory could be restored. It rested on his wife's shoulders now, the fates of so many beings of omnipotence and might.

He knew she was watching as he bid farewell to the king who had hosted them over the past few days. She stood aloof from the rest of them, the men and women who had dined with her only last night giving her a wide berth as they scurried about, an unconscious avoidance of the unnatural stillness of her stance, the unearthly watchfulness of her gaze.

His wife had always been alone, even when he had first known her—that rose-lovely girl with sand on her feet and drops of saltwater in her hair—as he had been too, until the welding of that enigmatic bond between them, carved from silver and steel.

A lump of bile flooded his throat as he thought of what else awaited them on the island of the gods—the inevitable sundering of whatever tremulous thread of the bond they had painfully, laboriously rebuilt over the past few weeks.

She could not honestly believe that he would let her keep his powers as her own.

Beside him, Flaithbertach cleared his throat, and Jamie shoved away his distraction, his dread, smiling with that false bravado, that debonair carelessness that he'd worn wrapped around himself like a second skin for centuries now, ever since he'd been the forgotten boy-child of the father of the gods, with his meager skills of changing flies into horses and the snow into sun. It was second nature to him still, even in this borrowed body. "I will never forget your kindness, Bertie. The gods will owe you and your children and your children's children a debt for all their days."

"Don't think that I won't expect to collect it," the king

huffed as he turned to observe Rozlyn where she waited for Jamie. "What of that wife of yours? What debt does she owe me?"

"None," Jamie said. "Although you might owe her one, seeing as how you are not, in fact, flat as a potato pancake on the floor of your courtyard as we speak."

Flaithbertach chuckled. "I've always liked a woman with balls." With this odd pronouncement, he gripped Jamie's shoulder in a wordless farewell and strode away, nodding to the soldiers he had tasked with seeing them across the narrow strip of sea at the northernmost edge of Dúnalde-ragh. Just across the water, hidden in the fog, lay Inis Trá Tholl and the Court of Shádach.

Steeling himself, Jamie came to stand by her side, and she slipped her hand into his without a word, as though she knew this was the last time that she would ever be able to do so and was already trying to distance her-self from this silver-threaded attachment between them. They stood in silence, shoulder to shoulder, staring into the fog that rolled off the silhouette of the island in the distance.

"Let's go tomorrow," he said. "We stay here tonight, en-camped on the ship, and we leave at dawn."

Rozlyn's ice-cold fingers relaxed ever so slightly in his own. "One more night."

"If you like. And as many nights as we want, Rozi, after this next one. I promise."

She stiffened, then slipped her hand from his as she walked away toward the shoreline, avoiding his eyes. "You'd better go tell the men."

They curled together in the smallest cabin on the wooden ship that night, arms and legs entwined around each other, so close that the tips of their noses brushed each time they exhaled, and their breaths intermingled in their sleep.

Rozlyn awoke wrapped in his arms when the pale cold moon was high above her in the sky, every drop of that preternatural power in her veins thrumming in urgent warning. She sat up, pulling free of Jamie's arms. He grunted, a sleepy protest, but she ignored him, listening to the utter stillness around them.

There—a faint crackling on the deck above, the slightest creak of wrongness that whispered through the wood over her head. She shook his shoulder. "Jamie. Wake up."

His eyes flew open, bleary at first, then they focused, bright and alert, at the sight of her face. "What's wrong?"

"Something is up there," she whispered, pointing at the deck above.

Jamie sat up, reaching for his bow and quiver. "I don't hear anything."

"It sounds like—" She listened again, straining with all her otherworldly senses. "It sounds like fire, falling from the sky like rain, a river of flames." She flushed. "That doesn't make sense, I know, but—"

"Seven shades of shite."

She jolted at the curse, his face gone pale and tight. "What?"

His fingers trembled as he reached for her hand. "Rozi. The Abhartach."

Rozlyn's face went white.

She remembered the story he had told her long ago—when it was nothing but a ghost tale, losing its horror beneath the bright springtime sun, Rozlyn munching on soda bread while he regaled her with stories of the myths and monsters of the realm of Éire. The Abhartach, he had whispered, lowering his voice to an ominous pitch, was the deadliest creature in all of Éire, one that hunted even the gods themselves for his own dark desires. The Abhartach was rumored to have been a brutal warlord of the eastern province of Leinster, Jamie had told her, centuries ago, back when Éire was still a young maiden in the first bloom of her youth. But despite his prowess as a warrior and his rumored might as a dark-magic druid, his people had hated him for his cruelty, his savagery, and they had conspired with a neighboring king to lay waste to his castle while he slept and to slaughter him in his own bed.

Rozlyn's awestruck lips had parted as Jamie had smiled at her, then told her how the warlord's people chose to honor him as a warrior even in his death, burying him upright in his tomb, his arms crossed over his chest, his spear in his hand. But they did not anticipate, Jamie had said, how he would rise from his tomb, a bloodless, stone-skinned monster—the king of the vampírs, the first of its kind, devoid of any lingering shreds of humanity, invulnerable to any weapons of iron or steel. The Abhartach was filled with rage at the treachery of its kinsmen, and it stalked through the land, devouring any innocent it found in its way, drinking their blood to feed its own strength, growing more and more potent with each victim it drained. Its sorcery, Jamie had claimed, grew a hundredfold, and the people began to lock their doors and douse their hearth-fires on the red nights, when the sky turned crimson, blotting out the stars, as though a river of fire suddenly surged through the darkness, a sure sign that the Abhartach had awakened from its grave and stalked the night in an eternal quest to slake its bloodthirst for vengeance and death.

Rozlyn shuddered as she remembered the story now, huddled beneath the hull of the ship. "That was real?"

"Of course it was real, Rozi. The dearg-dur was real enough, wasn't she, poor soul that she was." His grip tightened. "This is far worse. He cannot be reasoned with or contained, and he is most assuredly here for you, Rozi."

Sweat beaded along her forehead, at the base of her neck, and along with it, an all-too-familiar nausea clawing at her throat.

Guilt.

She was moving for the cabin door, toward the stairs that led up to the deck, where all those oblivious, hapless soldiers sat waiting, the too-easy victims of such an unstoppable force, when Jamie seized her by the shoulders, pinning her against the wall. "What are you doing? Are you mad? You can't go up there, Rozi."

"I have to! I have to protect them, to save them. Jamie, they will *die*."

"And so will you," he said, his grip tight and unyielding on her arms. "That creature has long been driven mad by thirst, a thirst for the same power you wield. It has not satisfied nor fed that appetite in three hundred years, and it has clearly been stalking you for a long, long time. It will not stop until it has drunk every last drop of your blood in its quest to rule over the entire realm."

An ice-kissed knife of fear sliced through her, but she ignored it, shoving him away as she fumbled with door to stumble out into the hall. "I don't care. Flaithbertach's soldiers—it will kill them; we have to stop it."

His hand wrapped around her wrist, yanking her

backward, and she yelped in shock. "It's too late for them, Rozi." His face was grim as he spun her to face him in the darkened corridor, weaving slightly as the ship rocked side to side in the harbor. "If the Abhartach is here, you can't save them."

"I can fight it! I can shift, and I can kill it, Jamie. I am the Beast of Connacht. I am the queen of monsters, Jamie, and I can defeat it, I can, like all the others!"

"This is nothing like the others, Rozi." She flinched as though he had slapped her. "Hardly even the gods them-selves can stand against this creature, forged as it was in the dark fires of the devil's own sorcery, do you understand? It is *invincible*."

"So am I." She shoved against him once more, trying to free herself from his unyielding grip, struggling to get to the stairs, to make her way aboveboard, to fight as she was born to fight.

"You have fangs," he said, urgency vibrating in every word, refusing to loosen his iron-tight hold on her arms. "And claws, and a tenuous command at best over the ele-mentals of the world. You are many things, Rozi, but you are not invincible, and I swear by the Dagda himself, you will not be learning that lesson this night."

Something snapped inside her, a crude splintering along the sutured lines of decades-old scars. "Jamie," she whis-pered, her fingers twisting in the soft fleece of his shirt. "I can't bear it, to stand by, to flee, knowing that they—" Her breath shuddered once, and even in the gloom of the cor-ridor, gripped by fear, she saw his eyes soften.

"Their blood is not on you, Rozi."

"Oh, Jamie," she whispered. "I thought we were no longer lying to one another."

A heartbeat, then two passed, before his hand came up to grip her chin, tilting her face toward his, bone-weary and sad. He leaned forward to press a kiss to the top of her head. "Shift," he said. "Shift, while you still have time, and go across the sea, as we should have done in the first place—if I hadn't been so damn selfish. It can't follow you there." For the briefest moment, he rested his forehead against hers, and through the growing scent of smoke, it washed over her, the smell of his sweat and pine sap and the faintest trace of the brackish scent of the sea. "Go now, before it finds you."

Rozlyn's heart stuttered to a stop. "Not without you."

"This is not your guilt to bear." He pulled away from her, drawing an arrow from his quiver and nocking it to his bow. "I will try and save as many of Flaithbertach's men as I can while you escape, Rozi. I brought them here; they were entrusted into my care. It is my responsibility, my obligation, to die with them."

"No."

"Free the gods," he said, backing away from her toward the stairs, and she made a keening sound at the sight of him, face tight with determination, white as a corpse. "That is your duty, a bhrèagha, and this is mine."

She opened her mouth to scream at him, churning with an internal tempest of wordless fury, when all hell broke loose above them—without warning, the boards of the ship quaked once, an ominous shudder, and then the night air was split in two with inhuman screams.

"Rozi, go." Jamie's urgent command broke through her horrified trance, and she whirled around to watch him disappear, his footsteps thudding up the stairs, even as the sound of the pandemonium rose to a fever pitch above them, punctuated with clanging steel and shrieked curses and vicious, unearthly hissing.

Distantly, through the wild, frantic shrieking from above and the roaring in her ears, she heard a heavy thud, then another, and another, a rapid-fire succession of bodies slumping to the floor.

She wondered if one of them was Jamie's.

Then she was moving, running for those same stairs, fingers curling into talons at her sides, fangs lengthening and tail sprouting, bounding up the stairs as her wings scraped against the narrow walls of the stairwell. She was strong, she thought wildly. She was powerful, a queen of beasts. She could fight this monster as she had all the others.

She could save them—save him.

Rozlyn burst through the door onto the deck of the ship, her paws sliding precariously in puddles of rainwater.

Not rainwater, she realized, and even in her beastly form she quaked with fear. Not water but blood, an endless sea of blood coating the deck, and the night sky burning with unnatural fire—and there, at the far end of the ship, wreathed in billowing pillars of smoke and flame, its face a bloodless white, was the Abhartach, corpses piled about its feet. She watched, frozen in horror, as it turned its face toward a soldier crouching against the rail of the ship, his arms clasped over his head, and swifter than she could see, it struck, fangs flashing, and the soldier slumped to the ground, eyes rolling into the back of his skull, his hands fluttering toward his crimson throat. The Abhartach hissed once, its tongue flickering between its teeth like a snake, bending toward the twitching soldiers, his mouth ajar as he shook with hunger.

Is this what she had once been, Rozlyn wondered dimly through the sobs and moans of the dying soldiers all around her.

How did this slaughter, this ruthless massacre of innocent men, compare to the carnage the people at Connacht had endured for so many years at her unwitting hands?

She shook herself free of her morbid epiphany, searching the shadows, straining to catch that familiar scent of cedar and salt through the bitter tang of blood lying heavy in the night air. Where was Jamie? Where was Jamie? She needed to find Jamie—

The Abhartach froze in the midst of feeding, as if sensing her scrutiny, and swiveled its head around until it stared directly at her with those preternatural yellow eyes. They widened, and she could almost see herself in their glow— as she truly was, a pale-faced girl with the faint shadows of magic sparking in her soul. It recognized her. It recognized her now, as the dobhar-chú, as the merrow, as the púca all had, a hollow kind of sisterhood.

It cast the limp soldier aside like an unwanted doll and rose with a stealthy menace, its mouth opening in a long, satisfied hiss.

And Rozlyn, the queen of monsters, cowered, her wings drooping, her tail tucked between her hind legs.

She knew, in that unearthly way of hers, by whatever gift had allowed her to command the dobhar-chú and to befriend the púca and the merrow, that this was not a fight that she could win.

She was outmatched in this game, and the only hope of surviving was to concede.

To run.

The Abhartach struck, faster than a snake, and she whirled away, panic clawing at her throat as she scrambled over him, wings flailing gracelessly as she scanned the corpse-laden ship, searching for a swatch of dark hair, a pair of sightless blue eyes. She slammed into the deck, on the far side of the Abhartach, clawing her way through the sea of bodies, and she heard it hiss again, furious and hungry. From the corner of her eye, she saw it bend its knees, preparing to strike.

There. A flash of brown hair, a black fleece doublet, and she lunged forward, catching the back of his shirt in her teeth.

His eyes fluttered once, twice, and she whined deep in her throat, too-human sobs rising in her bestial chest. She launched into the air, wings wheeling, and below a blurry shadow crashed onto the spot where she had stood only seconds before, and it raised its waxen face toward the sky and screamed, bloodcurdling and filled with rage. Jamie thrashed weakly in her grip as she hovered high in the air above the ship and stared down into the vengeful glare of the Abhartach where it stood, its head tilted back at the red-fire sky, his black cloak riddled with blood.

A handful of men still crawled about on the deck below, slipping on the blood of their companions as they clambered on their hands and knees toward the sides of the ship, toward the rickety wooden bridge that still moored them to the dock, to the ice-black waves that lapped at the side of the ship, anything other than the inexorable fangs of this most evil of monsters.

For a moment, she hesitated, ignoring that urgent screeching voice inside her that told her, beyond a shadow of a doubt, that this unnatural creature would be her final undoing. For a moment, she considered. If she could get Jamie somewhere safe, and then come back, come back and fight, kill it, kill this abomination, this monster that was nothing like her yet everything like—

"Rozi." His voice was a whispered croak, faint and raw with pain, a feeble twin to that same inexorable power within her that urged and begged her to flee, to fly fast and far away from this abomination that would surely destroy her if she gave it the chance. "Don't."

She whined once, and then Rozlyn felt Jamie go limp in her jaws, his arms dangling in the air. She watched as the Abhartach snapped its teeth at where she hovered above him, then turned away, its attention fixed on the faint outline of a one-armed soldier dragging himself over the side of the ship.

There was so much blood. So much death tonight, because of her.

She forced herself to suck the air into her lungs, one shuddered breath, and then another, a cacophony of harsh, ragged gasps, a lifeline to the here and now—because suddenly she was five years old again, standing in the doorway of her father's home, staring out across the mutilated grass of the courtyard, seeing for the first time all the victims who had died for her, the birthright of blood and pain that she had brought into the world. Innumerable souls, gone, wasted and destroyed, always because of her.

That fragile hope of a dream, that tremulous belief that someday, somehow, she could be free of her past sins, that heavy, ever-present burden of guilt, shattered.

She could not save them. There could be no saving of herself either.

Sobs broke free from her chest, and she clutched Jamie's sagging form more tightly in her jaws, then with a furious flap of her wings, tore away into the bloodred sky, winging their way toward Inis Trá Tholl and the Court of Shádach.

CHAPTER THIRTY-FIVE

She landed on the mist-shrouded rocky shore of the island with a crash. As soon as Jamie rolled away from her claws, she shifted in a single fluid motion, stumbling to her knees and burying her face in her hands as her shoulders heaved, convulsing with the violence of her sobs.

They were boulders—great gray stones, like the ones that lined the sloping hills of her valley, heavy burdens of unforgiving stone—these griefs she bore in her heart, all the lives that had been stolen away because of her.

So many lost. So many precious things lost, vanished forever on the winds of her cursed existence. It was too much, she sobbed into her hands, hidden beneath the black veil of her hair. It was too much for one woman to bear.

Jamie groaned on the frozen ground next to her and sat up, reaching unsteadily for her where she knelt on the frozen ground, her forehead pressed against her knees. "Rozi."

"They died, Jamie," she whispered through a cloud of

tears. "All of them, because of me, just like all the others, for so many years." She shuddered. "How many lives have I destroyed, Jamie, faces I can't even remember? How many more? Because there will always be more, always, and I can't take it any longer. I can't stand it—"

Jamie crawled across the ground to where she crouched. "It's not your fault, Rozi," he said, and she shied away from his touch. "It's no one's fault but hers."

"How can this end? I don't see how this can ever be made right."

"It can't, not fully." He ran his hand through her bedraggled hair. "But you have to trust, to believe that the Tuatha Dé Danann will help. This is their purpose, the reason that the earth-mother brought us into existence all those centuries ago. We care for the things of the earth, your people included, and the vicious monsters who ravage the realm of mortals will once more be leashed when my family again walks among you."

Rozlyn closed her eyes. It was that same coaxing tone, the sweet, honeyed persuasion, which he had wielded against her so long ago in her father's hall, the last time that she sobbed in his arms. It had been a lure, bright-colored and bedazzled, which he had dangled before her, a carefully laid trap that would ensnare her into whispering those fateful vows that would loose the bindings of her magic and set her free into the ether.

She found that she was too weary to care.

"I should have married you the moment that you walked into my father's castle and been done with it."

His hand stilled in her hair.

"I should have married you," she said, "and died there wherever you left me, and that would have at least been ten fewer years of suffering that I'd have wrought upon the world."

"I never would have let you die." It was a whiplike protest, a savage crack that echoed in the empty air. "I told you. We would have gone north to find whatever druids remained."

"There are no druids," she said dully. "Galena told me. She is the last of their line, their sorcery forever lost to this world." He pulled back to stare at her, his brow knitting together around an ugly black bruise forming on his forehead. He should treat that, she thought dimly. Some yarrow root and witch hazel would do it. "What would you have done, then, when you learned there was no hope to be found in the North, when the Beast inside me showed signs that it would soon claw its way free? Would you still have sought to save me, even then?"

"I would have found a way."

She ignored it, this feeble attempt at a lie. "We both know that my father should have thrown me from the tower to die on the night that I was born."

"Stop." Jamie staggered to his feet, looming over her, his expression dark. "First off, it wouldn't have mattered if he did. You would have been reborn again and again, and eventually, another three hundred years from now, you and I would have been right here where we are. She would never have relented so easily as that, Rozi." He sighed and pressed his fingers against his eyes. "I know that this guilt has been consuming you for years. There is nothing that I can say to take that away from you. You will learn to accept it, to live with it, to find what peace you can with the evil that has been done through you—done *to* you—but for now, I am offering you the best chance that we have to ensure that no more is done."

She lifted her tired eyes to his face, shrouded in the gloom of the early morning fog. "That was your argument the last time that you lied to me."

He flinched. "That's not it." He scrubbed his hands over his face. "You believe that I have been manipulating and deceiving you this whole time, Rozi, but I have been trying to save you, as I always have. To protect you, however I could, as I always have."

Protect. At the sound of the word, the memory of the king of the each-uisce, bloodied and torn apart on the beach, of the mutilated face of the gean-cánach, the ruined body of the mighty cú-sídhe, rose before her.

She did not need, she thought tiredly, protection from anything other than what evils, what injustices others had done to her long before she had ever been born, it seemed.

Jamie continued, still urgent. "I only wanted to spare you further sorrow, to give you some light of redemption in this dark world of despair that you have lived in for so long."

Rozlyn stared down at her hands, trembling on the mud-stained fabric of her breeches, and realized that she could never know the taste of redemption. No matter how this ended, it would end in darkness for her.

But she found that she was at last too broken to care.

She didn't protest when he crouched down and reached for her hand. "Let's go, Rozi. You told me once that all you have ever wanted is to be free to choose whatever path, whatever life, you desire to lead. Choose now to be free of guilt, of pain. Let's go so that we can both finally be free. So that we can all be free."

"Okay," she whispered, even as something in her cried out in dissent, weeping for this beautiful song of art and magic and light that had been used for such vile things, that somehow still hummed with such harmony in her veins. "Let's go."

She treated the mottled bruising on his forehead as best she could, with the meager supply of herbs she could find in the gloomy light of the early dawn. Not much grew on the island—a dry, barren rock of an isle whose austereness seemingly accommodated only frost and fog. She dabbed at Jamie's wound, her chest constricting at the thought— this place was nothing like her home. It bore not even the slightest resemblance to the rich, lush woodlands surrounding her vale, the wealth of flowering bushes and leafy green saplings that cocooned her keep, full of vitality and hope.

She ached for home.

She scraped away the poultice from Jamie's forehead and stood, rubbing her hands on her shirt. She looked around at the fog-shrouded island, its landmarks barely visible through the denseness, even as dawn twinkled dimly in the eastern sky. "Where is it?"

"The island is small," Jamie said, entwining his fingers with hers as he led her across rocky earth. "Really, it is just a pure slab of stone that protrudes from the sea, surrounded by treacherous inlets and dangerously shallow shoals. It is very, very difficult to reach its shores—if you cannot sprout wings and fly, that is. Had we sailed here as we intended, we would have been forced to encircle the island to its northernmost point, as it is only there that there is enough semblance of a beach to dock a boat."

Rozlyn shivered. "It's cold."

"No trees, very little greenery, subject to the winds

without relief. It is a cold, flat, hard place, Rozi." Through the gloom, she saw his mouth quirk into a smile. "But it is, for better or worse, my home." He pointed through the mist that swirled around them and clung to their hair in chilled drops of silver. "Look there."

Rozlyn squinted, and in the distance she could see the vague shape of a sheer white wall looming before them. "Is that—"

"The Court of Shádach. Made entirely of marble and wood, a palace fit for the gods." He stepped forward. "They sleep beneath us even now, Rozi. Let's bring them home."

For a long while, they walked through the mist in silence, and then there it was, peeking through the thick rolling fog. Rozlyn's breath caught at the sight of its magnificence. The polished white steps flowed down from twin mahogany doors, and above its gates were a myriad of gold-and-silver engravings of all the members of the race of the Tuatha Dé Danann. She peered at it, noting a tall, many-horned figure with a flowing beard, a broad-shouldered god wearing the skin of a bear, a long-haired female standing knee-deep in the midst of a river, a baby at her bosom. "There are so many."

"Too many to name," Jamie said quietly, a flicker of some long-ago memory dancing across his features.

"Where are you?"

Jamie gave her a smile, one that whispered of days long since passed, and pointed toward the bottom of the door. "There."

An inexplicable rush of excitement coursed through her, and she climbed the gleaming white stairs two at a time, eager to see him as he was truly meant to be. She squatted in front of the door and studied him, forever frozen in this gilded moment of glory.

He sat on a horse, long hair streaming behind him in the wind, a rich, fur-lined cloak swinging about his shoulders as he galloped across the plain. She could see the vague outline of his face, somehow still laughing and full of light even in this motionless rendering of a lost moment in time. There—that was his same smile, curving across the features of a face that was so foreign and yet so familiar to her. At his side loped a bear and a deer, predator and prey, running in perfect harmony with one another under the force of his will, and around him shone the midnight stars burning in unison with the bright light of the day, the gleam of snowfall under the sunlit sky of summer. "The elementals."

"Yes." She glanced back over her shoulder to see him behind her, his hands in his pockets. "They wanted to put me in robes and seat me on a bench—a judge, you know, as a joke—but my father overruled them."

"Who made this?"

"My cousin Goibinu. He's a smithy and fancies himself the god of art because of it." He shook his head, a fond gesture. "We keep trying to tell him that we are, all of us, artists in our way, but he's rather pretentious about it."

Rozlyn stared at the myriad of gold-and-silver portraits that adorned the smooth doorway. "They really are your family."

"They really are," he said, rubbing at his jaw. "For a long while, I thought that I mostly despised them, but three hundred years of being without them has taught me differently." He huffed, and she could see his shoulders bracing as though in preparation for some arduous task. "I'm going to have to ask you to wait here, Rozi, while I go into my ancestral home alone for a while."

"Why? What are you doing?"

"I'll be right back," he promised, his eyes steady and clear as they bore into hers. "But I do need you to wait here."

They stared at each other standing at the top of the smooth marble steps until she nodded, reluctant but accepting, and he turned away, laying his palm flat against the mahogany door in an unmistakably loving gesture.

"There's no handle."

"No, there is not," Jamie answered with that same rueful affection, then rested his forehead against the wood and whispered, "Crann taca."

Without a sound, the doors slid open, an invitation, and Rozlyn peeked over his shoulder at the dark foyer that awaited him. He stepped inside, his hands sliding again into his pockets, and a distant warning chimed within her at the familiar gesture, a bell-like foreboding. "I'll be right back," he repeated, and the doors swung closed soundlessly behind him even as she opened her mouth to object.

Then she was alone in the mist-sodden air, standing frozen on the marble steps. She huffed, sinking down with her knees pulled to her chest, resigned to wait. She leaned her head back against the door, studying the pictures that adorned its frame above her, the figures shimmering even in the gloom, and as she blinked up at them, exhaustion crept over her. Her eyelids grew heavy as she watched them winking at her through the fog, these long-lost gods whom she had come so far to rescue, until she was drifting to sleep in the chilled morning air under their gilded scrutiny.

She jolted awake, an urgent voice hissing some wordless warning in her ear, shattering her slumber, and she sat up, rubbing at her sleep-clogged eyes.

The sun was high in the sky, and the fog had lessened somewhat. She frowned as she took in her surroundings, a sudden tug of urgency, of anxiety deep in her chest. It was at least noon, and Jamie had not come back.

She stood up, her hands clenching over and over again at her sides. She paced back and forth on the top step, looking out over the barren, foggy rock toward the dim horizon of the ocean in the distance, until she could bear it no longer. Her heart thudded as she placed her palm flat against the door of the gods, just as he had done, and whispered, "Crann taca."

A momentous pause, the unseen sentry who guarded their keep weighing her merit, her worthiness, and then, as though they scented that faint drop of divinity flowing through her veins, the doors swung open. Rozlyn gritted her teeth, striding into the foyer before the swell of courage inside her chest vanished and she fled back into the open air where she belonged.

The doors clicked shut behind her, and she was swathed in darkness. She swallowed and held out a shaking palm, willing that fire to come to her, to guide her way, and the barest hint of a flicker appeared in her palm, even as her head throbbed with the exertion. The ache sharpened, intensified, as she poured her will into the flame, and it leapt higher and brighter.

Through her blurry vision, she could see the foyer, a shining wonder of marble and gold and black cherrywood. Rubbing at her temples, Rozlyn tentatively moved forward to the archway in front of her and peeked into the vast expanse of the great hall.

There were long tables and benches, so hauntingly familiar to her father's and her own. At the center of the back wall stood a commanding dais with a single silver throne and a massive wooden club, taller and wider than any mortal man, lying across its seat. A sparkling silver crown, long abandoned by its wearer, dangled from the arm of the throne. The Dagda's seat, she thought as her fire flickered along the shadows of the still and silent hall. Jamie's father—and hers by marriage, she realized, then swallowed the thick lump that arose in her throat at the impossibility of it, that she could ever look into another man's eyes and call him father without vomiting.

She had renounced one father and had no desire to ever know another.

The walls were decorated with countless draperies and tapestries, knit with the most delicate of needlepoints, all depicting the many triumphs of the gods. Rozlyn studied them, her scrutiny focusing, in particular, on an arras woven from deep-red silk. In its center stood a pale-faced woman clad all in black and gray, a trio of ravens perched on her shoulders. Her eyes were as black as night, her hair an ebony waterfall that cascaded around her shoulders, and she stood in the middle of a battlefield surrounded by dead and dying soldiers, her face void of all expression. They groveled before her, even as she stood weaponless and unarmed but for the silent promise of death rippling in the air around her.

The Mórrígan, Rozlyn realized with a shiver.

She whirled, hearing footsteps behind her, and the hair on the back of her neck prickled in a soundless scream of warning, when from a nearby doorway, Jamie appeared.

He halted at the sight of her. "What are you doing here?"

She blinked at the curtness of his tone. "You left me outside. You were gone a long time."

"I was busy."

Rozlyn huffed and crossed her arms. "Are we back to

your cryptic little remarks, Jamie? Because I'm not in the mood for it at all."

Jamie shrugged, some of that strange tension in his shoulders relaxing. "I'm not sure what you want me to say. It has been three hundred years since I've seen my home. I apologize if you felt a little neglected while I reacquainted myself with it."

Rozlyn felt a twinge of guilt at his flat tone. "I'm sorry," she said, but it felt wrong on her lips, the apology. "You scared me. I thought something might have happened to you."

He studied her, then prowled forward a few steps, a jungle cat with its claws out approaching its prey. "Let's get on with it, shall we?"

She nodded, then looked behind her to the far wall to where he pointed. Hanging on the white marbled wall from a single brass hook was a harp carved from the finest oak, studded with incandescent jewels, the strings barely luminous in the faint light of her fire. She inhaled sharply. "The Dagda's harp," she whispered. "Uaithne."

"What?"

"Uaithne," she repeated. "The name of the harp. I thought that's what you told me." A flicker of doubt. "Did I get it wrong?"

"Ah." His lips tightened. "No. That's right."

The silver-chimed bells inside her began to peal in earnest, and she swallowed. "It's just as beautiful as you told me."

His lips twisted briefly, then he gestured toward it. "Go on, then. Use it."

"To do what?"

"To wake the gods, of course." He studied it with an odd detachment. "You have my power, do you not? So. Shift into my father's form and then command the harp to awaken them. It's the only way." His eyes slid to hers, dark and unreadable. "Surely you can do that, can't you?"

The bells were screaming now, their silver rusted into strident brass.

Rozlyn stared at him, her palms slick with sweat. "You want me to do what?"

He looked at her, and she could almost taste it, the loathing that rolled off him in thick, putrid waves. "Shift into my father," he repeated, "and command his harp."

She shook her head. "I can't do that, Jamie."

"Yes, you can. You are not *that* weak." His eyes were burning with hot, furious anger, and something snapped inside her, because never, not once, even at her most beastly, both in shape and in spirit, had Jamie looked at her so, with such contemptuous rage. "There is no other way, and if you fail, then you will have no further use to me after all."

It was a lethal strike at the heart of her, bored and callous and cruel, nothing like the clever way that Jamie played, subtle and delicate. She knew it so well, his artful manner of maneuvering and manipulating, and deep within her heart, suspicion stirred.

"I can't do it," she whispered through the burning in her throat.

"No," he said. "You just don't want to."

Another savage strike, a full-tilt attack, sending her bishop stumbling headlong over the hem of his long bronze robes.

Rozlyn swallowed. "No," she said. "I cannot. I have no idea what your father looks like. I cannot shift into what I do not know."

"You do know him," Jamie countered, trembling with latent thunder. "You stood right there before him on that gods-damned dais and greeted him as your father. You know exactly what he looks like. Can't you *remember*?"

Even her queen, dauntless and all-powerful, trembled. This was no game, not even a war—this was a slaughter, a severing of her lifeblood right at the neck, the ultimate endgame.

"No," she said with a steadiness that she did not feel. "Because I am not Étaín."

"You think I don't know that?" he snapped at her, his face contorted with viciousness. "I am fully aware of what a miserable, mediocre imitation of my wife you are. I would have never deigned to so much as look at you had you not been born with her green eyes and my own damn magic. Spare me, Rozlyn," he spat. "You are not now, nor will you ever be, Étaín."

Match in three moves, a bhrèagha.

She knew.

"No," she said slowly. "I am not." She curled those tendrils of magic within her into a tight mass of vipers, ready to strike. "And you are not Jamie."

His face froze for the briefest, most finite of seconds. "What do you mean?"

"Jamie never calls me Rozlyn." The air sizzled between them. "It is always brèagha or Rozi, no matter how often I have told him to stop. But never—never Rozlyn."

His nostrils flared.

"And so you," Rozlyn continued, her fingers flexing at her sides, those coils of magic sliding and tensing around her, jaws parted and fangs bared. "You must be Fúamnach, my husband's fiancée."

Jamie smiled suddenly, and Rozlyn shuddered to see such a smile, devoid of warmth, of humor, flitting across those familiar lips. "Clever girl." His head tilted ever so slightly. "And you are my fiancé's wife."

CHAPTER THIRTY-SIX

Rozlyn stared at those dark blue eyes, their depth and hue distorted with such malice. "Where is Jamie?" she asked, silently summoning that elusive spark to the tips of her fingers.

Fúamnach waved airily. "Oh, he's fine, child. I would never hurt him, my one true love. Never fear."

"You don't love him. You hate him. You have tortured him mercilessly, relentlessly for three hundred years."

"Not in the slightest. I have only punished him for his naughty little dalliance with *you*, you stupid girl." His lips curled. "Really, it's all your fault. He was perfectly content with me before you came along with those big sad eyes and your virginal curves." She huffed. "No man can resist a virgin, it seems, though for the life of me, I cannot fathom why. They don't even know what they're *doing*—they just lie there."

"Maybe it's a territorial thing," Rozlyn said vaguely, her mind whirring, searching for what move to make, what strategy to use, what pieces to concede, in this all-important match that was unfolding before her. "Men do love to be the first in all things."

Fúamnach seemed to consider this. "I suppose. It makes sense, for those warmongering fools, with their insatiable greed, their thirst to own the whole world over." A careless shrug. "They're all the same, weak-minded and blinded by greed. So easy to deceive." She leaned forward conspiratorially, a facade of sororal accord, and Rozlyn stepped backward on instinct. "They did the same to me, you know, trying to marry me off to that beloved god of yours in the first place."

"What do you mean, 'married off to'?"

"Oh, that's right. You can't remember." Fúamnach grinned, her deviousness apparent, and Rozlyn forced herself not to shudder at the cruel twist of his mouth. "Shall I remind you?"

The air rippled once, and Jamie disappeared, and in his place a golden-haired man with noble bearing, a purple cloak cascading about him in regal waves. He lifted his head and looked at her, and the world spun around her.

For a moment, she was gone, transported to another time and another place, somewhere safe and secure, with white sand splayed across her feet and the sound of the gulls squawking above her and the radiance of the sun warming her hair.

Midir, she thought, *my love*.

Then it vanished, and she was back in the middle of the Court of Shádach, sunless and shivering, staring into the face of the source of all her sorrows.

"It was an arranged marriage-bond, mine and Midir's, as was your own at the time," Fúamnach said, brushing the stolen hands of the god down his robes. "You were betrothed as well, you know, when my own fiancé stumbled upon you on the beach that fateful day, but that stopped neither of you. I suppose you clung to the erroneous idea that since the two of you had not chosen your intendeds that absolved you of any blame when you callously abandoned them for each other."

"Who arranged it? Your marriage-bond?"

"The Dagda, of course. Long have the Tuatha Dé Danann and the cailleachs warred with one another, the two most powerful forces of magic in this world, ever since their kind arrived here on what was once our isle, a land of nothing but rain and fog and magic."

"The Cailleach? But she cursed me. She was there on the night that I was born."

"Och, enough, you stupid mortal." Rozlyn flinched at the sudden infusion of hatred that flooded through the god's silken voice. "Humans call her 'the Cailleach,' as though she were so special." The false Midir spat on the marble floor. "My blue-skinned sister with her hands of ice—pah. She is merely one in a long line of our kind, those who speak the ancient incantations; we are far older and more powerful than these so-called gods, and yet they are the ones that you revere. Imagine the injustice of it," the witch snarled. "Because I have to craft my art and learn to wield it, to shape it, to build its magnificence from the merest flickers of magic, because I must learn and study and slave over my spells, they consider me to be inferior to themselves, they who simply flick their fingers and wave some new truth into being." She huffed, and Rozlyn acknowledged a reluctant twinge of empathy. She knew what it was like to have to scratch and claw and fight for even the most meager droplets of power.

"That is the difference, you see," the witch continued, "between these supposed gods and my kind. We must speak our magic, and they simply think it and behold." Fúamnach gestured derisively. "It appears."

Rozlyn said nothing, but her skin prickled.

Speaking. Her magic relied on her speech.

It was a weakness, a flaw in her armor, a window through which to strike with her queen when she least expected.

Rozlyn's attention snapped back as Fúamnach continued. "So we have fought since they first wandered onto the shores of Éire, the Tuatha Dé Danann, but the Dagda—he had enough of wars, or so he said. We both know that men can never have enough of bloodletting, of warmongering. But so he claimed, and thus he called together the members of my clan and proposed a truce. As a sign of his goodwill, he would give the hand of his son in marriage to me, and the gods and the witches would at last exist in harmony." Fúamnach sniffed. "He whined and he complained, my fiancé did, begging his father for mercy, but when the Dagda speaks, the gods obey, and so eventually, Midir fell in line and took me to his bed"—she smirked again—"and promised to wed me by the midwinter moon. I grew rather fond of him, you know."

Rozlyn braced herself. "I am sorry," she said, and she was, because no one deserved to be so humiliated, whether it was for love or no. "I understand that you are grieving, that you are hurt, but it does not excuse what you have done."

"Don't be an idiot." Malice sliced through the air, like a dagger in the dark. "It was quite the blow to my pride, I admit, but don't be a fool, girl. My kind, few in number as we are, have been waiting for over a thousand years for such an excuse to strike against the Tuatha Dé Danann, these invaders who arrived on our shores so long ago. Here they were, all gathered together to greet their new daughter"—her teeth snapped once—"and my loving fiancé with his godlike powers, sleeping so peacefully beside his sweet little wife, and it came to me, the idea of stealing that oft-overlooked magic of his, to take the shape of whatever he so pleased, and use it to command the almighty harp of the Dagda himself, and with a single blow, wipe their existence from the face of the earth." Fúamnach clapped Midir's hands together and crowed in delight. "It was so easy! I could not believe that I had not thought of it before, you see. I slipped in through the window and whispered a simple siphoning spell. And the fool, he was so exhausted by you and that lovely body of yours—perhaps there is something to be said for virgins, after all—that he never even stirred as I drained it from his soul. To test out my newfound power, I changed him, shifted him into this." The air shuddered once, and Midir vanished, and Jamie stood before her again, with that wide, cruel smile. "And don't you know, I have to admit. It was wonderful, simply imagining my will into being. The flood of power that rushed through me was like nothing I had ever conjured before." Fúamnach smirked. "Being a god is not so bad, after all."

Rozlyn's fists clenched. "I want to see him," she said. "I want to see what you have done with Jamie."

Fúamnach stared at her for a moment, then she raised her hand, as Rozlyn herself had done so many hundreds of times before, and she shifted, more slowly this time, so that Rozlyn could watch Jamie's face blur, melt, and fade into something foreign and strange. It was deliberate, she knew, a self-satisfied flex of the witch's superior strength, a reminder of Rozlyn's own weakness. Fúamnach lifted her head, and Rozlyn shivered at the sight of her terrible orange eyes blazing against the backdrop of midnight curls.

She looked like a tigress who had grown tired of stalking her prey, and finally, after centuries of waiting and watching and savoring its fear, was ready at last to pounce.

Fúamnach smiled that same cruel smile, which slid along the curves of her fire-red lips far more naturally than it had Jamie's. "You want to see your husband, child? Very well, then," and she raised her voice to a high, cold pitch. "Come on out, my love," she called. "There is someone here who is *dying* to see you."

Rozlyn braced herself as she heard a shuffling in the corridor, a tortured whine, and then in from the darkened doorway crept a lean wolfish figure, his gray tail drooping, his tongue lolling miserably between his jaws. He raised his silver-gray head, and it dropped her to her knees, that heartbreaking sight of him. She stretched out her hands as he limped forward, a keening whine escaping from his snout, and he buried his muzzle against her neck as she wrapped her arms around his neck.

"Oh, Jamie," she whispered. "It's all right."

She knew, Rozlyn thought, those tightly coiled vipers beginning to writhe with fury within her. That witch knew what he most feared, and she used that knowledge with unbearable cruelty.

The wolf whined again and nuzzled at her neck with his wet nose, a wordless farewell, and the coils of magic within her hissed in rage. "It will be all right," she whispered again, as soft as she could. "I can do this."

Fúamnach pealed with laughter. "Do you really believe that you can stop me, you foolish child? You can barely begin to manage that minuscule drop of his power that I gave you on the night your mother first conceived you. Oh, I knew you even then." Her bared teeth glinted as she paced in circles around where Rozlyn crouched, her fingers entwined in the rough hair of the wolf. "Your father lay snoring beside his young blushing bride, and I slipped in, even as I did on your wedding night so long ago, and I whispered my spells and poured my potions down her throat as she choked and thrashed in my grip." Rozlyn made a wordless sound of distress, and Fúamnach laughed again. "Did they not tell you, child, how she, so hale and hearty and round when she first married your father, slowly began to wither and fade away over the long months while you grew inside her? Did you think that was an accident? No," she snarled, "that drop of magic inside you siphoned away her strength, dooming her to die the day she bore you—oh, I told her all of it, you know, on that night I forced my poison into her veins—so that you would be utterly alone, with no one to protect you, to care for you, because as we all now know"—her revulsion was a tangible thing as it reverberated through the air—"only a mother could ever love that monstrous Beast I turned you into."

Rozlyn's breath caught, the memories of those long, loveless years slicing through her, her bone-deep loneliness always centered around that ancient, ever-present longing for something that she had never had. A primal, powerful surge of magic, heaving and churning like the storm-swept sea, an upwelling of strength like she had never before known flooded into her fingertips, tail lashing and fangs glinting.

She rose, her fingers sparking, and Fúamnach's eyes widened. "Good girl," she said. "Come and fight. Let him watch as I destroy you."

The wolf barked at her feet, his hair bristling as he bared his teeth, then yelped once, a high-pitched, pain-racked sound. He collapsed to the ground, whimpering, as though an unseen hand had punched through his spine, and Fúamnach grinned. "Don't be brave, my love," she tsked. "You are under my power now, you know, as much as any of those beasts you used to command were once under yours. Do you remember how effortlessly they bent to your will?"

The wolf growled, his body convulsing, and Rozlyn's hands flew up, a crescendo of flames writhing through the air. "Leave him alone," she said as dark-gray smoke wheeled around them. "Your fight is with me. It has always, it seems, been with me."

Fúamnach turned her fiery stare to Rozlyn, a hungry, malevolent light gleaming in its depths. "You are wrong about that, girl," she said. "It has always been with him and his kind. You"—her crimson lips curled—"you were incidental to that, a stepping stone along the way. A worthless pawn."

A dam broke inside her, and she lifted her hand, fingers lengthening and curving into razor-sharp talons. "No," she growled. "I have always been a queen," and then Rozlyn was no more, and in her place rose a black-haired Beast with a serpentine tail. She roared, the tapestries shuddering on the wall from the sheer force of the sound, then lowered her head and prowled toward the witch.

Fúamnach licked at her lips, blatantly ravenous, Rozlyn knew, for blood—her blood. "This won't go well for you, little monster." A stream of raucous words poured forth from her crimson lips, and Rozlyn squealed, a thousand hot knives carving into her sides, into her skull. She collapsed, her claws scraping against the marble floor as she mewled, the white-hot blades burrowing into her flesh.

Distantly, she heard the wolf scream, heartbreakingly human, and then the pain was gone, and she was left panting and dizzy, sprawled across the floor, no trace of blood or gaping wounds, only hundreds of purpling scars, still tender and raw, patchworked across her skin.

"There now, my love," she heard Fúamnach say from above her. "You see? She is still that precious little damsel in distress whom you rescued all those centuries ago after all. Pathetic." She spat on the floor. "This mewling creature is what you chose over me? You miserable fool."

He whined, sorrow-filled and forlorn, and Rozlyn twisted on the floor, desperate to see him even as he was a beast, like her, aching to feel that strange silver thread that stretched between them go taut and tight with unspoken understanding. He turned his wolfish head and looked at her, and suddenly, Rozlyn remembered.

She was sitting on the hot sand of an unfamiliar beach, staring at the white-tipped waves of the ocean, the salt of the sea mingling with the tears growing cold on her cheeks. There was the golden-haired man from before, his eyes as bright as the sea, staring at her with such longing, begging for something that only she could give to him. She could see his lips moving, his hands pleading, and even without hearing him, she understood it, his urgency and his love.

She heard her own voice, tremulous and small, a voice that she had never before used in this life.

I want freedom. I want to be free—to choose, for myself, what my life shall be.

The golden-haired man nodded, a gesture of assent. His lips moved, and the thrum of some inaudible promise hovered in the air between them, and then he was gone, his deep-purple cloak swinging behind in the ocean breeze.

She opened her eyes, and the eyes of the wolf—of Jamie—were staring at her with that same hungry intensity, and she inhaled a ragged breath. "I remembered something," she whispered. "I remembered that I asked you to let me choose." His eyes lit up with a fierce, triumphant joy.

He turned his head and looked at Fúamnach, snarling as his hair bristled and his ears pinned flat, a wordless declaration of defiance and rage.

Fúamnach hissed. "So be it."

She turned back toward Rozlyn's prostrate form and screeched, a rush of unknowable, guttural words, and Rozlyn was flying through the air, her wings shredding and tearing underneath the weight of invisible blades. She crashed against the sleek marble wall with unthinkable force, and the thick-welded bones fused together under the ripple of sinew and muscle shattered as her right shoulder snapped against the stone, the ugly break of the bone echoing in her ears.

She slid, stunned, to the ground, while the wolf howled with rage. She blinked once, then a tidal wave of pain seared through her shoulder, and she roared, keeling over, her wings limp and ruined on the ground, her snout filled with blood. Fúamnach laughed. "I do not suppose that it will be much of a fight after all, my love." Dimly, Rozlyn watched as the witch glanced over to where the wolf paced frantically, trapped behind the boundaries of an invisible leash, and she smiled, an eternity of cruelty glimmering along her lips. "You chose wrong, Midir. You have always chosen wrong."

Rozlyn closed her eyes and breathed through her blood-clogged nose, trying to focus through the shriek of pain in her shoulder, on her beautiful black-feathered wings, which had once flown so high and proud above the earth, a boundless force of majesty and strength. *Ignore it,* she whispered to herself. *Ignore the pain and fight.*

It was a familiar refrain, she realized suddenly. Her

whole life, a litany of denying and hiding, shrouded in ig-
nominy, alone in the dark. She had hidden it then, this
heartrending pain, the years of loneliness in the joyless heart
of a loveless little girl. She had buried deep the raw welts of
guilt that scarred her heart, guilt for the sorrows she had
inflicted on her people by clinging so desperately to her
magic, her only lifeline in the rain-swelled river. She had
entombed her pain in the blackest caverns of her soul—that
heartrending ache of betrayal by the only two men whom
she had ever loved—never speaking of it, never thinking of
it, letting it fester and burn, an infection spreading to every
drop of her blood. She had closeted herself away, a cocoon
of self-sufficiency and independence, locked away in her
hall, watching over the villagers from a distance, a benign
remoteness, firmly rejecting their proffers of friendship
and affection. She had Galena and her magic, and that was
enough—enough to help her to ignore all the heartaches and
agonies of forcing herself to learn to harness and to wield
this beautiful, cursed power with which she had been born,
to bear the burden of so many years of griefs and guilts—that
was enough to ignore all of it, and to fight on. She sobbed
suddenly, one harsh sob of pain, as she saw how tattered she
was, all the way down to the depths of her soul. She was just
a brokenhearted girl, with the scars of a thousand fractures
splintering her surface, and she was utterly alone in this
world, with no one to tell of the sadness in her heart, and
there was no trace of a queenlike greatness in her after all.

You command the waters of the seas and the lochs, deirfiúr.

Rozlyn blinked, the soothing call of the merrow singing in her ear. She whipped her woozy head around, ears
pricked, but there was only Fúamnach's glowing orange eyes
floating in front of her, and the wolf whimpering anxiously

as he paced back and forth across the room, restrained by the unseen leash of her will.

She would never be able to win this game—their pieces were not equitable, not carved of white-gold and bronze, but of some obsidian-black metals mined from the depths of hell.

There was no way for her to win.

"I suppose we should finish this now, shouldn't we, my love?" Fúamnach asked of Jamie airily, but her hungry stare was locked on where Rozlyn lay crumpled on the floor. "She is in so much pain. It would be a mercy, really." She tilted her tigress head and bared her pointed teeth. "Don't worry, little girl. It will be painless and swift, like it was all the other hundreds of times, and you will recall none of this when you are reborn tomorrow as a snake in the grass."

The wolf threw himself against the invisible bridle that bound him, snarling and in helpless rage, but Rozlyn's chest continued to heave, the remembered song of the merrow still echoing in her mind.

Command the waters, deirfiúr.

And Rozlyn remembered it, that urge to build her own pawns from the sea and the sun and the sky.

The elemental forces of the world.

Fúamnach opened her mouth and more incoherent words of incantation flowed out. An invisible vise of iron and steel seized Rozlyn in its unseen grasp, and it was squeezing her, clenching its unforgiving metallic fingers around her beastly throat with an unbreakable band, choking the life from her lungs—

Rozlyn remembered the sea.

Her shaggy limbs quivered with something far more powerful than anguish and fear, and the skeletal ridges of her bones became fluid and flowing inside her skin. Even as the warm scent of salt and seaweed and brine permeated through the air, that tsunami of pain that had ripped and torn through her hirsute shoulder vanished, and for the briefest moment, she glanced up, savoring the way Fúamnach's red-fire lips fell open in shock. Then she was slipping across the floor, a monsoon of seawater crashing toward the witch, hurtling toward her as inexorable as the tides, her fingers outstretched with foaming white tips like the crest of the surf pounding into the shore.

Fúamnach opened her mouth to snarl a curse at her in that hateful ancient tongue, and another memory suddenly burst into life around her, as bright and brilliant as the sun cresting over the oceanic horizon in the east.

The girl who can become the sky.

Her speech, Rozlyn thought. The key was not to allow her to speak.

The haunting song of the slúag, crooning to her as she soared through the night-black sky, rang in her remembrance, and Rozlyn hissed as the beginnings of Fúamnach's curse began to lambaste her, heavy, jaw-jarring thuds from an invisible force slamming into her watery limbs and battering at her fluid form.

Rozlyn imagined flying through the air, her feathered black wings whole and unmarred, spread wide and proud, the wind screaming around her, the queen of the beasts, as she soared so far above the world.

The water of her limbs began to sizzle and mist, and then she was gone, an unseen entity of shadow and night, and in a violent gust of wind, she thundered through the gap between Fúamnach's half-parted lips, inhaling with an inescapable intake of breath, and the air hovering in the witch's throat shuddered once, then came rushing out of her lungs in unthinking obedience to her call.

Fúamnach fell to her knees, gagging and choking, her crimson lips abruptly tinged with blue, and distantly, Rozlyn heard the wolf howling, with approval this time rather than fear, a snarling challenge for more. In a cyclonal gust, she whirled away from where the witch wheezed against the oak-wood floor, gray of face and blue of lips, caught in the airless prison in which Rozlyn had sealed her and swallowed its key.

Rozlyn stared down at the witch suffocating on the floor beneath her and thought of her mother, dying in a river of blood in her bed, her first and last maternal benediction for the Beast she had borne into the world expiring on her lips as she breathed her last.

For that, and for that alone, she owed this witch a blood-price that she was bound to pay.

She remembered, suddenly, sitting in the sunlit quiet of her childhood terrace, lost in the pages of a half-forgotten poem of war and fire and a monster who slept far beneath the rocks of the great northern sea—*you are the mother of monsters, little witch*, she could almost hear the púca say—and even as she imagined it, this unstoppable force of vengeance and doom, she lifted her windswept arms to summon him forth. Far, far below, buried deep underneath the barren gray slab of rock, she could feel it—something stirring to life at the sound of her wordless call.

Rozlyn exhaled a satisfied rush of air, as the púca's merry voice chimed sweetly in her memory, mingling with a low, distant rumble beginning to rattle the ornaments hanging on the walls.

From deep beneath the floors of the palace, the barren

rock of the isle, came an earth-shattering roar. The oaken
floors of the hall of the gods juddered with an unknowable
force, and she could hear the scrabble of the wolf's paws as
they slid across the shifting floorboards. With a resounding crack, the wood split in two, and from the depths of
the world below came a great, black-scaled, leather-winged
monster with golden-red eyes and sharp-tipped horns curving over its massive head, clawing his way up from the dark
pits below, where he had slept undisturbed on his bed of
hoarded gold for so many centuries.

Lig na Paiste, Rozlyn thought hazily. The last dragon of Éire.

Even as she thought it, Rozlyn shifted from air to Beast,
and then shook her bloodstained head at the oilliphéist and
roared, a queenly command. Lig na Paiste bent his scaly head
in understanding, in acquiescence, his golden-red eyes as
bright as the fire that glowed beneath his ribs. He slouched
forward to where Fúamnach lay supine, raising herself up
on her elbows as her eyes wheeled, horrified, at the sight
of the creature before her stretching his bat-like wings, his
coarse black tongue hissing through its teeth. She screamed
once, a soundless squeal of terror, and the oilliphéist seized
her in his mouth, as a black bear seizes the unsuspecting
trout from the stream, and then swept his scaly tail along the
splintered wooden floor as he slithered back down, down
into the depths from which Rozlyn had summoned him, this
wild creature of magic and nature with whom she shared her
blood, vanishing into the gloom.

Mate, she thought. The end of the match.

Rozlyn knew the moment that the witch expired, far
down in the dragon's den of treasure and gold. The wolf
shuddered once where he crouched on the shredded remains of the oak floor, and he yelped as his fur receded,

his limbs growing smooth and fleece-clad once more. The air around him shivered, a blur of motion, and then he was there, kneeling on the ground, his chest heaving, his dark-brown hair soaked with sweat.

She shook her own head wearily, the white-hot flare of agony burning anew in the sinews of her shoulder, her ravaged wings alight with pain. A growl escaped through her clenched jaws as she focused all her strength, this newly unearthed magic of hers, into mending her injuries, smoothing and suturing the rips and tears in the delicate fibers of her feathered wings, carefully knitting back together the shattered tendons of her shoulder with painstaking stitches by an ethereal hand. She took a tentative step, fluttering her wings softly, and it thundered through her, a savage delight at the bottomless well of this newfound power of hers.

Thirty years, she thought. Thirty years lost, but a lifetime to go.

From across the hall, Jamie groaned, and she swiveled her shaggy head toward where he still knelt, his forearms braced against the floor, chest heaving. Panic seized her, and she shifted, running toward him with outstretched hands. She fell to her knees beside him. "Jamie," she wheezed. "Are you hurt?" His head drooped lower, and his shoulders shook. "Let me see. Let me make sure that you are well—"

He laughed, a sobbing, hysterical sound. "Rozi," he gasped. "I am very well indeed."

Rozlyn stared at him as he lifted his midnight-blue eyes, blazing with a boundless joy that she had never before seen. "Rozi," he whispered again. "We are free, a bhrèagha."

CHAPTER THIRTY-SEVEN

INIS TRÁ THOLL, ÉIRE, 1017

Rozlyn leaned her flushed face against the cool marble wall of the Court of Shádach, aching with exhaustion from the aftermath of her battle with Fúamnach, strangely numb from the force of her summonings.

Jamie knelt by her side on the broken shards of the oak floor, lifting a silver goblet filled with water to her lips. "Here," he said. "The freshwater streams of the island trickle down from the ice of the northern glaciers. It will help."

She drank deeply, slurping at the frigid taste of the water, then sighed and closed her eyes. He settled on the ground beside her; then his hand slid under the nape of her neck, his lips brushing against her forehead. "My brave brèagha," he whispered. "How my people will sing of your deeds today for centuries to come."

"Stop pestering me to awaken your damn gods and let me rest for a moment."

He huffed out a surprised laugh. "I'm not, Rozi. Truly.

The gods know I certainly am not bold enough to hurry you, after what I have seen you do this day." He hesitated. "Rozi, what you did to Fúamnach—"

"She deserved it."

"Without question." He stroked her sweat-matted hair, a rhythmic sequence of gentle, reassuring pats. "She was far more of a monster than any of the others that you have slain. I have no doubt about that."

Perhaps it was the exhaustion, or the dullness in her brain from the ache in her bones, or perhaps she no longer had the strength to strive to hide the depths of how much she truly cared for him, but she opened her eyes and looked at him wearily. "I killed the cú-sídhe."

Jamie's hand dropped away. "I know."

"You do?"

"Rozi." His fingers brushed across his lips, and she could have sworn she saw his mouth twitching underneath. "You disappeared into the night, incandescent with rage, and then came back the next day to take an unusually long nap in the sun. Clearly, you found an outlet for your 'nasty little tantrum.'" A tug of recognition, of that first war of words that they had exchanged so many weeks ago in the familiar warmth of her hall. "And your choices were somewhat limited."

"Why didn't you say anything?"

A half shrug. "Why didn't you?"

She fidgeted, suddenly conscious of how close he sat, the way his gaze never wavered from her face. "I didn't do it for you," she clarified hurriedly. He bit his lip, and she knew he was fighting not to smile. "I didn't."

"Obviously."

"It was a monster, a menace to others, and it was my

duty to protect any innocents who might wander into its path."

"I agree."

"It wasn't for you."

He said nothing, only waited patiently, and she cleared her throat before she spoke again. "Are you angry with me, about Fúamnach?"

"Of course not. What do you think I came inside to do when I asked you to stay outside?" His eyebrows lifted. "Obviously, in hindsight, that was a mistake."

"You knew she would be here?"

"I suspected." He raised his hand as she opened her mouth to protest. "Don't, Rozi. It was wrong of me to try and shield you." He eyed the shattered floors, the cracked and ruined marble of his father's hall. "Clearly. But I was afraid, a bhrèagha. The last time that you and I were in a room with Fúamnach, I watched you die for the first time of a hundred different lives, so perhaps a little leniency for my lapse in judgment, born of centuries of remembered trauma, is called for here."

"Perhaps." She leaned her head back against the wall with a sigh. "Fúamnach tried to taunt me by telling me to shift into your father's form, to command the harp. She seemed to think that was what you brought me here to do." A meaningful, expectant silence greeted this pronouncement, and her eyes widened as she spun to face him. "Jamie— that's not your plan, is it? There has to be another way to awaken them."

"The call of the harp imprisoned them, Rozi. Only its music can free them."

"It won't work, Jamie."

"It might."

"How could it? I have never seen him. How can I shift into him? I don't know what he looks like, or how his voice sounds." Rozlyn gripped her hair, her nails digging into her scalp. "You must have realized this, Jamie. Why would you bring me all this way? Why drag me here, for nothing?"

He sighed, reaching out to skim his fingers against her flushed cheek. "Well, at first, as I believe I mentioned to you right before you exploded with rage and stormed away, I was fairly confident that it would be a moot point, that I would be able to persuade you to yield to my charms—"

"I'd sooner be charmed by an eel than by you," she said reflexively, and his lips quirked into the shadow of a smile.

"Our twin histories would prove differently. But then I realized that there was a far better solution."

"What?"

Jamie shrugged. "You become Étaín again, of course. You can remember her. I know you can. You remembered your other lives easily enough, and clearly it is there in the shadows of your memory—and you recalled that day on the beach." The muscles in his throat jumped. "You simply have to truly want to *be* her again."

"Jamie—"

"We can go back," and she ached to hear it, the longing in his words. "We can go back to who we were, who we were always meant to be. You could remember what it was to be Étaín, to love me like you did when I was Midir and you were that girl, in that other life. No beasts, no curses, no scarred wounds of sorrows in your soul. There will be no more tension between us. You won't need or want this power any longer, and it can be mine again, and all will be as it used to be."

Rozlyn's hands trembled. "No," she said.

"Rozi—"

"Jamie, please." Her voice cracked, her face crumpling with exhaustion and despair and decades of grief. "I only want to go home."

His face softened as she fought back her tears. "A bargain, then."

"I am done with your bargains, all our worthless games."

"One last bargain, Rozi, for old time's sake. Let me prove that I see you, that I know *you*. Rozi, daughter of Saoirse, queen of the vale, lover of books filled with brave deeds and less love, and fine dark chocolate, and honey-lavender teas—"

"I only drink those to diffuse the bitterness of the rowan's juices," she said, and this time when he smiled, it was full and bright.

"I thought so." He hesitated, then touched the back of her hand with his. "Let me show you that I know she's still there, hiding inside you, the girl I first knew, who adored the sea and the sand and the smell of the salt wind in her hair, and the only woman in almost a thousand years ever to touch my heart. If I can guess," he continued, "what it is that snapped that key to your summoning into place, that allowed you to become water and wind and to call forth the dragons in the deep, then you will try, just once, to remember who you once were, to free my people as you swore you would. If I can't"—his throat spasmed—"then go. Shift, and fly home to your vale and leave me here to live out my days on this barren rock of my family's tomb."

For a moment, she remained frozen in place, so still that she could hear the faint thump of her pulse as it beat in her wrists, that live-wire spark of magic that laced its way through her blood. Which girl, she wondered, did he truly love—the beauty who danced heedless and free on the beaches of Ulaid, or the Beast who embraced the darkness in which she had been born, alone and unsmiling?

They were not, she knew, the same woman.

He stepped closer to her, taking her silence for acquiescence, and reached out to cup her cheek with unutterable tenderness.

"For water," he whispered, "you pictured the sea, boundless and free, as you have always longed to be, and for the air, the wind as it thunders under your wings as you soar through the sky, the nearest thing to that freedom you could ever achieve."

Rozlyn's eyes stung, even though she would have thought that the fire in her heart had burned away all her tears.

"And for the oilliphéist"—Jamie's voice gentled—"you pictured your mother, whom you have never known but always have mourned in those secret corners of your soul, who knew your nature even as she bore you, but loved the beauty in your beastliness in the most unconditional of ways, just as you have always longed to be loved."

Rozlyn shuddered, and she stepped into his arms, burying her head in his shoulder as his arms encircled her. "I know you," he whispered. "No matter what name or shape or form you have taken, I have always known you, as you have always known me, whether you realized it or not." He pulled back slightly. "And I know that you can do this now, Rozi—for me, for yourself, for the people of Éire. You can, and you must."

She stood with her head against his chest for a long time. "All right," she whispered. "The merrow made me promise, that day on the beach. She called me 'sister,' as the púca did. For them, I can try."

Jamie stroked her hair, and Rozlyn tried to ignore the
approval, the relief in the gesture. "That's my brave brèagha.
Only a few more minutes now, Rozi, and the gods will take
this burden from your shoulders that you have carried so
unfairly for far too long."

She nodded, then looked over his shoulder past him
to where the oaken harp called Uaithne hung glinting on
the wall, taunting her as its golden and bejeweled adornments shimmered in the dim torchlight of the great hall.
She squeezed her eyes shut, straining to recall those brief
flashes of half-faded memories, sieving and sifting through a
hazy waterfall of images of a long-forgotten life, the pictures
blurring together in a kaleidoscope of incoherent colors, a
fresh-painted mural on a gray-stone wall caught too soon
in the rain. She hissed through her teeth. "I can't remember," she said. "I can't do this, Jamie. I can't remember how
he looks, or the sound of his voice, or—"

"Hush." Her eyes flew open as Jamie placed his hands
on her shoulders and spun her around to survey the impos-
ing expanse of the room. "You can though. You have seen
him, my love. Imagine him there." He pointed toward the
dais of polished mahogany, inlaid with an endless parade of
gold and jewels. "See him standing there, his red hair falling about his shoulders, his arms outstretched as he greeted
you when I first escorted you into our home."

Rozlyn stared at that now-empty dais, an ominous tightening in her chest, then sank to her knees, her forehead
pressed against her fists.

"Let go of Rozi for a moment, a bhrèagha. Let her go
and listen."

His hand pressed against her back as she sat frozen on
the ruined floor, trying to recall what it might have been

like to have been a girl so simple and soft, free from sharp edges and bitter thoughts and guilt-riddled scars.

"You knelt before him," Jamie whispered close by her head, his breath tickling her ear. "You were so unthinkably beautiful in your gown of white-gold, with my crown on your black hair, and you knelt before him, his mortal daughter, as he laid his hands on your head in benediction." She heard him breathe out, slow and soft. "You were so happy, as the Dagda blessed you, promised to you his protection and his love, and named you as his own kin."

Rozlyn flinched. *Never*, she thought. Perhaps this other girl, this other woman whom she might once have been, but never her, Rozlyn Ó Conchúir, ever wary, ever watchful, never needing any strength other than her own.

She shook her head, lips tight.

Jamie sighed and sat down next to her, running his hand through his hair. "Do you truly remember so little?"

"Only flickers of memories."

Jamie leaned his head against the marble wall and stared at the harp, the inoperative key to his family's revival. "Try this instead, then. I have been telling you stories for all these years. Perhaps it is time to return the favor." His fingertips skimmed the scars on her clenched knuckles. "Tell me what you see, in those brief flashes of memory of our past."

Rozlyn swallowed. "The sea," she whispered after a moment. "The gulls soaring over the waves. My bare toes burying themselves in the sand, the hem of a pale-blue gauzy gown caught in my hand as the surf crashes around my legs."

"Go on."

"A purple cloak, deep violet and soft, trimmed with fur. I'm lying on it on the beach, watching the clouds drift across the sky." She hesitated, but Jamie remained preternaturally still beside her. "The scent of cedar and pine, somehow, even though I'm on the shores of the ocean." She glanced at him, his hands gripping his knees with his head bowed. "Is any of that right?"

"Yes." He looked up, and she jolted to see tears on his cheeks. He laughed, a breathless sound. "Étaín," he said, the name like a prayer on his lips. "You see? You do remember me, a bhrèagha."

She stared into his eyes, bright with happiness, unburdened of all the sadness that had lingered in their depths ever since the first time that she had seen him so many years ago.

It was an expression of unbridled joy, and she remembered it.

More accurately, she realized, she remembered the taste of that joy, the citrus-chocolate sweetness of it melting on her tongue. It was the sensation of lying in the shade by a cool mountain stream, lazily licking the remnants of its tart flavors from the pads of her fingers, blinking in contentment against the brilliance of a midsummer sun.

She jerked backward at the clarity, the concentration of the flavor of that joy pooling in her mouth, and then like a dam bursting, other flavors were there too, edible remembrances from a long-ago life—a rough, masculine hand clasped in hers as they sank to their knees, side by side, an indivisible force. She saw that what was now a flimsy, slender thread between them was once an unbreakable chain of silver and steel, of perpetuity amid their two intertwining souls. Before their bowed heads, a tall figure rose—broad, muscled arms outstretched to welcome them home, an aloof benevolence that radiated regality and power, booming out across the crowded marble hall, an innumerable blur of pale-faced graces of unimaginable divinity and power. "Let the witch renounce her claim on my son," and she could hear the rumble of unquestioned authority in his sonorous voice. "For so does love supersede all strife and sadness in our world, and so does my son love his black-haired beauty of a bride."

The crowds of watching gods roared, and his hand tightened around hers, their shared joy sparking from his fingers to hers, and she raised her head to meet his gaze and smiled—freely, boundlessly smiled.

The vision vanished, and her hands twisted into the fabric of her shirt.

Rozlyn had never once smiled like that, like Étaín had.

Her head bowed, her lungs constricting in her chest at the thought, and Jamie's hand hovered just above her fingers where they trembled, splayed out and tense, on the shattered wooden floor. "Rozi?" he asked. "What did you remember?"

Without a word, she gathered the exhausted dregs of her power and shifted, her hair reddening as half-ripe apples in the warmth of the sun, her arms growing thick-muscled and raw with power, her newly broad limbs vibrating as the strength of the king of the gods flowed through her. She lifted her head, registering Jamie's awestruck expression, and then turned toward the harp, a siren's call of welcome to its lone master. She strode toward it, her heavy booted feet booming along the fractured wood floors, and then lifted the harp of the Dagda from where it hung on the wall.

The harp lay smooth and sparkling in her meaty hands, waiting with bated breath, a soundless question hanging in the air between them.

"Uaithne."

The instrument quivered once, its strings twanging faintly in answer to its master's long-lost voice.

"Play," she commanded. "Play mirth."

The command resonated along the marble walls, and softly at first, then with increasing vigor and tempo, the harp began to play—soft, tinkling melodies of a myriad of joys: of first steps taken by small, shaky legs into a mother's waiting arms; of a first kiss between shy-hearted lovers underneath the cool blue rays of a summer moon; of a son, tall and bearded and strong, handing his firstborn into the arms of his white-browed grandfather, trembling with pride; of a bright-eyed maiden astride a wild stallion, the ground trembling beneath them as they fly across the thick green grass of the lowlands, hair and mane streaming in the wind; of two blue-veined trembling hands clasped in the warmth of the other as they slip across the whispering veil between the realm of the living and the eternity of Magh Meall, hand in hand as they enter the valley of death, content and serene.

So the harp sang, and the unending warmth of its joys rushed through her, bliss like she had never before tasted. Distantly, she heard Jamie laughing aloud from the unassailable force of the song—long, rich peals of laughter that shook the room from one end to the other. Then the final notes faded, that brief glimpse of joy slipping away and vanishing into the air, and she stood with the harp clasped in these hands that were not her own, solemn and sad eyed as ever, even in this borrowed form.

From outside the castle came a resounding clap, the shattering of megalithic rocks, and she glanced down to see the luminous glow of the harp dimming, returning to its former muted oaken sheen, and she bowed once before she rehung it on the marble wall.

It is done, it seemed to whisper as it drifted to sleep, its duty fulfilled. *Farewell.*

"Rozi."

She flinched at the sound of his voice, still breathless with laughter, then shifted, her black hair tumbling about her shoulders. She turned to look at Jamie, the lingering traces of enchanted mirth still rippling across his features, but he was already staring at her, blue eyes blazing bright, fierce with satisfaction.

With victory.

"They are here."

Chapter Thirty-Eight

They walked out the great mahogany doors of the Court of Shádach together, side by side, their hands hanging close but apart. The anticipation rolled off him in waves of unbridled excitement, and she swallowed, fighting the surge of nausea that rose within her as he hurried away from her side to greet his kin, leaving her lingering, uncertain, behind him.

The granite expanse of rock that stretched in front of the Court of Shádach was sundered in two, jutting toward the fog-encrusted sky in looming shards of gray stone. From the depths of the world that lay beneath the rock, the shadowy forms of the gods emerged, staggering toward the rush of the open air that yawned before them.

Rozlyn watched them, a reluctant sense of awe flooding through her as the figures of the Tuatha Dé Danann materialized, their features so foreign yet oddly familiar to her, these creatures of grace and power sprung straight from the myths that she had loved, those stories that the man who now strode to greet them had beguiled her with so many years before.

She saw the many-horned god of the forest—Cernunnos, she remembered was his name, who wandered between the isles scattered across the northern seas—green-and-brown branches of fir and oak threading through the towering antlers that he wore atop his leafy head, his thick arms entwined with ivy and thorns. Behind him came Lir, god of the sea, blue of hair and green of skin, and with him came the rich aroma of salt-scented air, the strands of seaweed that twined about his sea-soaked legs glinting in the light of the sun. She recognized the goddess of healing and song, Brigid, her red hair piled atop her head, a rich crimson crown, adorned with the flowering herbs of her arts, her bare arms a deep golden brown against the pale blue of her gown as she cradled a finely crafted flute in her hands.

Against the gray sky appeared a pair of delicately feathered wings, as white as the purest winter snow, fluttering tentatively against the cold bite of the air, and a face was soon visible beneath them, pale-eyed and gorgeous as the dawn—Aengus, the god of youth and summer and love. Ecne appeared next, the god of knowledge; and with him Lugh, the legendary hero of Moytura, the god of cunning and the harvest, with his scythe in his sun-browned hands; and Goibinu, the god of the smithy, his cheeks flushed with the remembered heat of his forge; and with them dozens of elegant figures, glimmering with the luminous sheen of divinity and power. And there behind them, the earth quivering underneath his steps, came the Dagda, his dark-red beard falling almost to his knees as he climbed out of the pits of the earth where he had been confined for so many years, and he threw back his head toward the open sky and breathed in deep the biting winter air.

Jamie stepped forward, his hands trembling as he sank to his knees before his father. "Father," he choked, and even Rozlyn's shuttered heart ached to hear the regret, the pain flowing through his voice. "It is I, Midir, stripped of my powers by the witch Fúamnach, cursed to endure a deathless existence while robbed of everyone I ever loved, trapped forever in this mortal body. It is because of me, my abandonment of our promised marriage-bond, that you have suffered this fate for all these years." He keeled over at the waist, his forehead pressed against the ice-kissed rock of the island. "Forgive me. I have failed you all."

The king of the gods surveyed Jamie as he knelt before him, his palms flat on the ground, outstretched in supplication to his immortal father, and in one smooth motion, he dropped to his knees to embrace his son. "Midir," he boomed. "No, my son—you have saved us all."

The gods roared as one, and Rozlyn sank to the ground as well, clutching at the frost-kissed rock of the island as the ground shook from the sound of their cheers, and she watched from a distance as the Dagda wrapped his arms around Jamie and embraced him.

The Dagda pulled away from him, surveying his changed son, and his lips twisted. "What you must have suffered, my son," he murmured. "Trapped away, alone, stripped of your divinity in this mortal form." He let out a rumbling growl, and in unison, the entirety of the Tuatha Dé Danann howled with him, a promise of retribution for their oft-forgotten son. "And yet," the Dagda continued, and the gods fell silent. "This is not the time to grieve, to rage against the injustices that we have faced, the suffering that we have endured. There will be time for that." His attention drifted away from Jamie, and Rozlyn froze as the king of the gods' gaze met her own.

Jamie stood and turned toward her, where she still crouched against the ice-kissed rocks, and held out a hand. "Áthair," he said, his eyes latched onto hers with a wordless plea. "You remember my wife, Étaín."

At the sound of the name, the gods fell silent, an impenetrable hush of utter stillness descending on the barren stones of the island. Rozlyn rose on trembling legs and looked at them as they stared at her, their expressions flat and unreadable. It was because of her, she realized suddenly with a shiver, that they had been condemned to this living death for so many centuries, for her sake that they had been trapped in the dark caverns of the earth. She swallowed and slipped her hand into Jamie's, then bowed her head before her new father-in-law. "My king," she murmured.

"Daughter." Rozlyn could not stop herself from flinching, to hear that unwanted word on another's lips. "You are welcome again to my home, to the house that my son has restored for his people." He turned away from her, an inconsequential wife of another innumerable son, and raised his arms above his head as his family chanted again, the deep-throated roar of the most powerful beings in all the world. "Children." His sonorous voice echoed across the barren expanse of the island. "Sisters, brothers, wife—now is the time to rejoice, for at last we are free!"

The gods erupted once more into a bone-shaking cheer, stamping their feet and clapping their hands, until the whole island shook with the force of their roars. "In!" the Dagda boomed, waving his hands toward the Court of Shádach, which sat looming behind them, an ominous shadow of a palace that was aptly named indeed. Rozlyn shuddered once at the thought of reentering its walls, but then she was caught in the rush of immortal bodies cheering and shouting in celebration as they swarmed toward their home, and she gripped Jamie's hand as he pulled her forward, back into the castle of the gods with its splintered floor and shattered walls.

"It's all right," Jamie whispered in her ear as they were swept along with the procession of the shouting gods. His palm was warm and reassuring against the clamminess of her shaking fingers, and he squeezed gently. "We're home now. All is well."

She remembered her vale, the thick green trees that grew tall and broad-leafed around her small stone castle, the familiar corridors and sunlit rooms, her sandstone hearth, and the sweet scent of herbs and ink and fresh-brewed tea, of Galena's gray eyes and her villagers' smiles.

No, she thought as he tugged her back inside, back into the cool dark shadows of the Court of Shádach. *It's not.*

It was during the feast that everything went to hell.

She sat by Jamie's side at the long mahogany table in the great hall, her heart pounding with wonder. It was staggering, what the full might of the gods' magic could do when it was unleashed on the world. The oaken floors were restored to their original polished sheen with a mere flick of the mighty Dagda's wrist, the jagged cracks from her battle with Fúamnach that scarred the marble walls smoothed away by the slightest touch of Goibinu's calloused hand, and when Lir and Lugh and Brigid raised their arms above their heads in a unanimous, silent command, the tables groaned and sighed under the weight of a feast of unparalleled bounty—spiced sea trout and roasted salmon, legs of mutton and silver plates piled high with steaming sausages, wide-mouthed bowls overflowing with potatoes and cabbage, leeks and onions, fat brown loaves of sweet-smelling veda bread, lush red strawberries and green apples, tankards overflowing with mead and stone jugs of wine. Through a haze of exhaustion and bone-deep weariness, Rozlyn watched as the gods ate long into the night, hours upon hours of banqueting and carousing and drinking, and yet the piles of food never seemed to diminish, an unending bounty of rich, sumptuous feasting.

There were toasts and songs and lengthy orations about duty and desire, and after a while, the sounds of their speeches became incoherent and slurred to Rozlyn's ringing ears, the unnatural boom and thunder of their voices reverberating through her aching head. She rested her temple against Jamie's shoulder, memorizing that faint smell of cedar and sea salt, and he turned his head slightly and pressed a light kiss against her hair in response.

The room fell silent without warning, and she sat up swiftly, palms damp, the sudden, reverent hush roaring in her ears far more stridently than had their cheering and shouting. The Dagda had risen from where he sat across from them, his large hands now pressed against the edge of the table as he leaned forward to stare directly into her eyes.

"Daughter," he began, and just as before, it was like ice in her veins, to hear this unearthly being claim her as his own. "For three hundred years, my people have lain imprisoned beneath the earth, trapped in the throes of a living death, awake yet slumbering, unable to move or to speak or even hardly to breathe. For three hundred years, my last remaining son has been alone, entombed in a mortal prison, the magic given to him by the earth-mother herself unlawfully stolen from him by an unnatural witch." A hiss resonated among the listening gods, their teeth snapping at the mention of Fúamnach, and Rozlyn clasped her sweaty palms in her lap, her fingers trembling. "But my son has prevailed," the Dagda continued, and the gods rumbled their wordless approval. "He has fought long and hard, suffered in unimaginable ways, to do his duty and free his people from this witch's curse, and now the time has come to restore him to his former glory."

The sweat beading on Rozlyn's forehead turned to ice.

The Dagda raised his hand and extended it toward her, his expression flat and unforgiving even as his voice stayed deep and mellow and smooth. "It is time," he said, "for you to do your duty as his wife, as my daughter. You must return the magic that was stolen from him, the birthright of the gods alone. Restore to him his power, Étaín."

Étaín.

She thought of that green-eyed girl from so long ago, smiling in her wedding gown, rising up on her toes to kiss her bridegroom with nothing but joy in her heart.

She looked down at her hands, the faint scars on her knuckles, the tips of her fingers, trembling with power, the calluses on her palms, stained with decades' worth of unwitting sins, and made her choice.

Jamie was waiting at her side, tense and watchful. She leaned away from him slightly as she looked up at the king of the gods without flinching. "My name," she said, "is Rozlyn, and that power belongs to me now."

His chair clattered to the floor behind him as Jamie

rose, his hand coming to rest on Rozlyn's shoulder. Before he could speak, the rest of the gods murmured violently among themselves, and at the far end of the table, Cernunnos stood, his chair scraping against the floor. He leaned forward. "This cannot be," he said, and even as her heart pounded with fear, Rozlyn could not help but notice the surging rush behind his words, like a thousand rivers flowing through the heart of the earth. "The girl may be like us, but she cannot wield this power as one of the immortal gods." His handsome features were distorted, lined with contempt. "She will never be one of us."

All around her, in silent agreement, the rest of the gods rose, their shadows falling across her where she sat at the table, her fists clenched in her lap and sweat pooling at the small of her back.

With unsteady hands, Rozlyn pulled herself to her feet as Cernunnos continued to frown at her from beneath the canopy of the dark-green leaves winding their way through his antlered horns. Her fingers were beginning to burn with that surge of power that had been stolen away from these gods who now towered over her so threateningly. She watched from the corner of her eye as next to her Jamie held up a reassuring hand to his horned cousin. "It is not her fault," he said, and even though he was as steady and as calm as ever, she could almost taste his fear in the air. "Fúamnach cursed her even as she doomed us all. She imprisoned my powers within her, and she has learned to use them as her own, it is true." Jamie's gaze flickered to hers ever so briefly, bright with an unmistakable warning, before he looked away at the gods who still watched her with pitiless eyes. "But I know that she will return it to me now that she has done what I could not and has awoken you back into the world of the living." His lips tightened. "After all, it is she who has freed you, Áthair, not I."

The gods muttered among themselves as the Dagda's unflinching stare roamed over her where she stood, straight-backed and proud. "Well, daughter?" he asked, and this time his full lips curled into a sneer at the term. "It is true? Will you restore my son's godhead to him and resume your place as his mortal, beloved wife?"

Jamie's fingers brushed against hers, a silent plea, and she pulled her hand free of his and raised her chin in the air. "I will not." Jamie reached out and gripped her elbow, but she shook herself loose and continued. "It no longer belongs to you or your kin. It is mine now by right. I won it for my own and claimed it as mine when I defeated the witch who imprisoned you. I will not give it back."

The Dagda's face darkened, but Aengus stepped forward, his wings fluttering in the bright light of the torches that lined the marble walls. "Child," he said, his voice a gentle contrast to the hard, unforgiving lines of his mouth. "Do not so grieve my brother by condemning him to lose his bride so soon after he has found her."

From beside him, Ecne spoke up next, his fingers thrumming against the table in an impatient rhythm. "You're a fool if you believe that you can keep it," he said, and Rozlyn recoiled at the venom in the god of all wisdom's indictment. "The power that runs within your veins belongs to the Tuatha Dé Danann alone. It is ours to wield, as so decreed by the earth-mother, Danu, herself a millennium ago. You will give it back," he commanded as his pitiless gaze bore into hers, "or you will die, and we shall watch your power vanish into the ether rather than be so defiled in the hands of a mortal."

Rozlyn flinched even as Jamie clenched his fists. "Do not threaten her, cousin," he snapped. "She is my wife by right, and therefore under my protection. It is forbidden to harm her under this roof."

Ecne tilted his head, and a chill unlike any she had ever known slipped down her spine at the sight of his face. "True," he said. "So I suppose we must first take her outside." He jerked his chin, and Cernunnos began to prowl around the table, the muscles in his green arms flexing as he stalked toward her.

"No!" Jamie shoved Rozlyn against the wall behind him, his hands outstretched. "No," he repeated, his breathing ragged. "She will yield, I promise you. She will soon see reason, and then I will claim my power from her this night." He turned toward her, frantic.

Rozlyn stood still and silent, as unmovable as the snow-capped mountains that loomed on the far-off shores of Éire, while the divinities who still hovered around the table glided forward, encircling them where they stood.

She looked at them one by one, these gods from the stories that she had so loved, and saw no hint of remorse, of pity or understanding, in their immortal faces.

She thought of her father, locking her away in a cold, lonely tower for all the years of her early life, the helplessness and the impotence of her youthful existence, longing to be her own queen, the sole arbiter of her fate, good or bad.

She would not be left powerless ever again.

"No." Rozlyn imagined the squares of a black-and-white board, her pawns long lost and her pieces in disarray, but her queen survived still, and she would never yield. "Kill me, then, but I will not concede."

CHAPTER THIRTY-NINE

She was so pale. Jamie's heart, which had for so many centuries belonged only to her, grew cold and leaden in his chest at the sight of her defiance, her fear.

"Rozi." Her gaze flitted away from him as he pleaded with her. "It is time. Give back to me my power and let me again be whole."

"No."

"Rozi." His lungs ached from the sudden coldness in the air as the gods prowled about them, the threat of their magic rolling off them in waves, and even as he shuddered, it sang to him, that ominous rippling in the air, like a touchstone to his divinity, that long-lost diamond-bright piece of his soul. "It is mine, a bhrèagha. It does not belong to you."

She looked up at him then, and he could see in the determined set of her shoulders, the hard lines of her mouth that there was no hope of saving her now. "It does though. It does belong to me, because I have made it mine." She gestured between them, and he knew it for what it was—a wordless appeal to him and him alone. "You saw it yourself, Jamie. It answers to my call now, not yours."

The gods tightened their ranks around them, around *her*, and his stomach clenched as their features grew dark and bottomless as the night sky.

"Rozi." His voice was tremulous with dread, those two great passions of his immortal life roaring at one another in confusion. "Don't do this, my love."

He saw her fingers flex, in and out, and he leapt forward, seizing her wrists. "No," he said, and her eyes snapped back to his at the urgency, the terror that flowed through his command. "Don't fight. Please, Rozi. They will kill you."

Behind him, he heard one of them snarl—Brigid, he thought distantly, only Brigid could make a snarl sound so melodious and smooth—and Rozlyn ripped her arms free of his grasp, shoving at his chest as she pressed herself up against the marble wall. "Stay back," she hissed. "Don't touch me."

"Rozi." He stepped backward, his palms raised in the air, as he eyed the gods looming over his shoulder, watching her with hungry eyes. "I'm not going to hurt you. I told you, only a few hours ago. Do you remember, a bhrèagha? I told you that I have never been like them, never truly been one of them, not really. They could never feel what I do for you. Trust that I will care for you, as I have unwaveringly, for so many centuries. Trust me, please, and yield this power back to me, my birthright that was stolen from me."

She swallowed and shook her head, her fists clenching in an unspoken resolution, and his heart sank in his chest as the gods behind him growled in unison.

"Enough," Cernunnos snarled, shaking his sharp-tipped antlers at Rozlyn. "Just take it from her, then. It has been three hundred years since we walked the earth, and our patience for the foolishness of mortals has long since vanished. Take it by force and let us be gone to tend to the cares of the world as we were born to do."

Jamie watched Rozlyn grow rigid, her knuckles whitening as she clenched her fists in the fabric of her shirt. "No," he whispered, and she looked at him, chest heaving. "I won't do that, Rozi."

A collective shout burst from the gods pacing behind him, but Rozlyn kept her eyes fixed on his, and they stared at one another, a silent conversation between only the two of them. "Jamie," she said as the roar of the gods grew louder and more feral around them, the air between them crackling with sparks of unseen power. "I'm sorry."

Even as he opened his mouth to speak, the air inside the hall grew unnaturally still and deathly cold, as frigid as the winter winds thickening into an ice-black mist of an eternal blizzard. The gods surrounding them suddenly vanished, reappearing again in complete stillness in the far corners of the room, each of them bowing low at the waist as they turned to face the silent figure who stood in the entryway, their immortal faces shuttered and tense with fearful reverence. Slowly, she emerged into the light, dressed in a gown the darkest of grays, her midnight hair cascading about her shoulders, mingling with the ink-glossed feathers of her ravens where they sat perched on her shoulders, and Jamie steeled himself before stepping forward to greet the arrival of the Mórrígan.

His mother.

"A mháthair," he murmured, and she raised her bone-white hands to cup his face.

"My child," she whispered, sending tendrils of ice

crackling across the marble floors. "You have saved us all, even as I foresaw so many centuries ago."

"I missed you, a mháthair," he said, kissing her palm lightly. "I thought that perhaps the dark underbelly of the earth suited you too well for you to rejoin us here in the light."

Her black eyes remained cold and joyless. "I have never cared to mingle with the rabble, my son." She withdrew her hands, and he shivered at the crinkles of frost forming in the lines of his face where her fingers had lain. "I arrive when it so pleases me, not when it is expected."

He bowed slightly, and her midwinter stare sliced over his shoulder to fix on Rozlyn where she stood behind him. He turned to see her still pressed flat against the marble wall, her face pale with defiance even now, in the presence of the most dreaded divinity in the entire cosmos, the arbiter of fate, the very mouthpiece of doom. "So this pretty thing has stolen away my son's magic," she continued in that gentle tone, which rippled with the ice of a thousand corpses. "You will return it to him, child, or you will soon find that there are worse fates to be devised for a young girl like yourself than being the lowly wife of an all-powerful god."

Rozlyn's face grew whiter, and Jamie could see her hands shaking, despite her defiant posture, caught in the throes of the primal terror that ensnared the heart of any mortal who dared to look upon the face of death herself. "A mháthair," he said, "please."

She did not remove her deathly stare from Rozlyn's face when she answered him. "Do not interfere, my son. This is between myself and my lovely daughter-in-law." Her lips moved, pitiless and unhurried, and even the frost of her footsteps that covered the marble floor shivered in answer to the iciness in that smile. "Would you like to remain a member of my family, child, or take your chances with that power that throbs so weakly in your veins? You may be the match of that spineless little witch, but you do not know me, child. You will never be able to command that power as it was meant to be wielded, and you will die screaming in the cold, even as you try to brandish it to protect yourself from the darkness of my arts." Her voice grew even softer, its gentleness belied by the malevolent glitter in her eye. "I do not wish to see my son so grieved, little girl. Go with him now and give to him what is his by right."

Jamie watched as Rozlyn's face—her strong, beautiful face, this clever, boundless girl whom he had loved for so many years—crumpled, like soft powdered snow crushed under a careless boot, the callous destruction of its pristine beauty.

She lifted her stricken gaze to his, and suddenly, he found himself remembering the dearg-dur—another lost girl, sitting wasted and sad at the table of her all-powerful husband, forever grieving the memory of the life she had lost. He shook his head as the image flashed through him, that hollow-eyed face, and he watched as Rozlyn's shoulders sagged in defeat, as she prepared to yield to the wishes of the gods, bound to their will.

Then he was moving, placing himself unwaveringly between her and the looming darkness that stood before her. "No." He met his mother's stare, his gaze as cold and implacable as her own. "Let her go."

The Mórrígan's dark eyes burst into flames of black ice. "You foolish boy," his mother hissed. "You will die if you do this. I have seen it." Her teeth snapped together as she spoke. "Fúamnach is dead, and without her art, you are fully mortal now, my son. Without her craft to keep you alive, you will grow old and die as the rest of mortals do. It is not within our right to so manipulate the ordering of the mortal world. None of us can save you. Your immortality is bound to that drop of power in her veins," and the Mórrígan raised her bone-white finger in accusation as she pointed at his wife.

"I know," he said, turning his attention to where Rozlyn stood behind him, her face pale.

"And so will she," his mother added with a hint of venom coating her voice. "Your power does not grant her that eternal thread of life that runs through our veins, my son. It will not bestow on her that immortal folaíocht that pulses in our blood. You will both die, and your power will vanish with her. Do not—" She reached out and brushed her icy fingers down the side of his cheek. "Do not deprive me of the sole child of my womb for the sake of some headstrong girl."

Jamie said nothing, and his mother stepped closer, laying a coaxing hand on his arm. "She would not do the same for you, my son. Do not be so weak, as these humans are weak. You are infinitely strong, one of the immortal gods who holds the power of the world and all its wonders in the palm of his hand." She stared at him, burning with intensity. "Do not forget who you are."

He reached down and gently removed his mother's hand from his arm. "I have not forgotten," Jamie said. "For three hundred years, that is all that I have remembered. Be assured, a mháthair, that I have come to know myself in ways that I never once fathomed to be possible, and believe me when I tell you that no part of who I now am or who I ever will be would want to see her broken and bound, as you would have me do, no matter the cost."

The gods snarled around them as the Mórrígan stared at him. Her nostrils flared, and she turned away, her beautiful face growing even colder with disdain. "Let him die, then," she said to the Dagda, who watched her with a wary expression, his shoulders tense. "I had seen his death in the half-formed thoughts of the sky, but now it has become embedded in the earth itself. He has chosen it, and none can deny its happening."

Cernunnos growled. "Kill the girl too, and let them both be gone from this world, for a mortal cannot wield our powers."

"Yet she will." The Mórrígan's words were flat and implacable. "I have spoken, boy. My son has made his choice. Go back to your rivers and your trees and see to your own affairs whilst you still can."

The air grew tense with cold as the Mórrígan stared at the Tuatha Dé Danann, and the Dagda strode forward a single step. "She has spoken," he repeated, the boom of his voice dimmed with sadness. "And thus, so have I." He turned to Rozlyn, his face unforgiving with the storm of his rage. "You have doomed my son to a living death, and he has chosen to spare you with his final request of his immortal nature. Go, before I change my mind."

Distantly, through the roar of protest that followed, that shard of ice that had once been Jamie's heart shattered in his chest as he watched his wife shove away from the wall and run, past the leering gods and down the length of the great hall, out the door and into the waiting mist without a backward glance.

CHAPTER FORTY

INIS TRÁ THOLL, ÉIRE, 1017

Rozlyn ran through the midnight fog toward the edge of the island, stumbling and tripping over the rough, barren rocks and brush that littered its flat, bare surface. The memory of the king of the gods' fury burning across his all-powerful face flashed before her; a bone-deep shudder blurred her vision and tumbled her steps. She fell, scraping her palms against the sharp flint rocks scattered across the island, and she lowered her head to the ground, gasping with pain, with a bottomless grief.

A hand wrapped around her elbow, steady and strong, pulling her to her feet.

She could barely see his features in the misty gloom surrounding them, but there was no mistaking the paleness in his face, the grim line of his mouth. "Rozi." His expression was weary with resignation even as he searched for an answer that she would never be able to give. "Why?"

"It is all that I have, Jamie." Soft red welts began to

bloom on her skinned palms, and she clenched her fists and dug her nails into the wounds, relishing the burn, so much easier to endure than the hurt scarring his face as he looked at her. "I'm sorry, I am. But I cannot let you take it from me. Perhaps it is selfish, and perhaps it is wrong, but I cannot give it up to you. It is all that I have ever had, and I cannot let you take it from me and leave me powerless and empty."

His face shuttered. "So you would condemn me to die, then, Rozi? You fly away with what is mine by birth, by right, what was stolen from me because I chose you over all else—this is my reward?"

"You would condemn me to die by taking it from me. Is that to be *my* reward?"

"Rozi, I told you. You wouldn't die. The might of the Tuatha Dé Danann could easily heal you, that shredding of your soul. Do you really imagine that I would risk losing you again, a bhrèagha?"

"I told you not to call me that," she whispered, and he spun away, slamming his fist against the sap-soaked trunk of a pine tree.

"I would not risk you," he repeated with his back to her. "I would never let you die."

She ached to touch him, to hold him. "How can you not see that there is more to death than merely dying? To live a life that you do not want, as someone you are not? It is a fate worse than death." Rozlyn forced her hands to remain still at her sides, to refrain from reaching out to entwine her fingers with his. "Surely you, of all people, can understand that."

He wheeled around to face her, desperation scarring his features. "Once you dreamed of being my wife, content with that same power that won you your freedom in the first place belonging to me and me alone. Once that was enough for you. Why is it not now, Rozi? Why am I no longer enough for you?"

He still did not understand. He would never be able to see it, to know beyond a shadow of a doubt that she was not that girl whom he had once loved, that the Beast she had become had killed her as surely as it had slain all the innocent souls who had been so unfortunate as to venture into its monstrous path.

End it, something whispered inside her. *End this thing between you now, before it is too late.*

She forced her fingers to uncurl, to flex at her sides, in and out, and she saw his eyes snap down to where the ember of her magic—*their* magic—was beginning to glow with a cautionary fire.

"Fúamnach was right about one thing," she said, but he kept his gaze fixed on the curve of her fingers, the faint trail of embers glimmering in their wake. "I am not Étaín. I know that you loved her, and I know that you grieve for her, that you will always grieve for her, but, Jamie." She forced herself to continue. "She died all those years ago, and she can never come back to you, no matter how much you wish her to." At last, he looked up, and she flinched to see the ocean of hurt swimming in his eyes. Her voice softened even as she stepped back, away from him. "I could never be her, you know, with or without this magic. I am as much a Beast in this form as I am in my other, not a beauty as she was."

"You're wrong," he said, but it was hollow and weak, and they both knew it.

She swallowed. "I am not the girl you loved, that woman who could smile on her wedding day and not feel pain. That has never been me." He opened his mouth once more to object, then slowly, painfully closed it again, and she turned away. "You have your family, your kin, the balance and order of the world restored. I am sure that those all-powerful gods of the earth and sky can find a way to restore to you your immortality. Only let me go home, Jamie."

"Rozi."

She froze at the touch of his hand on her forearm, his fingers icy. "Give me what you promised, Jamie, that day in my hall." Their eyes met. "What you once promised to Étaín." His lips trembled once. "Give me my freedom."

The thread between them broke, its frayed and fragile ends floating away across the endless churning of the ice-ridden sea, the sad remnant of something that once had been bright and full of promise.

He studied her for a long moment, then wordlessly withdrew his hand from her arm and stepped away from her one final time.

Rozlyn's throat burned, then she launched herself into the sky, her wings exploding from her shoulders as the black-blue pelt of the Beast sprouted from beneath her skin, her fingers lengthening into sharp, curving claws protruding from her massive black paws, and with a few feverish flaps, she was soaring high above the ground, up and up, until she could barely discern the outline of his shoulders against the stone-gray earth, his hands in his pockets, his dark head tilted back as he watched her flight across the endless night sky. She watched him grow smaller and fainter, a mere whisper of a half-forgotten shadow, until the swirling mist of the clouds hid him completely from her sight.

She turned south and flew toward home without a backward glance.

EPILOGUE

Rozlyn was cocooned in her solar with a book and a mug of hot tea, a gray ball of fur snoring by the fire, when she was interrupted by a tentative knock on her door. It eased open before she could answer. "Someone to see you, a bhanríon," Isleen, the young maid from the village, whispered. "A man. He says that he knows you."

Awareness prickled across the back of her neck. "What does he look like?"

"Handsome," Isleen said, cheeks red. "So tall, and such thick brown hair and the most wonderful blue eyes, and oh, his smile—"

"That will do," Rozlyn said, closing her book and rising to stand, steeling herself for battle. "Show him in."

Isleen gestured to the unseen figure waiting in the corridor, then peeked at the queen of the vale, bright with curiosity. "How do you know him?"

"In every conceivable way," Jamie answered, ever

cheerful, ever smiling, as he strode into the room, his hands in his pockets. "Hello, a bhrèagha."

"Don't call me that. Isleen," Rozlyn said, ignoring his answering grin as she settled back into her chair, "this is my husband."

Isleen's eyes widened, a wordless apology, and Rozlyn waved her hand. "It's quite all right, Isleen. We are very much estranged."

"Not for long, though, if all goes well," Jamie added, winking at the girl, and Isleen blushed again.

Rozlyn shot him a wry look. "That will be all, Isleen," then waited until the girl slipped back into the hallway, shutting the door quietly behind her.

They looked at each other in silence for a long moment, measuring and assessing and scheming.

Always plotting. Always pitted against each other.

She straightened her shoulders, preparing for a new game, as he smiled at her. "No lovers waiting in the wings this time?" he asked, and she almost believed it, the idle carelessness in his tone.

He had clearly practiced.

"Is it any business of yours if there are?"

His lips flattened. "No. Yes. Damn it, Rozi, don't you know—"

"You can relax," she said, reaching for her book. "No lovers. Now if that's all?"

"Not even a little bit. I have decided," he announced, his attention flitting about the room as he took in the scraps of parchment strewn across the table, the half-eaten slice of potato cake grown cold on the windowsill, "that I am going to win you back, a bhrèagha."

"So your many missives over the past few years have told me.

I see that you have decided to try your luck in person instead of sending one of your silver-tongued letters to do your pleading for you." She folded her hands across one another on the table. "Do you think that you will succeed where they have failed?"

"I'm pleasantly optimistic." He smiled again, leaning against the wall in that casual way of his, even as Rozlyn saw, with a sudden throb of awareness, the faintest glints of gray in his dark-brown hair.

"Did you have anything in particular to say, or can we escape the meaningless banter and skip to the part where I throw you out on your arse?"

He laughed. "You love our banter, Rozi. You always have. It is the only reason that you ever gave me the time of day in the first place. You know as well as I do that you were horribly bored by those dull-witted boys who wooed you with flowers and sweet words for so many years. The moment that I showed up with a few cheeky grins and a couple of well-placed barbs, your falling madly in love with me was only a matter of time."

"Perhaps it was due to some other, far more interesting things that you could do with that clever tongue of yours."

He laughed again, a delighted sound that thrilled her in those deliberately forgotten corners of her heart. "I was thinking about something," he said after a moment, "and I was suddenly overcome with the burning desire to tell you myself what I was thinking, and so I rode for a full fortnight, all the way to your doorstep, so that I could tell you my radical thought."

"I can barely contain my excitement."

"Here's my epiphany." He ignored the sarcasm simmering

in her voice. "You were right not to cede your power to me after all, Rozi."

"This is hardly a revelation."

"Furthermore," he said, "I decided that it is too intolerable, us spending what meager time is left to both of us on this earth apart from one another. So I am here to stay, whether you welcome me into your bed or no."

"That would be a no."

"Regardless," he said with a shrug, "here I stand, the prodigal husband returning to the unwelcoming arms of his frigid wife. Such a lucky man."

"You *are* aware that I can still rip out your throat at any moment, are you not?"

He grinned. "If you were ever going to kill me, it would have been that first moment I stepped foot in this hall of yours, Rozi. All things considered, my life seems relatively secure in those monstrous hands of yours."

Rozlyn crossed her arms, but before she could answer, the fuzzy gray-brown ball of fur in the corner yawned and stretched its long limbs into the air, then registered the presence of a stranger, a new set of legs on which to leap and unfamiliar hands to lick. It burst from its cushion, barking with joy, tail whirring faster than the wings of a dragonfly, and Jamie balked, horrified. "By the harp, Rozi. What the hell is that?"

The half-grown puppy rolled over onto its furry back and waved its paws in the air at him invitingly. "This is Conan," she answered, her lips trying very hard not to twitch in laughter at his outraged expression. "His mother was one of the hounds in the village, and she found herself impregnated with a litter of strangely large pups, and her master brought her here to me so that I might help ease her labor."

The faintest shadow of a smirk appeared on her face as she noted his revulsion. "Conan here was presented to me as a gift of thanks from her owner, for which I'm very grateful. He is swift and strong, and fearless as any wolf, and has already proven himself to be a marvelous hunter." The puppy trotted over to her, tail wagging, and she stroked his velvet ears. "He does look a little like a wolf, doesn't he? A wolfhound, if you will. I think that I shall breed more like him. He's such a sweetheart."

"For the gods' sake," her husband complained, nose wrinkled in disgust. "Aren't there enough of these hateful creatures prowling your realm without you making more?"

She had missed this, she thought. She had missed him.

She considered conceding, considered smiling at him, just one time, if only to see what it would feel like.

She scowled instead as Conan loped away into the hall, seeking a more receptive audience for his attentions, and preferably a hunk of bone. "Why are you really here, Jamie? You know that I have no intention of taking you back."

"While I was brooding on your decision to leave me standing there jilted and heartbroken on that barren rock of an island in such a gloriously unapologetic fashion, I also realized," he mused, as though it were inconsequential, a small matter of no great significance, "that you were right about something else. I do not in fact love you as I once loved Étaín."

Rozlyn ignored that still-sharp stab of pain in her heart. "I don't care."

"I love you infinitely more." Her face did not even flicker at his pronouncement. "Ironic, I know, given that I am irrevocably finite in my personage for the first time in almost a thousand years, but make no mistake. I have held eternity in my hands, breathed in the silver-scented essence of its core, and taken the full measure of its worth as it nestled, sphere-like, in my palms. So you see, I know all too well what infinity feels like, and it has exactly the same width and height and breadth as how much I love you, so I stand by my statement, improbable as it may sound."

She responded with stony silence.

"A bhrèagha," he said, "I am going to need you to say something, anything, in response, before I run screaming from the room, driven stark raving mad by the suspense."

"That was quite a speech," she said, and she watched as his eyes lit up, to hear his own words from that morning as they faced one another once more, after so long apart, in the dim torchlight of her hall. "Have you been planning it for very long?"

"Nearly three years."

"That is a long time." She eyed him warily—how he stood and how he smiled, always so charming, so damn tempting. "You still lied to me," she said. "On several occasions. Before, when I was young and foolish. More recently, when I was not. How do I know that you will not do so again?"

"You don't. And most likely, I will do just that, and you will subsequently threaten to flay me alive as a result of that nasty temper of yours. We are neither of us perfect, and I do not promise you perfection, but, Rozi," and the muscles in his throat jumped as he swallowed. "Poetry aside, I do love you, you know."

"Jamie."

"I do though. I choose to love *you*, not as you once were, three hundred or fifteen or even four years ago, but who you are now, the woman standing in front of me, with all her virtues and all her flaws." A shallow, shaky breath. "As I hope that you will accept me."

Her heart swelled. It was, she thought, just like him, to topple from the board both of their kings and invite her to play, not for the sake of vengeance or victory, but for the sheer joy of the game. It was a well-played move, one that she knew she would be hard-pressed to defend against.

Rozlyn sighed and stood to face him. "It is irrelevant, Jamie. I cannot give up my power. I would be nothing without it."

"Rozi," he said, "you are everything without it." He sighed and rubbed his hand across his jaw. "I am not trying to trick you. There is no longer any threat to your well-being, since, as you can see, the folaíocht in my veins has gone cold and dry." He pointed to the silvery strands of hair glinting in the sunlight that dappled over the floor through the open windows. "I will never be able to take that power from you and make it my own, ever again. You would lose it—that is true." He looked directly at her, with no trace of deception or guile. "But not to me. It would simply be gone, vanished into the ether, back into the arms of the earth-mother, who first brought it into being at the very beginnings of time."

"Forgive me if I find myself disinclined to believe you."

"We would be equals, Rozi." The humor vanished from his tone, and the hairs on her arms tingled, because there was no desperation or greed or hunger in his plea, but a quiet longing, a loneliness that whispered of the same faint echoes in her own heart. "No one greater or more powerful over the other, no advantages, no laddering of our worthiness. Just you and I, in the most final of adjournments, together, side by side."

She studied him carefully, his smiling face, his steady

eyes and determined mouth. "What do my beloved in-laws have to say about this idea of yours?"

Jamie shrugged, a shadow of grief slipping across his features. "They are all but gone as well." Her mouth fell open, and he smiled more sadly at her. "The world has changed too much over the past three centuries while they have slumbered beneath the earth," he said. "They have fulfilled their duties and renewed the confinement spells of the sídhe, once more locking away monsters that have ravaged the land for these last few years, but alas, Éire has changed. Humans have changed. They—" He winced slightly. "*We* fear the magic of the Tuatha Dé Danann now, rather than revere it, and mortals have learned to cultivate the earth and its beauty on their own. The Dagda has spoken, and the gods will return to their barren isle north of the world, of their own free will this time, to sleep until they are needed again."

"All of them?"

"The Mórrígan, as you know, adheres to her own rules, her own will, and she does not relish the idea of exile. She knows too much about the intricacies of the universe to leave it in the hands of hapless mortals. She will continue to walk among them—among us—for so long as she pleases."

"And will I have to fear her wrath, if I steal away her son?"

"She has forgotten me," he countered. "I am no longer of value to her in this brief, broken state of mortality. She sees eternity, and I am the smallest drop of rain in the vastness of the ocean." His fingers wandered over to fiddle with the edges of a blank scrap of parchment on the table. "I am truly alone in the world now, but for you."

"I have always been alone."

His eyes met hers. "You do not have to be." Another pause. "Only if you choose to be."

The flicker of a memory flashed through her—she was again sitting on an unfamiliar beach, the sand warm and heavy between her bare toes, her face stained with the salt of the sea and her own tears, whispering to the figure who leaned over her of her longing to be free, to choose for herself the life that she wished to live.

You shall have it, a bhrèagha. I swear by all the gods, you shall have it.

She swallowed. "You know that it is not that simple."

His stare grew more intense, darker than she had ever before seen. "Do you remember the story of Medb that I told you so many years ago, Rozi? 'Let there be no imbalance between us.' We are imbalanced, my love, and have been since we first began this story of us all those centuries ago. I would like the chance to be balanced, to be equal, and to see what magic that we can make all on our own, you and I together."

Rozlyn eyed him warily. "Jamie."

He held up his hand. "I know that you are not willing to give up your power, Rozi, nor would I force you to do so, as I have proven quite thoroughly, I would argue. But should the day come—tonight, tomorrow, in a fortnight or a decade or an entire era of humanity, I don't care—should that day arrive when you are content with the simple, mortal, magic-less life that we could build together, the good that we two can do as one, and desire to be truly equal with each other in all things, then I will be here waiting for you. All you need to do is come to me, and I will know that it is time, and that you have chosen, for yourself, to do so, to accept this union between us, simple as that. No more resentments, no more traps, no more games. Just the two of us, one soul in two hearts, as we were always meant to be."

She was quiet for a long time. "Only when I am ready?"

"Not a moment before." He nodded at her once, a gentle

assurance. "I have waited for you for over three hundred years, a bhrèagha. I can wait a little longer."

Rozlyn studied him, his wry smile, those creases at the edges of his temples that crinkled a little more deeply than they had the first time that she had seen them, fifteen long years ago now, awash in the light of the midmorning sun, and her heart swelled at the memory of him, with his teasing and his tales and his never-wavering fidelity and devotion.

She loved it, this magic of hers that burned within her, the power of the sun and the stars and the sky that soared from her fingertips with the effortlessness of a falcon in flight, but it had bound her to this other girl, this scowling, solemn-eyed girl who was so afraid to smile, to let herself be loved—bound her to centuries' worth of sorrows and griefs, and immeasurable guilt.

She found that she might love the idea of being free of it, of herself, a little bit more.

"I do not know," she admitted, "how long that I will be able to wait."

The grin that broke across his face was as joyous as the dawn. "In all fairness, I plan on making it as difficult for you as possible."

"I would expect nothing less."

They continued to watch each other across the narrow expanse of the room as the sunlight danced around them, the mirror of the brightness that leapt within them, and he stepped toward her. "Rozi," he said, a velvet-soft caress against her skin. "I would very much like to kiss you now."

She held up a finger. "Just one kiss."

He crept closer. "You said that once before to me."

"I mean it this time."

"You meant it last time too."

Then he closed the distance between them and cupped her face in his hands. "But I should be able to restrain myself better this time. I hear that you have become quite beastly in your dotage."

After thirty-three years, Rozlyn—the princess of Connacht, the queen of the vale of Inagh, the mother of monsters—allowed her lips to curve upward, full and happy and free of shadows.

She truly was a beauty when she smiled.

ACKNOWLEDGMENTS

Thank you so much to my wonderful agent, Jill Marr, who has championed *Unbound* fearlessly since I first signed with her and has been so incredibly supportive and enthusiastic. Forever grateful that we connected over our shared love of baseball and mythology, and for everything that you've done for my writing career and for *Unbound*.

Thank you to my editor, Daniel Ehrenhaft, for believing in *Unbound* and giving it so much love and enthusiasm; thanks also to the entire team at Blackstone who has worked so tirelessly on it—Madeline and Josie and Ember, and Larissa too, for my gorgeous cover, and everyone who helped behind the scenes to bring this dream of mine to life. Thank you all so, so much.

Special thanks to Read Between the Wines book club, who generously agreed to read a truly—and this cannot be stressed enough—*terrible* rough draft of this book in its earliest stages to confirm that yes, there was in fact something there worth salvaging. Without your encouragement, I doubt

I would have had the nerve to pursue this, so my everlasting thanks!

To my writing friends, which is the majority of the '24 Debut group: I love y'all so much. Floundering my way through the confusing and very stressful process of publishing a book would have been much more daunting and scarier without all of you. Eliza in particular: you've been incredibly supportive and encouraging, such an amazing friend, and I am so thankful that we found each other!

To Sarah and Serene: I don't have words to express how happy our friendship has made me—our ongoing group chats that encompass multiple platforms and which are my primary support for all publishing-related doomsday scenarios (Sarah) and weird jokes (also Sarah) and peptalks and video calls (both of you), but I think we all know that I am most especially thankful for our beloved collab work, which is by far the most I've ever laughed out loud while writing. Serene: thanks for being the best critique partner I could ever ask for—love you, boo.

To my incomparably wonderful and incredibly supportive group of girlfriends: Melissa, Anna, Basil, Owen, Allie, Wilson, Sara, Amy, and Briana—your friendship means the world to me, and I would be lonely and lost without you all. Thanks for always laughing with/for/at me, and especially for loving me.

To Tessie: My dearest friend, my most faithful reader, the light of my life, the Gus to my Shawn, the Taylor to my Swift, the peanut butter in my Reese's cup, and the cool-cool-cool side of my pillow. Growing up, I used to be so sad, being the only girl in a horde of brothers, always wishing that I had a sister, but it turns out that I just hadn't met you yet. I love you so much; I will forever cherish our friendship as one of the most precious blessings of my life.

To my parents: Thanks for so many things, but especially for all those years of indulging my bibliophilic ways, and then later, your enthusiasm for my writing career. Special shout out to my mom, for so many years of shuttling me back and forth without complaint for my biweekly trips to the library, her eagerness to read this book even though she "doesn't really care for magic stories," and most importantly, for giving me the gift of reading; without your patient teaching and your encouragement, my life would not be full of books and wonder, and thus be so much emptier than it has been. Thank you, and I love you.

To my brothers: You're all idiots, but you're *my* idiots, and I have loved you madly for my entire life. Thank you for always supporting me, always loving me, no matter how much of a little shit I was/am.

To my children: What can I say except what I try and tell you every single day of your lives? I love you always; I'm so proud of you; you are my greatest and most beautiful creations, as well as the most exhausting. You will forever be my highlight reel of what has been a rich, full, and wonderful life. On our best days and our worst, I love you, love you, love you, endlessly and perpetually.

And to Joey: I never would have dreamed, all those years ago, when you showed up at my dorm room with a tub of ice cream and Chutes & Ladders to challenge me to a board game duel, that this is the life we would build together. We've had plenty of bright days with clear skies, but I know, too, that we've faced many storms along the way that neither of us could have foreseen or prevented, but I'll always be glad that you were the one with whom I weathered them. Also, I love you more.

Lastly, to you, reader: I wrote this story a long time ago, for my own amusement, during the quiet nights and lonely afternoons of early motherhood. At the time, I never dreamed anyone other than myself would ever read it. I hope that—whatever stage of life you are in—it has brought you a small measure of the happiness that it brought me then. Thanks for reading!

AUTHOR'S NOTE

I have been fascinated by mythologies my entire life. Perhaps it was growing up in Appalachia, said to be one of the most ancient and ageless mountain ranges in the world. Perhaps the looming presence of their majesty, their grandeur—their secrets—engendered a deep and burning desire to accumulate knowledge, to hoard legends and myths and primeval, undying tales from all the other cultures on earth, to clutch these treasures to my chest like the tiny, introverted, story-loving dragon that I was. By the time I was eight or nine, I had read every book in my local library about Greek and Roman mythology, and it was no doubt my grandfather's influence, his deep and abiding love of Ireland's evergreen shores, that inspired me to turn next to Celtic mythology, in all its rich, intricate, gorgeous glory. *Unbound* is my love letter to those stories—and to him as well.

It is, however, important to note that *Unbound* is a work of fantasy, and while it has been inspired by ancient Irish mythology and culture, it is not intended to be representative of any particular era. The "dates" utilized at the start of each chapter merely act as guides for the reader to mark the passage of time as it occurs over the course of the multiple timelines used. Readers should remember that there are four major periods, or "cycles," in Irish mythology, which altogether constitute a body of work spanning over a thousand years. Since I have included several different myths and tales from different time periods, there really is no single era in Ireland's history that suits this particular narrative.

Furthermore, there are several anachronisms used throughout the work—chocolate did not arrive in Europe until the late 1500s, nor did pockets exist until the twenty-first century—but since both of these things are essential to my own personal happiness, I blessed my characters with them as well. Also, some of the myths told during the novel have been condensed and adapted to fit the narrative; for example, the central tale utilized is the myth of Midir and Étaín. Their story, which spans centuries and is much more complex than the condensed version retold here, is found in the ancient text of *Tochmarc Étaíne* ("The Wooing of Étaín"), partially preserved in a larger body of work known as *Lebor na hUidre*, the oldest extant manuscript written in Irish. *Unbound* has been inspired by this myth, among others, but is not an exact replication of this tale, although there are several homages paid to the original story throughout the novel, which readers who are familiar with the myth will hopefully appreciate. If you enjoyed my simple reimagining of this fascinating and compelling myth from ancient Ireland, please visit my website, christyhealy.com, for recommendations to learn more about the primary texts that inspired this book. I also highly recommend that you check out the works of Shauna Lawless and Morgan Llewellyn,

Irish authors who write gorgeous and compelling stories about their culture and their history.

One last note concerning the geographical descriptions found in *Unbound*: Many of the places mentioned are real, but some have been embellished in the interest of cohesive storytelling; the Vale of Inagh, for example, is based upon a real place in Ireland, but I have taken fictional liberties in inventing a unique location for Rozlyn to make her home. Also, the trees indigenous to Ireland described herein are all but nonexistent in the present day. This is due to the deforestation of Ireland, which began in early medieval times as the need for farmlands increased, and escalated after the Anglo-Norman invasion of Ireland in the late twelfth century, at which point Irish woodlands were routinely harvested by the British (most infamously in 1666, after the Great Fire of London); deforestation also increased dramatically in the eighteenth century after the rise of the Industrial Revolution, until over 90 percent of Ireland's trees had been lost. Despite many efforts to reverse the damage, the destruction of so many of Ireland's indigenous forestry can never be undone and is one of the great environmental tragedies of Western civilization.

So, in my story, I gave the earth-mother her trees back.

I hope you enjoyed reading about Rozlyn and Jamie as much as I enjoyed writing about them.

Sláinte,

Christy

PRONUNCIATION GUIDE

The pronunciation of Irish words often depends on the region/mood/intention of the speaker. This is my best rendering of the terms used in the text, but there will be differentiations among Irish speakers according to the factors listed above. Also included are the vocative pronunciation for some of the Irish terms used; the vocative case is used for direct address, also known as the "calling" case, and is often indicated by the use of the vocative particle "a" before the name in question along with a slight spelling and pronunciation change, which can vary depending on the region of the speaker. So please consider this merely a helpful starting point and remember the most important thing is to enjoy the tale.

NAMES

Aengus—AHN-gus

Ailain—ALL-in

Aillil—AH-lil

Aodh—AH-yuh

Balor—BAY-lor

Cailleach—CALL-ea-haa

Cathbad—CAYF-ah

Cernunnos—SEAR-nair-nowz

Connacht—KAH-nuhkt

Corchenn of Cruach—CORE-kin of CROO-hagh

Crom Dubh—CRAHM DOOV-fuh

Cúchulainn—KOO-koo-lane

Dagda—DAHG-duh

Dáire mac Fiachna—DYE-ray MOCK FEE-ock-nah

Deirdre—DEER-druh

Donn Cúailnge—CU-wail-nyuh

Ecne—ECK-neh

Eochaid—YOCK-eye

Eochu—OH-kah

Étaín—EY-teen

Étar—EH-tar

Fearghal—FUR-gull

Finnbennach—FINN-bah-nick

Flaithbertach—FLAH-ber-tah

Fomorian—FOH-moh-ree-an

Fúamnach—FOO-ah-mah-nah

Goibinu—GO-ree-new

Kenai—KIN-eye

Lig na Paiste—LIG NAH PEST

Lir—LEER

Lugh—LOOG

Magh Meall—MAH MALL

Maimeó—MY-mo

Medb—MAY-vuh

Midir—MEE-deer

Mórrígan—MOR-i-gin
Neit—NEAT
Niall Frossach—NEIL FRO-sah-cuh
Nuada—NOO-ah-duh
Ó Conchúir—*OH KON-coo-err*
Ó Corraidhin—OH CORE-raid-hen
Padraig—PAH-drig
Saoirse—SUR-shuh
Uaithne—OO-win-ay

PLACES

Aasleagh Falls—AH-sleeg
Aileach—AL-yuh
An Bhearú—AHN BEER-oo
Ard an Rátha—ARD-un-rah
Beanna Beola—BAE-nah BOW-lah
Bhanna—BAN-uh
Bréifne—BREF-nuh
Brug na Boinne—BREW-nah BOYNE-yeh
Cionn Mhálanna—SEE-yahn MAH-lahn-nah
Cnoc na Loinge—KNOCK AH LONG-ee
Dubhais—DOO-vish
Dúlachán—DOO-lah-han
Dunach—DON-eek
Dúnalderagh—DOON-al-dur-ah
Éireann—AY-ren
Éire—AY-ruh
Gougane Barra—GOO-gone BAH-rah
Grianán—GRAY-none
Inagh—EYE-nuh
Inis Trá Tholl—IN-ish TRA-hull
Latharna—LAYH-thur-nah

Leinster—LEN-stir

Lough Neagh—LOTH NEE

Maghera—MEG-era

Mhám Toirc—MAAM TURK

Moytura—MOY-toor

Oichén—EE-chin

Osraige—OSS-rye-gah

Sámair—SAW-mar

Shádach—SHAH-dah

Sléibhte Dhartraí—SLAY-tur DAR-try

Sliabh Gamh—SLEEVE GAH-muh

Tech Duinn—TECK DOO-in

Tír Sogháin—TEAR sah-in

Uí Néill—EE NAIL

Ulaid—YO-lay-id

TERMS

a *bhanríon—AH VAHN-ree-yun*

a dhia—AH YEE-ah

a dhaidí (vocative form of daidí)—AH YA-dee

a rí—AH REE

a bhrèagha (vocative form of brèagha)—AH VUH-ree-yah

Abhartach—AW-ar-tah

áthair—AH-her

bean-sí—BAN-shee

brèagha—BREE-yah

chailín—KAY-lin

chodán—KO-dan

crann taca—CRONN TAH-kah

cú-sídhe—COO-shee

daidí—DAH-gee

dearg-dur—DARE-ick-DOO-ah

deirfiúr—DEER-fur

dia—DEE-yah

dobhar-chú—DOOR-who

each-uisce—ICK-ish-kuh

fear céile—FAIR KAY-lah

fidchell—FI-key-ell

flaith—FLAY-ah

folaíocht—FOH-ley-oh-sat

gean-cánach—GONE-key-on

mháthair—WAH-hair

midithir—MID-yee-teer

oilliphéist—OH-lee-fay-sheet

púca—POO-kah

sídhe—SHEE

slán abhaile—SLAWN AH-wal-ya

slán agat—SLAWN AH-git

slúag—SLOO-ah

Tuatha Dé Danann—TOO-ah DAY DAH-non

HELPFUL LINKS AND RESOURCES

https://www3.smo.uhi.ac.uk/gaeilge/donncha/focal/features/irishsp.html

https://www.scoilgaeilge.org/lessons/fuaimniu.htm

https://www.teanglann.ie/en/